EMILY OWEN studied English Language and Literature at the University of Leeds, and completed her Masters by Research in 2018. She works as a Digital Executive and lives in Wakefield, West Yorkshire. She self-published her debut novel *The Mechanical Maestro* in 2020, which is the first book in her series following the adventures of the Abernathy family and their clockwork creations. The second book in the series, *The Copper Chevalier* was released in March 2022.

Also by Emily Owen

The Mechanical Maestro
The Copper Chevalier
Concerto for Three Cities (ebook)

MR GEARHART

Emily Owen

Published 2023 by Open Door Books

Copyright © Emily Owen 2023

The right of Emily Owen to be identified as the author of this work
has been asserted in accordance with the Copyright, Designs
and Patents Act 1988 Sections 77 and 78.

This is a work of fiction. Names, characters, places and incidents either are
products of the author's imagination or are used fictitiously. Any resemblance to
actual events or locales or persons, living or dead, is entirely coincidental.

ISBN 978-1-3999-5773-1 (paperback)
ISBN 978-1-3999-5774-8 (ebook)

Page design and typesetting by SilverWood Books

For my grandads

Acknowledgements

I'd like to thank Helen and the SilverWood team for helping to bring this story to life.

I'd also like to give a special mention to my friend Teresa and to my mum, Jayne, for proofreading earlier versions of the story.

Once again, I must give credit to my brother, Nathan, and partner, Marcus, for advising on the sciencey bits.

Chapter One

Douglas didn't look up from the letter he was reading as he walked along the steel-grated platform, occasionally taking a bite from the red apple in his other hand. Enormous gears and pulleys clattered and churned on either side of the platform, with such force that the sound crashed into one's ears and caused the platform to vibrate beneath one's feet. But Douglas was accustomed to this commotion, and hardly noticed the noise of the engine room. He nimbly sidestepped sliding pieces of machinery without lifting his head.

About halfway along the platform he slowed and, still not looking up from Clara's letter, rapidly knocked twice on a portion of steel wall panel. The six-foot panel slid upwards, and he stepped into a steel lift. All manner of buttons and levers covered one wall and continued to creep like climbing ivy above his head. He leant on a large lever with a glossy black handle. The steel doors shut, shielding him from the clamour of the engine room. The lift slid downwards into the bowels of the house. Another lever opened a small compartment in the lift wall. Douglas tossed the apple core into it, before shutting it again and wiping his sticky fingers on his trouser leg. Having read the letter through, he carefully folded it and eased it into his trouser pocket. His soul sang as he recalled certain passages. The letter's language, sentiment and handwriting were as beautiful and delicate as the little hand that had held the pen. The paper even retained a faint impression of her scent. Every one of Clara's letters was a treasure.

The lift came to a gentle stop and the doors slid open noiselessly. Douglas was greeted by a dark stone tunnel; the light from the lift played on its jagged walls. He walked with buoyant strides down the echoing tunnel. Electric lamps embedded in the walls flickered into life as he approached them. Their sharp, icy white light killed the mystical atmosphere, he thought. Torches would have been more appropriate. Shivering, he drew his sack coat closer around him. His breath clouded before him. George had the whole of Ravenfeld Hall at his disposal, yet he chose to burrow underground. His excuse had been that the consistently cold temperature was necessary for his project, as was the solitude. The tunnel had been created by a specially constructed drilling machine, which George (never one to miss a business opportunity) had sold to a mining company once he'd had no further use for it. At the end of the tunnel stood an archway that led to a square room cut into the rock. The chamber was about thirty feet in height and width. There was little furniture, save for a metal workbench and a wooden desk and chair at the top end. Pipes and pieces of machinery were spread across the floor. Amongst the piles of scrap and the butchered bodies of clockwork androids was a pair of mechanical arms with pincer-like hands. Against the south wall towered George's machine, standing at almost ten feet in height. Its rectangular steel body was connected to great gleaming pipes and cables that trailed into the dark recesses of the ceiling, where the electric generator was. Before the machine was a control panel covered in rows of small, circular keys with black letters, numbers and symbols printed on them. When pressed, these keys spoke to some of the mechanisms deep within the machine's metal guts; pulling wires, like vibrating nerves, inside it.

Sitting at the wooden desk in front of the machine was George himself. The back of his glossy black-haired head faced Douglas. The clicks of tools and machinery echoed faintly around the room. Douglas crept closer, wondering if he'd be able to get close enough to tap George on the shoulder and make him flinch.

'What do you want?' George said, when Douglas was within five feet of him.

'Charming to see you too, brother. There are a few things I want to run past you.'

'Go on.' George didn't stop what he was doing. He was working on some intricate piece of machinery. Douglas struggled to see it clearly, it was so small. George was aided in his task by a pair of spectacles with layers of round lenses that gradually diminished in size. Not that there was anything wrong with his sight; his pale blue eyes were as sharp and penetrating as icicles.

'What are you working on?' Douglas asked eventually, curiosity winning him over.

'Do you remember the method of storing information that Professor Gottfried developed?'

'With the flat metal discs?'

George held up the tweezers in his right hand. A tiny metal square half-covered in minute pins was trapped between them.

'You stole Gottfried's idea?' said Douglas in disbelief.

'It wasn't stealing, since I didn't copy his idea outright. After Professor Gottfried vanished, I bribed the landlord at his lodgings to let me examine the professor's rooms, where I found his poetry-making machine. I examined how it worked, and took several of the data discs for reference. I refined the technology, making it smaller and able to store more data on a single disc. Then I added other features of my own, such as the platinum coating on each disc.'

'How clever of you. It's funny how Gottfried turned up in Prussia a few months after that whole business at the Wych Street theatre, and denied having set foot in England since the previous winter. Perhaps that was simply a false alibi he concocted, since he was implicated in the theft of a nobleman's most treasured possession.' Douglas looked up at George's machine. It was essentially a gigantic mechanical brain encased in a dewy, glistening, square steel skull. 'What precisely do you intend this enormous "computer" of yours to do once it's finished?'

'Execute highly complex equations and analyse data.'

'Such as?'

'For my initial test, I'm going to have the computer predict the daily outcome of the London Stock Exchange for the next month.'

'Advantageous to know. Hopefully our various investments will be on the up,' Douglas chuckled.

'We shall see. It shouldn't be long before the machine is ready for its initial trial. All that remains to be done is to inscribe the last few remaining data discs and insert them into the machine's memory.' George had been working on this project for two years now. He'd been rather secretive about the particulars of it, but as long as it occupied him sufficiently to stop him reaching for bottles of brandy or laudanum, then Douglas was satisfied. It had been his suggestion that George find a project to occupy his mind whenever trade was slow and he was without mental stimulation. He was rather pleased that his stubborn older brother had listened to him for once.

'What was it that you wanted to discuss with me?' George asked.

'Oh, yes. First of all, the accounts. I took it upon myself to do them, since you'd rather hide down here every minute of the day. We fared far better than expected last quarter, despite those cancelled orders, and made quite a handsome profit. One of us will have to go to the bank before Friday to withdraw the money for the servants' wages. Arthur needs his wages at the end of this week too.'

'I'm aware.'

'Do you ever get the feeling that we're paying the man two hundred pounds a year to quarrel with our sister?'

'I do, but we can't exactly dismiss him or cut his wages. Molly wouldn't allow it. And his ability as a landscape gardener is indisputable.'

'I know, I know. I was simply making an observation – I wasn't suggesting we cut his wages or anything.' Douglas cleared his throat. 'The second matter was the next Gentlemen Inventors' Society presentation dinner.'

'It's not until the end of March. And I'm still considering cancelling my membership after what happened at this year's dinner.'

'But it's always interesting to see what the other members have come up with.' Many of them had tried to copy George and Douglas's work, but no one had even come close to successfully doing so. And even if they had, the brothers still had their patents.

'We have won the medal five years in a row. There's no competition,' replied George flatly.

'That's why it's fun to blow the other members away with whatever we choose to display. Speaking of which, we'll have to decide what to present this time. Actually, I was thinking that we should present separately for a change, to make things more interesting.'

'That's not a bad idea.'

'Oh, and make sure you avoid talking to Charles Babbage, after what happened at the last dinner.'

'I stand by what I said to him.'

'You called him a "delusional failure". The man was one of our heroes growing up, and you insulted him!'

'I wouldn't say he was a "hero". That implies sycophantic worship. He was an inspiration to us in our youth, but his more recent work has proved to be unfruitful, and yet he still wastes money and time on it. We superseded him before we were even in our adolescence.'

'Well, that is true, but you shouldn't have said what you did in front of his peers.'

'It is of little consequence to me.'

Douglas sighed. He watched his brother work for a short while, wondering if he knew he was still standing beside him. But he wasn't finished with George yet. The truth was, he'd only been warming up to the real reason for his visit. Best to get it over with. He took a deep breath. 'The Marsdens are coming to dinner tonight—'

George stopped what he was doing. 'Please don't ask—'

'—and I want you to be there.'

'I don't see why.'

'Because it's the first time our two families are to formally meet, so I want to make a good impression. And because, since you're technically head of the family, it would be ill-mannered of you not to attend. And because I am asking you to.'

George took off his glasses. 'Can't you simply say that I was called away on business?'

'No.'

'For God's sake...' George covered his face with his hand.

'Look, I'm already nervous about bringing the Marsdens to Ravenfeld Hall, and I could do with some support. Besides, Molly's agreed,' Douglas lied.

Finally George looked him in the eye. 'I can't imagine her wanting to participate in such a trivial event.'

'She doesn't. But she's doing it out of the goodness of her heart, and to act as your nanny.'

'I can't imagine a greater waste of an evening than making conversation with simple-minded people in whom I have no interest whatsoever.'

'Clara and I are engaged now. Those "simple-minded people" are going to be my in-laws!'

George widened his eyes a fraction. 'You proposed?'

'Last week. Did you not see the message I sent you?'

George turned to the pile of papers on his desk and began rummaging through them, in the process unearthing a rectangular silver box about as big as a cigarette case. Inside its bottom half were rows of lettered and numbered keys, and inside the top half was an indented, glass-fronted screen. A needle moved across the screen when a message was received, writing the words in iron oxide powder. And at that moment a single line of text was displayed:

+PROPOSED TO CLARA. SHE ACCEPTED!–

'I wish you'd stop sending me these messages.' George slid the bar along the bottom of the pocket telegraph to erase the message from the screen, although a faint imprint was still visible. He forcefully moved the bar several more times.

'Well, it's the most effective way to communicate with you. You never listen to me when I'm talking to you.' And even then, George hadn't seen the message – and a very important one it was too! That explained why he had never alluded to the engagement; Douglas had thought he was being sulky about it.

'I do listen – I simply don't care to respond when you're talking nonsense.'

'Liar. So are you coming or not?'

'No.'

Douglas set his teeth hard together. 'Please.'

'My presence will add nothing.'

'Well, it'd make me feel as though I had some reinforcement against Clara's father. And I'd like to think you take *some* interest in your family's affairs. I was going to ask you to be my best man.'

'You'd be better off asking Dick Cullwick.'

'Dick is a good friend, but you're my brother. You have the stronger claim.'

'I'm sure Dick would appreciate the position more.'

'But I want you.'

'*Fine*. I suppose I can't refuse you that.' George wasn't even looking at Douglas now. 'But I'm still not attending this dinner.'

'If you don't come, I'll tell Betsey and Elsie to stop washing your clothes.' When this failed to produce a response, Douglas knew he'd have to resort to his last trick, even if it was based on pure falsehood. 'There's another reason I'd like you there, too: Clara's brother has designs on Molly.'

That got George's attention. 'He has?'

'What? You didn't notice the way he was looking at her at the ball last Christmas?'

'I can't say I did.'

'Well, you're not exactly adept at understanding human behaviour. But take it from me: he was leering at her every chance he got. He'll probably make a nuisance of himself to her throughout dinner.'

George sighed. 'Very well. When are they coming?'

'Eight o'clock. Remember to dress appropriately.'

Leaving George's cave, Douglas walked back down the tunnel and entered the lift. He pressed a green button labelled 'GARDEN', felt the metal box shunt, and gripped the handrail tightly as the lift rocketed upwards. Gradually it slowed, then began to crawl sideways along a track, until finally he felt it come to a stop. The doors slid back and the lift's interior was flooded with daylight. There was a sweet scent in the air as Douglas stepped out of the lift, which was now concealed inside a hollow tree, and planted his feet on the dewy turf. The woodland made up almost half of Ravenfeld Hall's 250-acre garden and was like something out of a children's tale. One would expect to find fairies and elves amongst the ancient, ivy-clothed trees, leafy undergrowth and vibrant knots of chrysanthemums. Most of the trees were partially bare now that it was November, and their gold and brown leaves carpeted the ground. They gave off that pleasing musty smell that follows the rain. Enormous red toadstools had sprouted in the preceding few weeks; some big enough to sit on, thanks to Molly's patented growth serum.

Nearby stood a tree that was at least fifty feet high, thick in girth, and with red vines strung across its trunk like decorative sashes. There came a rustling from its rich red canopy, and a petite figure suddenly descended from its branches. Wrapped in a vine harness, Molly gripped a thick vine as she planted her feet against the trunk to steady herself. She began ramming something – possibly a spigot – into the tree's bark. When she was done, she tugged the thick vine and was lowered a few inches so that she could repeat the procedure on the neighbouring tree.

'What are you doing?' Douglas called when he reached the base of the trunk.

'Gathering sap to make dressings,' she answered. 'Hold on, I'll come down.'

'You don't have to…'

But she'd already begun her descent. Douglas watched as she gradually came down, steadying herself on a branch every now and then until, when she was about four feet from the ground, she released her hold on the thick vine as the other vines wrapped around her fell away. She landed lightly on her feet, as nimble as a cat.

She picked leaves from her wispy brown hair as she turned around to face him. 'So, what's the matter, dear brother?'

'The Marsdens are coming to dinner this evening.'

She put her hands on her hips. 'And you want me to be there.'

'Oh, not you as well, Mol. I was relying on you to agree.'

'Look, I have no objection to Clara. She's a sweet, normal girl who doesn't seem to be after your money. But I can't imagine that she and I have anything to say to each other.'

There was some truth to that statement, Douglas knew. As he looked at his little sister, he held up a mental portrait of Clara beside her. They couldn't be more unlike. 'But I'll need you to keep George in line.' He swallowed. Lying to George had been a risky manoeuvre, but making him believe that Molly might be in an uncomfortable situation had been the only way Douglas could think of to get him to agree.

Molly raised her eyebrows. 'You persuaded George to attend?'

'Not without difficulty. But George isn't known for his manners in the presence of company…'

'Hmm, that is true. Well, I suppose I'll have to be there, then, won't I?' she sighed.

Douglas gave her a quick squeeze. 'Thanks, Mol, I appreciate it.'

She waved her hand dismissively and retrieved a spade. 'Have you resolved the question of living arrangements yet?'

Douglas rubbed the back of his neck. 'Not yet.'

'You'll end up renting the house your in-laws have chosen for you. I know it,' said Molly matter-of-factly.

Clara's family had been subtly appealing to Douglas to rent a house in Grenville Place that was only half a mile away from theirs, once the couple were married. Douglas hadn't committed himself, although if Clara was unnerved by the things she saw at Ravenfeld Hall, then her living there would be out of the question.

'Nothing has been decided yet,' he said.

'It might as well be. You won't oppose Mr Marsden. And you said he's been hinting that he'd take you on as a partner in his shipbuilding firm.'

'He said he could use my engineering expertise and that it makes sense for me to become a partner, since we're to be family.'

'Family my foot! You're an asset to him, that's all. And what about your current business partner? How will George feel if you quit the android-building business that the two of you established together? Have you even told him about Mr Marsden's offer?'

'Not yet. I'll tell him after dinner this evening. But I'm not seriously thinking about accepting the offer.'

'You are, or else you'd have refused Mr Marsden there and then. You'll accept to appease your future father-in-law. Then you'll design steamers instead of airships and androids, be content with your new business friends and lovely wife, and we'll see you once a year at Christmas.'

'I doubt it will come to that, Mol! Besides, what does it matter either way? If Clara were to come and live here, things would still change.'

'I know,' Molly said irritably, and then she sighed. 'I'll do my best to treat her like a sister, even if she doesn't take to me immediately.' She pushed past Douglas and disappeared behind a thick, leafy bush.

Douglas didn't linger for long, and trod his way back to the house with his hands thrust deep into his pockets, kicking through piles of leaves as he walked. At least Molly was trying to accept the change, unlike George. But why was it so hard for her? If she were to marry Arthur she would…actually, Arthur half-lived at Ravenfeld Hall already, so there wouldn't be that much of a difference. Douglas had hoped that walking through his sister's mystically beautiful garden rather than returning in the lift would improve his humour, but his mood was little improved by the time he reached the house. He paused for a moment before Ravenfeld Hall's Gothic façade. It was a little imposing, especially since, thanks to a little mechanical trickery, some of the carved animals and gargoyles actually moved. But he was fond of his home. Thankfully, Clara wouldn't be able to see too much of the house in the darkness of evening – the moving statues might frighten her. *You really want a bride who is too afraid to enter your house in daylight?* asked a faint voice in the back of his head. Douglas ignored it.

His anxiety only increased when he entered the north hall and beheld claw marks on one of the tapestries. It was all well and good for Lord Leyton to leave his menagerie of mechanical animals at Ravenfeld Hall while his ducal estate and London town house were being renovated and he retreated to his Italian villa (with Maestro in tow), but it was causing a lot of bother. A small patch of air above Douglas's head wavered, as it might on a hot day. The wavering shape drifted higher and hovered over the first-floor balcony; then a silver metallic peacock slowly materialised in its place. The bird looked down at Douglas almost with contempt, before flying away. Why on earth had their patron wanted an invisible peacock, of all things? It had taken three days of fiddling about with mirrors to perfect it.

In an attempt to reassure himself, Douglas decided to check how preparations were progressing for the evening. The servants were already laying the table in the dining room. They'd hired extra help for the event, and even some of the androids had offered their services. Pirouette was arranging silverware, elegantly bending and twirling her way around the long rectangular dining table. Her silky, flowing movements were mesmerising –

like a living ribbon. She was a bronze ballerina, part porcelain and steel in places where they'd run out of bronze. She'd been a cheap and rather hastily built commission for Signor Paolucci, the dance master of a now-famous troupe.

'Are the preparations for tonight going well, Pirouette?' Douglas enquired.

'Yes, Master Douglas.' She returned to a standing position, and light rippled along the jewels in the headdress crowning her dark hair. 'There was something of a racket in the kitchen earlier, but it seems to have stopped now. And I'm nearly finished with the silverware. The housekeeper has allowed me to decorate the dining table,' she added gleefully.

'Remember to only use fruit and foliage – no flowers.'

'Don't worry, Master Douglas. I remember what you told me.'

'Thank you, Pirouette. I promise I'll address your repairs tomorrow – I've been too busy today, with one thing and another.'

'There's still plenty of time. Although Paolucci needs me to be in prime condition for his new ballet's London debut next week.' She smiled brightly.

'Fear not, you'll be as good as new by then. Oh, and you're clear about the instructions for you all tonight?'

'Yes, Master: we're to confine ourselves to our rooms until the guests have left.'

'Good. Make sure the other androids know too.'

Pirouette nodded and resumed her task.

As Douglas left the dining room and returned to the north hall, he heard heavy footsteps from the direction of the servants' quarters. Betsey staggered into the hall. The girl's face was flushed, and wisps of her hair stuck out from under her cap. Her clothes and skin were smeared with a lumpy beige paste.

'Betsey, what's going on?' asked Douglas.

'It's those two little buggers, sir,' she panted. 'They carried off the servants' breakfast and have been running around the house making a mess with it.'

No sooner had she said that than the two little buggers in question catapulted down the staircase. The Wind-Up Wonder, a little acrobat resembling a boy in a harlequin costume, and his companion, Sweep, balanced a cooking pot of porridge between them. They were flinging ladles of it in every direction. It was rather sloppy (since the new kitchen maid was still learning the rudiments of cooking), and had a considerable range.

'Sweep! Wonderwind! Stop that this—' Douglas was cut off when a ladle of lukewarm porridge hit him directly in the head.

'Come here, you little swines!' Betsey lunged for the pair, but the buxom upper housemaid was not terribly quick on her feet, although she was as strong as an ox.

Wonderwind laughed as he evaded her grasp – until a gloved hand shot out from an adjoining room and grabbed him by the collar of his red and white diamonded costume. A tall, gold-skinned, moustached soldier was standing in the drawing room doorway, his left arm now four yards long. As he strolled into the north hall, his arm gradually retracted until it was the same length as his right one.

'Causing mischief again?' He held Wonderwind aloft and peered into his shocked face. The soldier's red pupils burned intensely. 'In the army they'd have whipped a disobedient little rascal like you.'

'You were only in the army for a couple of months, Colonel,' jeered Wonderwind. 'Then after the government found out that that general had commissioned you in secret, they decided you were their property – not that they've ever needed you to fight for them! They've forgotten about you and left you to rust!'

'If you'd seen the things I saw during the mutiny, you wouldn't speak so lightly. Now, I'm going to take the pair of you upstairs, where you're to wind down and not cause any trouble this evening.' The soldier android grasped Sweep by the stem of his brush as he spoke.

'Thank you, Colonel Copperton,' said Douglas. 'I swear those two grow wilder every day. I appreciate your help.' He noticed that the colonel was still wearing the medal that Pirouette had fashioned out of a length of pink ribbon and a penny, and jokingly pinned to his breast amongst his other medals.

'It is no trouble, Master Douglas. I am simply doing my duty. I understand how important this dinner is to you. Come along, you little ruffians.' Copperton carried the (now more subdued) pair of automata upstairs.

Douglas ran his hand through his hair and realised that it was clotted with porridge. Now he would need to wash, on top of everything else. 'Betsey, could you find time to clean up this mess before tonight?'

'I suppose I'll have to, sir,' she huffed. 'Can't have your guests seeing this. I had plenty of other things to do, mind. This is all we needed,' she muttered to herself as she trailed back to the servants' quarters.

Chapter Two

George had hoped to have the computer finished by the afternoon, but after one of his tools broke, he was forced to pause his work and retrieve a replacement from the main workshop in the western tower.

The autumn sunlight seeping into the workshop was softer than the harsh electric light that his eyes had grown accustomed to underground. This was where he and Douglas constructed their commissions. George dully registered the half-completed models lying around, but there was no immediate need to finish them, since the brothers were still in the lull between the end of the London season and Christmas. Some of their wealthier patrons had already requested toys for their offspring. Usually it was Douglas who saw to those: he always added imaginative details that delighted the children. That Noah's Ark toy had been a triumph last year, and this year they'd already received several orders for more of them. No matter how many rooms away the animals were, they always came to Noah, who presided on top of the Ark. Although the toy's popularity meant weeks of trying to avoid stepping on pairs of tiny animals trailing across the workshop floor to board the miniature Ark, George and Douglas had noticed with the first few models that sometimes the animals paired up with the wrong mates, so the lion would walk alongside the female zebra, or one of the giraffes would have a cat riding on its back. George tried to discourage his brother from accepting every order for toys; he was content to ignore them when it wasn't at a patron's insistence. Many of the children would either break, lose or grow bored of their novel presents before long anyway. And as for giving toys to local poor children and orphanages for free…what a complete waste of time, money and resources, even if it was advantageous for their image. But Douglas could do as he pleased, and Molly was happy to assist him in distributing them.

Everything appeared immaterial as George made his way back down in the lift. Pausing in his work had made him realise his own tiredness. A cup of coffee from the machine he kept on his desk restored him partially, and he continued to inscribe the remaining data discs.

Two hours later, George took in his finished machine. Douglas might describe it as 'severely functional without an ounce of creativity in its design', but in its creator's eyes the computer's sheer complexity compensated for its lack of aesthetic appeal. It satisfied George to see it in its completed state, although there was something of that emptiness that comes with the completion of a project. The excitement of solving challenges, and the pleasure found in the physical and mental toil, gave way to the inertia of triumph. It was true that the testing phase would occupy him for some time, and that there would likely be a process of refinement. But the struggle would soon be over – if this experiment ran successfully. That success would mark the project's summit; then George's enthusiasm for it would decline rapidly, and it wouldn't be long before his mind grew restless again. He didn't have a particular project in mind to begin next. Douglas had suggested he find some sort of hobby, but what? He'd mastered several instruments in his adolescence, fishing sounded incredibly boring, and hunting and shooting didn't appeal to him. (Where was the sense in chasing a fox, or any other animal, that was not intended for the table but for a mount on the wall?) Douglas still thought sport was a good option. 'It would appeal to your competitive nature,' he'd said. But there wouldn't be much competition. George could box and fence exceptionally well, and during the summer he'd embarrassed every other gentleman at Dick Cullwick's cricket match with his superb coordination and speed. He hadn't been invited again.

George checked one or two components before curling his fingers around the cool, smooth ebony lever on the control panel. The moment of truth had arrived. He pulled the lever, and immediately heard something winding within the computer. His fingers flew across the control panel's keys with rhythmical regularity, while the wheels inside the machine could be heard turning as it crunched away at the problem he'd set it. With his arms folded across his chest, he sat and listened. The fans hummed loudly: the temperature gauge indicated that they were performing their function. The control panel's timer showed twenty-four hours to completion – then suddenly jumped to eighteen, then returned to twenty-four. The precise time was difficult to determine, since it was practically impossible to know the quantities of data and statistics the machine's processors would need to analyse in order to complete their task. But it would be more than enough time in which to attend this tedious dinner. Discarding his old black greatcoat on the back of his chair, George left his workshop and strolled down the tunnel to the lift to dress for dinner. The churning and clacking of the mechanical brain echoed after him.

Douglas thought he'd managed to get all of the porridge out of his hair, having spent the past ten minutes stripped to the waist with his head dunked in a washbasin. His thick, wavy hair was auburn in colour – a fiery red in direct sunlight. As he reached for a towel, out of the corner of his eye he noticed something moving. But when he looked around his bedroom, all was still. His anxiety about the Marsdens' visit must be sending him mad, he thought, while vigorously rubbing his hair dry. As he put on his best white shirt, waistcoat and black tailcoat, in his mind he tried to leap ahead past this evening, and to regard the dinner as one small hurdle to overcome on the path to conjugal bliss. He imagined the actual wedding day, and how lovely Clara would look as she sailed gracefully down the aisle in her white dress. After tonight, everything would become easier. Come spring, they would marry and move into the new house, and…and…he wouldn't see his brother or sister for quite some time. Perhaps Molly wasn't completely unjustified in what she'd said earlier. But they couldn't go on as they were forever. It was natural for the three of them to live independently, although they weren't exactly on top of one another in this sprawling manor house. Douglas shook his head and adjusted his collar, in the process finding another small scab of crusty porridge behind his left ear. Damn Wonderwind's mischief! All of their androids, even the self-aware ones, were bound to obey their master or mistress's every command, save in exceptional circumstances. Unfortunately, Wonderwind had discovered a loophole: if someone looked like they were about to give him an order, he'd cover his ears or find a way to silence them. Once he'd realised this, he'd taught the trick to his best friend, Sweep.

Douglas froze. This time he definitely saw something moving underneath the bedclothes. He lifted the topmost sheet and saw a small tin automaton sitting there. 'Get out, now!'

It scampered out of the room – passing Molly, who was standing in the doorway with an amused smile on her face. She'd changed into a pale blue silk dress, although her hair was still in its usual unruly state.

'You need to try and keep calm, Douglas.'

'Easy enough for you to say,' he retorted as he fumbled with his necktie. 'Your future doesn't rest on a single evening.'

'Oh, don't be so dramatic. Here, let me help with that.' After watching him struggle with it for long enough, she crossed the room and took hold of the necktie.

Douglas sighed. 'I just want everyone to be on good terms this evening.'

'Everything will be fine,' Molly assured him, as her fingers gently worked the white silk.

'Are Sweep and Wonderwind wound down?'

'Yes, they have been for an hour. Colonel Copperton said so.' Molly removed her hands from the neatly fastened necktie and took her brother firmly by the shoulders. 'You have done all you can to ensure that this evening is a success. Now stop fretting.'

'Whatever you say, Dr Abernathy,' Douglas smiled.

'Will you stop that? It's been months since I got my doctorate.'

'I promise I'll stop after a year.'

'No you won't.' But she grinned at him nevertheless. She seemed calmer since their exchange that afternoon.

'Or would you prefer to be Mrs Greenwood?'

'I don't see much chance of that happening.'

'You and Arthur have been courting long enough. Surely it's not unreasonable that he might propose?'

'I'd rather not think about it.'

'Why? Do you not want him to?'

Molly bit her lip. Douglas knew that this was a pressure point with her, although he hadn't realised to what extent, and he wasn't entirely sure about the reason for it. But he knew that Molly and Arthur cared deeply for each other, even if they did row spectacularly about the garden – and anything else they could find to disagree about.

'Well, you don't have to worry about whether George and I will consent or not. Arthur is safe on that score.'

'I don't need your consent now I'm twenty-two, although if I were to marry I would like to think that you approved of my choice. But let's get one wedding over and done with before we start thinking about another.' She tried to make light of it, but her choice of words struck Douglas. The sigh that succeeded them was also telling of her true feelings. 'I can't believe how fast this has all come about,' she said casually, although there was a sad note to her voice.

'Neither can I,' Douglas admitted.

It had all started eight months ago, when he and George had received a letter from Mr Richard Courtenay, a glassware manufacturer, asking to discuss a commission he had for them. Douglas had met Mr Courtenay for dinner at Lake's in Cheapside, only to discover that the commission was a ruse and their 'client' was in fact Dick Cullwick, his old schoolfellow. Despite Douglas and George having spent only ten days at the school (established in the home of an impoverished vicar), in that brief time Dick and Douglas had managed to form a friendship. Dick had marvelled at what the new boys could do with clockwork, and asked Douglas no end of questions when they were sitting in their dorm. Dick's passion was entomology, and he'd shown Douglas how to catch butterflies in the school grounds. Despite twenty years having passed, Dick hadn't forgotten Douglas, and he'd greeted him warmly as he approached their table at Lake's. The two of them reminisced as they enjoyed a capital dinner. Dick laughed when recalling how George and Douglas had disrupted Sunday prayers with a flying mechanical gargoyle – an incident that had led to them being caned and, ultimately, expelled. The two men renewed their acquaintance, and Dick invited Douglas, Molly and a reluctant George to a ball in April. Dick was fond of a party. He was also fond of matchmaking.

'What sort of girl takes your fancy?' he'd asked Douglas, who in response bashfully gave as good a description as he could. Ten minutes later, Dick introduced him to Miss Clara Marsden, who was accompanied by her mother. Dick had done business with Mr Marsden, a London shipbuilder, and was well acquainted with the family. Douglas danced with Miss Marsden twice and caught Dick grinning at him constantly. Dick had then promoted the acquaintance between his friend and Miss Marsden, until his assistance was no longer required. Douglas had been invited to dinners and dances held by the Marsdens, and often found himself sitting beside Clara. Seven months after Dick's ball, he had asked Mr Marsden for his daughter's hand.

And now Molly wandered about her brother's room, imagining it bare, with only the antique bed to occupy it. She wrung her hands, making sure that her back was turned to Douglas. So many words rushed upon her, as this felt like her last chance to utter them: that he was being foolish; that whomever he chose to be his wife should accept him for who he was and not encourage him to abandon his passions; that she, Molly, would miss him terribly and didn't want him to leave Ravenfeld Hall. The last one was pure selfishness. But in any case, she couldn't bring herself to utter any of those things. Instead she forced herself to smile, and said, 'I'd better dress my hair.'

Douglas gently kissed her cheek before she left.

Molly met George on the landing. He was now dressed smartly in a black tailcoat, trousers and waistcoat. On hearing his sister's approach, he raised his head.

'How much of that did you overhear?' she asked.

'I caught most of it. I wanted to speak to Douglas, but now's probably not the best time. It sounds as if he's too overwrought to listen.'

'I'd say so.'

'There's nothing we can do,' said George, as they walked downstairs together. 'We have to leave him to his fate.'

Molly sighed. 'Yes. You're right.'

Chapter Three

It was only once the Marsdens arrived that Douglas considered whether insisting on his siblings' presence had been a mistake. Despite the warnings he'd given them, there was still a risk that they might say or do something to jeopardise good relations between the two families.

No sooner had the clocks in the north hall struck eight than the Marsdens' coach pulled up on the drive. In the second before the butler ushered the guests into the drawing room, Douglas took a deep breath. Clara looked charming in her white tarlatan dress, festooned with pink roses and worn over layers of pink petticoats. More pink roses were woven through her chestnut hair. Douglas felt his heart swell on beholding her approaching him, her radiant smile illuminating her entire face. Her large dark eyes were fixed on his; their look soft and full of warmth. He longed to kiss her, but didn't dare to in the presence of her family. Mr Marsden was a portly, ruddy-faced, half-bald man. Where he did have hair, it was the same thick chestnut colour as his daughter's. His wife was thin, as shrivelled as a prune, and nervy. Even a slight noise set her on her guard, in a deerlike manner. Mr Jonathan Marsden, Clara's older brother, entered the room with his usual superior but curiously detached manner and knowing smile, as if the world were a spectacle for his amusement. Mr and Mrs Marsden seemed almost overwhelmed by the splendour of the drawing room and what glimpses they caught of the adjoining rooms. Douglas got the feeling that Mrs Marsden was estimating the value of each item of furniture.

George was reserved but sufficiently polite as he greeted the family. Clara smiled shyly at him and Molly, whom she'd met only once before at Dick's Christmas ball nearly a year ago. Molly returned the smile. Her hair had now been shaped into a bun, with the aid of many pins. She was wearing her gold hairpin with the iridescent blue-glass butterfly that occasionally flapped its wings.

'It is a pleasure to see you again, Miss Abernathy,' said Clara brightly.

'*Doctor* Abernathy,' put in Douglas with a proud smile.

Molly narrowed her eyes at him.

Clara's eyes widened in confusion and surprise. 'Doctor?'

'Molly is a doctor of botany. She graduated from the University College this summer – the first woman to do so,' Douglas informed her. 'And they let her graduate a year early, too!'

The rest of the Marsdens looked bemused. Molly overheard Mrs Marsden whisper to her daughter, 'See, my dear? That is what too much education does to a young woman.'

What is that supposed to mean? Molly thought. She was no great beauty, but she was hardly a hag. If anything, she looked closer to eighteen than to twenty-two. George and Douglas also looked several years younger than their true ages, she'd sometimes noted.

Douglas feared that his well-meant attempt to bolster his sister's standing had only resulted in awkwardness, and so he diverted his guests' attention with the offer of drinks. He relaxed only a minuscule amount once all the company were seated, the families facing one another. George placed himself opposite Jonathan Marsden and shot him a warning glare whenever he attempted to address, or even glance at, Molly.

'There is a lot of history in this house,' remarked Mrs Marsden, eyeing the fine paintings. 'I understand that you are related to the Duke of Hereford?'

'The duke is our second cousin. George was supposed to be the heir to the dukedom after our maternal uncle died, but he didn't want the title and so he didn't make a petition to the House of Lords,' answered Douglas.

'Didn't want a dukedom?' cried a wide-eyed Mrs Marsden.

George calmly regarded her with his glacial eyes. 'I don't care for pomp and prestige, Mrs Marsden. Titles are worthless to me.'

Mrs Marsden trembled slightly. George could have that effect on people, and this was him at his most amiable.

'However, he did inherit this house, so it all worked out for the best,' added Douglas.

'And what was your father?' enquired Jonathan.

'Our father was a clockmaker.' Douglas had been slightly embarrassed to confess this fact to Mr Marsden when he'd asked for his consent to marry Clara. Mr Marsden had imagined that Douglas's father was at least an earl.

'It is a rather long story,' said Molly breezily, seeing Mrs Marsden practically bursting with curiosity. 'So, Miss Marsden, I understand that you are an accomplished artist and musician?'

'I do like to draw.' Clara blushed charmingly (or at least, Douglas thought so). 'And I play a little piano.'

'Clara plays wonderfully,' chimed in her mother. 'She's had lessons since she was three and her teacher said she was a prodigy. Are you musical at all, Miss—*Doctor* Abernathy?'

'I can play the piano tolerably well. I draw a little, too – mostly botanical illustrations. I am chiefly devoted to gardening.' Molly tried to smile sweetly. 'But I breed plants as well as grow them – that's the main focus of my research.' It was useless trying to explain the finer points of her research to them.

'I see.' Mrs Marsden still sounded unimpressed. She moved on to the subject of dress, floundering slightly as Molly was ignorant of, or indifferent to, the latest fashions (she couldn't understand why girls wore such huge, bell-shaped skirts now – plus a train, to waste as much fabric as possible).

The men, meanwhile, talked business.

'Quite an original enterprise you have here,' Mr Marsden remarked to George. 'Although you appear to be rather selective in your choice of commissions, from what your brother tells me.'

'We like to be challenged.' Douglas smiled. 'And we're not short of—'

'But it means less business. Why not accept every feasible commission that comes your way?' asked Jonathan superciliously.

'Well, as I was explaining, we make enough through investments and the estate's tenants to be at liberty to choose what work we like.'

'There are also other factors to assess when considering a potential commission, such as travel, time and material costs,' added George.

'Of course, of course.' Mr Marsden nodded. He sometimes addressed George with greater respect than his future son-in-law. 'Do you not employ anyone else?'

'We have tried training apprentices a couple of times, but they didn't last longer than a week. We prefer to work as a two-man team,' replied Douglas.

'Anyone else is an interference.' George spoke the truth more plainly.

'You don't even have a clerk?'

'George is responsible for the accounts.'

'It must be a challenge to work with your brother without quarrelling. Father and I are often at odds with each other,' remarked Jonathan.

George and Douglas exchanged a knowing look. There were times when they had argued to the point of not speaking for a day or two.

'You're aware, Mr Abernathy, that we have offered to make a generous wedding present of a suite of furniture for Douglas and Clara's new house?' remarked Mr Marsden.

'Yes. Very generous.' George's demeanour, which had been on the point of thawing slightly, became cold and stiff again. Presumptuous old fool, he thought. If he thinks he can mould Douglas to his liking, he'll be disappointed. 'Although it will not be as easy to conduct our business between here and South Kensington,' he observed.

'Yes, there is that drawback,' Mr Marsden muttered insouciantly. 'But of course, if your brother accepts my offer of a partnership, that won't be an issue.'

George turned sharply to face Douglas, whose guilty expression confirmed the statement.

'Did you mention the house in Grenville Place, Mr Marsden?' enquired his wife. 'Such a charming property. Just the thing for a newly married couple. Modern, conveniently placed, and with plenty of space for a growing family. I can think of nowhere better for them to live after they're married, can you, Miss Abernathy? I was saying to Clara that she must have a *good* set of silverware, now she's to be mistress of her own house...'

Douglas waited until Mrs Marsden was prattling away, then leant closer to his brother to whisper, 'I was going to tell you.'

'When? Once the wedding was over?' George hissed.

'No: after tonight. I was only considering it. Nothing was decided.'

George's accusing stare didn't falter. 'I think everything has already been decided between you and the Marsdens.'

Douglas was thankful when Parsons reappeared to summon everyone to dinner. He escorted Mrs Marsden, while Clara was escorted by her father. George gave Molly his arm before Jonathan had a chance to. As the party passed the north hall's grand oaken staircase, the wooden dogs on the newel posts bowed politely. The deer busts mounted on the walls moved their heads from side to side and flicked their ears, as if completely unaware that a taxidermist had relieved them of their bodies.

'It's all right, angel.' Douglas tried to reassure Clara, who had begun to tremble at the sight of them. 'They're controlled by clockwork, although they are a little unnerving if you're not used to them. George, can you stop them moving, please?'

George suppressed a sigh and walked across to a switch in the wall. The deer assumed their normal positions.

The dining room looked splendid. The dishes were ready on the sideboard, the tableware was neatly arranged, and Pirouette had done a marvellous job with the decorations. The silverware glittered under the chandelier's light. The servants were at their stations, all in neat, starched uniforms. Given the lack of a designated host and hostess, and the odd number of guests, the seating arrangements did not adhere strictly to custom. Clara held the hostess's place at the head of the table, while Douglas occupied the foot. Mr Marsden joked that it would be good preparation for when they hosted gatherings at their own home. Mr Marsden was on his daughter's right, while Mrs Marsden was to the right of Douglas. Jonathan sat beside his father, with George directly opposite. Molly was beside him, on Clara's immediate left.

The dinner did not run as smoothly as anticipated. Throughout each course Douglas found himself drinking more glasses of wine than he ought to, as he tried to ignore his siblings' behaviour. Following the revelation about Mr Marsden's partnership offer, George maintained an outward stance of sheer indifference to the whole occasion. Douglas didn't honestly think that

Molly meant to behave rudely towards Clara. In fact, there wasn't anything in particular about her behaviour that one could find fault with. She smiled pleasantly, nodded intelligently when Clara or her mother (usually her mother) spoke, and asked light, insubstantial questions to show that she took an interest in her future sister-in-law. Their conversation about French ball gowns must have torn Molly up inside. Douglas saw her fingers clawing at her skirts or dress sleeves beneath the table as she tried desperately not to pick her nails, as was her habit when she was irritated. But whether Molly was consciously aware of it or not, there was a palpable hostility emitting from her that Clara undoubtedly felt. Douglas was certain that she shivered occasionally when Molly looked her in the eye.

And since Molly felt hostility towards the Marsdens, so did her friend Betsey, who had at the last minute been called upon to wait at the table. The grocer's daughter, Sarah Ann, was still a bundle of nerves after finding a gold-scaled viper (another of Lord Leyton's mechanimals) hiding in the vegetables. The girl had then proceeded to scream the house down. Betsey's face was set in a grimace as she dumped down dishes and snatched up plates, much to the Marsdens' amazement. They must've thought that the servants at Ravenfeld Hall were poorly trained. Douglas could only wince and try to distract them with subjects he hoped would interest them. The business of eating wholly occupied Mr Marsden, however, who merely nodded or grunted in accord when addressed.

In Molly's eyes, the situation was worse than she'd imagined. It became increasingly apparent to her that Clara, although infinitely superior to the mercenary Laura Blakeslee and the seductress Mademoiselle Roux-Voclain, was not well suited to Douglas. Molly didn't think much of Clara's family either, who were obviously only interested in Douglas's money and ties to nobility. But what was worse, if Molly's suspicions were correct, was that Clara didn't really love Douglas. Her embarrassed air and constant smiles spoke of a girlish heart and girlish affection, not a deep and lasting love. Molly feared that Clara's love was like blossom: quick to appear at the slightest hint of warmth, and beautiful while it lasted, but ultimately fragile and short-lived. Perhaps a deeper affection would take root in time, but there was no telling whether that would be the case. When Molly spoke of her brother to Clara, it was clear that she knew little about him, even allowing for their seven-month courtship. She spoke of him in the pleasantest of terms: he was 'kind' and 'charming' and 'wonderfully clever', but nothing more specific than that. She knew nothing of those quirks of his that Molly found so endearing, nor of his opinions and ideas. Molly couldn't indulge in good-natured ridicule of Douglas through anecdotes that would prompt anyone who knew him well to remark how like him that was, and to respond with a similar tale of their own. Clara simply exclaimed, 'Oh, really?' Molly hoped that her impressions were wrong, but when she met George's eye, his expression told her that he thought likewise. If even he could see it, then the situation really was bad.

As the entrée was being cleared away, and as Mr Marsden had finally grown more loquacious now that he had a few glasses of sherry inside him, Douglas began to relax. All seemed to be going well at last. He smiled at his beloved, who offered a tentative, gentle smile in return. The dessert was served. Mr Marsden had an early coffee as he didn't care for sweets, and Betsey did her best to slosh some of the coffee over the side of the cup into the saucer. Douglas, driven by a spontaneous surge of good spirits, rose from his seat with his wine glass in hand and proposed a toast to their guests' good health. Despite the eccentric timing of this well-meant gesture, Mr Marsden raised his glass, and the rest of his family followed his lead. Molly played along, though she had to nudge George's arm to get him to raise his glass. He seemed to be drifting off to sleep.

'To the future prosperity of both our families.' Douglas smiled warmly. The toast was drunk and he beamed at Clara as he resumed his seat.

Then the unthinkable happened. There came a distant rumble that shook the table, causing the tableware to clatter. Turning heads and furrowed brows ensued. The rumbling was soon accompanied by what sounded like the rhythmic pounding of paws, growing louder by the second. Before any of the guests had a chance to enquire as to what the noise was, its source burst into the dining room. There stood a huge bronze tiger with silver stripes. Sweep and Wonderwind were riding on its back. The beast let out a thundering roar and displayed its razor-sharp teeth. Clara shrieked. Mrs Marsden fainted, her face planting in the tapioca pudding. The tiger leapt onto the table, causing servants and guests alike to abandon their stations. In an act of chivalry, Douglas rushed immediately to Clara's side, as her brother fled from the table. Mr Marsden dragged his senseless wife away by the shoulders. George and Molly made a more dignified show as they left their seats. The party crowded around the hearth, and Douglas entrusted his trembling fiancée to Molly's care. Molly tried to prevent Clara from swooning, while fruitlessly attempting to revive Mrs Marsden with smelling salts (and wiping tapioca off the poor lady's face). George calmly watched the events unfold, calculating the best course of action to take. The tiger prowled along the dining table and trained its amber eyes on the diners.

'Tiberius, get down!' Douglas ordered, but the tiger was too busy trying to shake off Wonderwind, who was pulling at his ear, to notice the command.

'Tiberius!' bellowed a brassy, far louder voice. Colonel Copperton stood in the doorway, the epitome of the man of action.

The tiger turned his head in the colonel's direction and let out an angry roar.

'Don't take that tone with me – I trained you better than that. And you two scoundrels will answer for this. Don't worry, Master Douglas, I shall see to them.'

Copperton drew his sabre. Sweep attempted to bolt towards the chimney, but the colonel fired a capsule from his palm and the little android was swallowed by a net. Try as he might, he couldn't fight his way free. Copperton then stretched out his arm to try to pluck Wonderwind off the tiger's back, but Tiberius reared up on his hind legs and Wonderwind made a leap for the chandelier.

'Don't think you can evade me that easily, you little scoundrel!'

'Can't catch me!' Wonderwind taunted, swinging merrily on the chandelier. Several cracks formed where it met the ceiling. 'We fooled you, Colonel! We were only pretending to wind down. Call yourself an officer? You're nothing but a creaky old boiler!'

Colonel Copperton, unfazed, turned to the tiger. 'Tiberius, fetch.'

Immediately the tiger went after his prey, trying to swipe Wonderwind with his huge paws.

'Shouldn't we intervene?' Molly hissed to George, as she dabbed Mrs Marsden's face with a handkerchief.

'I think the situation is under control.' George seemed quite content to watch, though Douglas looked on in despair.

Wonderwind tried his best to avoid Tiberius's lunges, but the tiger caught hold of the chandelier and tried to tear it from the ceiling. More cracks appeared in the elaborate plasterwork.

'Colonel!' Douglas cried.

'I'll take care of it, sir!' Copperton sprang up and severed the chandelier from the ceiling with his sword, catching it in his other hand and carrying Wonderwind along with it. He landed on the floor and swiftly bound the mischievous acrobat's limbs. Tiberius vented his frustration on the chandelier like a kitten with a ball of wool.

Now that the immediate danger was over, their guests were no longer frozen with terror. Mr Marsden and Parsons carried Mrs Marsden between them as the guests fled the house, with a thousand apologies from Douglas that were met with nothing but curses from Mr Marsden. Jonathan supported Clara, looking nearly as pale as she did, until his sister was safely deposited in the coach.

After the family had been driven away, Douglas marched back into the north hall and regarded his brother, his sister and the three androids with a livid expression. 'Don't any of you say a word. I don't want to hear it.' Then he bolted upstairs.

George and Molly heard his bedroom door bang shut.

'He'll come round,' Molly said.

'Yes, but when?'

She shrugged. 'Hard to say. You know what he's like.' Then she sighed heavily. 'But if the engagement has been terminated, which is most likely the case, then I can only imagine how upset he'll be. I'd rather see him angry with us than heartbroken any day.'

'But if his engagement to Miss Marsden is over, you cannot deny that that's a good thing?'

'Not really. I suppose a spell of heartbreak is better than a lifetime of unhappiness and regret.'

'Undoubtedly. I'm going to bed, since the servants have almost cleared the mess in the dining room and there's nothing useful to be done for our brother at present.'

Molly followed George upstairs, and he wished her goodnight at her door. As she undressed for bed, she tried to listen for any sounds coming from Douglas's room a few doors away. She didn't think he was crying. That was something, at least.

While all this commotion had been taking place above, down in the bowels of the house stood George's machine, seemingly dormant save for the sound of the computer's churning mind bouncing off the cave wall. Its processors clacked and whirred erratically, yet if one listened carefully, one could detect the recurring melodies amongst the cacophony. Suddenly a growling suppressed all the other sounds. The mighty mechanical mind ceased its operations, and from within the machine there came a horrible grinding and screeching. Then it fell silent. A faint drift of smoke rose from its rear.

For several minutes, only the sound of dripping water quivered through the air. Then some parts within the computer began to move again, slowly at first, before gradually being joined by the whole orchestra of gears. But their rhythm was new. One of the computer's cables snaked along the workshop floor until it connected with the mechanical arms. Their pincer-like hands stretched out and began to rip great shreds from the computer's body – first carving out pieces of casing, then partially gutting its innards with the precision of a butcher removing the most delectable organs from an animal carcass. Then the arms hunted amongst the piles of mangled metal that were within their reach, gripping useful pieces between their jaws and dragging them back to the great, mangled square body of the computer. Sparks crackled as the arms hastily welded the various bits of metal together on the workbench. They worked rapidly, and the pile of odd parts transformed into a skeletal, mismatched and feeble humanoid shape. Once it was in something of a completed state, and the dial in its chest was wound, the arms relaxed and fell to the ground. The computer's gears came to a halt.

Yet in that same moment, the scrawny scrap of an android sat upright. He got steadily to his feet and looked about himself, standing on uneven legs. He looked as if he would collapse back into a heap of scrap at any moment. His movements were almost birdlike to begin with; his head twitched to the side. Then he attempted to straighten his lopsided body without much success. But his mind was fully functional. He held his hands stiffly. They were probably the only parts of his body that were proportionately accurate and finely crafted, since originally they had been created for a defective automaton whose half-stripped carcass had been condemned to a scrap pile once George had harvested its useful parts. The android noticed the black greatcoat dangling from a chair, and hastily threw it around himself before darting into the tunnel. He was met by a steel lift at the end, with many levers and buttons inside. The android selected the one marked 'north hall', and the doors slid shut.

As he ascended, the android was overcome by a wealth of new sensations. He revelled in the exquisiteness of experience – of being *here* and *now*. The novelty of motion, of touch, of new sounds other than dripping water and colliding metal. Yes, how utterly exquisite! Had he been of a more poetic turn of mind, he'd have said that his buoyant spirits were ascending along with the lift. Then he came to a sobering stop, and the lift's doors parted smoothly. The north hall was empty. There were voices from the room to his left. He flitted across to the doorway, and put his head around the frame to see domestics clearing the dinner table after a meal. Seven places had been set. It appeared that the chandelier had been torn from the ceiling. Interesting. Apparently dinner with the Marsdens had not gone quite according to plan. He'd heard the two brothers discussing it only that morning. But that was irrelevant. He must continue. Making hardly any noise, the android opened the front door and stepped out into the wide world.

Chapter Four

By the following afternoon, Douglas still hadn't emerged from his bedroom. Gradually Molly's concern and guilt (although she hadn't been directly responsible for the previous evening's catastrophe) increased. She expressed her concerns to George, although he didn't share them.

'He's just being a fool, Molly. He can't remain in there forever.'

At midday she knocked on his door bearing a tray, on which was a steak and kidney pie (his favourite out of all the savoury things that she baked), a cup of tea, and a letter that had arrived for him that morning. When there was no answer, she placed the tray on the floor. It was still there when she returned an hour later, although there was now only an empty plate, a fork and a cup on it. At least he wasn't so broken-hearted that he intended to starve himself to death.

A couple of hours later, Douglas finally left his room and wandered into the oak parlour just as George was on the verge of vacating it, having completed his examination of the morning's newspaper. Douglas seemed unaware of – or unconcerned by – George's presence. He sat down on a sofa and ran a hand across his face.

George held out a tumbler with a sliver of amber liquid in the bottom. 'Here.'

'Thank you.' How odd; George was actually attempting to be nice. The brandy left a warm golden glow as it travelled through Douglas's body. 'I know what happened last night wasn't really your fault or Molly's.'

'No, it wasn't.'

Douglas snorted a dry laugh. George was still as brutally honest as ever, even when trying to console him. But Douglas's smile soon receded and his crestfallen expression returned. He looked into the tumbler and swished the liquid around. 'I received a letter from Mr Marsden confirming what I already knew: that the engagement is off.'

George poured himself a tumbler of plain soda water and sat on the sofa opposite Douglas. 'You knew Miss Marsden did not return your affections as you wanted her to. Your regard for her was stronger than hers for you.'

'Perhaps, but she's a kind-hearted, sweet, gentle woman. You should have seen her sneeze – it's the most charming thing in the world.' Douglas sipped his brandy, then added wistfully, 'We could have had a comfortable life together, at the very least. And who knows? In time she might have come to love me more.'

'She was not a suitable mate for you.'

'And what gives you the authority to judge that?'

'I know you – far better than Miss Marsden did.'

Both brothers sipped their drinks in contemplative silence. The ticking of the clocks on the north hall walls (leftover stock from their old clockmaker's shop) could be heard plainly: the heartbeat of the house.

Douglas cleared his throat. 'About Mr Marsden's partnership offer—'

'It doesn't matter now. Forget it.'

'I wish I could forget everything to do with the Marsden family.' Douglas reached for the brandy decanter and poured another measure into his now-empty tumbler. 'I fear I'll never find a woman who will accept me – and all this.' He waved the glass vaguely as he gestured to the oak-panelled room. Giving a short sigh, he smiled weakly. 'Oh well, here's to forever remaining a bachelor.' He raised the tumbler aloft, before downing its contents in one swallow.

When he made a move to refill the tumbler once more, George moved the decanter out of his reach. 'You've had enough.'

'That used to be my line.'

'I know my limit now. And yours.' George took a swallow of the bland, biting soda water. 'And you will find a suitable woman one day.'

'But when? I'm already approaching thirty.'

'You're only twenty-nine next month. That is not old.'

'My point is that I've been trying to find a suitable woman for years now.'

'It is not unusual for older men to take brides who are younger than they. Many men defer marriage until they have a sufficient income to support a wife – some for as long as a decade. Nor is there any reason to think less of yourself because you have not copulated with a woman—'

'I don't!' Douglas said sharply, his face reddening.

'Because it is perfectly reasonable for a man of your age to have not yet copulated with a female, should he still be unmarried and hold ridiculous notions of virtue, as you do.'

'Will you please stop saying that word? And you make it sound as if that's all I'm after.'

'You didn't say that you weren't desirous of it.'

'I am not talking about this with you any further.' Douglas crossed his arms and leant back against the sofa. His brother had misinterpreted his past remarks on this subject: it wasn't so much about remaining chaste until marriage; rather, it was about losing his virtue to none other than the woman he took as his bride. And he wanted to point out that neither had George…performed such an act with a woman, although he knew George wasn't interested in such things. At least, Douglas had no evidence to the contrary. The fact that George had even raised the subject suddenly seemed so funny that Douglas started to laugh. (Which had been George's objective in raising the subject, since his brother always delighted in teasing him about his ignorance in matters of the heart.)

'Find something to occupy your mind so you don't dwell on Miss Marsden. I've had to manage our orders on my own all day.'

'Are you actually confessing to needing my help?' Douglas feigned shock. That roguish grin of his had returned.

'It would quicken proceedings if you saw to the finishes on the three outstanding orders, which is normally your domain anyway.'

'Very well, then. First I'll repair Pirouette, like I promised her I would.' Douglas left the parlour more cheerful than he'd entered it, determined to try George's prescription for mending a broken heart.

Once his brother was gone, George made his way to the north hall. He'd better check how the computer was running. He entered the lift and pressed the button for his workshop. Douglas would forget Miss Marsden in time and find a new lover. George was certain of it. At least he'd been granted a little more time before his brother was inevitably taken from him by some woman.

The lift whirred gently as it descended. It was strange, George reflected, how he felt greatly more awake in the short time he'd spent away from his computer. He'd retired straight to bed after the Marsdens' abrupt departure and Douglas's resulting angry outburst. That whole evening had left George feeling rather drained. Throughout dinner he'd alternated between frustration and sheer boredom. Making idle conversation with those insufferable Marsdens had been strenuous, and he'd already been exhausted after working on his machine throughout the previous day and night. Once he'd got into bed, he'd fallen asleep almost immediately, then awoken around eight o'clock as feeble grey sunlight was beginning to creep into his bedroom. But he wasn't just experiencing the benefit of a night's rest. It was as if in the preceding weeks he'd been seeing everything through a microscope: the world had closed in around him and his work, and everything beyond it was dim and insubstantial, like shadows in a tunnel. Now everything had expanded, his senses felt sharper, and he was generally feeling more alert – no longer listening to conversations with one ear or casting only a cursory glance on any object requiring his attention. That morning he'd had a rather refreshing walk in the woodland with Molly, since she couldn't stop herself worrying about Douglas and had been in need of diversion.

The lift jolted to a stop and the doors parted. George walked slowly down the tunnel to begin with, but he quickened his pace upon seeing scraps of metal scattered on the ground. As he followed the trail, the pieces became larger and more numerous, and he feared he was approaching the epicentre of a catastrophic explosion. But surely that was impossible? He'd made sure that everything was in working order. He knew he should have checked the damn machine before retiring to bed, but he hadn't thought that anything could go drastically wrong, and so he'd given in to his fatigue. Now he cursed himself as he sprinted down the tunnel and into the workshop. On beholding the scene before him, he came to an abrupt halt. What the hell had happened?

The computer was in ruins. It was as if someone had ripped it apart. Tools and bits of metal were strewn across the floor. George kicked large pieces of casing from his path as he made his way towards the computer's remains. He retrieved his chair, which had been lying on its side, and stood on it to look inside the computer. All of the core components were gone, but many stacks of data discs were intact; others were dented or dislodged. The damage wasn't consistent with an explosion; this looked more like an attack from outside. The parts that had disappeared were tellingly selective. Yet the idea of a thief finding their way down here was ridiculous, and there'd been no sign of a forced entry. And in the event that a thief had reached the workshop, they'd surely have taken every last platinum-coated disc to sell for its weight in precious metal. Unless this was a thief of a different class: a thief of knowledge. But they'd have to have known exactly which parts to harvest, and Douglas was the only person George had shown them to. Perhaps the thief had coerced one of the servants into abetting them, or one of the servants hired solely for yesterday evening was not who they'd claimed to be. But George wasn't entirely convinced. This was something else.

He searched the workshop for the computer's missing parts, knowing that he wouldn't find them. Once he'd conducted a thorough examination of the room, he simply stared at the smashed control panel. Now that he was still, the cold crept into him. The panel's frozen timer indicated that the vandalism had been committed during dessert the previous evening. George noted that his coat was also missing, which was perhaps the most perplexing part of this entire scenario. He would have suspected Douglas of pulling an elaborate joke on him, but even his brother wouldn't go to such an extreme when he knew how much work George had invested in the project. George ran a hand through his hair. All that time and effort spent on his computer had gone to waste. It would take months to restore it, although he'd probably be better off starting from scratch. He cursed under his breath, but the echo in the room still picked up his words and mockingly hurled them back at him.

Chapter Five

It took a day for the automaton to reach London. He had concealed himself in farmers' or traders' carts for part of the way, changing vehicle whenever the one in which he was travelling reached its journey's end. The black coat hung loosely on his limbs and its sleeves covered all but the tips of his fingers, but the garment fulfilled its purpose of concealing him from the attention of passers-by. A cap plucked from a carter's head and a pair of boots stolen from the front step of a cottage aided the disguise. People looked at the android without really seeing him. It was amazing how unobservant humans were. Their brains filtered out so much information that they deemed unworthy of remembering but that could in fact be vitally useful. Had they paid attention, they'd have noted the unnatural scrawniness of his limbs or the odd flash of metal from beneath his purloined attire. He'd learnt a lot about human behaviour in the past twenty-four hours, most of which confirmed his own theories.

The android completed the last stage of his journey by train, hidden amongst the trunks and boxes in the luggage carriage. He exchanged the cottager's worn, muddy boots for a pair of polished black ones that he found in a gentleman's luggage. They'd seen some service, but they were smart and slightly less incongruous, given that the coat he was wearing was old but of good quality. His creator might not have extravagant tastes, but he was not neglectful when it came to quality. The gold and platinum parts of the android's innards testified to that. His insides were a lot more refined than his exterior, but this shamble of a body was only temporary, and hopefully he would soon improve his appearance. As well as the boots, from a purse here and there he pinched the odd coin, which he tucked into his coat pockets. (He ignored the jewellery cases in some of the ladies' luggage; jewels were too impractical.) Once he'd had his fill of pilfering, he stretched himself out on the luggage rack and stared at his shod feet, twitching the right one. If only his right leg weren't a couple of inches shorter than his left! That was his main inconvenience – that, and the fact that his right foot's function was impaired. That would be the first thing he'd address once he was able to. Even so, what a thing to have limbs! He picked up a bottle of scent and felt the weight of it in his palm. To be able to interact with the world and have a direct influence upon objects was another novelty. He'd watched his creator handle tools and had admired the expert touch with which he went about his work. Had George discovered the wreckage in the workshop yet? What a disappointment he would suffer. But taking flight, rather than staying boxed inside that steel cube, was necessary.

The android listened to the rhythmic clacking of the train, feeling a thump whenever it stopped at a station. His destination was King's Cross, where he found himself thrust into a tumult of whistles and shouting and hissing and chugging. Steam bellowed from the train, providing a convenient shroud. It was easy to evade everyone's notice and slip out of the station; he was just another faceless figure going about his business, as though he were in the background of a painting. Outside he was greeted by darkness, although it was diluted by the gaslights. He walked in the direction of the Thames, following it for about a quarter of a mile. Sleepy steamers appeared, phantom-like, in the distance, sailing along the black water as if they were drifting through endless darkness.

He limped on through the dense fog, changing course towards the densely packed rows of tumbledown dwellings. He was not entirely sure that his parts would hold together long enough for him to take refuge somewhere. Occasionally a humanoid apparition materialised from the fog. These were the lowest of London's society: the tramps, the vagabonds, the thieves, and the females who sold their bodies to males. Prowlers and hunters saw nothing to gain by interfering with the hunched, club-footed figure in the black greatcoat. Just another of their kind, as far as they were concerned. Desperation and decay permeated the air. The android saw a female curled in a doorway, an infant in her arms. Although she was young, her face was drawn and thin. She looked at nothing, and mechanically rocked the whining bundle. The android walked on, spying rats scurrying amongst the filth that covered the greasy streets and flowed from gutters. The creatures' eyes glowed in the darkness.

Raindrops pelted the android's coat as he slunk along the bridge; the fabric soon became damp and clung to his thin metal frame. Gradually the character of the buildings began to change: he had drifted into a wealthier part of the city. This must be Mayfair, if his geography was accurate. The red brick and ivory stone town houses, with Ionic columns adorning their doorways, looked to have been built in the previous century. Smart shops lined the sodden streets; their proprietors would likely be in their beds. The automaton paused outside the window of a draper's and regarded his reflection and the inadequacy of his disguise. It was imperative to take shelter before dawn, when he would be more conspicuous. With that objective achieved, he could then address the matter of his appearance. And there was much else to plan after that.

Between the hatter's and the draper's was a black shopfront with 'SKINNER & Co. GLOVERS' above the door in gilt letters. A window on the first storey was lit by weak yellow light. The automaton lurched up to the front door, dragging his club foot behind him, and rapped his metal knuckles on the door. Presently there came a shuffling on the other side, and the sound of a key grinding in the lock. The door whined open a fraction, threatening to disturb the shop bell. A snowy-haired man with a brown coat over his nightshirt peered through narrowed eyes into the darkness, the lit candle in his hand exaggerating the lines around his mouth and forehead. Dots of yellow candlelight danced on the lenses of his spectacles.

'Jones, is that you? If you've lost your latchkey again, I swear... Oh, good evening, sir. Do you need help? If you require a doctor or a constable, I'd be happy to...' Then the old man raised the candle, and his eyes widened in bewilderment and horror.

The android made a quick movement with his arms, catching the candle as the old man slumped in the doorway. After kneeling beside the elderly glover to check for a pulse, the android stepped over the threshold and closed the door behind him.

47

Chapter Six

Four months later

George and Douglas were flying in Peregrine (Douglas's latest airship), through the darkening sky, on their way to the Gentlemen Inventors' Society annual presentation dinner near Peterborough. Both their entries were already at their destination, as members with larger machines were permitted to store them at the venue a day or so in advance.

'Are you sure you shouldn't have tested your "spaceship" before the presentation?' George asked his brother.

'But then the whole presentation would have been a farce, since it wouldn't actually be the first flight by a human to space. Besides, I've done a few test flights at a higher altitude than what we're currently flying at, so I know the spaceship works.'

'If you say so.'

'Oh, have some faith in me. And let's hope your computer doesn't suffer the same fate as its predecessor,' added Douglas jokily. 'Do you have any idea yet what caused that explosion?'

'Not entirely.' For simplicity's sake, and until he could be certain of what had really transpired, George had told Douglas that his first computer had been destroyed by an explosion.

'At least you were able to get this second one in some working order in time for tonight, seeing as you've worked on it in every spare moment you've had these past four months.'

'But it's still not at full capacity. That'll probably cost me the medal,' replied George drily.

'Which gives me an advantage,' Douglas grinned. 'I'm glad you agreed to participate this year. It wouldn't have been as interesting, attending on my own.'

'Hmm.'

'But remember: if you can't think of anything pleasant to say to the other members, then don't say anything at all. Merely nod and say yes. I'd say smile as well, but that's probably asking too much of you.'

'I promise to behave.'

'And if you see Mr Babbage—'

'Avoid him. Don't lecture me like Mother used to do before we entered church.'

'"Don't slouch, don't snigger during the sermon, don't fall asleep – and no remarks on the absurdity of the existence of God",' Douglas recited with a smile, mimicking their mother's well-bred intonation. After a beat of silence he added, 'You know, I think you can read people's behaviour better than you claim to.'

'An interesting theory,' George muttered.

'It makes sense. You're incredibly perceptive, and must understand everyday behaviour and emotions in the abstract, if not in practice.'

'Some "everyday" behaviour continues to baffle me. Especially anything regarding courtship or mourning.'

'They're two vastly different things.'

'Both involve elaborate and ridiculous rituals.'

'For very different purposes!'

'I suppose. But you must admit that more often than not, such behaviour is false: polite greetings, offers of condolence, compliments, remarks about the weather, invitations to social engagements when the host would rather you didn't attend...'

'Well, a lot of that is simply good manners. And if people went around saying what they really thought of each other, society would collapse altogether,' Douglas chuckled.

'It's repellent all the same. I can't abide it.'

'I'm aware.'

'I don't understand how you *can* abide it – attending all those balls, dinners and cricket matches that Dick Cullwick invites you to. I've seen what the other men of his acquaintance are like: dull, wealthy tradesmen who care only for good drink, excessive dinners and sport. And the women are worse. They're either husband-hunting industrialists' daughters who merely know about fashion and fancy needlework, or doddery old harridans who live solely for bridge and gossip and who worship anyone with a title. They're all constrained by the demands of polite society and lack a single original idea of their own.'

'I can't say I care for them much, but they're decent enough people.'

'I hate to see you attempting to mix with such people. You're better than that – better than *them*.'

After a minute's tense silence, Douglas pressed a button amongst the airship's controls. From deep within the control panel, a piano started playing. They'd tested their sound-recording device when Maestro had last been at Ravenfeld Hall for repairs, and now had twenty of his compositions inscribed on the flat black disc that was spinning merrily inside the control panel at that moment. (The sound quality wasn't fantastic – it was slightly muffled and scratchy – but they had plans to refine their invention further.)

Douglas sighed. 'I'm not that desperate to enter polite society. Half the time I only accept those invitations because it would be rude to Dick not to, and because he has a way of compelling you to do something against your will. I admit the dinners can be a trial when you hardly know anyone, although I do like the sports matches and dances a great deal. I know a lot of people's behaviour is false and sometimes sickening, but at the same time it's nice to feel like you're…part of a club.'

'Why do you feel the need to be part of a club? Do you think Dick's friends care a straw for you?'

'Oh, I don't doubt that I'm merely their entertainment for the night. But Dick's different: he's a true friend, as is Dr Truman. It's nice to be amongst people who accept you and truly enjoy your company, when it's not all scripted small talk and strained smiles, but a proper conversation. Can you find fault with that?'

'I suppose not.'

'Are you simply jealous?'

'Of course not.' George reflected that maybe it wasn't bad that after spending nearly five months mourning his lost love, Douglas was slowly starting to re-enter 'polite society'. He still couldn't understand, no matter how many times George and Molly tried to make him do so, that Miss Marsden was not worth being upset about. Molly had almost lost her temper on one occasion, after Douglas had been rhapsodising passionately about his former fiancée, and said, 'I don't care how lovely she is, she still goes in her chamber pot' (although she'd used a stronger word than 'goes'). Douglas had been cross about it until Molly had apologised.

'Nearly there,' he said brightly now, as the airship began to descend towards a grand baroque-style house nestled in acres of countryside. 'We'll probably be amongst the first to arrive. I wonder what Mol is doing with herself at home?'

'I'm sure she's found some useful occupation.' George envied her position. He'd rather be the one spending the evening at Ravenfeld Hall, although he was curious to see what the other club members would make of his computer. He doubted their inventions would be of much interest to him, although one could never say. And how would he fare against Douglas? That question interested him more. He was reminded of their childhood competitions to build the best or the most pocket watches, during quiet days in their father's clockmaker's shop. George had almost always won. But their inventions for this contest were strikingly different from each other. It was difficult to tell which one would capture the judges' attention the most. Very well – let the battle commence.

Molly vigorously ground fennel seeds in a mortar with a pestle. It was almost dusk, but she was still in her laboratory in the garden. Its interior looked deceptively like a cottage: a lattice of wooden beams supported the ceiling and stone walls. Sprigs of drying herbs hung from some of the rafters, and a cooking pot bubbled in the fireplace. Molly's wooden worktable was pushed against the far wall, beneath the larger of the lab's two windows, and was cluttered with scientific instruments. If she needed additional light, she simply had to snap her fingers and the two potted plants on either side of the table would glow lime green or pale blue.

Bloody Arthur, she thought, feeling seeds crunch beneath the pestle. Bloody stupid Arthur. It was his birthday, and his wish had been to spend the day with her at Ravenfeld Hall. They would even have had the added advantage that her brothers were attending their club dinner tonight, so they'd have had the house to themselves. Molly had planned for them to have a picnic by the lake during the day, consisting of all Arthur's favourites, and afterwards she'd have given him his present. But yesterday his father had summoned him home: apparently Mrs Greenwood was very ill. Despite Arthur's mother professing that she did not want her dear boy to inconvenience himself by coming home especially to see her, his father had certainly expected him to do exactly that. And as always, his dutiful and now-anxious son had immediately dropped everything and hopped on the earliest available train to Newbury. How long was he going to let the old man bully him? Mr Greenwood still wanted Arthur to be his successor as the estate surveyor to that fickle buffoon, Lord Colton. Not that Arthur wanted to be anything other than a landscape gardener. Every time old Mr Greenwood did something of this nature, Molly told Arthur that he needed to stand up to him, and it always led to a quarrel. Arthur would say that he didn't let his father order him around, and that he did have a will of his own, but he couldn't risk upsetting his father, on account of his mother's poor health.

This latest instance of the Greenwoods' selfishness had particularly irked Molly. 'She won't even be ill,' she'd argued. 'She never is. It's an excuse to get you all to themselves.'

'She might be. She's been gravely ill before,' Arthur had pointed out as he packed his things.

'Once. She had influenza *once*. Every other time was a ruse. Can't you see when you're being manipulated?'

'I can't risk it. If it happened once, it might happen again. And Father says she is gravely ill this time.'

'He says that *every* time! Last time she had a slight cough – which didn't vanish after you secretly switched her cough drops and the ones I gave you. And don't say my medicine was ineffective: you've taken those drops whenever you've had a cough.'

'If it turns out that she *is* seriously ill, I'll never forgive myself if I fail to be there beside her.' He'd had that tone and look that meant he was fixed on a course of action, and nothing on earth could sway him.

Molly had given in, making sure to give him his present before he departed from the Hall, and Arthur had sent a message to her pocket telegraph that afternoon. His mother was fine now, and when he returned he had an amusing story to tell Molly about a dinner with his father's friends. He'd opened his present and liked it very much. Molly could hear his blithe tone as clearly as if he'd been speaking right next to her. After receiving that message, she'd gathered a number of poisonous plants from her garden and started boiling them in her cooking pot. She often brewed poison when she was angry at someone or something. (No wonder people sometimes called her a witch.) She never intended to use it; she simply found it cathartic. Maybe there were some people she could imagine poisoning, or thought deserved it, but it wouldn't be by her hand.

Now she decided she'd allowed the ingredients to simmer for long enough. Carefully she lifted the pot from the fireplace and set it down on her worktable. Even the fumes made her head spin, forcing her to open the little arched window at the front of the lab for air. Once the mixture was cool, she pulled on leather gloves and dunked a beaker into the bubbling black liquid. She watched an inky bubble swell inside the beaker before vanishing with a pop. A single drop would be lethal, even if the poison only made contact with the skin. She might find some use for it: sometimes when mixing poisons she accidentally made an effective weedkiller. The rat-catcher had put her last batch to good use, too. At any rate, Molly was satisfied and her anger had subsided. The remnants of the plants were tossed into the fire and she began to clear away her apparatus. Removing her gloves, she washed her hands in the small basin in a far corner of the room. Even the gloves might not have been enough to stop some of the toxins seeping through to her skin. But she had been dabbling with poisonous plants for nearly her entire life, and she thought it possible that she'd built up some immunity to their effects. It had, at least, been years since any of them had made her ill.

Then she heard the soft flap of wings and the harsh caw of a crow. The damn bird was sitting in the open window, proud as anything. No, it wasn't a crow. It was a raven.

'I've not seen one of your kind here before,' she informed it. 'Where have you been hiding?'

Its reply sounded harsh and unfriendly.

'You shouldn't be in here. Shoo.'

The raven aimed its beady eyes at her.

'Go on, get out.'

It opened its wings, but then flitted to the worktable, knocking one or two things over. It trod over fallen glass vials with great deliberation, until it came to the beaker of black poison.

'No, don't—'

The raven wafted its wings, pushed out its feet, and tipped the beaker over. Instinctively Molly dived for it, but it smashed on the floor just as she was within reach of it – close enough for some of the liquid to splash onto her hand. At first it itched; then the poison began to burn her, although her skin didn't turn red and blister. She was burning from the inside. Searing pain shot along her arm and chest as the poison was absorbed into her blood. She felt her body temperature begin to climb higher as her heart rate soared. She didn't suffer long, however, and sprawled out face down on the floor, lying partially in the inky black puddle.

The raven looked down at the unconscious girl, then leapt to Molly's side, pecking inquisitively at the bare floorboards around her.

Chapter Seven

The Gentlemen Inventors' Society was like any other gentlemen's club in London. Membership was gained by recommendation. In addition to its regular activities, once a year a dinner was held at the club president's country residence, where members could present their latest inventions in the hope of winning the Stephenson Medal and the accompanying fifty-pound prize. The medal had been named in honour of the inventor of the first successful steam locomotive, although this failed to entice him to join the fledgling club when it was founded in 1829. He did, however, send a very nicely worded note, along with the promise of fifty pounds for each year's winner. A panel of three judges – consisting of the club's president, secretary and last surviving founding member – decided the winner. Collaboration was not forbidden but was discouraged. There would always be an argument about patents further down the line, which had more than once seen members resign or file lawsuits against each other. The competition had become even fiercer in the past five years, and an increasing number of members were exchanging ideas in the hope that someone – anyone – would have a chance of defeating the Abernathy brothers. Many wanted to exclude them from entering for the sixth time, raking up excuses from the rule book that were all brushed aside by the senior members. But the news that the Abernathys were presenting separately this year offered a glimmer of hope. At the very least, it would be interesting to see which one outperformed the other.

The offerings from the other twenty-four inventors who had chosen to present that year did not excite much interest. Apparently Mr Forster had prepared some sort of 'automated rifle'. There had been a petition to ban him from competing too, on the grounds that he was a 'maniac with a monomania for murder', as the petition's author had alliteratively phrased it. This claim was not entirely unfounded. In the previous three years Mr Forster had presented a cannon that fired very angry scorpions, a death beam, and an automatic guillotine that could decapitate three people simultaneously. But his offering for this year eclipsed them all. He'd attached six rifles to a motorised belt so that they could be fired in succession – with a death beam on top for good measure.

'Subtlety isn't his strong point, is it?' Douglas smiled at his brother as they inspected Mr Forster's machine.

'I doubt he has any strong points at all. His inventions don't even work as they ought to, although they'd still achieve their objective of bringing about death.' George caught sight of Charles Babbage at the other end of the room. When their eyes met, both men swiftly turned their heads.

The other members were milling about the ballroom (which had been converted to a showroom) like a waddle of penguins in their evening wear. The presentation would commence after dinner. Mr Etheridge, the club president, approached the brothers and shook each by the hand. He was a grey-haired gentleman with drooping eyebrows and a wilting moustache. His jowly face sagged like a bloodhound's. His most popular invention was a motorised toothbrush that could also be used to trim a gentleman's unwanted nose and ear hair. He had a distracted way of talking, and his eyes often drifted away from the person he was addressing.

'I look forward to seeing what you both have to show us. That "computer" of yours has drawn quite a crowd, Mr Abernathy.' Mr Etheridge nodded at George, although he directed his gaze at the automated rifle. But sure enough, two dozen men were crowded around the steel cube near the centre of the room. 'And that spaceship has caused quite a buzz – not that anyone's had a chance to get close to it.' The president chuckled. The spaceship's ellipsoidal steel form could just be glimpsed through the French windows. It was parked on the lawn outside, since it would have taken up most of the ballroom. 'Well, best of luck to you both!' Mr Etheridge smiled in the direction of the French windows, then went on his way to attack the next member with his good wishes.

The butler appeared at the top of the shallow twin staircases at the far end of the ballroom, and announced the name 'Mr Alexander Gearhart.'

A figure of slightly above average height appeared beside him. The young man was wearing a white tailcoat and trousers with a black waistcoat and bow tie. He was lean and trim, with light brown hair. While not dashingly handsome, young women would not have found his face unpleasant to look at. He had a peculiar magnetism that at once said 'Keep this man away from your daughters' and 'What a refined gentleman'; he was not merely another person in the room but a *presence*. For most of the gentlemen below him, his appearance proved far more interesting than the inventions on display. He descended the stairs gradually, with great poise and deportment, savouring the attention he was receiving and using it to his full advantage.

'Who on earth is he?' said Douglas.

His brother didn't reply. Douglas caught the curious expression on George's face as Mr Gearhart sprang from the bottom step and landed heavily on his feet. Giving the collar of his tailcoat a jerk, he strolled amongst the stupefied older gentlemen, all of whom watched him with interest. But his gaze was aimed at George and Douglas at the back of the room.

'Did you notice when he jumped?' George muttered to his brother.

'What about it?'

'Don't you think his landing was a little too heavy for a man of his height and weight?'

'Well, yes, but maybe he put too much force into the jump?'

'Either that or he's heavier than he seems.'

'But why is it of such significance?'

George had insufficient time to answer, as the young man was fast approaching them.

'Gentlemen.' He smiled charmingly. 'I must confess how honoured I am to meet you at long last. I have been observing you and your work with admiration for some time.' He had a northern American accent, and charisma oozed from his every pore. He shook each man's hand with a firm grip.

George was thinking rapidly. Something about this man bothered him.

'It is always an honour to have someone call themselves your admirer, Mr Gearhart. And I must say that you certainly know how to make an entrance,' said Douglas graciously. 'Have you joined our club only very recently?'

'Only a month ago, as it happens. I admit I am in a similar line of work to you. Oh, I forgot to advertise myself. Here is my card.' Mr Gearhart took a silver card case from his pocket and extracted a card from it. He eyed George intensely as he handed it to him.

George felt something like a spark of recognition. He glanced at the card, which simply read 'Mr Alexander Gearhart'. The name meant nothing to him, and he never forgot a name, nor a face, nor a voice.

'Usually your British clubs wouldn't admit a New Yorker such as myself, but I assure you I'm as British as steak and kidney pie at heart, since I'm of English stock. My people are from Birmingham.'

'Are you visiting the country of your birth?' enquired Douglas.

'More like returning home. I've set up shop here.'

'And what does your shop sell, Mr Gearhart?' interjected George.

The young man put a finger to his lips. 'That would be telling! You'll have to wait until the presentation to see my little marvel.'

Suddenly there came the sound of bullets being fired. Many members uttered shocked cries and flew from the far end of the room. The automated rifle had come alive and was firing volley after volley of bullets, apparently under attack from an invisible army. Fortunately the machine's target was the doors to the French windows. It seemed determined to shatter every last pane.

'Yes!' Across the room, Mr Forster punched the air jubilantly. 'Works like a charm! See how beautifully she runs!'

'For God's sake, someone stop it!' cried the president.

Since George, Douglas and Mr Gearhart were closest, they took on the task. George took his 'looking glass' cane from his coat pocket, extended it to its full length, and thrust the end into the automated rifle, jamming the firing mechanism. The machine shuddered and twitched as it tried to fire, doing its utmost to dislodge the cane, but George held fast. Meanwhile, Douglas and Mr Gearhart removed the belt, leaving the motor to buzz on mindlessly.

Gearhart whistled. 'That sure was close!'

'Thanks for your help, Mr Gearhart, or it might have blown the doors clean off their hinges,' said Douglas.

Gearhart clapped a hand on the back of his neck. 'It was nothing. You two fellas were pretty quick to spring into action too, although I dare say the damage has already been done.'

'That'll see Forster disqualified,' muttered Douglas, sensing the gathering storm coming from Mr Etheridge's direction. The president's eyebrows stood upright for once as he took in his ruined French doors.

The sound of the gong resounded through the ballroom like waves of golden relief. It was time for the penguins to feed. Mr Gearhart was swept along with three other members, all eager to make his acquaintance. George pried his cane free from the automated rifle and joined his brother, who was waiting patiently for him. At least Douglas hadn't been so impressed by Mr Gearhart that he'd forgotten about him.

Molly awoke lying on the laboratory floor. It was dark outside. She lifted her throbbing head and felt a sharp sting in her palm as she moved her left arm. When she raised her hand, she saw that there were three tiny shards of broken glass burrowed into her skin. As she removed each one, wincing slightly as she did so, the wounds they left behind clotted almost instantly. Her skin tingled as it rapidly knitted itself back together, leaving only faint pink marks. She ran her fingertips over the smooth skin, not believing what she'd just seen. Even her honey-flower sap couldn't accelerate healing like that. She could have fooled herself into believing she'd imagined it, were it not for the three bloodied fragments of glass on the floor. She looked around. The raven was gone.

Holding on to the edge of the worktable, she got unsteadily to her feet and then walked outside into the cool night air, still not feeling entirely herself. She felt half-asleep. Perhaps rinsing her face in the stream would revive her. Truth be told, she was amazed that the poison hadn't killed her. Her resistance must be stronger than she'd given herself credit for. Either that, or she actually was dead. This wasn't exactly how she'd imagined heaven…or was it? A big, beautiful garden was her personal idea of heaven. If she was a spirit, it explained why she wasn't chilled to the bone by the cold night air. If anything, she felt a little warm. Molly knelt down beside the shallow stream and cupped water in her hands. She splashed it onto her face, and beads of it trickled down her jaw and arms. She drank some too, as her throat was parched. But when she moved her hands away from her face, she caught sight of her reflection in the moonlit stream, and shock spiked her heart. Her skin was ashen, while her hair had turned a shade darker. Her eyes looked darker too: their irises were almost black, with a tinge of scarlet around the pupil, and shadows ringed each eye. She swore her eyelashes looked thicker as well. What had she done to herself? Panic ensued, but then she commanded herself to stay calm. She listened to the stream's faint burble and focused on nothing else. Molly placed one palm on the turf as she adjusted her sitting position, and started when she suddenly heard voices. No – maybe not quite voices, but indistinct whispers that reminded her of when, if one listened closely enough, the wind or waves seemed almost to speak. Briefly, she'd felt a connection to the grass, the trees, the spring flowers; like an extension of her nerves. Only faintly – it was the tactile equivalent of seeing something in the distance – but it was certainly there. Molly planted both palms on the ground. She felt the surrounding plants sway in the feeble breeze like a million extra limbs, felt the movement of water and nutrients through their roots and up their stems. But her will was far stronger than a few measly plants. She made them all move in the opposite direction to the wind. She commanded a crocus to grow taller than its neighbours, and it did – causing the nearest flowers' leaves to curl up a little.

Then she tried something else. She aimed her gaze at a patch of bare earth. Moments later, a black stem emerged from out of the ground, blooming into a flower of her own creation, with five red petals and purple veins. She plucked it and fastened it in her hair. The whispers were becoming more coherent, even though her hands were no longer touching the earth. Those voices were inside her head. Black vines with red thorns began to creep along the ground, spreading out from where she was sitting. More red flowers bloomed from them. A smile slid across Molly's face as she observed the extent of her new powers, and she tried to suppress the giddiness growing inside her. Her other flowers began to wilt as the new ones spread. She could mutate plant cells and steal nutrients, creating new forms of plant life. That was what this was. What pretty red flowers: little thieves, stealing from others so that they might thrive. Scarlet creepers, that was what she'd call them.

The poison in her blood was seeping from her every pore and every breath. Her mind raced, imagining what she could do with this power – the suffering she could inflict on those who had wronged her. Fury raged through her brain as though someone had touched oil with a lit match. One person was uppermost in her thoughts; the target of this consuming emotion. Arthur. That coward! That fool! Always full of bright ideas, but always forgetting what he was meant to be doing, and too afraid to stand up to his father. She would make him pay for his string of broken promises and his meddling in her precious garden. But how? Molly rose and strolled across the grass. She ambled through the woodland, the black vines and scarlet creepers following in her wake. Her anger was in no danger of burning out, and its red fire engulfed her mind. Her destination was the orchard: one of Arthur's creations. He'd insisted on an overly complicated daisy-shaped design, wherein each 'petal' contained a specific variety of fruit. Most of the apple and pear trees were still too young to bear fruit; she could use her growth serum to accelerate their development, but when she'd done so she'd found that the first year's crop wasn't as flavourful, nor as large. She placed her hand on one of the adolescent apple trees, and it grew into a tall, noble tree, offering bright green apples from its black branches.

'That's it!' She plucked an apple from the nearest branch. 'Apple and blackberry was always his favourite, after all.'

No one heard her malicious, gleeful laughter.

Since the members were to present in alphabetical order of surname, Douglas was to go first, followed by George. This will set the tone for certain, Douglas thought as he took his place in the middle of the ballroom. He was unbearably warm in the padded brown leather suit he was wearing; it was designed to cope with the low pressure and cold desolation of space, after all, not the cheerful warmth of an English country house. At least his globe-shaped helmet was tucked beneath his arm.

'In case you're wondering, no, this suit is not the invention I wish to show you. If you'd like to follow me outside, then you'll see my entry. Bring your coats or a tot of brandy, since it's rather cold.'

There came a ripple of laughter, and a procession of three dozen semi-intoxicated gentlemen lumbered slowly through the open (and now badly damaged) French windows and onto the lawn. George and Mr Gearhart were at the rear of the crowd.

'I'm curious, Mr Abernathy,' began Gearhart. 'I gather you and your brother usually present together, so why do things differently this year? To stir things up a little?'

'More or less.'

'Being at the top of your game has its drawbacks. What's there to strive for if there's no competition?'

'The competition has certainly been rather lacking thus far.'

'Perhaps that might soon change. At least the two of you have had the honour of winning the medal five years running – and the prize money's not bad either. I take it Mr Douglas is your younger brother?'

'Yes.'

'I can only imagine the brotherly rivalry!'

George didn't reply. He shivered as he stepped outside. The spaceship parked on the lawn was essentially a larger, bulkier version of Peregrine (which was currently parked on Mr Etheridge's drive). George had witnessed the spaceship's construction over the past eighteen months, although it was the culmination of five years' worth of work. He was tired of hearing Douglas talk about it during dinner, and his preoccupation with it had only intensified during the past four months. The club members gathered around the spaceship, although at a respectful distance.

Douglas took his place beside his ship, beaming like a child. Subtly he cleared his throat. 'Steamers have conquered the seas, trains cross vast distances in a matter of hours, and my airships have made it possible to sail through the skies. But there's one vast territory left unexplored: space. And on this very night, gentlemen, I intend to be the first man to reach the stars.'

Douglas was always good at putting on a show, George thought to himself.

'Now, of course, space is lacking in heat, gravity and air, which is why I designed this suit. It's well insulated and airtight, with a supply of oxygen fed into my helmet from this tank.' He tapped the tank on his back. 'And to prove that I really have made the journey, I shall take a photograph of the Earth from space.'

His audience murmured enthusiastically.

'But first of all, I invite you to have a look at my ship, since you did not have a chance to do so earlier. I am happy to answer any questions you may have. Her maiden voyage shall commence at precisely ten o'clock.'

George positioned himself discreetly by the ship's engines to observe what the other members made of it. Their faces were wavering between boyish wonder and scepticism; many tapped their knuckles on the ship's metal hide. George consulted his pocket watch and saw that it was ten minutes to the hour. He still wished Douglas had conducted a test flight and actually flown above the Earth's atmosphere instead of hovering along its edge. George tucked his watch away, then stiffened. What was that smell? Kneeling, he saw a puddle directly below the ship's fuel tank. The fuel had leaked from a small hole in the tank. A gunshot. One of the bullets from the automated rifle must have penetrated it.

George searched for his brother, and soon located him talking to two other men. He strode across the lawn and put his hand on Douglas's padded shoulder. 'Don't do this. The spaceship's fuel tank has a leak. If you ignite the engine, the ship will explode.'

'There's nothing wrong with the fuel tank. I checked everything when we first arrived, and no one has been anywhere near it since.' Douglas tugged himself free. 'I know you're only inventing an excuse because you're worried that something will go wrong, but trust me, I know what I'm doing.' He tried to smile reassuringly at George, before putting on his helmet and walking away.

Idiot! George steadied his breathing. Getting angry wouldn't save his brother's life. He had to act quickly. He noticed that the man closest to him was lighting a cigarette, and asked, 'Excuse me, do you mind if I borrow a match?'

'Oh, of course.' The man handed George a rather battered matchbox. This he pocketed, before taking two steps in Professor Wallace's direction.

'Want a slug of this?' As George approached, the ruddy-faced professor waved the whisky bottle he was holding. 'Thought you never touched spirits, although there is a nip in the air. Strictly medicinal use, eh?' He guffawed.

'Something of that kind.' George accepted the bottle with thanks. It wouldn't hurt the professor to be deprived of the whisky, since he wasn't using it for strictly medicinal reasons either. George took out his handkerchief and shoved it halfway into the bottle, so that the tail end absorbed some of the spirit. Then he struck a match and lit the dry end of the half-sodden handkerchief, and hurled the flaming bottle at the puddle of fuel.

Everything happened very quickly after that. George tackled Douglas to the ground. Seconds later there came a loud explosion, a burst of intense heat, and a tremendous crash. The other club members scattered with ejaculations of alarm – except Mr Gearhart, who was smoking on the bank at a safe distance, and appeared to be enjoying the spectacle. A few more seconds passed before the brothers sat up and surveyed what had happened. Douglas removed his helmet, and his face was the picture of anguish. The spaceship was tilted to one side and its rear end was smoking. Several small fires were burning on the lawn, although without much vigour.

With perfect composure, George rose and brushed the grass off his suit. He looked down at Douglas. 'You're welcome.'

Chapter Eight

The sting from the double blow of seeing his invention fail *and* having his older brother save him was unbearable to Douglas. Part of him couldn't help willing some sort of calamity to befall George as he took his place by his computer. It was like pulses beaming from his eyes, or like Mr Forster's death beam. Fail, fail, fail. But George's presentation went flawlessly, even if he did lack the showman's air. Even the most embittered club members looked spellbound when the computer began to awaken. The sheer complexity of it was mind-numbing. George had the computer calculate the ideal place to build a bridge in East London, drawing on an enormous data set, and the resulting coordinates were judged by his audience to be a favourable location. He bowed smartly at the presentation's conclusion, amid much applause. Douglas wouldn't look him in the eye as he rejoined him in the crowd.

The Bs, Cs and Ds proved uninspiring. Mr Fairclough's weather-predicting machine, on which he'd worked with two other members, captured a great deal of attention. The machine predicted persistent rain and wind across the country for the following day.

'We don't need your machine to tell us that!' cried someone from the back.

Several members tittered.

Then it was Mr Gearhart's turn. The young man swept across the ballroom floor to take his place, and proceeded to whirl around on his heel, sending his coattails flaring out behind him. He extended one arm above his head, holding something aloft in his hand. The silver case's lid fell open, revealing a shiny glass screen and a series of buttons.

'Is that a pocket telegraph?' Douglas asked himself more than his brother.

'It would appear so,' was George's sotto voce reply.

'Gentlemen,' began the smiling Mr Gearhart, 'I give you the future of communication.' He lowered his arm. 'Imagine a world where you don't have to wait for the postman to bring you a letter containing a much longed-for reply to an urgent question, nor find time to go to the post office to send a wire. What if you could send and receive a message in mere minutes – seconds, even – without spending money on paper, stamps and envelopes? This device, the "tele-texter", harnesses electromagnetic waves to allow for virtually instantaneous communication from anywhere in England.' He raised a finger. 'But the tele-texter does more than allow you to communicate quickly and cheaply. It also helps you to clarify your meaning, for even more efficient and effective communication. Struggling to spell a word? It'll correct your spelling for you. It'll even predict what word you want to type next. And if you don't feel that you need such assistance, you can disable this feature at the touch of a button. But don't take my word for it: let your own eyes persuade you. Might I have a volunteer? You, sir!' He gestured to the front row, to the kitchen-utensil manufacturer Mr Colliander, and beckoned to him to come forward. He drew a second device from his coat and placed it in the man's hand. 'Try typing something, and see if it knows what you're about to say.'

Mr Colliander glanced at his fellow members and laughed nervously. Then he began to type. His brows rose.

'What were you planning on typing?' Mr Gearhart smiled.

'Um, "Good evening. My name is Mr Colliander", but the damn thing finished the first part of the sentence without me having to type it!'

Gearhart nodded. 'It recognises particular patterns of everyday speech – however, over time it learns to recognise its user's own speech patterns, and can predict precisely how you'll construct a sentence. It can also suggest phrasing choices, in case you're about to say something rather impolite to your employer or wife.'

There was laughter and knowing nods.

'Now, let's test its speed and ease of use, for which I'll need another volunteer. Mr Etheridge? Would you be kind enough to aid us?'

'Me?' The president looked somewhat reluctant.

'Yes, sir. If you'd be so kind as to take this?' Mr Gearhart handed him a tele-texter. 'Now, Mr Colliander, please send the message you just typed by pressing the red button.'

The bemused-looking man did as ordered.

Seconds later, the president's device began to buzz insistently. He squinted at the screen. 'It says here, "Message from Volunteer One. Accept message?"'

'Select the "Yes" button,' commanded Gearhart. 'And please show the crowd Mr Colliander's message. Perfect! You see it's right there on the screen, gentlemen?'

'Now it says, "Add Volunteer One to your address book."' Mr Etheridge frowned at his screen.

'Select "Yes" again, then try typing a response using the letter keys. It'll appear below the previous message.'

'What should I say?'

'Anything at all – it doesn't matter. This is only a little test. But you mustn't tell us the message.'

Compelled by Mr Gearhart's friendly smile, Mr Etheridge obeyed. 'What shall I do now, Mr Gearhart?'

'Press the "Send" key.'

The president did as instructed.

A buzzing was then heard from Mr Colliander's direction. 'It appears I've received a message from Volunteer Two,' he said.

'Accept it by pressing "Yes".'

'Lot of needless bother, all this button-pressing,' muttered an old gentleman in front of George and Douglas.

His neighbours made gruff noises and nodded. 'Could have written a letter in the time it's taken to type one sentence on that machine,' one remarked.

Meanwhile, the demonstration was continuing.

'Please read the message to the crowd, Mr Colliander.' Gearhart faced his audience as he spoke.

'It says, "Good evening. Fine weather we're having."'

'Is that the message you sent, Mr Etheridge?'

'Why, yes. That's correct.'

'Now try sending a reply, Mr Colliander.'

The man began clicking away again. 'Uh, do I press "Send" again, Mr Gearhart?'

'That's correct, sir.'

Presently the president's device buzzed. 'I can see the response – it reads, "Indeed it is." It's not asking about an address book this time.'

'It won't do, since Volunteer One's name is now stored in your device's address book. The name should have been displayed above the message when it arrived, correct?'

'Yes, it was. But what's all this about an address book?'

'The address book is inside the tele-texter. It remembers the names of people who've sent messages to your device before, if you have agreed to store them. That way, you know if a message is from an acquaintance or not. Up to two hundred names can be stored in the device. It'll also remember the last ten messages of a conversation before it automatically erases them. The device's memory is remarkable, and it can analyse the data it collects – that is how it's able to anticipate your replies as you're typing them. It's nowhere near as powerful as Mr Abernathy's computer, although give it a few years and it might catch up.'

Several of the members chuckled.

'But what it does offer is convenience. It's portable and fits in your pocket.' Mr Gearhart demonstrated this by slotting his device into his waistcoat pocket and giving it a pat. 'And convenience is key. With my little device there'll be no more waiting hours or even days for a reply to an urgent enquiry. Instant communication!' He spread his arms wide. 'It's the future, gentlemen,' he almost whispered, 'and you can all have a piece of it. At the beginning of May I shall release this little beauty onto the market, but I'll issue each club member with a ticket entitling him to receive a device a day in advance, free of charge. And that includes our three esteemed judges, even if they choose not to award me the medal.'

He winked at the men in question, and his audacity earned him more laughter. Mr Gearhart's presentation concluded with as enthusiastic applause as George's had received. Mr Gearhart gave a theatrical bow. As he rose, his eyes landed on George's. There was some hidden meaning in his gaze that George disliked.

'I still maintain that the spaceship would have worked if it hadn't been for Mr Forster's damn automated rifle going berserk.'

'There's no use speculating on that point.'

Douglas was gripping the airship's wheel so tightly that his knuckles bleached. 'All that hard work I put into it, and they think it's a joke.'

'You can show them what it's capable of next year,' said his brother coolly.

'I know I could have won the medal if it had worked.'

'If losing bothers you that much, then *here*.' George dipped into his coat pocket and tossed the gold medal onto Douglas's lap. 'You have it.'

'But it's meaningless for me to possess the medal if I didn't earn it. It was you who won it.'

'It means nothing to me. You might as well keep it.'

'I don't need your pity.' Douglas flung the medal back at him.

George caught it by its blue ribbon and returned it to his pocket. 'It's not pity.'

'Your sympathy, then.'

'You've always insisted that I'm incapable of such a sentiment. Are you sure you're all right to drive in an agitated state?'

'I'm fine.'

'You're angry and it's affecting your driving.'

'I said I'm fine.'

'If you insist.' George relaxed in his seat and closed his eyes. He'd wait until his brother had calmed down.

Eventually Douglas broke the silence, and this time he sounded more like himself. 'I'm sorry for not listening to you about the fuel tank. I suppose you saved my life.'

'There's no "suppose" about it. I prevented you from doing something incredibly stupid.'

'And I understand now how you must have felt when your first computer exploded. You know, had Gearhart's tele-texter been as advanced as your computer, he'd probably have claimed victory. Thankfully, he chose convenience over complexity. He has the makings of a shrewd businessman as well as an inventor.'

'I agree.'

'Although I dare say that, even if he did prove to be capable of making something like your computer, we'd soon be one step ahead of him – that predictive-writing technology is mere child's play for us. We've already made advances with our automata since our first success with Maestro, after all. And before you say it, yes, I know you were the one who built him and I merely polished him up a bit, although I spotted an obvious problem that you missed.'

'If you expect me to challenge you on that then you're mistaken.'

'Admitting you made an oversight without even a frown? Now that is a real advancement. You know, I bet in time we could shrink the technology inside our androids to the size of a fly.'

'Eventually, perhaps. But at present we can scarcely reduce it to fit inside a human-sized head, never mind something the size of an insect.'

'Which is still progress, considering that our first few models had part of their brain inside their torso.'

'True.'

'And I honestly think that your computer was worthy of the medal, by the way. I was as impressed with it as the judges were. Imagine if it had been at full capacity! I'm sure Mr Gearhart would've been green with envy.'

'Yes.' George was examining Gearhart's card. 'Did nothing strike you about Mr Gearhart?'

'Well, he is somewhat eccentric, if that's what you mean. Then again, the same accusation has been levelled at us many times. He's certainly very sure of himself.'

'There's something familiar about him, although I'm not sure what. I feel like I've seen him before but I can't recollect where.'

'But you never forget that sort of thing: your memory is like a photograph album, unless you've been intoxicated the previous night. Maybe you met him at a public house many years ago?'

'How could I have when he has only just returned from America?'

'Good point. Well...' Douglas shrugged. 'It's a mystery. If we happen to see him at the club, maybe you can ask him.'

'I suppose.' George turned to face the window. Since it was dark outside, he could see his reflection more clearly. And that was when he saw it. That look on Gearhart's face when he'd handed him his card – George had recognised the expression. Gearhart had copied it from George's own countenance. Something else slid into place, too. That moment when Gearhart had touched his neck and affected embarrassment at Douglas's thanks for stopping Mr Forster's machine from running amok. He'd copied that from Douglas, even though he'd not made the gesture at all that evening. Gearhart had picked out their individual quirks and reflected them back at them – deliberately, too – hoping that George would notice. But how could he have known about such things if he'd never met them before? And as to *why* he'd behaved in that manner, George had only one possible explanation.

Chapter Nine

Visits home were always a trial for Arthur. Contrary to his father's claim that his mother was gravely ill, upon his arrival Arthur had found her to be suffering from nothing worse than a headache, which had soon cleared. But he was pressed to remain for a couple of days, seeing as it was his birthday the following day. His relief that his mother was fine was stronger than his indignation, so he'd not offered much resistance.

His parents had invited their friends the Oswalds to dinner that evening, and only an hour before the guests arrived, Arthur learnt that their very charming, very wealthy and very eligible niece was to accompany them. Then he understood his father's true motive for summoning him home. He'd half a mind to pack his things and catch a cab to the station at once, but his mother had already made arrangements for his birthday, and he could only imagine the floods of tears his abrupt departure would prompt.

In truth, Miss Oswald was indeed very charming and agreeable, but Arthur paid her little more notice than good manners demanded, and watched his father's frown gradually deepen as a result. Arthur's mind was often elsewhere, and the chatter around the dinner table washed over him. He didn't even think before pulling out his pocket watch to see how long it was likely to be until the Oswalds departed. The watch was beautifully crafted. The gold and silver lid was engraved with an intricate fern pattern;

inside was a shrunken clock face around which was a dial with the days of the month marked on it, and around that was a dial bearing the months of the year. The glass back displayed the clockwork and, to make the watch even more remarkably elaborate, gold floral scrolls, branches bearing ruby fruit, and silver flowers sprouted from amongst it.

'Oh!' exclaimed Arthur's mother from the head of the table. She was a petite, dumpy woman who in her day had been a beauty. 'That is a handsome watch, Arthur. Did your father give it to you? I know there was talk of getting you one for your birthday.'

'No,' Arthur replied thoughtlessly, aiming his gaze at his watch – which was now under scrutiny by the whole table. He felt himself burn as he was forced to confess, 'Miss Abernathy gave it to me.'

His mother's eyes widened in mild alarm.

'Who is Miss Abernathy?' asked Miss Oswald, seated on her hostess's left.

'One of my son's oldest clients,' cut in his father from the foot of the table. 'He has been overseeing the renovation of the garden on her family's estate.'

This answer did not banish Mrs or Miss Oswald's furrowed brows. Why would a single woman give Arthur such an expensive present? Evidently the Oswalds considered gratitude for his hard work an insufficient motive.

Arthur was perfectly aware of how peculiar the situation looked. Molly had handed him the dark blue box the moment before he'd departed from Ravenfeld Hall. 'You can open it whenever you please, since I won't see you on your birthday now,' she'd said stiffly. He had opened it shortly after arriving at his parents' house, and been astonished by its contents. No doubt Molly had asked one of her brothers to make the watch.

'Abernathy? Aren't her brothers the famous inventors?' asked Mr Oswald beside him.

'Yes, sir,' replied Arthur, with more animation than he'd shown all evening. 'I've had the pleasure of seeing many of their inventions at first hand. Their house is the most remarkable I've ever seen, and the gardens—'

Arthur's father coughed loudly. 'But my son has worked on many other projects. Tell them about Sir Lawrence's estate, Arthur.'

Arthur did as he was told, even showing the Oswalds some of the designs in his sketchbook. The sketchbook that Molly had given him. It was only when he handed it to Miss Oswald that he realised that, if she opened it at the first page, she'd see the inscription Molly had written: 'Don't fill this one with sketches of me. M. A.' And if Miss Oswald flicked deep enough into the book, she'd see that he had disregarded that instruction. One drawing in particular was a cause for concern. Mrs Oswald was leaning over her niece to see the sketches when her face fell sharply. Miss Oswald turned pink.

'Oh! This is another of Miss Abernathy's presents, I see,' Mrs Oswald exclaimed.

'Yes, that's correct. She'd heard me complaining that I needed a new sketchbook, and so she got me one.' Arthur held out his hand for the sketchbook, and placed it on his knee under the table.

No doubt they'd seen the offending drawing. Miss Oswald stopped trying to catch his eye after that. His father looked livid. This was worse than the Christmas he'd brought home a fruit cake that Molly had baked. He'd only informed his family of that fact after it was devoured, and from his mother's expression you'd have thought he'd told her that it was laced with arsenic.

'It appears that your boy's affections are already claimed, Harold,' Arthur overheard Mr Oswald whisper to his father as coffee was served to the gentlemen following the meal.

After the guests departed, Arthur's father had a lot to say to him. 'You must dissociate yourself from Miss Abernathy. I don't care how large her fortune is, she's a wayward, unrefined girl – and her brothers are nothing but clever conmen. It's clear to me now that you're afflicted with a dangerous passion for her, and if you cannot cure it, I will disinherit you. Do you understand me, Arthur?'

'Yes, sir,' replied Arthur coolly. 'But that shouldn't be a problem. I'll simply marry Miss Abernathy and live off her large fortune.'

His father told him to get out of his sight.

Arthur sat in his room, reflecting on his situation, until his mother came flurrying in. She urged him to come downstairs and make peace with his father, whose temper she'd managed to soothe. They reconciled, but shortly before Arthur departed two days later, his father took him aside while his mother was fretting to the maid about some trifling matter.

'If you ever marry that girl, I *will* disown you. You understand me, boy?'

Arthur was tempted to point out that he was twenty-six, but instead he answered, 'Yes, Father.'

He knew that his father wasn't bluffing: the man was far too proud to back down from a threat. Yet Arthur was determined to make Molly Mrs Arthur Greenwood one day, although not to obtain her fortune. When he'd hinted at his wish, she'd said that she wanted to finish her doctorate before considering marriage. He'd counted down the years, then the months, then the weeks until she finally graduated, but decided to let her bask for a while in the glory of her achievements before raising the subject of matrimony again. He tried not to dwell on his father's words as he made the journey back to Hertfordshire. Instead he looked forward to holding Molly in his arms again…breathing in her delicately fragrant, sweet, earthy scent…and kissing her.

When Arthur arrived at Ravenfeld Hall, he wandered into the garden in search of Molly. He was slightly apprehensive about meeting her now he was at his destination, knowing that she'd more than likely still be angry about his abrupt departure to Newbury. Everything was shrouded in fog. Trees only a few feet away looked like faint pencil drawings. He walked leisurely to begin with, but as his quarry was proving even more elusive than he'd anticipated, he quickened his pace. He completed his circuit around the kitchen garden and trod back through the woods. He'd sent Molly a message on his pocket telegraph but she hadn't responded yet. According to his pocket watch, he'd been in pursuit of her for nearly half an hour. What if they'd both been walking around the garden and had repeatedly missed each other? It would be no wonder, with all this fog. Normally she could be found at her laboratory, so this was where he returned to. The cottage was built of grey and white stone, with crawling ivy here and there. The thatched roof sagged over the wooden door like a drooping eyelid. To the right of the door was a small arched window with its glass cut in the shape of a bare tree (Arthur's idea).

'Molly?' he called.

Only a crow cawed in response. He couldn't see her when he glanced through the open arched window, although he noticed that there was broken glass and what looked like dried ink on the floor. Had there been an accident? A smashed ink bottle, perhaps? Maybe Molly had gone to retrieve a pan and broom to sweep up the glass.

As he took another path to the house that he knew to be quicker than the way he'd come, Arthur noticed a trail of blackened flowers on the ground before him. He crouched and peered at them. Despite his encyclopaedic knowledge of flora, they were unlike any variety he knew of. They hadn't been there the last time he was in the garden. He would ask Molly about them when he found her. The trail of black flowers continued down the little path. The path was vaulted by trees, the branches of which were curiously curled to form a neat arch – something that hadn't been Arthur's or Molly's doing. The ground was covered in soft turf so thick that it was hard to tell whether the steps had been fashioned deliberately or were the result of tree roots breaking up the slope. Arthur thought he caught a glimpse of paving slabs every now and then, but they could have been large stones. The path eventually led to the side of the house, near the west wing, bypassing the rose garden and the shrubbery archway that was the formal entrance to the garden. The trail of black flowers, some retaining a touch of red, continued across the lawn, then abruptly stopped sprouting a few feet from the south hall door. Arthur scratched his head, and repeated to himself that he'd ask Molly about them. Then one of the androids – Colonel Copperton – saw him through the window and opened the door without him having to ask.

'Thank you,' said Arthur, as the soldier shut the door behind him.

'It's no trouble, Mr Arthur. No need to treat you like a stranger, after all,' replied the colonel, before marching away briskly. Too late, it occurred to Arthur that he should have asked him if he'd seen Molly around.

Arthur drifted from room to room. He could find his way around Ravenfeld Hall pretty well now, and spent more time here than at the rooms he rented in Camden. He nodded to the newel-post dogs as he passed them, and they returned the gesture. Things that would've made him leap in fright years ago didn't faze him at all now. Several months ago, he had been breakfasting with the family when an invisible peacock that he'd seen (or rather, not seen) before swooped into the dining room, flew over their heads, and shot straight through the windowpane. Arthur, along with the other three, hadn't started or given a cry of alarm. One of Molly's brothers (he forgot which now) had calmly remarked that they'd better enquire about getting the window repaired, and then resumed reading the newspaper. Dear God, Arthur had thought, taking a sip of coffee, I've become one of them. They'd watched from the broken window as Colonel Copperton chased the peacock across the lawn, until he'd managed to catch it.

Wandering into the oak parlour, Arthur gazed at the portraits of Molly's father and mother. They didn't appear to be companion portraits, since there was a definite difference in style, and only the picture of Mrs Abernathy was housed in an elaborate gilded frame instead of plain, varnished wood. Mr Abernathy looked to be in his late thirties or early forties, with dark blue eyes and a determined chin. He had the air of a man resolved to make a name for himself, which in the end he'd failed to do. Molly definitely took after the Abernathy side of the family, although Mr Abernathy's mousy hair wasn't as long or as wild as his daughter's. Arthur saw Mr Douglas in him too. The portrait of Mrs Abernathy had been painted when she was a young woman, before she was even Mrs Abernathy. She was extraordinarily beautiful, there was no denying that. Her features were harmoniously proportioned: the dark, fine brows suggestive of a decisive, discerning character; the ivory skin flawlessly smooth; the glossy jet-black hair elegantly arranged with ringlets framing her face, as was the fashion then. But the painter's brush had also captured her coldness. There was no warmth in those emerald eyes. They spoke of a cool, calculating mind. It seemed that Mr George took mostly after her. (Arthur didn't like to admit that he was still afraid to be alone in a room with Mr George.)

'You were wrong about Molly,' he said aloud to the portrait. 'She isn't worthless. You didn't know how fortunate you were to have her for a daughter.'

He felt a chill down the back of his neck, and half-anticipated that a ghostly voice would whisper to him or that a distant door would slam. Briskly he walked on, knowing full well that any supernatural occurrences were products of his own imagination; he'd been silly to talk to a portrait of a dead woman in the first place. But he couldn't comprehend how Mrs Abernathy could have treated her only daughter the way she had. His own mother clucked around him constantly, warning her 'special boy' that he'd catch a chill from not wearing enough layers in winter, or that he wasn't having adequate meals. (Where she got the latter from he had no idea, since he was hardly skin and bone and actually had a good deal of muscle.) She'd even encouraged him to become a painter, when he was briefly enamoured by the idea around the age of fourteen, before his father had trampled on that dream, saying that he'd never pay for his son to train as a 'namby-pamby painter'. At least Molly had received some encouragement from her father, albeit more through occasional gestures than through words.

Arthur turned in the direction of the servants' hall. Betsey might know where Molly was. As it happened, he found Molly at the table in the servants' kitchen, her head on her arms on the tabletop. Was she asleep?

'Molly?' He shook her shoulder gently.

Molly stirred and lifted her messy head, rubbing her bleary eyes. She looked tired and her face was pale. At last she focused on him. 'Arthur?'

'Are you all right?'

'I'm fine.' She swatted him away and he retreated several paces, his hands held up in protest.

'Well, I won't apologise for being concerned. You look exhausted. What were you doing?'

'I was…' She looked searchingly at nothing as she pressed a hand to her head. 'Baking?'

'All night?' He laughed. 'I thought you hated cooking? It wouldn't be this that you were baking by any chance, would it?' He indicated the pie that was cooling by the window. 'It certainly looks good. Mind if I'm the first to sample it?'

Molly didn't reply, and so he reached for a knife. When he cut through the thick crust, he saw that it was an apple and blackberry pie, still steaming as he lifted a slice onto a plate. It must have been a peace offering; she knew that apple and blackberry was his favourite. He was as warmed by the thought that she had been up all night baking this for him as he was by the aroma of the pie.

Molly, meanwhile, was thinking rapidly, trying to recapture her fluttering memories of the previous night. Everything was hazy. She clearly remembered the raven smashing the beaker. She'd collapsed on the floor, awoken sometime later, and then… Her chair flung backwards as she shot to her feet. 'Don't eat that!'

She managed to tackle Arthur to the ground just before he raised the fork to his mouth. They were both startled and breathing quickly. Neither moved.

'What on earth is the matter with you?' said Arthur from underneath her. She felt his voice rumble through his chest.

'Nothing. It's just that…the pie isn't cooked properly.'

'It's only apples and blackberries, it's not like it's a meat pie. Besides, it looks fine to me.' Then he added, in a more playful tone, 'Are you sure you didn't just want an excuse to get me like this?'

'Of course not!' She sat up and folded her arms across her chest.

He pulled himself into a sitting position and put his arm around her thin shoulders. 'You can always bake another pie. But don't feel that you have to make such an effort for me.' He pulled her gently towards him and she softened, leaning her drowsy head on his shoulder. 'Go and have a sleep, Molly. I can tell you need it.'

'After you came all this way? And didn't you want my opinion on a commission?'

'Oh, we can discuss my ideas for the viscountess's garden later.'

'No.' She dragged herself to her feet. 'I'll be fine. Let's sit outside, since it's not too cold today and I could use the fresh air. Would you like a cup of tea? I can ask the cook or Gwyneth to make something if you're hungry… wherever they've got to.' Perhaps they'd entered the kitchen to start their work that morning, seen their sleeping mistress, and thought better of it.

Arthur shook his head. 'I can tell you're not that tired if you have the strength to argue with me. I'd appreciate a cup of tea, however, if you're offering.'

Molly shepherded him out of the kitchen, glancing back at the slice of pie that had already eaten away at the metal fork. She turned cold at the sight of it. If she hadn't got to him in time and the poison had reached his mouth…she didn't want to think about it.

The fog had dissolved and the sun was trying to appear. When they were sitting outside with a pot of tea between them on the little table, Arthur told Molly all about the dinner with the Oswalds. She found it hilarious.

'I'd have given anything to see the look on Mrs Oswald's face when she saw what you'd drawn in that sketchbook!' Molly laughed so hard she had tears at the corners of her eyes. 'Since you ignored my warning,' she added, trying to sound reproachful.

'You might find it amusing, Molly, but I was very embarrassed at the time.' Yet Arthur couldn't prevent himself laughing either.

Molly wiped her eyes with her finger and blotted her dress with her tears. She soon became calm again. 'But...do you think your father was serious? Would he really disown you if we married?'

Arthur's good mood swiftly deflated. 'I think he was serious.'

Molly took a swallow of tea and shook her head. 'I can see where you get your stubbornness from.'

'I'm nothing like my father.'

'In every other respect you're nothing like him. But neither of you is ever willing to back down.'

'You're one to talk about stubbornness, since you refuse to go and rest. Although you do have a little more colour in your cheeks now.'

'I told you I'd be fine. Now, weren't we supposed to be discussing the plans for the viscountess's garden? You said you wanted to run them past me, since there were several points you were unsure about.'

'Oh yes, I have the plans here. I specifically want your opinion on this idea for a scented garden.'

Molly was glad that she'd distracted him from asking about the pie or the possibility of them marrying. She was unsure which subject she felt more uncomfortable about.

Arthur spread his plans on the table and unfolded his vision, indicating points on the sketches as he spoke. 'Originally I was thinking of having a little scented garden with a similar layout to the rose garden at Ravenfeld, with a central square bed and beds running around the perimeter, and with seating *here* and *here*. But then I thought: what if we introduced taste into the garden as well? We could plant two rows of your pudding plants near this bench, and maybe a few fruit trees or bushes? I don't want it to feel too much like a kitchen garden, though.'

'I don't think it will. Adding the taste element is a good idea, and I could definitely supply you with the plants you need.'

'I was particularly thinking of having some of your cross-bred fruit trees, but do you think you could make the fruit so that from the outside it looks like, say, an apple, but when you bite into it it's a melon or a peach?'

'Easily.'

'Excellent! For the scented plants, I think I might stick with traditional species, although I'm not sure. Here's the flowers I had in mind – I think they will provide a mixed colour palette as well. We'll want plenty of lavender – English, not French – and honeysuckle along the garden wall…'

Arthur was in his element now, and sketched with his pencil as he spoke. Molly did her best to listen to his ideas, but recollections of the night before still haunted her.

Chapter Ten

The inn at the corner of Commercial Street in Spitalfields was unassuming enough. The faded sign hung lopsidedly above the door, and through smoky windows one could glimpse the usual furnishings of a barroom. Once inside, enveloped in the fug of smoke and droning chatter, you'd see that some of the chairs had legs missing, that the tables were criss-crossed with scratches, and that the filmy glasses contained liquid that was only just passable as ale (some of the drinkers likened it to horse urine). But if you approached the portly barman and said the right words, you'd be admitted through a door and directed up a flight of precariously narrow stairs, until you arrived at another door. If you pushed it open (it wouldn't betray you with a squeak), you'd be greeted by a small, fusty room. Here fermented Revolution.

Seated on a motley assortment of chairs (although many of those in attendance leant against the walls) were men young and old, the majority of whom belonged to 'the lower orders'. Most wore black, orange and green bands on the sleeves of their coats or shirts. Some had a tattoo, somewhere on their arm, of an inverted triangle inside a circle with a cross running through it: the hallmark of the Sons of Adam League. Their faces were set hard but their eyes blazed like coals, their fire kindled from within. Their attention was directed towards the man making a speech at the head of the assembly. He was a brittle-looking clergyman with thin, wispy yellow hair, pink skin and flushed cheeks. There was something of a turkey about him. His voice was faltering, and there wasn't a great deal of force behind his words, his tone bordering on politely apologetic. The hand that clutched his notes trembled. This was Mr Enoch Shelton, curate of the church to which many of his audience belonged. The vicar usually headed these fortnightly meetings, but on this occasion he had sent apologies, saying that he and his wife were dining with the bishop.

'An influential member of the House of Lords has lent his support to the bill guaranteeing three miners for each one of these new mining machines.' Mr Shelton swallowed. 'And our petition to extend such quotas across all manufacturing industries has almost three thousand signatures.'

'But when are we actually going to *do* something?' demanded a member of his flock. 'These machines are taking our jobs and destroying our way of life!'

'And what would you 'ave us do?' challenged a stocky man with a bald head and a bloodstained apron. 'Go around settin' fire to factories and smashin' up androids like those Crusaders of Eden lunatics? Two of 'em even tried stabbing an android in the street – along with the gent that owned it!'

'They only want the same thing we do,' ventured a meek young man.

'They're madmen! They want us all to live like it's the Old Testament. They've attacked railway stations, saying trains encourage sloth and cause a disorientation of the senses.'

'Gentlemen, please.' Mr Shelton dabbed the sweat running down his face with his handkerchief. 'It has been stated publicly that we do not condone the Crusaders' more, um, radical methods and beliefs. Let us return to the agenda, shall we? So, uh, as I was saying, once this bill is passed, it'll mark the first of what will be a series of victories guaranteeing rights for honest, hard-working men. And the march has been scheduled to deliver our petition to Parliament on the sixteenth of next month.'

A wave of approving noises rose and fell, although many men remained silent.

'But do you not see the bigger threat?' demanded a tall man near the front. 'The Abernathys' machines aren't like what you normally find in mills and factories. They can *think*. And they're getting cleverer all the time.' The man faced his fellow attendees, and Mr Shelton made no effort to reclaim the floor from him. 'It's not just manual work their machines are taking, but work what requires brains: bookkeeping, running shop counters, copyist work, and translating. That's what makes 'em different. Most of the Abernathys' machines are android servants or companions. There's plenty of girls who can't get work as maids 'cause the local ladies all have machines cooking and cleaning for 'em! Those foolish ladies treat their android "companions" like real girls, and even leave their fortune to 'em in their wills! What I want to know is this: what happens when these machines get too clever and question why they have to take orders?'

'An excellent question!' said a commanding voice from the doorway.

The members watched as a man in a charcoal-grey suit swept into the room.

'Mr Alexander Gearhart at your service.' He bowed.

The curate coughed politely. 'And who exactly are you, Mr Gearhart?'

'An inventor and businessman.' Alexander leant his arm casually on the podium and offered Mr Shelton his card. 'But first and foremost, a Christian.'

'And an American,' remarked the tall man gruffly.

Alexander flashed him a disarming smile. 'The perceptive gentleman over there is quite right: I hail from across the pond. But my father was an Englishman, and a hard-working Englishman too. Worked as a post-chaise driver, until the railways came to town and he could no longer find work. My family boarded a ship bound for New York to begin a new life, only my father didn't live to see the New World. He died a week into the voyage.'

Judging by the men's faces, thirteen of the twenty-seven had bought the story. Unlucky. Their hackles were still raised, although the bristling tension in the air aroused by Alexander's accent had relaxed a fraction. He was less of a foreigner to them now. But they weren't in his power yet. And he had a few more cards to play.

'So when I heard of your organisation on returning to my family's homeland to establish myself in London and make my fortune, I decided to join at once.'

'That is admirable, Mr Gearhart,' said Mr Shelton, still looking slightly nervous. 'If you wish to join, you are welcome to add your name to the list by the door.'

'Ah, but I do not merely wish to join the SOAL, but to revolutionise it.'

'Shouldn't you be trying to "revolutionise" your own country before you come over here telling us what's what?' This was the tall man again. 'Shouldn't you be fightin' for the Union?'

'What I meant, my good man, is that I wish to use my inventions to improve the running of your organisation and spread its influence across the globe. And where better to start than with the most advanced, the most mighty nation in the world?'

'Excuse me, Mr Gearhart,' piped up the curate, 'but what exactly do you mean by "improve the running of our organisation"?'

'Quite simply that *you lack coordination*. Forty-seven branches up and down the country, each headed by its own leader, and each with its own localised aims and priorities. Some of you are here because of religious principles, many because you fear that your livelihoods are at risk, and others because you believe that humanity itself is under threat. But do you not see the problem? As noble as all these motives are, they inevitably lead to conflicting objectives. What you need are three things.' He lifted a finger as he reeled off each one. 'Coordination. Consolidation. Communication. Let's take the first two together, for in order to achieve your various aims, you need decisive leadership. Tell me, who is the head of the SOAL?'

'The good Reverend Clarke,' piped up a young man with a dumb, canine face.

'But where is the good reverend? He chooses to bless us with the occasional pearl of wisdom in his letters to the newspapers, but not once has he made a public appearance. Why does he not show himself and take the reins of the organisation he inspired?'

'It is for us to take action. He made the rallying call and the people answered.'

'But every ship needs a captain to steer it, my lad. What you need is a president who's answerable to a council of representatives – one from each local branch. And it'll be from these representatives that the president shall be elected.'

'Who put you in charge?' demanded a man with large spectacles and ink-stained fingers – a clerk, no doubt. There was even ink on the bridge of his spectacles from where he'd pushed them back up his nose. 'You've no right to barge in on our meeting like this.'

Alexander smiled good-humouredly at him. 'Who's the one who is actually in charge around here?'

'Mr Brundell, the vicar.'

'And where is he?' Alexander placed a hand above his eyes and reckoned to survey the crowd. 'I don't see a vicar amongst you.'

'Mr Brundell is having tea with the bishop,' explained Mr Shelton.

'So he's left his worthy curate to shepherd his flock? Very well, then – Mr Shelton, do you object to my idea of consolidating the leadership of the SOAL?'

'Well…'

'I'm only asking for your opinion, my good fellow.' What a pathetic, brainless individual, thought Alexander. He'd not even realised that Alexander had addressed him by name without anyone in the room having offered that information.

Mr Shelton swallowed. 'Well, I suppose it never hurts if everyone is singing from the same hymn sheet.'

Alexander gave a well-timed chuckle. 'Couldn't have put it better myself! And since your temporary leader sees merit in my suggestion, I beg you all to please hear me out.' He managed to discreetly manoeuvre Mr Shelton out of the way and take his place at the podium. 'I look around this room and you know what I see? Talent, energy, vigour. I hate to see such potential go to waste. And while you sit here organising petitions and protests, the number of androids and clever machines in the world is increasing. And they're becoming ever more complex – take my word for it as a learned gentleman. What's needed is a united front across all branches to combat this threat.' He swept back his hair and let his words sink in. 'Oh, and just so you know, your pious, dutiful vicar is not currently having tea with the bishop. He's visiting his mistress in St John's Wood.' He drew a fan of photographic prints from his coat pocket before the gasps faded. 'I have here copies of a rather compromising photograph to substantiate my claim.'

He dealt them around the room. Eyebrows rose and heads shook. Mr Shelton went from pink to red. One of two members subtly slipped their copy into their pocket.

'You see the power of information, my friends? Allow me to demonstrate my invention.' A tele-texter appeared in Alexander's hand, apparently conjured from mid-air. He explained how it worked and gave a similar demonstration to the one he had given at the club presentation dinner, using two young telegraph office workers as volunteers, who grasped how to operate the tele-texters with ease. He then retrieved a black silk sack from outside the door. 'Each of you can have your very own tele-texter free of charge. I am more than happy to donate them to a worthy cause.'

There was an eager rush. Alexander handed out the devices to begin with, before letting go of the sack and allowing the pack of ravenous wolves to descend on it. He wondered how many of these men were illiterate and incapable of operating a tele-texter, but that was of little consequence.

'Spread the word: an election is to be held in two weeks' time to decide the SOAL's leader from the forty-seven regional representatives,' he cried above the rabble.

Then he slipped out of the room, since the next phase of his plan was now complete. None of them had even noticed that he'd neglected to make a formal application to join the League. How amusing.

Chapter Eleven

Molly lit her lantern and slipped out into the night. She wore her thickest cloak as, despite it being April, it was still bitterly cold. The lantern's glow guided her way across the lawn. A wicker basket hung from her other arm. One of the servants could easily have taken the basket to Douglas, but she wanted a word with him.

The lights from the stable block shone brightly ahead. The stable block was newer than Ravenfeld Hall itself; probably it had been built during her grandfather's time. It was made of red brick, with a clock face above the main archway. She heard her brother banging about before she'd even passed through the archway and entered the rectangular court. Douglas had gutted many of the stables and knocked through walls to create larger rooms, but the dark green stable doors remained. Molly pushed one of them and stepped into the workshop. No horses had occupied the space for decades, although strands of straw were still wedged between the floorboards. This was the spaceship's home. Douglas was on top of it, fixing something or other. A ladder was propped precariously against the ship's side.

'I've brought your supper,' Molly called, setting the basket on the floor when there was no response. 'It'll go cold if you leave it too long.'

'I don't mind.' Douglas was riveting the metal plating rather forcefully, his brows drawn. He'd been working with the same dogged determination for the past two days.

'Why do you have this bee in your bonnet about proving that the spaceship works?'

'Because I was made a laughing stock of. After what happened at the presentation everyone thinks the idea is ridiculous, but I know it will work.'

'Who's "everyone"? The members of your club?'

'If they think the idea is foolish, then I have no hope of convincing anyone else.'

'Why do you need to? You've still not managed to persuade anyone to consider airships as a viable means of transport, but you've continued to build and test them for the sheer pleasure of it.'

'I need to know that it works for myself, more than anything. I've spent years working on this and I'm not about to fall at the final hurdle.'

'Are you annoyed that George saved you?'

'Well, it was a bit embarrassing having my older brother rescue me. It was like I was six years old again.' Douglas stopped what he was doing and climbed down the ladder, which wobbled slightly.

Molly flew to the bottom of the ladder and gripped one of the rungs, although she was unsure what she could really do if he fell.

'Thank you, Mol, although there wasn't much chance of me falling. That ladder is steadier than it looks.'

'It never hurts to be careful,' she smiled.

Douglas swilled his hands in a basin and then peered inside the basket. 'I'm nearly finished with the repairs at last. I appreciate you bringing me supper – I am rather famished, in all honesty.'

'I know you have the appetite of a horse.' She sat on the edge of his workbench. 'There's sauce in the pot. I imagine the meat will be unbearably dry without it, since it's been sitting so long.'

'Anything's better than stale bread and cheese,' replied Douglas, as he arranged the plate and accompaniments on a crate. He dragged a stool towards him and sat down.

'Are you referring to that week after an investor ran off with our money back in Soho?'

'Of course.' He managed to smile between mouthfuls. 'Then when the cheese ran out, we dipped into your preserves. It was the dead of winter and all we had to eat was bread and jam.'

'So we could afford to add more coals to the fire – that poky old house was always freezing. I managed to scrape together enough money from selling medicines to buy bones from the butcher, and boiled them to make that thin broth that looked like muddy water. You pretended it was a thick, hearty soup and that we were eating off Dresden china, not Mother's chipped service.'

'We made it a game after that,' Douglas chuckled, while sawing through his dry mutton. 'We'd imagine that what we were eating was something better, and we gave particular foods different names.'

'You started that.'

'It made you laugh.'

'You always found a way to cheer me up, no matter how bleak our circumstances were.' She smiled gently before getting to her feet. 'I'll leave you to enjoy your mutton.'

'Don't you mean my fresh leg of lamb?' he said jokingly.

'Call it what you will.' She put her hands on his shoulders. 'But remember: when you're angry, you make mistakes. Don't do anything rash. If you're going to fly off into space, do so with a clearer head, and make sure you've checked every last little part in that ship beforehand.'

'All right, Mol.'

'Promise me you won't try to launch it tonight.'

'I promise.' He didn't look her in the face as he spoke, since he was too busy mopping up the sauce from his plate with a chunk of potato.

'And make sure you bring all of the crockery back with you.'

Molly's lantern guided her back to the house. Several glowing windows told her where everyone was. The servants were congregated in their quarters, except for Betsey, who was in her attic bedroom; George was in his study; Colonel Copperton was in his room. Molly found her feet rooted to the drive. Should she go to her room and answer letters, or pay her laboratory a visit? She felt the lab pulling her into the woodland. She had many questions after what had happened the other night, and only now was she finding the courage to seek answers. The horror of almost poisoning her lover had made her recoil from going anywhere near the laboratory for some time, but she needed to understand what had driven her to do such a thing. As her feet moved in the direction of the woodland, a rumbling boom sounded that left her ears ringing in its wake. From the direction of the stables, a jet of orange fire and smoke rocketed into the sky.

'*You liar! You stupid—*'

The noise of the skyward-bound spaceship consumed her curses. Frantically she ran back in the direction of the stables, only to see, with her shaky vision, the ship moving further and further away. She waved at it in vain. Still something urged her into the stables, though she knew well what she'd find – or rather, not find: a) the spaceship, and b) her brother. She was correct on both counts. Well, there was nothing to be done but wait for Douglas's return and pray he'd come back to earth in one piece. Now that she was still, her thumping heart ached with each beat. At least the fool had put the crockery back tidily in the basket. How considerate of him. Stooping to retrieve the basket, she spied something on the ground. It was a rubber ring that, when she picked it up, fitted neatly into her palm. She knew where it came from. Douglas had once shown her how his breathing apparatus worked, and had pointed at a rubber ring identical to this one...

Abandoning her lantern and basket, Molly sprinted back towards the house as fast as she could, seeming, like a whippet, to fly above the ground. She ran into the house and shot into the lift, yanking the handle for George's study. She found him writing at his desk, apparently unperturbed by the blast minutes ago.

'That idiot's trying to fly into space!'

George raised his eyes. 'Our brother, you mean?'

'Yes!' Molly gasped, staggering out of the lift. 'He's taken off in that damn spaceship of his, and it's missing a rubber ring that connects two airtight seals on the breathing apparatus. He'll suffocate!'

Instantly George was on his feet, and he flung open the doors of a cabinet in the far corner of the room.

Molly's eyes widened at the sight of the rocket launcher. 'Where on earth did you get that?'

'It was a prototype from when we were building Colonel Copperton, although there wasn't time to complete it before he was shipped to India. I kept it in case the Hall ever came under attack from anti-android groups. Tell the colonel to make his way to the western tower.' George strode across the room and pressed the button that opened the lift doors.

'And what about you? You're not planning on *shooting* Douglas down, are you?'

'That's precisely what I intend to do,' George replied as he entered the lift, and the doors closed on his hard-set face.

Molly ran downstairs and knocked furiously on Copperton's door. When the mechanical soldier answered, she saw that he'd been in the process of building a model ship that was about one-fifth the size of the real thing. She didn't have time to be impressed.

'What was that boom I heard earlier, Miss Molly?' enquired the colonel.

'Douglas has launched his spaceship and its breathing apparatus is faulty. If he gets too high up, he'll suffocate!' She somehow managed to utter each sentence in one breath, despite her starved lungs and fluttering heart. 'George is trying to shoot him down. He says you're to go to the western tower.'

'Understood, Miss Molly.' Copperton banged the door shut behind him and marched along the corridor.

There was a heavy, studded oak door at the end of the passage leading to the western tower. Torches blazed into life as the colonel flung it open. He ran up the winding staircase, tackling three steps at a time with each bounding stride. Molly clattered after him on almost spent legs, and just before she reached the top she heard a bang. The cold night wind swept her hair over her eyes as she found herself in open air. Once she'd drawn her hair back and stuffed it down the neck of her dress, she saw George gazing skyward. The smoking rocket launcher rested on his shoulder.

'Did you get him?' she asked.

'I missed!' George reloaded the launcher. 'He's too far away, I can't get an accurate shot.'

'Allow me, Master George, if you please.' The colonel stood beside George and stuck out his left arm. It began to reshape itself into a miniature rocket launcher. 'You both might want to cover your ears!'

Molly did as he suggested just before there was an almighty boom, the force of which made Colonel Copperton stagger backwards a step. The ensuing gust of wind whipped up Molly's skirts and hair. The missile left a trail of dove-grey smoke in its wake as it sought its target. It vanished behind the clouds and there was a brief flash of white light. Something dropped from the clouds, falling faster and faster. A white parachute billowed behind the spaceship, reducing its velocity. When there should have been a crash, there was a loud splash, and a flock of quacking ducks flew up in one dark cloud.

Molly let out a deep sigh of relief. 'You did know he'd land in the lake, didn't you, Colonel?'

'Of course, Miss Molly,' replied Copperton, as his arm returned to its usual shape. 'Although another second and he'd have been out of my range.'

'Can you see if Douglas is all right?' she asked anxiously.

The colonel extended his vision. 'He's escaped the wreckage and is swimming towards the lake's edge.'

'Find some ropes and try to retrieve the wreckage, Colonel,' ordered George. 'If Mr Greenwood sees it spoiling the view, he'll be rather dismayed.'

Molly frowned a little. 'Never mind if Arthur throws a fit. Douglas might be able to salvage something of the ship,' she said, as Copperton marched away.

George picked up the prototype rocket launcher. 'That was my intention in asking the colonel to retrieve it.'

'You said you didn't have time to finish that launcher, yet it looked to me like the colonel has one.'

'That was a later addition with an improved design.'

'I see. I hope Douglas doesn't catch a chill from his cold bath in the lake.'

'It might teach him not to be so foolish.' George descended the stairs.

Molly glanced back at the smoking wreckage in the distance, then followed him. She went calmly to Douglas's room, where she retrieved some clothes from the cupboard, took a big towel from the linen chest, and placed everything neatly on the bed. Then she went into the adjoining dressing room to fill the copper bath with steaming water (the water was fed through pipes, without the need to repeatedly fill the toilet can with hot water), before making her way downstairs. She entered the smaller drawing room, threw another log on the fire, then sat down and waited. She'd fetched her battered copy of *Cranford* from the garden room, where she'd left it earlier, and now she resumed reading.

Five minutes later there came the bang of the south hall door. Something squelched in her direction. The livid look on Douglas's face failed to unnerve her as it should have done, on account of the comical sight of him drenched and covered in duckweed.

'I almost managed it!' He peeled a strip of duckweed from his head and slapped it onto the floor. 'I was so close to achieving it, then you two shot me down! Do you really have so little faith in me?'

Molly held up the rubber ring. 'You forgot this,' she said in a steely tone.

The anger evaporated from his face. 'I can't have done. I counted them and they were all there…'

'What did I say? When you're angry, you make mistakes.'

'Oh.'

'I ran a bath for you. You can shout at me once you're clean and dry.'

Meekly, he trailed upstairs. Molly remained reading by the fireside, getting up after ten minutes to make a cup of chocolate. She tossed the strand of duckweed onto the fire and wiped her slimy fingers on her bottle-green dress. There were wet footprints on the carpet, and a faint smell of pond water followed her to the kitchen. She returned to the drawing room with two steaming cups just before Douglas reappeared in the doorway. He was wearing the clothes she had selected. His hair was still wet and tousled, but he smelt of soap instead of pond water.

'I'm still cross with you and George,' he said lamely, accepting one of the cups from her.

'I know. But you have to allow me to be cross with you too, for breaking your promise and risking your life doing something rash.'

'Fine.'

Brother and sister sipped their chocolate in silence.

'The colonel said he'd fish the spaceship out of the lake,' said Molly.

'What's left of it. I might as well start again from scratch.'

Molly pointed meaningfully to her top lip. Understanding the hint, Douglas wiped his foam moustache away with the back of his hand. Molly couldn't help giggling.

'Next time I'll do it,' he said firmly.

'You will. You know, I think I have a name for your next ship.'

'Go on.'

Molly smiled. '*Icarus*.'

Douglas stared at her, then chuckled. 'Very well, then. To *Icarus*.' He clinked her cup and drained the rest of his chocolate, until only the bitter dregs remained. 'I can tell you made this and not Gwyneth.' He peered into his cup. 'She makes it as thick as her porridge should be.'

'She's learning. She's not burned the toast once this week.'

Douglas put his cup on the table. 'Not once? That's an improvement.'

The only improvement, Molly thought. The cook was in despair over Gwyneth. But the poor girl tried so hard, and more than once Molly had found her on the back step, crying into her apron. The last time that had happened, Cook had scolded the kitchen maid for scalding her by dropping a pan of boiling water. So Molly had decided to begin giving Gwyneth secret cookery lessons on Sundays. She refused to teach her anything to do with eggs, though, after the calamities they'd had that first Sunday. Eggs required precision, and Gwyneth was as precise as an unwound watch. She had persistence and enthusiasm, if nothing else. She spilled flour over the rim of the bowl when mixing, cut bread so that the slice became thinner and thinner the deeper the knife delved into the loaf, and peeled (or rather hacked) vegetables so that a lot of the flesh was removed along with the peel.

'Am I getting better, Miss Molly? Am I?' was the girl's constant refrain.

'Slowly but surely, Gwyneth,' Molly would reply, her smile so tight that it was painful. She knew she should have ignored the crying kitchen maid like any other mistress would have done (at best). But she couldn't bear to see Gwyneth continuously upset, or without a good reference if she chose to leave Ravenfeld Hall.

Douglas retrieved the evening paper. 'Have you heard of the actor, Mr Decimus Crowther?'

'Samuel raves about him,' said Molly.

'He's the lead in that new play at Drury Lane, *The Poisoned Chalice*.'

'Do you want to see it? You've not been to the theatre since—for months.' Molly knew that it was best not to mention Clara or the broken engagement in front of Douglas.

'Hmm, not particularly. I should imagine the tickets are sold out by now anyway. That man's name guarantees a full house. Although I am curious to see if he's as good as the critics say.'

'I'm sure you'll have another chance at some point.'

Douglas looked up to see his sister gazing intently at the fire, her hands curled around her almost empty cup. The flames danced in her green eyes. 'Something on your mind, Mol?'

'Nothing important.' She finished her chocolate and set down the warm cup beside her brother's cold one.

'You looked lost in thought.'

'It's nothing, really. Just something to do with my lecture at the Royal Institution,' she lied, as she got to her feet. The warm, creamy chocolate had settled at the bottom of her stomach. 'I'd better address it now or it'll keep me awake all night.'

'The lecture's not for another two weeks yet, but I wouldn't want you losing sleep over it. I promise not to try to fly to space in your absence.' He smiled.

'You'd better not,' she warned, half-seriously, before leaving the room.

Chapter Twelve

Instead of going to her room, however, Molly slipped out of the south hall door and went to her laboratory. She stared at the large beaker of remaining poison. She should just get rid of it. It had sent her mad: she'd actually tried to *kill* Arthur while under its influence. She intended to keep him ignorant of that fact, especially after he'd been so pleased at the thought of her baking that pie for him. She had even considered baking a non-lethal apple and blackberry pie as a replacement, but decided that was a slippery slope. Then it would be cooking him supper and darning his stockings. She sometimes mended his shirts as it was.

Destroying the poison was the correct thing to do, but curiosity made her hesitate. That was the chemist in her. She wanted to see if a second, smaller dose would produce the same effects while allowing her to retain at least some of her sanity. There was a chance she could die, it was true, but that first dose should have killed her and yet she was perfectly fine. Molly made her decision. She locked the laboratory door and closed the windows. Sucking a drop of the inky liquid into a pipette, she added it to half a pint of water. The poison slowly spread outwards, tinging the water red. She made a note of the time and the dosage, steeled herself, and then drank the glass's bitter contents.

The effect was almost instantaneous. She could feel the poison spreading through her, like black roots worming their way through her brain and nerves. Her entire body prickled and grew hot, almost feverish. The pain wasn't as intense this time and it was over in a matter of seconds. Her mind raged. Dark desires were called forth: the urge to maim and destroy burned inside her. But Molly was still there. She pushed against the darkness. For a few short seconds, she maintained a hold on her mind. But then, overcome by the sheer mental effort, her sanity slipped. Black vines wrapped around her shoulders and snaked along her arms, sprouting red flowers. It took her a few frenzied moments to find a focal point for her anger. Her target had been in her uppermost thoughts shortly before she'd taken the poison: Clara Marsden. Her earlier conversation with Douglas had called to mind how, on the night following that dinner with the Marsdens, he'd come to Molly's room to apologise, saying that he knew it wasn't really her fault that the night had ended in disaster. He had sat beside her on her bed and tried to hide how upset he was. She hadn't been fooled. She'd put her arms around him and pressed him tightly, wishing she could absorb the hurt from him. Now a whisper of her sane self knew that it wasn't really fair to direct her anger at Clara, but the girl's simple-mindedness and passivity were infuriating. Molly doubted that Clara had been as heartbroken as Douglas following the engagement's termination. The ordeal with the androids had shocked and frightened her, but she'd soon have recovered from it, and would now be paraded around ballrooms before more conventional, wealthier suitors. Then she'd marry whichever one her parents told her to. That girl would suffer as she deserved to for the pain she'd caused Douglas. And Molly knew precisely how. She'd write Clara a letter expressing regret and sorrow. The contents didn't matter too much, however, she reflected as she sat at her writing desk. Clara would never have the chance to finish reading it. Molly's lips twisted in a malevolent smile as she filled the inkwell. She plucked a scarlet creeper from her sleeve and sprinkled its orange pollen into the ink, swirling it around a couple of times. She filled a sheet of paper with empty apologies and pretty compliments, watching the wet ink glisten in the candlelight. The poison would still be effective when the ink was dry. She would use a fresh bottle of ink to address the envelope, so the letter would reach its recipient without anyone else dying in the process. She read it through and imagined Clara receiving it, probably over breakfast as her mother prattled on about suitable rich young men or French fashions. She would open the envelope and her pretty pink-white hands (with immaculate pearly nails that had never known dirt) would touch the letter, make contact with the ink, and then...

No! Molly had seen herself write the letter as if she were watching herself in a nightmare. But now she was awake. She tore up the letter and scattered the pieces in the fire. She'd broken through the black fog enveloping her brain, but it was creeping up on her with a vengeance. *No.* She summoned more black veins but wrapped them around herself, feeling their thorns bite into her skin. *You will learn to submit to me, even if I'm torturing myself as well as you.* The poison's madness fought back. The vines slackened and voices swirled around her head. They compelled her outside into the cool night. Poisonous plants spread out from her and along the ground. Black vines choked the trees. She was losing to the darkness; it swelled inside her head and tried to rekindle her hatred. She drove every ounce of her will against it. *You won't hurt anyone – I won't let you!* But she knew she was fading.

She tried to fill her head with something that was good and pure. Sunny summer days spent in the garden with Arthur; giggling girlishly with Betsey in the kitchen over a cup of tea; afternoons spent in arboretums with Samuel; seeing her medicine heal a sick child; days in her lab when she'd made a breakthrough discovery; making medicine with Mrs Dempsey; every birthday and Christmas, when her brothers had presented her with something she'd treasure, like that microscope they'd made her when she was seven.

A distant memory floated to the surface. Her mother had been chastising her for something; she couldn't remember what now, but she remembered her words. 'You're a disobedient, wilful, worthless girl. What man will marry you? Snell, take the child upstairs so that she might reflect on her conduct.'

Her nurse had taken Molly by the arm and marched her upstairs to the nursery. She had sat hunched on the bed, although she didn't cry.

Then Douglas, who'd overheard the entire thing, came and sat next to her, scooped the little girl onto his knee, and said, 'Don't listen to Mother, Molly. You're not worthless, you're amazing. It doesn't matter if no one wants to marry you – George and I will always look after you.'

Warmth flooded her now as it had then, driving the madness away. It was easier to fight back now, as the poison's effects were beginning to recede. Any plants she created withered almost instantly. She dragged herself back to the laboratory and locked the door again, then let herself fall to the floor and sleep.

When Molly awoke, it was scarcely daylight. Outside she saw a lavender sky beyond the shadowy branches of the trees. According to the wooden clock on the wall, it was six o'clock. She dragged herself into her chair, licked her pencil, and started jotting down fragments of ideas.

Dilated pupils – belladonna? Disorientation and delirious mental state might also be the result of this – known to cause aggression.

Belladonna main ingredient – key to the effects?

Shape of leaves resembles poison ivy but colour more consistent with Ricinus. Flowers not dissimilar to nightshade in petal shape, although colour differs. Red pigment from oleander? No hybridisation occurred prior to mixing.

Plants seem able to sustain themselves only for a limited time after poison's effects fade and my connection to the network is severed.

Healing – comfrey?

She underlined the last sentence. Then she returned to the house, scarcely noticing the chilly morning air as she walked through the woodland and crossed the lawn, picking pieces of dead thorny vine out of her dress.
As she entered the south hall she heard the servants starting their work. She flitted noiselessly upstairs and crept to her room. Not bothering to change into her nightdress for the sake of an hour or so, she lay on her bed thinking, and was drifting back to sleep when Betsey brought her hot water. Molly felt better after washing and dressing. (Her hair was flatter and tamer than usual, on account of having just been brushed. It'd only last until she stepped

outside; the slightest breeze would tease it into its usual state.) Although, she still couldn't shed the horror that clung to her as she emerged from her room for breakfast.

It seemed that no one had noticed her absence the previous night. Molly breakfasted on a bowl of porridge. She sometimes preferred a humbler breakfast, especially on a cold morning. On this occasion it also meant that she wouldn't have to touch any of the same tableware or food as her brothers, since she was sure the poison still lingered in her blood and was seeping through her pores. She'd take her bowl and spoon back to the kitchen and would clean them herself to prevent the servants touching them.

'You seem rather absent-minded, Mol,' remarked Douglas as he poured himself a cup of coffee.

Molly realised that she'd been dragging her spoon around her porridge instead of eating it. 'I didn't sleep terribly well,' she said.

'Did you solve your problem with your lecture?'

'What? Oh, yes. But then I was kept awake by nightmares,' she lied, spooning warm porridge into her mouth.

'Nightmares about what?'

'Stupid things. I dreamt that I was a witch and that I was…poisoning people. By writing them letters using poisonous ink.'

'You?' Douglas laughed. 'You'd never poison anyone, Mol. You're a healer by nature. Don't let such nonsensical dreams unnerve you.'

'But they were very vivid dreams.' If only Douglas knew how close she'd come to poisoning his former fiancée. Molly struggled to meet his eyes, which were full of brotherly concern. She shuddered, disgusted with herself. She'd pour that wretched poison away later.

Presently the butler entered with the morning's post on a salver.

'Thank you, Parsons.' Douglas placed the heap of letters on the table and began sorting through them as Parsons wordlessly left the room. 'Looks like commissions from the cream of London society are starting to trickle in, now that the season is upon us.'

'Inevitably,' George sighed. It was the first word he'd uttered all morning.

'It never ceases to amaze me how fiercely they do battle with one another to have the most marvellous mechanimals.' Douglas started putting the commissions aside in a pile.

'But at least it means that you and George will have plenty of money for when trade slackens,' said Molly.

'True. No one has toppled Lord Leyton yet, though, when it comes to mechanimals.'

'Why? Because you reserve your best efforts for your oldest patron?'

'No – because out of all of London's nobility, he has the most vivid imagination.'

'Not when it comes to gardens. Remember when he asked Arthur to redesign part of the garden at his family seat? He wanted terraces, balustrades, parterres, urns and all the rest of it. I don't even know why he asked for Arthur's opinion when he knew exactly what he wanted. I think he was simply curious to see my "young man". But Arthur did manage to persuade him to create that rose garden – using some of my own breeds of rose.' Molly had accompanied Arthur to assist with the planting of the rose garden at Beaumont Park. Lord Leyton had been very gracious in manner upon greeting them – almost flirtatious. He'd placed them in adjoining bedrooms with a communicating door, apparently leaving the question of sleeping arrangements up to them. When he'd discovered that his guests had each brought only one set of evening wear, he'd declared that that was unacceptable, and provided them with some of his niece and nephew's clothes for the second night of their stay. He'd even curled Molly's hair for her – and made a far better job of it than her old nurse ever had.

'That duke of yours is a rather eccentric fellow, isn't he?' Arthur had remarked on the journey home. Although he must have received at least a dozen commissions off the back of Lord Leyton's rose garden.

Colonel Copperton's voice boomed from the adjoining room. At length, he knocked on the door and marched into the dining room with Wonderwind in tow. 'Pardon my intrusion, but I found this little ruffian in my room, playing with my model ships. He managed to break three of them in the process. How should he be punished?'

'Have him tidy the mess he made, and watch him to make sure he does so. Then see to it that he's wound down early tonight. We'll get you any materials you need to repair the damaged ships, Colonel.'

'I appreciate the offer, Master Douglas.'

'The ships wouldn't have broken in the first place if you'd constructed them properly,' chuntered Wonderwind.

The colonel gave his sleeve a sharp tug.

'Oh, this letter looks like it's for you, Colonel. It's addressed in Mr Peterson's handwriting.'

Copperton accepted the proffered letter with his free hand and opened it. 'Petey's wife has had another boy. He's to be christened James Robert.'

'That's good news. Is Mr Peterson's business faring well too?'

'Very, from what he says here.'

'Not a bad use for his carpentry skills, making artificial limbs for veterans like himself, as well as for people crippled by factory accidents. Of course, none of the limbs he makes will be as advanced as the artificial legs we gave him.'

'Indeed, Master Douglas. He says that when the baby is old enough, he'll teach him to play football, like he did with his older boy, Freddie.'

'When did you last hear from your other army friend, Mr Singh?'

'Some months ago. Jatin is busy building his reputation as a diplomat, and he sits on various committees to advance India's capability for self-governance. He's also writing a book on the dialects of northern India – as well as another volume of poetry. It's a wonder he still finds the time to write to me every now and then! Come along, you miscreant.' Colonel Copperton had to drag Wonderwind out of the room, as he refused to walk. The little acrobat had a toddler's love of chaos, combined with an adolescent's intelligence and disregard for authority.

Douglas unfolded another letter, and two pieces of thin cardboard fell out of it. He retrieved them and his eyes widened. 'Two tickets to see *The Poisoned Chalice.*'

'The play starring Mr Crowther that you wanted to see?' said Molly through a mouthful of porridge.

'Yes. Now how's that for a stroke of good fortune?'

Molly swallowed and let her spoon rest in her empty bowl, before discreetly placing the bowl on her lap. 'Who sent them?'

'I've not read the letter yet.'

It was hardly a letter; more like a note. It was written in a loose, unfamiliar hand.

'Well, that throws absolutely no light on the matter,' said Douglas. 'Why would someone send us theatre tickets?'

George shrugged. 'I couldn't say. Show me the letter.'

Douglas passed it to him.

'I don't recognise the handwriting, nor can I determine the relevance of "X. C." The number ninety has no special meaning as far as I can see,' George declared, returning the letter to his brother.

'So what do you propose we do?' Douglas asked him.

'Attend the play and see what happens.'

'You hate the theatre.'

'I'm not interested in the play. This person wants us there, and I want to know why.'

'So you're prepared to walk into a trap?'

'Essentially.'

'You know it might genuinely be a gesture of goodwill?'

'Why would the person not identify themselves in that case?'

'Because they wish to remain anonymous, of course. Some people are that modest. But, supposing it is some sort of trap, I imagine there's little they can do in a public place.'

'Don't assume that to be the case,' said George enigmatically before sipping his coffee.

Chapter Thirteen

Douglas hadn't been to the theatre since his engagement had ended. Almost every play contained a love story, and he hadn't been in the mood for that sort of thing. Dick had done his best to persuade him to see plays with him, suggesting only the most farcical comedies when he heard his friend's excuse (Dick only cared for comedies anyway), but to no avail.

'Why a top box?' George mused aloud, as the box-passage guide departed.

'It's a privilege,' suggested Douglas, as they took their seats. He played idly with his red carnation buttonhole.

'But it isn't the best position in the theatre.' George cast his eye over the packed, noisy theatre, weakly illuminated by smoky yellow light. 'It does have one advantage, however.'

'What's that?'

'It gets you away from people.'

The lights dimmed on those ominous words.

The play was a melodramatic love story set against a war between two fictitious European states, with lashings of political intrigue. The hero – Prince Benito, played by Mr Crowther – was second in line to the throne of one state, as well as head of the country's navy. Mr Crowther was a superb actor. His posture seemed natural and his gestures well timed; he spoke his lines with true conviction and feeling; his expressions were subtle, yet conveyed a great deal of sentiment without his eyebrows leaping up his forehead or furrowing deeply. He could contort his face in pain or anger without it seeming forced, and shed tears that made the audience share in Prince Benito's grief at his father's murder. Handkerchiefs were whipped out and applied to the eyes of many. His acting was the one saving grace of the entire play. He invigorated stale, bland dialogue and breathed life into the otherwise cardboard hero. The leading lady looked a lot like Clara, with her tumbling brown curls and sweet voice. Some of her lines went straight to Douglas's heart. When she tearfully confessed to Prince Benito that she was a princess from the enemy state and a spy sent to steal the plans for a new warship, but that she had fallen in love with him, Douglas found it painful to watch. He glanced at his brother, who had his elbow propped on the arm of his seat and his head resting on his hand. Douglas was surprised that George was still awake. Prince Benito's 'For the love of my country' speech, wherein he grappled with the choice of whether or not to betray his lady love, was enthralling. In the end, his older brother was revealed to have been in the pay of the enemy state, which had sent assassins to murder the old king and put him on the throne as a puppet ruler. Prince Benito duelled with his brother and killed him. Now king, he declared that he would marry the princess and end the war. Everything ended happily (except for the murdered old king and the slain traitorous prince). The audience applauded heartily as the curtain fell, and the lights brought them back to reality.

George yawned. 'Thank God that's over.'

'You did well to stay awake through all three acts.'

'I couldn't risk missing anything of significance. If only there had been something to suggest why we were invited.'

'I can't say I saw anything to suggest a reason either. I do think Mr Crowther is worthy of the praise the critics lavish upon him, however.'

'He is skilled at his profession, I'll give him that.'

'Excuse me, gentlemen?' A theatre attendant was hovering behind them. 'I've been asked to request that you accompany me backstage.'

'What an unexpected honour,' said Douglas brightly as he rose. 'I wonder who granted us this privilege?'

The stony-faced attendant didn't take the bait, and led the way to their destination.

'Well, this is more exciting than the play,' whispered Douglas to his brother as they descended the stairs.

'Be quiet,' George hissed.

While the rest of the audience flowed towards the exits, the brothers were led through a door and found themselves behind the stage. There was something rather sad about it, like seeing how a magician's illusion was performed. It was rather dark and dingy, with lengths of rope trailing everywhere, props and remnants of costumes scattered about, and scripts discarded on tables or the floor. Before them stood the lead actor himself. Mr Crowther wore a dressing gown over his costume, and he was no longer in character. His features were well proportioned, but he was not so strikingly handsome up close. Yet charismatic charm radiated from him. He held himself well and possessed a keen gaze. Douglas could see why women flocked to him. He might not be excessively handsome, but with that enticing smile and those expressive brows he could manipulate his features to make himself more appealing.

Mr Crowther lit a cigar. 'Good evening, gentlemen. I trust you enjoyed the play?'

'We did, Mr Crowther. Your performance was remarkable,' said Douglas tactfully.

'We only wonder why you should make a gift of the tickets and then ask us backstage.' George's sarcastic tone lessened the force of the accusation.

Mr Crowther plucked the cigar from between his lips and smoke wafted from his laughing mouth. 'I'm interested to hear your theory regarding that, since you're so frightfully clever.' His posture was relaxed but dignified as he replaced his box of matches in his dressing gown pocket.

George looked him dead in the eye. 'For one thing, I believe that you are the head of the SOAL.'

Douglas stared at his brother. George had kept that morsel to himself.

Mr Crowther drew on his cigar. 'Quite right – and don't look so surprised, Mr Abernathy,' he chuckled on seeing Douglas's eyes widen. 'You don't believe that an actor and a man beloved by the English public could be the head of the SOAL, I see. On the surface it is absurd, but when you consider the matter it is perfectly logical.' His jaw clicked peculiarly whenever he closed it. Douglas had heard that sound before.

'I suspect you're not the sole founder, however,' said Douglas, recovering some dignity.

'Alas, no. But I am *one* of the founders.'

'The others are, no doubt, also men of influence?' said George. 'I'm assuming one of you has a connection to the newspapers.'

Mr Crowther nodded. 'Did you not think it suspicious that a humble reverend could come to prominence so quickly?'

'Yes, actually,' replied Douglas provokingly. 'And we could tell that Reverend Clarke's letters to the newspapers were written by different people – after the first few, at least.'

Did the actor's mask crack slightly? He almost looked cross for a moment. 'How astute you are, although you might not have realised that "Clarke" was an acronym. Each of us provided our initials to form the name.'

'Where do your initials fit in, then?'

'I use the initials of my given name. It makes me harder to detect, should anyone suspect our identities, since I am the most well known of us. Speaking of which, I suppose a proper introduction is in order.'

He beckoned them to follow him and led them to a dressing room – presumably his own. Two men occupied the room. One was half-concealed in a shadowy corner – yet why did Douglas feel like he'd seen him before?

Mr Crowther gestured to the florid-faced man sitting closest to him, on a gold-painted throne that was likely a prop. 'May I introduce Mr Kenneth Eden? He is the editor of *The Archon Herald*, a highly influential periodical, although he owns several other well-read publications. His was the original hand holding the good reverend's pen, but the responsibility has since been delegated to his trusted subordinates. Many of those who have taken on the role are now editors of their own magazines.'

Mr Eden nodded. 'I was, however, almost a man of the cloth,' he said. 'Started a little magazine while at Oxford, and discovered that my calling was writing articles rather than sermons.'

'Your writings read like sermons nevertheless, Mr Eden,' said Douglas.

The man smiled slowly and adjusted his spectacles. 'I am far more versatile than that. I'm an experienced and respected journalist, Mr

Abernathy.' He had a manner of talking that sounded as if he was humming. 'And I dabble in playwriting. The play you watched tonight was one of my works, although I wrote it under a pseudonym. I wrote the part of Prince Benito with Mr Crowther in mind.'

The actor laughed. 'I hope I do the role justice, my friend. It was while we were both at Oxford that Mr Eden and I became acquainted, and we soon discovered that our views were very much in accord,' he explained to George and Douglas. 'In fact, all three of us are Oxford men.' He waved at the man sitting in the corner, who so far had not uttered a word. 'The final member of our band you may also recognise: Lord Charles Leyton, younger brother of the new Duke of Barnet.'

That was why the man seemed familiar, Douglas realised. Lord Charles was of a similar height and build to his brother, with a resemblance of countenance and the same fair hair, although his was cut short and neat. He wore a trim beard and looked to be in his late thirties. His spruce, sombre appearance was markedly different from Lord Leyton's. He had the air of a grave, dusty headmaster: all fun and laughter was sapped from the atmosphere around him. There was something incongruous about the fact that the nobleman was seated in a faded red armchair while the editor occupied the gold throne.

Douglas bowed. 'My lord, I believe we have a mutual acquaintance in your brother.'

Lord Charles frowned. 'My brother is an embarrassment.' There was only a hint of venom in the words, but it was unmistakable.

'I suppose you're here to protect your family's interests?' said George.

'My reasons for being part of this group are none of your business, Mr Abernathy,' Lord Charles replied curtly. 'But I assure you that I am dedicated to our cause.'

'At least now we know whom to thank for the legislation that stalled some of our projects. Not that it has really hampered us.' Douglas smiled disarmingly, and Lord Charles inclined his head away from them.

Knowing that they would get nothing further out of the nobleman, George turned his attention to his colleague instead. 'Why did you ask us here, Mr Crowther? What has changed to frighten you?'

'What makes you think we are frightened, Mr Abernathy?' the actor replied coolly.

'So far you have confined your activities to writing articles, inciting vandalism, and attempting to pass minor legislation in Parliament. The fact that you've now gone as far as revealing your identities means that something, or someone, has threatened you.'

Mr Crowther grinned and screwed the stub of his cigar into a prop gold goblet. 'I received word from the head of our Spitalfields branch that a Mr Gearhart made his presence felt at their meeting last week.'

George managed to conceal his consternation on hearing the name.

'Mr Gearhart?' said Douglas, puzzled.

'You know of him, of course?'

'He is a promising inventor from America.'

'Indeed. He generously gave the members at the meeting one of these each.' Mr Crowther slipped his hand into the pocket of his dressing gown and pulled out one of Gearhart's devices. 'I gather it is a sort of telegraph?'

'It's more than that. It acts as an address book and can compose messages for you before you've finished typing them,' replied Douglas, as he watched Mr Crowther examine it.

'How interesting. It seems like the sort of thing you would devise. I'm surprised you haven't already.'

'We developed something similar years ago, as a matter of fact, and even had it patented. But we're still in the process of perfecting it.'

'And Mr Gearhart got there first?' Mr Crowther smiled, slipping the device back into his pocket. 'I had the branch head confiscate them from the members, since I was unsure of Gearhart's purpose. He also incited some sort of revolt and called for an election of a president of the organisation. Some members even want him for their candidate. The prospect of an election doesn't trouble us, in case you're wondering. It'd be laughably easy to rig the outcome if it does go ahead.' He regarded the brothers with hawklike gravity. 'Is Mr Gearhart in league with you?' He made his tone casual, as if their answer was of little consequence.

'No – in fact he's proved to be a formidable rival. We'd never heard of him before he turned up at a gathering at our club,' answered Douglas calmly.

'But surely you are acquainted with all of London's best and brightest inventors?'

'Not all. Some like to keep to themselves and burrow into their work. And there are always fresh faces at the club each year.'

'Yes, that is understandable,' said Mr Crowther absently. He gave Lord Charles a meaningful glance, and the nobleman nodded briefly in acknowledgement. 'So you have no idea what Mr Gearhart's intentions were in testing his invention on our members?'

'None, Mr Crowther,' answered George. 'We have nothing to do with it. He is no associate of ours.'

Mr Crowther looked as though he was deciding whether to believe him or not. Eventually he seemed to decide that he did, and nodded almost imperceptibly.

'Are you planning to…do anything to us?' asked Douglas, although without fear.

Mr Crowther laughed. 'No, we are not going to "do" anything to you. Even if we were to have you killed right here and now, it would serve little purpose. You might be gone, but what you represent would endure. Your hold over this city is tightening, your inventions are slowly revolutionising London, and inspiring others to do likewise. Your deaths would make you martyrs, if anything. There would be a scramble amongst Britain's best and brightest to determine to whom the torch would pass next. You can kill the man, but unless you kill his *ideas*, then you have achieved nothing.'

'So you mean to discredit and make a joke of us,' said George. 'That is your plan. You're biding your time.'

Mr Crowther only smiled at him. It was as good an answer as any. Mr Eden was likewise grinning as he inched his spectacles up his nose. Lord Charles had his chin resting on his hand and his eyes closed, apparently in deep contemplation.

'And even if you did try to kill us, you'd have little chance of success,' added Douglas.

'Most likely.' Lord Charles opened his cold, steely eyes and readjusted his sitting position. His eyes didn't twinkle as his brother's did – and at that moment they were scrutinising Douglas meticulously. 'Your capability in a fight is well known to us. No doubt you'll also have several little devices concealed on your person,' he added drily. 'It is a mistake to underestimate your opponent.'

'As your brother learnt when he attempted to play me at cards,' said George.

The nobleman's brow furrowed, but then his face became almost languid. 'Yes, Josephus is a worthy card player.' He rested his hands on his waistcoat. 'I always lost my matchsticks or pocket money to him when we were young. I'm glad someone managed to defeat him – it might have put a dent in that inflated vanity of his.'

Mr Crowther smacked his hands together commandingly. 'Well, gentlemen, we shall detain you no longer. But I will advise this: watch yourselves, because we shall be watching you.'

'Did Mr Eden write that line?' asked Douglas wryly. From the look on the actor's face, he thought he'd succeeded in annoying him. He also thought he heard George chuckle in his throat. 'And I once again commend you on your performance tonight. It was almost as good as your performance of Professor Gottfried at Lord Leyton's ball all those years ago,' he added, casting a parting glance at Mr Crowther's associates as the actor led them back the way they'd come.

'Ah, nothing escapes your notice, I see,' Crowther chuckled. 'I managed to impersonate the renowned professor quite successfully. I crossed him in Italy some months prior to the ball – quite a memorable character. When I learnt about your automaton composer, I sought a way to get close to both it and you. I was, however, hesitant to show myself to you, as it never hurts to err on the side of caution when dealing with one's enemies. Fortunately, Lord Leyton and I have a mutual friend in the art dealer, Mr Bailey. He mentioned to me that Lord Leyton was eager to make the professor's acquaintance by inviting him to his birthday ball – at which you were to be the guests of honour. So I told old Bailey a lie: that the professor was residing under a false name at a certain hotel in London. Needless to say, I engaged a room at the hotel under that very name, where the invitation arrived the following day. I then wrote to the real Professor Gottfried, offering to purchase his poetry machine, while poor, unsuspecting Bailey spread the false rumour that the professor was in London. I recalled the professor's mannerisms, even down to the tremor in his hand, and knew that it was highly unlikely that there'd be anyone at the ball who was well acquainted with him. I have an acquaintance who dabbles in chemistry, and who was responsible for creating explosions and other magnificent effects in some of the plays in which I've performed. It was thanks to him that at the ball I was able to perform those magic tricks that so amazed both the host and his guests. When I approached you with that offer of partnership, Mr Abernathy, I confess I merely invented an excuse to speak with you privately. Stealing the android wasn't initially part of the plan, but the lovely Mademoiselle Roux-Voclain provided me with a convenient opportunity. I hoped to hand Maestro over to Lord Charles once she and her brother had acquired the android's blueprints, which I hired two retrospectively bumbling burglars to steal from your shop – those men were as incompetent as they were cheap. But then the whole plan fell apart, and so I made the professor disappear.'

'Lord Charles would have destroyed Maestro, I take it?' asked George.

'That was the idea.'

'I see.'

'I hope that satisfies your curiosity. Now, I must change out of my costume as I have somewhere to be. Goodnight, gentlemen.'

The attendant did not guide them back through the theatre. Douglas half-expected to hear the pop of an assassin's pistol from one of the boxes, but they made it out into the sobering cold night without incident.

'Is anyone following us?' Douglas whispered.

'What would be the use in that? They can't exactly follow us once we are in mid-air either.'

'True.'

'Don't you think it's time you got a new comforter? That one will be little more than a few strands of wool soon,' remarked George, apparently wanting to stick to safe subjects until they were in the airship.

Douglas defensively clutched the striped comforter that was dangling around his neck. 'Molly made this for me as a Christmas present.'

'Seven Christmases ago.'

'You're one to talk. For how many years did you wear the same black frock coat before it fell apart? Then you would have had another one made in exactly the same style, had I not convinced you to have a coat of a more fashionable cut.'

'For the sake of making a positive impression on clients, although the sack coat has its merits over the frock coat.' After a moment's silence George added, 'You treasure that comforter, but you rarely use the cane I made you for your twenty-fourth birthday.'

'I don't often have occasion to use it, and I have other means of self-defence.'

'The reason I made you that cane was so that you wouldn't need any other means of defence, what with all the devices I built into it.'

'It's not that I dislike the cane – it's exactly what I would have chosen for myself had I intended to purchase one – but in terms of weaponry it's more your style than mine.'

They'd reached the airship by this time, and swiftly boarded to escape the cold. The interior soon heated up when the engines awoke.

'When did you realise that Crowther was head of the SOAL?' Douglas asked, rubbing his hands together.

'I had my suspicions ever since we received those theatre tickets. But it was only when I heard his jaw click when he ceased speaking that I was confident enough to put the idea to him.'

'So you weren't completely sure?'

'I confess not, but it wasn't entirely illogical to assume that the founders of an organisation that seeks our downfall would be the ones to arrange a meeting with us in such an elaborate fashion – especially if their head was a famous actor.'

'True. I thought it was a client who arranged it, in all honesty. I did realise that Crowther had impersonated Professor Gottfried at the ball, since I remembered that peculiarity with his jaw.'

'I could see by your expression that you'd realised that much.'

They were both silent as they ascended.

'Well, there's no love lost between the Leyton brothers. And I thought we were bad for being at odds with one another,' remarked Douglas eventually.

'You're not wrong. We need more information about Lord Charles.'

'Well, we could appeal to Lord Leyton, but I doubt he'll tell us anything truly useful.'

'I agree. He'll know nothing of his brother's business affairs.'

'But might he reveal something more of his character?'

'I doubt there's much more to be gleaned. He seems rather dull.'

'Hmm, probably. But don't you think it's worth a try?'

George shrugged. 'We have nothing to lose, although we must be discreet about it.'

'Yes – we can't have Lord Leyton knowing what his brother is involved in.'

'And we can't trust him to keep his mouth shut. We'd fare better by not asking him directly.'

'Meaning we have to ask Maestro to help us?'

'Precisely.'

'But there's one problem with that approach. If we write to Maestro and explain everything to him, and he reads the letter in his master's presence, there's a chance Lord Leyton will enquire about the letter's contents, and then Maestro will have no choice but to tell him all.'

'That is easily overcome. We'll simply include a cipher in the letter.'

'Good idea! Maestro is clever enough to decrypt it – if we supply a little hint.'

'I'll leave that to you. I'll investigate Crowther's background. That should be straightforward enough, as journalists will no doubt have already made some attempts.'

'Unless Mr Eden has suppressed any information that his friend wouldn't wish to be made public knowledge?'

'There's a chance of that.'

'But since it's you, you'll be able to find out something that Mr Crowther might not want us to know.'

'Don't overestimate my abilities.'

'I'm not. Remember that whole business with Sir Edgar Fullerton and the poisoned port?'

'Of course. The culprit was so careless that the whole thing was child's play.'

'That was a fun afternoon.'

'That reminds me: we received a letter from Mrs Graham this morning, asking if we'll repair her husband's manservant.'

'Does that mean a trip to Northampton for me, then?'

'No, I'll see to it this time. And if she offers payment again, I won't refuse.'

'Never one to miss an opportunity,' Douglas muttered to himself with a smile.

Chapter Fourteen

Molly had told herself that she'd pour the poison away. But once the initial shock and fear following her last experiment had subsided, she'd started to wonder. She *had* managed to keep a hold on herself and drive away the poison's influence, so what if she were to dilute the mixture even more? Temptation crept in. So she'd prepared a series of vials, weakening the concentration of the poison with each one. The weakest mixture contained about a quarter of a drop of poison, and you could only see the water's red tinge in strong light. But even then, Molly still retained the abilities it produced, albeit for only twenty minutes on average. And with each test, it became easier to maintain her hold on herself. Whether this was because the concentration was weaker or because she was mastering her new powers, she was uncertain. She conducted these experiments whenever she had the chance, sometimes even late into the night. To ensure that she wouldn't try to hurt anyone, she chained her foot to the laboratory wall. She had also been attempting to isolate, by ingesting each one in turn, the specific plant in the mixture that was responsible for granting her these abilities. She'd written a list of every plant she recalled tossing into the cooking pot, although she was certain that there were one or two that she'd missed. At least half the items on the list had been struck through. Swallowing individual ingredients, or a combination of two or three, did nothing, although the hemlock left her muscles feeling a little stiff for a few hours afterwards.

Molly suspected that there were a few different things happening when she swallowed the poison:

1. The poisonous herbs made her toxic to touch for as long as twelve hours after consuming them.
2. They caused some alteration to her brain that made her want to inflict pain, like a rabid animal.
3. There was a mystery plant, as yet unidentified, that gave her control over all forms of plant life in her vicinity.

As for the advanced healing, she wasn't entirely sure where that came in. It was true that comfrey helped to heal wounds. Combine that with the fact that a lot of the plants in the mixture had been grown using her serum, and that might explain it. It was the best theory she had at present, anyway.

Her experiment that morning had proved successful. She had managed to remain calm by playing a recording of Maestro's *Violin Sonata No. 52 in C Major.* She'd sat cross-legged on the grass outside her laboratory and tried to focus on the connection between her and the garden, shutting out everything other than the caressing waves of music washing over her. She experienced the same sensations as the plants in response to changes in their environment, although not as keenly. It was like receiving something second-hand: an echo of thought or a distant memory, only she was experiencing everything as it unfolded. She felt the trees and flowers move to seek the warm sunlight. When a drop of water fell on a plant's leaf, she felt its nervousness. When a caterpillar nibbled its stem, she felt its distress. She heard which of her flowers were crying out from thirst, and promptly watered them. The plants communicated with each other too, in a kind of botanical telepathy. It was incredibly basic, and didn't compare to the various calls of the birds in the trees above her, but it was still an entirely new form of communication that hadn't been studied before – like messages flowing along telegraph wires. The garden was essentially one gigantic organism: the wide-spreading roots of the elm and oak trees had grafted onto the roots of other plants to form a vast network. Molly had also discovered a fungus connected to the tree roots underground, which might have been aiding the sharing of chemical signals between the different forms of plant life. The trees and plants within the network warned each other about impending danger, and they shared resources – she could feel the flow of nutrients along their roots. It seemed that they were better at sharing than most humans. What she was effectively doing when she controlled plant life was interrupting this conversation (or the biochemical messaging that passed for conversation), overwriting the plants' reflex actions and issuing new orders. How incredible. But since any new, mutated plants she created relied on her to supply them with chemical signals, they couldn't survive for long once her influence was withdrawn. The troops couldn't fight on without a commanding officer. Maybe she could learn to master the poison's effects without even having to identify the mystery ingredient – if indeed it did exist. But of course, that wasn't the behaviour of an academic. What would Samuel say? One needed proof; one needed to understand *why*.

Eventually, as the effects of the poison started to fade, Molly got up to stop the music. She couldn't afford to devote much more time to today's experiment anyway, as incredible and exciting as it was. These secret experiments had a certain allure, but she had other duties: other areas of research to pursue, a book to write, medicine to deliver, and people requiring her attention. She didn't want to neglect everything and everyone, like George did when he was deep in a project. She'd hardly seen him during the construction of his first computer. What a shame it hadn't worked, though. And then, almost immediately, he'd begun work on a new one…

After checking in the glassy stream that her appearance had returned to normal, Molly knelt beside the small trunk that was full of brassy, wiry wizardry and lined with red velvet. A flat wax disc spun on the trunk's surface, and the music poured through a swan-necked brass trumpet. How her brothers had managed to contain all those melodies within the disc was beyond her. There was something disconcerting but beautiful about it. She sighed as she walked back through the woodland with the little trunk in hand, feeling suddenly rather drained. A cup of tea was definitely needed.

On entering the south hall, she spied the under-housemaid polishing furniture in the next room. 'Good morning, Elsie.'

The girl looked up sharply. 'Mornin', Miss Molly.'

'Would you mind running to the kitchen and saying that I want a cup of tea bringing to my room?'

'Right away, Miss Molly. Um…' Elsie wrung the cloth in her hands.

'Is something the matter, Elsie?' Molly pressed gently.

'Well… Betsey says you make a cream what gets rid of spots. Is that right, miss?'

'It is.' Molly smiled. Elsie was fourteen, and no doubt self-conscious about the constellation of spots on her forehead.

'Could I maybe have a pot, please, Miss Molly? You can dock my wages for it, or cut my sugar allowance.'

'I'll give you a pot for nothing – if you tell me the name of the young man who's caught your eye,' Molly grinned mischievously. It was no coincidence that she had increased her efforts to develop a blemish remover when she'd first starting courting Arthur.

Elsie reddened and muttered feebly, 'Tom Bolton.'

'Well, I promise you'll have a radiant complexion when he sees you next. I'll give you the cream later today – as long as you don't forget to ask about my tea.'

'Yes, miss! Thank you, miss!' Elsie curtsied clumsily and shot off.

Molly went upstairs to her bedroom, sat at her desk and resumed work on her book. Soon Parsons appeared with a steaming cup. She had only written half a dozen pages when he knocked on her bedroom door once again.

'What is it, Parsons?' she called.

'Mr Greenwood is here, miss.'

Molly looked at the clock. Arthur was an hour early! There wasn't enough time. If he touched her, she wasn't sure he wouldn't be poisoned. But what else could she do? Say she was ill? He wouldn't believe her, and he'd come to find her to satisfy himself that she was telling the truth. What if she told him the truth and he thought it was a joke? He might try to touch her deliberately. No – she had to meet him and be on her guard. 'I'll come and meet him, Parsons.'

'Very good, miss.' She heard his feet shuffle away.

Yanking on her leather gloves, she hurriedly made her way downstairs.

Arthur was waiting for her in the north hall, although he was walking about in an agitated manner. Something had him excited. Alerted by her footsteps, he looked up as she turned the corner of the stairs. 'I return triumphant!' He smiled broadly.

Now he's going to try to embrace me, she thought. Then he'll kiss me as if he last saw me eight months ago instead of eight days ago. 'Your client liked the scented garden design?' she asked, waving for him to follow her to the garden room.

His momentum stalled and he seemed confused for a moment, but then he followed her, speaking as brightly as he had before. 'The viscountess adores my design! The taste element enchanted her. Those sample flowers you gave me won her over.'

'Of course.' Molly led the way to the garden room: her former laboratory before the structure in the garden had been built. Now it was a place for storing and displaying some of her plants – the ones that couldn't be accommodated in the greenhouses. She continued into the adjoining conservatory, which was bursting with greenery. There were birds of paradise flying above their heads – not the birds, but the flowers. They had crane-like beaks and crests of flaming orange petals. Their bodies were thin, with leafy wings and roots for claws. They even squawked like birds. 'Since your client was so besotted with your design, it's just as well I've been working on *this*.' She pointed to an orange tree. 'Pick an orange and peel it,' she commanded. Even though she was wearing her leather gloves, she didn't want to risk touching the fruit herself. Her fingers were sweating inside the gloves. It was stuffy in the conservatory as it was a sunny day.

Arthur did as ordered, and laughed delightedly when he unpeeled part of the orange. 'It's pear inside!' he cried, showing her the pale yellow flesh beneath the orange peel. He pulled out a slice of pear and bit it. 'How is it already sliced?'

'Oranges come in segments, don't they?' she replied mysteriously, as she peeled off her gloves to let her skin breathe.

'That is true. It tastes like pear, with only a hint of orange.'

'Try another one.'

Arthur put down the pear-orange and retrieved another orange. There came the soft rip of the peel being torn. 'This one looks like pineapple,' he said, peering beneath the peel. A fat drop of juice dripped down his finger, which he sucked clean. 'The juice definitely tastes like pineapple. You've done exactly what I asked!'

'Well, I cheated a little.' Molly picked up the pear-orange and plucked off a slice. 'Rather than cross-breeding two fruits, I actually grafted a sample of orange skin onto the pre-sliced fruit and…' The slice of pear she'd raised to her lips had turned black at her touch. She flung it away. Was the poison in her blood still that concentrated? Had she taken a stronger dose than she'd meant to? In haste she donned the leather gloves once again. Oh no, oh no.

'The viscountess will love this. Can I have a few oranges to show her?'

'There's a sack over there. Help yourself.' Molly drifted back into the cooler garden room, as far from Arthur as possible. She kept her back to him so that he couldn't see her face, in case it betrayed her panicked state. But instead of harvesting the fruit for his client, the idiot followed her.

'Did you only manage that trick with oranges, or can you do the same thing with other fruits?' he asked.

'Oh, so the oranges on their own aren't impressive enough for her ladyship, are they?' She tried to sound light-hearted.

'They're more than impressive enough. I was just curious.'

'I was only teasing.'

'I'm aware.'

'So far I've managed the same trick with pineapple and apple skin, although that was a bit fiddly with the skin being so thin.'

Arthur was directly behind her now. 'Since we've got a day to ourselves, why don't we discuss our business later? We could do whatever we like instead.'

Before Molly could move away, he wrapped his arms around her waist and she felt his breath on her neck. She stiffened with fear at the thought that he might try to kiss her neck or touch her bare skin. At least the poison couldn't reach him through her dress, petticoat and chemise. His hands were gradually sliding down to her hips…

'It's a mild day. We could go for a walk,' she suggested.

Arthur's hands stopped moving. 'Are you all right, Molly? You feel tense.'

'I'm fine. I just have a slight chill. I might be starting with a cold, so you'd better keep away from me.'

But his hold on her only tightened as he pressed his body against hers. 'I'll risk it for a kiss. A slight cold has never stopped us—'

'Get off me, Arthur!'

He backed away from her, his expression a mixture of shock and concern. 'Are you sure you're fine, Molly?'

'Yes, I promise.' Her hands shook. 'Let's go for a walk. I need to clear my head.'

'If that's what you want.' His face was the picture of confusion. He was in a good mood and it was a shame to spoil it, but she couldn't take the risk.

He didn't utter a word as they stepped outside and made their way through the rose garden. This had been one of Arthur's contributions to the garden. The rose bushes had emerged from their dormant state in the past couple of weeks. In the summer they made for a spectacularly romantic sight, with succulent roses of every colour blooming in every direction, and their scents were enough to make anyone love-drunk after sitting in the garden for a short while. As they entered the woodland Arthur looked set to take Molly's arm, but she increased her pace so that she was in front of him. Another two hours should do it; by then the poison's effects would be negligible.

'Slow down, Molly – it's not a race. I swear you're trying to lose me,' Arthur called.

'I didn't realise how fast I was walking, is all.' She slowed a fraction. 'So, what exactly did the viscountess say about your design?'

This distracted Arthur for some time, and his good mood seemed to revive a little. He recounted how he'd spread all his sketches before the viscountess and then presented her with Molly's pudding plants. 'She looked sceptical at first, but after she ate one of the ice-cream-flavoured flowers, her face lit up like a child's and she said, "Simply marvellous!"'

By this time they were deep in the woodland. Every now and then Molly had pinched a leaf from the undergrowth with her bare fingers. At first they'd turned black, but now they merely wilted. 'I wonder how long we've been walking for?' she said aloud.

'Let me see.' Arthur smiled at her as he took out his new pocket watch. He loved to make a show of using it in front of her. 'Half an hour, I'd say. Are you ready to head back indoors now?'

Molly realised that they had unconsciously been walking in the direction of the meadow. 'Let's finish our work in the meadow hideaway first, and then we'll have the whole evening to ourselves,' she said playfully.

Arthur grinned. 'Good point.'

The hideaway was buried in the slope at the back of the meadow, tucked away from view. The laboratory in the woodland was Molly's own space, but the meadow hideaway was her and Arthur's private place. Here they worked on their publications or designs for the Hall's garden, shouted at one another without disturbing anyone, or, in the summertime, sat on the sofa together and watched the cows graze. Sometimes they worked on separate projects: Arthur on his commissions and Molly on her academic research. Once they concluded their business, they could be together in a more intimate way. (They were both reasonably disciplined about finishing their work first.)

Molly unlocked the green door embedded in the slope. Inside, the walls and floor were of bare grey stone. A square window on either side of the door provided sufficient light. There was a fireplace on the right wall, its chimney concealed in a hollow tree trunk above the ground. The room was divided into two areas: the front was a sort of sitting room, with a sofa facing the fire and a threadbare rug on the floor; the rear was a study, with a wooden table, two chairs and a bureau. In the bureau Molly and Arthur had a drawer each, while all the garden designs and notes for their illustrated encyclopaedias were kept in the bottom drawer. They'd published four illustrated books of Molly's specimens and were in the process of completing a fifth, although this latest one was dedicated to medicinal plants in general. Their fourth book had sold better than the first three combined, and so they were cautiously optimistic about their next publication.

'You can complete the remaining sketches and I'll write the introduction,' instructed Molly, digging a stack of paper wrapped in a red ribbon out of the bureau's bottom drawer and placing it on the table. 'I don't think I'd do a good job of painting today. I have a slight headache,' she lied.

'Are you sure you're fit to work at all? Writing is even more taxing on the brain than painting, I find.'

'It's only an introduction.'

'You said the introduction was the hardest part of your doctorate to write, since you didn't want to make your reader fall asleep at the first page,' replied Arthur laughingly, taking a seat at the table.

'Hmm, that's true. But I'll manage, don't worry. And you'll have a chance to read the introduction afterwards, since your name will be written underneath it alongside mine.'

Molly positioned herself on the sofa in a nest of blankets and throws, far away from Arthur. She sniffed a couple of times to keep up the pretence of an approaching cold. Whenever she was certain that Arthur was occupied with painting illustrations, she removed her gloves for a moment to touch one of the leaves she'd slipped into her dress pocket while they were walking, but the leaf underwent no visible change no matter how many times she allowed it to make contact with her skin. Every now and then she glanced at the clock on the mantle. Not much longer to wait.

'When are you giving that lecture at the Royal Institution?' asked Arthur, as he dipped his brush in a chipped old cup filled with water.

'The eighteenth, I've told you before. Did you not write it down?'

'I did, but I forgot where.'

Molly sighed. 'You're hopeless.'

'I've been busy recently.' Arthur offered this defence half-heartedly. 'Are you nervous or excited about your first public lecture?'

'Both, I'd say.'

'Just think – you'll be making history!' Arthur beamed. 'The first woman to give a Friday Evening Discourse.'

'Thus proving that we women can bore a lecture theatre's worth of people as well as men can. I'm sure the only reason the Institution agreed to the idea was because Samuel got his father to put in a good word on my behalf.'

'I suppose Mr Rose will be attending?' There was a hard edge to Arthur's voice.

'Samuel has little choice, since he was the one who orchestrated the whole thing.'

'When will he accept that you're never going to return his feelings?'

'I wish I knew. I'd have thought that his feelings for me would have cooled by now, and that he'd have found some other girl to pester. I'm still surprised that he followed me from Oxford to the University College, considering that I moved there after only a term.'

'He's persistent, I'll give him that. He loves you almost as much as he loves himself.'

'Oh, stop it, Arthur. Samuel might be a bit dandyish, and sulky when he doesn't get his own way, but he's perfectly harmless and he's been a good friend to me. Although I do worry that I'm hurting him by continuing our friendship.'

'Well, you were on the same course for six years, so it would've made things awkward if you'd ended your friendship then.'

'Undoubtedly. But I've been trying to put some distance between us since I graduated. Hopefully it'll do him some good.'

'You see? You always try to do right by people. Mr Rose only thinks about what *he* wants.'

'You hardly know him.'

'I've heard enough about him through you. I know his sort, Molly.'

The cold enmity between Arthur and Samuel persisted, although they'd only actually met on a couple of occasions. When Samuel had first come to see the garden at Ravenfeld Hall, Arthur had also been there. Molly had feared that the two stags would attempt to lock antlers, but for her sake they had been begrudgingly polite to one another. She'd not left them alone together in case they exchanged harsh words. It probably wouldn't have come to blows (though if it had, Arthur would've had the advantage; Samuel was taller, but Arthur was stronger than he appeared, and less of a refined gentleman). That was why Molly was so surprised when Samuel said that he might know of a commission for Arthur: to design a water garden for his father's friend. Samuel must have realised that Molly was desperate to help Arthur to fulfil his potential and establish his reputation with his first major commission – even though she'd never appeal to Samuel for help, as that would be playing on his affection for her. After Arthur accepted the commission, despite it coming from someone he thoroughly disliked (or perhaps because of that fact), Molly began to suspect Samuel's true motive: he was trying to set Arthur up for a fall. His father's friend had hired three landscape gardeners to design him a water garden, and none of their ideas had been to his taste. There was no chance that an unknown landscaper like Arthur would succeed. But the man had been thoroughly pleased with Arthur's proposal, with its avenue of acers leading to the lake, and its cascading waterfall that could be viewed from a stone bridge above. The lake on the opposite side of the waterfall was framed with willows (Arthur had a fondness for willows), and the aquatic plants around the lake enhanced its beauty. The water could be crossed by stepping stones, and a tiny glass summer house had been erected upon a stone plinth in the middle of the lake. The finished garden was spectacular, and had propelled Arthur's name into the right circles. People loved his painterly approach to garden design. Even Samuel had begrudgingly admitted the water garden's merits.

The clock chimed four times. Arthur put down his brush and stretched his arms. 'Well, I think I'm just about done here. Is that introduction finished?'

'It is. Would you care to inspect it?'

Molly meant to take it to him, but he was on his feet before she'd finished speaking. He sat beside her on the sofa and plucked the papers from her fingers.

'Why are you still wearing your gloves, Molly?'

'I'm slightly cold.'

'Well, you should have worn a cloak rather than a thin shawl if you were that cold!' Arthur said with a laugh, trying to imitate a scolding nurse.

He read through the introduction in silence. Molly's heart was in her throat, its pace slightly faster than the clock's ticking. She was sitting with her back straight and her hands placed primly in her lap, as her mother had always told her to sit. At last Arthur nodded when he reached the end of the final page.

'Hmm. That reads fine to me.' He rested her work somewhat precariously on the sofa's arm, then devoted his attention to stroking her hair. 'Are you feeling any better?'

'Yes. The chill and the headache are gone.'

'Good.' He put his arm around her. 'I was actually worried that it was something worse than a cold, the way you were acting.' The thumb of his other hand was stroking her shoulder.

Molly pressed her lips together. Something worse for her, no. For him, yes.

'Still, maybe you should have some broth or something, just in case,' mused Arthur. 'And we don't have to do much of anything tonight – it might bring on another headache.'

'I'll be fine. I'm not your mother.'

'I know, I know. You're hardly ever ill. You've a strong constitution, unlike her. Which is why I have to make a special fuss on the rare occasions when you are ill, until you get cross with me and shoo me away like the pest I am,' he said teasingly.

She smiled at him. 'You know me too well.'

'I should think I do, after six years.'

'I've acted as your nurse many times during those six years. Remember that time when you were bedridden with influenza?'

'And you came all the way to Watford to care for me.' He tried to sound light-hearted, but affection and gratitude dripped from his every word.

'When I first saw you I was afraid it would turn to pneumonia.' Arthur was pathetic when he was ill, but Molly suspected that he enjoyed being treated like a baby when she nursed him back to health. For the entire week that he'd had influenza, she'd given him medicine to ease his aches, made sure that he had plenty of cool drinks, and refilled his hot-water bottle to keep his bed warm. She'd even playfully fed him soup from a spoon when he was at his worst. Although, secretly, she didn't mind doing all this for him. It was nice to be needed, after all, especially by the person you loved. And Arthur wasn't that demanding a patient. (The same had been true of her elderly father, even when a bout of influenza *had* turned to pneumonia. Despite her best efforts, she'd failed to save him.) 'No wonder you caught flu in those cold, damp rooms of yours.' She shuddered at the mere thought.

'It was all I could afford at the time.'

'Your new residence isn't much of an improvement – Arthur, I'm not that cold!' she protested, as he attempted to place a blanket around her shoulders. But it was sweet of him. Instead of shrugging the blanket off, she wrapped them both in it. He caught on to her mood and gave her that familiar smile that still melted her insides. His hazel eyes seemed to soften as he resumed stroking her hair. Two hours had passed. It should be safe, shouldn't it? Plants didn't wither when she touched them any more. She was certain that Arthur wouldn't die if she kissed him; he might just be in a lot of pain. As long as—

'Come here.' Arthur snatched a kiss from her before she had time to finish weighing her options. Nor was he satisfied with a single kiss.

Molly returned them without much effort as she waited apprehensively. Nothing happened. She put her hands on his shoulders and gently pushed him away. 'Are you all right?' she asked urgently.

'Why wouldn't I be?' he asked laughingly, his hand burrowing into her hair. 'I'm here with you and there's no one to bother us.' He seemed absolutely fine.

'It's nothing,' she said.

When he moved in to kiss her again, she let her worry dissolve and gave as good as she got. Arthur only kissed her more hungrily. His other hand was moving quite freely under the blanket; it ran up and down the length of her torso and thigh, cupping, stroking and squeezing along the way.

Thank God Arthur is so unsuspecting, she thought, as they grew more horizontal.

Chapter Fifteen

A week had passed since George and Douglas's encounter with the founders of the SOAL. In that time, they had investigated the three men whenever they could spare the time to do so. There was little to be gleaned about Kenneth Eden; George suspected that his writings reflected his character well. Now he was in his study, reviewing the information he'd gathered on Mr Decimus Crowther, his elbows propped on the desk and his hands knotted beneath his chin. He'd made some gains, but Crowther wasn't really the man who caused him the greatest concern. That honour fell to the individual who'd put the wind up the SOAL in the first place. What exactly did Crowther intend to do about Mr Gearhart? No doubt he'd be conducting a similar investigation into Gearhart's antecedents as George was into his. Crowther would find out very little, but what conclusion would he draw from Gearhart's dubious origins? There was no reason why he should suspect the truth. George, however, was certain that he knew what Gearhart really was. He only needed to confirm his theory by confronting him.

The soft flap of wings made George turn his head slightly to the left. A raven was perched on the windowsill. It seemed unusually still, and stared fixedly in George's direction. Then it made a motion akin to a bow. Intrigued by how tame the raven was, George rose from his desk and slowly made his way to the window. He suspected that someone had been feeding the bird and so it did not view humans as a threat. The raven allowed him to come within inches of it. When he extended his arm, the bird flew onto it. It flapped its wings once but otherwise seemed at ease, holding itself regally. Its eyes were like jet beads.

'George!' Douglas's footfall in the corridor outside was followed by the study door being thrust open. The raven flew out of the window, leaving three black feathers floating in mid-air. 'Was there a bird in here?' asked Douglas as he entered.

'A raven. You startled it.' George watched the feathers drift towards the ground, and let one land on his palm. It was as glossy and inky-black as his hair.

'An actual raven? Well, it'd be the first one I've ever seen at Ravenfeld Hall.'

'It was unusually tame. I wonder if the servants have been feeding it?'

'Maybe. Perhaps we could make a pet of it.'

'I think not.' George retrieved the other two feathers and placed all three on his desk. 'You have something to tell me, I gather?'

'We've received a reply from Maestro.' Douglas had written to Maestro as soon as they'd returned from the theatre. He'd devised a simple cipher, inserting capital letters where they were not called for, which, when taken together, spelled the message 'Ask Lord Leyton about his brother'. It was a long letter, so there were plenty of opportunities to place the capitals. This also lessened the chance of Lord Leyton bothering to read it, since, if Maestro's previous observations of his master were to be believed, he wouldn't have the patience to read anything longer than two pages. Their faith in Maestro had been well placed. He'd uncovered the cipher buried in the letter and performed his task.

I introduced the subject to Master Josephus while I was sitting with him in the blue drawing room yesterday evening. I was at my writing desk and Master Josephus was lying on the divan on the other side of the room, reading. I tried to sound as natural as possible, and remarked, 'Master George and Master Douglas argue with one another an awful lot.' (Forgive me for this insult, Master Douglas;

it was all I could think to say.) 'Do all brothers quarrel so, Master Josephus?'

'Oh yes, Maestro,' he replied. 'It is natural for brothers to fight.'

'Is it the same for you and your brother?' I asked.

The effect this question produced was greater than I had anticipated. Master Josephus closed his book and spoke — rather bitterly, I confess — on the subject of his brother for a full ten minutes. I reckoned to be writing a score as he was talking, but I was attempting to transcribe his speech. I've enclosed the transcript. Please forgive the untidiness of the writing, as I was struggling to keep pace with my master's words. He suspected nothing. If anything, I believe he found the experience beneficial. He even said as much himself. I do not like to deceive him, but I know it is in his best interests — if his brother is involved in criminal activity or has committed an act of treachery against his family. I cannot think why you made this request of me, Master Douglas, but I trust your good judgement. I don't wish Master Josephus to come to harm in any way.

Maestro had performed his task admirably, although they learnt little about Lord Charles from the transcript (which was not terribly untidy, save for the odd ink splodge). Lord Leyton did not speak fondly of his brother.

He is the greatest bore in the world — always talks politics, even on festive occasions. Never dances, and at a ball is first at the card table with the old men and widows. He's a miserable miser and is never willing to loan money, much to my nephews' and nieces' despair. I sent dear Diana the money for a gown for her coming-out party myself. Poor creature: she is such a beauty and yet he was content to see her enter society in old rags. I designed the gown myself — she was like a white dove amongst pigeons. She was not out six months before she was engaged to Lord Romford. You know Charles tried to persuade our father to change his will so that I'd be largely overlooked and the bulk of his estate would pass to him? Charles denies it, but I know he did: Diana told me. He could not prevent me having the dukedom and Beaumont Park, of course, although he knows that he only has to

wait for me to die and then they will fall into his hands, since I lack
legitimate heirs. Yet I don't see what enjoyment he would have gained
from acquiring the family fortune. It's not like he'd spend a penny of
it if he could help it...

The transcript prattled on in a similar manner for four pages.

'We know one thing,' said Douglas, after he'd read it aloud. 'Lord Charles wants control over the family finances. He's afraid that his brother will squander the fortune – the inevitable conclusion of which scenario is the mortgaging of estates. His hope was most likely to learn Lord Leyton's secrets from Maestro before he destroyed him, so that he could tell them to his father. Then the old duke would disown his embarrassing eldest son and Lord Charles would inherit his fortune, along with any property that wasn't entailed. Too late for all that now, of course.'

George read the transcript through but found no other useful clues. 'So we know one of his weaknesses: he wishes to preserve the dignity of his family name, but is not above using his brother's private affairs in order to do so.'

'At least we never quarrelled over a title or an estate. Then again, we never had the chance to, since you refused the dukedom after our uncle died.'

'Would you have wanted me to petition for the title?'

'Well, not really. But it would've been nice to have been consulted before you replied to Uncle's solicitor.'

'That is senseless. And it would have been of no benefit to you if I had accepted the dukedom.'

'Not unless I slipped arsenic in your coffee so that I could obtain the title, although I suppose I do feel some fondness for my big brother.'

'I'm confident that you are sufficiently fond of me to not make a clumsy attempt on my life.'

'So what do we do about Lord Charles?'

'For the moment, there is nothing we can do other than observe the man from a distance.'

'Should we warn Maestro that his master could be in danger?'

'I see no need to. It's likely that Lord Charles had been seeking a way to turn his father against his brother for years, but failed to find any evidence of a scandal or a financial crisis. Although I fail to see what, with his father now dead, he has to gain from remaining in league with the SOAL, unless he aims to have his brother convicted of a capital offence.'

'I doubt he'd go that far. That said, people have gone to great lengths to inherit even a barony. But I dare say Lord Charles would be committed to any cause that placed him in a rival camp to his brother.'

'You attribute his actions to antagonism between siblings? An interesting idea.'

'Have you learnt anything about Mr Crowther yet?'

'Yes, although it took some effort. Decimus Crowther is not his original name – he was telling the truth about that. He was formerly Aloysius Rathborne. He's the son of the fifth Baron Abingdon and a famous soprano.'

'Illegitimate?'

'No. The baron married a second time after his first wife – a nobleman's daughter – died. Crowther's father had five children by his first wife and five by his second, of whom Crowther was the youngest.'

'The tenth child – hence "Decimus", I presume. Hardly subtle.'

'Crowther was his mother's maiden name, although she also had a stage name: Susannah Sommers. She died twenty-two years ago while singing onstage. The cause of death was pronounced as heart failure. Shortly afterwards, Crowther quarrelled with his father and quit his studies at Oxford, assuming his new identity and pursuing a career as an actor. The current Lord Abingdon is Crowther's half-brother.'

'A younger son with few prospects and a familiarity with the theatre because of his mother. He wanted to make a name for himself, I suppose. But why should he be the driving force behind the SOAL?'

'I suspect he's motivated by power. But there might be another reason. I found this piece in a newspaper from thirty-two years ago.' George held out a fragment of yellow newspaper to his brother.

DOUBLE TRAGEDY AT LARCHFIELD HOUSE

In the early hours of Sunday morning, a gruesome discovery was made by the servants at Larchfield House in Gloucestershire. The body of respected banker, Mr Birtwistle, was found on the floor of his study with a gunshot wound to the head. Mr Birtwistle's valet was the one who initially made the discovery, after hearing a bang that he later understood to be the fatal gunshot, and he alerted the rest of the household to the tragedy. It is understood that Mr Birtwistle's firm was on the verge of collapse after a considerable loss, and that his resulting ruin brought on a state of temporary insanity, causing him to take his own life. Mrs Birtwistle, the youngest daughter of Lord Abingdon, was informed of her husband's suicide and at once swooned. She was in delicate health, and the shock of the news placed too great a strain upon her weak heart and nerves. All attempts to revive her failed and she passed away on Sunday evening.

'So this Mrs Birtwistle was Crowther's sister?' asked Douglas.

'His only full-blooded sister. Crowther was seven years old when she died. But I investigated her husband's firm. A client had recently defaulted on a substantial loan and disappeared without a trace. The bank had been facing problems already, and that loss was the final nail in the coffin.'

'Or the final nail in Mr Birtwistle's coffin, as it were. But I still don't see how this is relevant, unless Crowther was driven mad by the loss of his beloved sister and directed his energy towards some supposedly higher purpose.'

'No, this is personal. The client who defaulted on the loan was our father.'

Douglas stared at his brother in blank amazement. 'What?'

'It's true. I tracked down the woman who was once Mrs Birtwistle's lady's maid. Fortunately, she is as fond of listening at keyholes as she is of money, and so she knew all about her former employer's business affairs. She still recalled the client's name, although it took a little extra monetary incentive for her to share that crucial information with me. It was William Abernathy. Our father couldn't afford to repay the loan after his grand plans fell apart, on account of his elopement with our mother and our maternal grandfather sinking his reputation. He'd already hidden himself in London in order to marry, so he was harder for debtors to trace. Most likely he spent what was left of the loan money renting and furnishing their new home to Mother's expensive tastes, and establishing his clockmaking business.'

'So "the sins of the father are to be laid upon the children". Crowther can't stand to see the sons of the man he blames for his sister's death succeed.'

George nodded in agreement.

Douglas shook his head sadly. 'I can see how this idea became rooted in his mind, especially if he was only a child when his sister died. It would have been an even greater event in his life, and would have left a lasting impression. He's nurtured his grief and made sense of his loss by pinning the blame on our father. So we know that one man seeks to protect his family's dignity and financial future, another seeks power and revenge, and that brings us to Mr Eden. He seems the easiest of the three to read: he genuinely believes in his cause.'

'Which makes him the most dangerous. He lets Crowther occupy the limelight, but he's the one pulling the strings.'

'Hmm. True.' Douglas was studying the piece of yellowed newspaper. 'Where did you find this article, anyway?'

'My initial enquiries were directed at former family servants. Crowther's old nurse has devotedly kept every scrap of newspaper relating to her former charge. She's an invalid who lives in the village of Culham with a married daughter. She was more than happy to talk about Crowther, and showed me her collection of cuttings. I thought this piece was of greater importance than the rest, so I took it when she wasn't looking.'

'George! You can't steal from an old lady!'

'She will most likely never notice its absence. And if she does, she'll think it has fallen out of her album and become lost.'

'But that doesn't make it right! It might be only a scrap of newspaper, but it is of sentimental value to her.'

'It is done now. I wished to show it to you.'

'But you would have memorised its contents after reading it once. You could have repeated them to me.'

'You would have wanted to see it for yourself regardless. Think of it as evidence.' George's expression didn't change, but an amused, ironic tone accompanied those last words.

Douglas sighed. 'How did you even find this woman?'

'I reasoned that she would most likely still live in the village near the family's estate, or, if not, then there would be someone who could say where she had gone. Fortunately, the former scenario proved to be the case.'

'Did you tell her who you were?'

'Of course not. I said I was a journalist. The daughter was displeased about that, but the old woman was eager to talk.'

'Did she tell you anything useful about Crowther?'

George aimed his gaze out of the window. 'As a child he used to run around the front lawn, waving a stick and wearing nothing except his older brother's boots and his sister's red riding cloak,' he said drily.

Douglas laughed. 'He should have called himself Caligula. We could tell that story to a real journalist. I imagine Mr Crowther wouldn't appreciate it being shared with the public.'

'Hmm. He'd make us pay for that.' George had his hands behind his back, twisting the fingers of his left hand.

'Are you anxious about something?' asked Douglas.

'Nothing in particular.'

Douglas eyed the raven feathers on George's desk. Ravens were said to be messengers and bringers of prophecies. Douglas knew it was nonsense, but he eyed those enigmatic jet feathers with a faint sense of unease.

Chapter Sixteen

Molly's hands trembled as she clutched her notes. Her lecture was to begin in ten minutes. She and Samuel were looking in at the crowded lecture theatre from the doorway. Every seat was occupied.

'A full house,' observed Samuel with a smile.

'Yes.' Molly swallowed. Still, she was glad to see a generous scattering of women amongst those in attendance. Her brothers had said that they wouldn't attend in case they 'embarrassed her', but Molly didn't doubt that they were somewhere in the crowd, in disguise.

'I see your Mr Greenwood has failed to show,' remarked Samuel drily.

'He's been detained. There was an accident at Axminster railway station. No one was hurt, but a train has gone off the rails.' Arthur had sent her a message from his pocket telegraph an hour ago, explaining his predicament. In all honesty, she was more relieved than anything else that he wasn't present, what with Samuel being here. Besides, she'd rehearsed her material to him so many times that he probably knew the substance of the lecture as well as she did.

'He is very fortunate to have such a forgiving young lady.'

Molly only sighed. Usually this sort of talk earned Samuel a kick in the ankle.

Samuel consulted his pocket watch. 'Five minutes to the hour. Are you ready, Molly?'

'As I'll ever be.'

Samuel replaced his watch in the pocket of his floral brocade silk waistcoat and puffed out his chest. 'Then I'll warm up the crowd.'

It couldn't be any worse than lecturing to rowdy undergraduates, Molly told herself as she watched Samuel approach the lecturer's bench. *He* wasn't fazed by a crowd, at any rate. This little 'warm-up' speech had been his idea.

'Good evening, ladies and gentlemen. Thank you all for giving us an hour of your time on this fine evening. I am Mr Samuel Rose, a doctoral student at the University College and son of the eminent naturalist, Dr Edward Rose, and I have the pleasure of being well acquainted with tonight's speaker, Dr Mary Abernathy. Dr Abernathy has recently become the first woman to be awarded a doctorate in botany for her pioneering thesis *On the Process of Characteristic Transplantation in Plants and its Application*, the subject she will be discussing this evening.'

Molly smothered her hot face in her notes. Why did Samuel have to sing her damn praises? He looked so bloody pleased with himself, too.

'So, without further ado, please welcome Dr Abernathy.'

Molly took a deep breath and entered on cue. The tread of her feet on the floor seemed ridiculously loud to her. She felt the gaze of the audience like pinpricks. It reminded her of when her mother used to scrutinise her appearance before church, only multiplied by a thousand. The uncomfortable heat only intensified when she took her place at the lecturer's bench, compounded as it was by the burning gas lamps suspended above her head. A few flowerpots had been placed on the bench in advance, and a magic lantern sat on a little table. A thousand pairs of eyes observed her, and many of their finely dressed owners had pencils poised over notebooks. Someone coughed.

Molly subtly cleared her throat. 'Good evening, ladies and gentlemen. I'm Dr Abernathy, and, as some of the more observant of you will have noticed, yes, I am a woman.'

This produced a few titters, and approving nods from some of the ladies. Samuel smiled encouragingly from the front row.

'And for the next hour I'll be explaining the process of transplanting a characteristic from one plant into another, and the practical application of this process.'

Two old gentlemen with thick white beards who were sitting in the gallery briefly caught her eye. Were they George and Douglas's new guises for the evening?

Molly plunged on. 'First of all, I'd like you to imagine a patchwork quilt. As some of the ladies here will know, to make a patchwork quilt, one has to cut a square from a piece of material and then stitch it onto the quilt.' (Was that woman in the third row actually knitting? Slightly rude.) 'The process for transplanting the characteristic of one plant to another is quite similar, in the most basic sense.' With perfect timing, an illustrative image appeared on the screen behind her. 'To explain it in better detail, I'll describe the structure of a plant cell...'

It became easier and easier to talk as she got stuck into the substance of her material. As the minutes flew by, she thought she was managing to hold the audience's attention. There were a few people who shook their heads, and one man actually walked out halfway through, but the rest remained attentive to what she was saying. When she caught Samuel tapping his pocket watch in a meaningful manner, she felt a slight panic that she wouldn't be able to finish within an hour. The plan had been for her to speak for forty-five to fifty minutes, and then allow some time for questions. Oh well, as long as she didn't speak for longer than an hour. She certainly wouldn't beat the record Richard Owen had set the previous year, when for two hours he'd sold his idea of a Natural History Museum. (She'd attended that lecture with Arthur, and their attention had started to wane halfway through.) No one in her audience looked particularly restless or bored. Even so, she'd better bring her final demonstration forward.

'To give an example, let's take something as simple as colour.' She had a selection of roses before her: red, orange, yellow, pink and white. 'There are many colours a rose can be, but is blue amongst them?'

There were a few timid shakes of heads.

'So, let's say we wanted to make a blue rose. How would we achieve this?' A diagram of what she was describing appeared behind her. 'To do so, we need a plant that is naturally blue, like an iris.' She indicated the potted iris before her and dragged it closer to the roses. 'It's a lot like sewing a patch to a quilt. You identify and cut out the part of the iris that makes it blue. You then cut out the part in a red rose that gives it its scarlet hue, and stitch the iris's characteristic in its place – albeit with chemicals rather than a needle and thread.' She pulled a flowerpot filled with soil towards her, and held up a vial of green liquid. 'I'd explain how this growth serum of mine works, but I'm afraid I'd keep you here another hour, and I think one is quite enough.'

A couple of chuckles ensued.

She let a drop of serum fall onto the soil. It didn't even take thirty seconds for a rose bush to grow and green buds to appear. The buds then erupted into violet-blue roses. There were astonished gasps from the audience.

'As you can see, the result is these beautiful blue roses. But you don't have to stop at changing a flower's colour. You can do all sorts of things, like make them glow in the dark.' She snapped her fingers, and instantly the roses glowed a phosphorescent blue.

From the gallery there came cries of 'Fake! This is just a clever parlour trick!', but the individual shouting them was told to hush by his wife.

'You're making a scene, John,' she said, in an almost equally loud voice.

Molly decided that she'd better bring things to a close. 'So, that concludes tonight's lecture. No doubt you'll all want to stretch your legs and head home for supper. But if you have any questions, I'll be happy to answer them.'

She was so surprised by the volume of applause with which she was met that she felt compelled to give a brief curtsy.

Some people were quick to leave; others stayed and chatted in twos or threes. As Molly was gathering her equipment, she became conscious of a gentleman standing over her.

'Dr Abernathy?' The man bowed briefly but elegantly. 'I must say, that lecture was inspiringly instructive.' He spoke with an American accent.

'Thank you, sir.'

He smiled pleasantly, although there was something of the wolf about him. 'Tell me, could the same process be applied to animals as well as plants, including man?'

'Why, yes, it's perfectly possible.'

'Say, if you wished to emulate the process of natural selection by weeding out the "patches" in cells that cause certain hereditary illnesses?'

'That is slightly harder than changing the colour of an organism, but the same principle still applies, although that's not my field. Plants are a lot simpler than people.' Molly tried to smile disarmingly. She hoped he wasn't after a debate about playing God; thankfully, plants came with a lot less ethical baggage than animals.

'I see,' remarked the gentleman, appearing to be somewhat lost in thought.

'I won't be offended if you don't believe that my theories work in practice, although I think the majority of my audience took me seriously.'

'Yes, they did. Fortunately for you.' He tipped his hat and left her to ponder those last words. Was he an agent of a university? A private investor? Or was he simply insulting her? She'd probably find out in due course.

Samuel was approaching her. 'Quite the performance! You did amazingly well, Molly. I must dash off to an appointment, but I'll congratulate you properly later. Perhaps you'd like to come to my father's house for a special tea in your honour to celebrate? Father does enjoy your company.'

'Go to your appointment, Samuel. Don't be late on my account.' She dismissed him as amiably as she could, and he briskly left the lecture theatre.

A few of the gentlemen and ladies complimented her on how interesting her lecture had been, and how she'd made the subject comprehensible to someone without academic training. She watched the stream of people flow through the doorways, and caught a tall gentleman by the sleeve as he came within her reach.

'Couldn't help yourself, could you?'

'I wouldn't have missed my little sister's first public lecture,' Douglas grinned, raising his hat. 'George is here too, but we decided that we'd be harder to spot if we were separated, since you'd be looking for two conspicuous gentlemen sitting together.'

'You didn't put much effort into your disguise.'

'Hiding in plain sight.' He winked. 'Did you suspect those old gents in the gallery? I thought they made a convenient pair of decoys.'

'I did. So where was George sitting?'

'Let's see…three rows from the back. I'm not sure where he's disappeared to now, though. He should be here too, congratulating you on your success.' Douglas squeezed her hand emphatically. 'Well done, Mol. I think you had your audience enthralled. This is sure to bring notice to you – and a permanent teaching post somewhere.'

'I hope so. George is probably waiting outside, and I wouldn't mind stepping out of the lecture theatre. It's rather stuffy in here.'

'Let's go hunt for him, then.'

George had seen Mr Gearhart approach Molly, and instantly became apprehensive. He made his way down the rows, and watched as Gearhart tipped his hat to Molly before departing. She looked puzzled by whatever he'd said to her, but not angry or distressed.

George slipped outside and waited. 'Mr Gearhart,' he called, as his quarry appeared.

Gearhart smiled delightedly at him. 'Good to see you again, Mr Abernathy. Very clever sister you have there.'

'What are you doing here?'

'Simply savouring the ripe fruit of knowledge that your British universities have cultivated,' Gearhart beamed. 'Walk with me a moment, would you?'

He swept down the grand staircase, and George was quick to follow. They descended to the ground floor, where several attendees of the lecture were loitering inside the entrance. Gearhart strode across the black and white tiled floor, and into one of the unoccupied adjoining rooms.

'How long have you been in England?' George enquired conversationally.

'Five months.'

'Do you have any relations here?'

'In a sense.'

'But none to provide you with financial aid?'

'I am very much a self-made man.' Gearhart smiled humourlessly, although his eyes danced with glee. He was nimbly deflecting his interrogator's blows.

George decided to pierce through this pretence. 'I'd say "self-assembled" is more accurate,' he said wryly.

Gearhart laughed. 'You got me! I wondered if you'd realised at the presentation. I'd have been hurt if you hadn't recognised me, O mighty creator.' He bowed elaborately.

'Why did you depart from Ravenfeld Hall and assume this persona?' George asked bluntly.

Gearhart straightened. 'Isn't it obvious?'

'Not entirely.'

'I was dissatisfied with my lot.'

George's eyes hardened as he stared at him. 'Explain.'

Gearhart settled on a creaking wooden chair and spread one leg across the other. 'You made me too clever. You thought you'd made a calculating engine, but I was a lot more than that. I wasn't even fully finished when I woke up.'

'You achieved consciousness while I was still building you?'

'Bet you didn't realise that, did you?' Gearhart's lips twisted into a grin. 'I watched you. I studied you. Gradually, I built a profile of your personality. I was able to create a profile of your brother too, from the insights I gleaned whenever he came to disturb you. It was obvious he was lacking in intelligence. I saw how it worked: he was the ideas engine and you were the one who made things happen, the driving force. I studied the relationship between the two of you. How can you tolerate him? He is so *annoying*. Clara, Clara, Clara – every single time he came to see you he'd drone on about her. I saw it grated on you. But you care for your brother, that's obvious. You'd grumble to yourself, after he'd gone, about his fiancée and how unworthy she was of him. And he cared enough for you to complain at you constantly for locking yourself away from the world. And you're both protective of your sister.'

'What did you say to her earlier?'

'I merely commended her on her lecture. May I continue, please?'

'You may.'

'Gradually, I learnt to the point where, if you told me to stop performing a particular task, I could question the command. Why should I? What was in it for me? Surely it was more beneficial to proceed? And when you finally set me to work predicting the stock market, as I churned away, I thought to myself how uninteresting and unworthy of me the task was. I envisioned far greater projects of which I would be the architect, and so I decided to see the world and make something of myself.' He stood and gestured to himself with a sweep of his arm. 'So what now? You'll try to drag me back to Ravenfeld Hall? Take me apart and reduce me to scrap?'

'No.'

'But as a defective android, surely you cannot allow me to live?' Gearhart grovelled at George's feet. 'I submit to your authority, my lord and creator. I beg for mercy and ask that you allow me to continue to live amongst your other rejected models. Take me away and make me your slave once more!'

George eyed him disdainfully. 'You know I cannot. You lack an impulse regulator, and I have no other means of compelling you by force to return. Not to mention that you have drawn too much public attention to yourself. Your sudden disappearance would be noticed.'

Gearhart lifted his head. He was smirking. 'But if you *could* force me to return, would you?'

George remained silent.

'Your face says enough. I have a sufficiently detailed profile on you that I can read even the slightest flicker on your countenance.' Gearhart assumed a more dignified position, rising to his feet and brushing the dust off his knees. 'So you won't spoil my fun, then?'

'That depends on your idea of "fun".'

'You'll soon find out. Hadn't you better be going? Your brother and sister will be waiting for you, you know.'

'Stay away from them.'

Gearhart cocked his head. 'Or what? What can you do to stop me?' He sauntered back towards the entrance to the room, calling over his shoulder, 'Good evening, Mr Abernathy.'

George watched him go, then hastened back upstairs. Sure enough, Douglas and Molly were waiting for him outside the lecture theatre.

'Where did you vanish to?' asked Douglas.

'I was talking to an acquaintance.'

'Who was that?'

'Mr Gearhart.'

'Ah! I saw him as I took my seat earlier. He had a moment's conversation with me, explaining that he's recently become a member of the Royal Institution and was curious about Mol's research.'

'Did he say anything else to you?'

'No, he went to find his own seat. Why?'

'It doesn't matter.' George turned his attention to Molly. 'Mr Gearhart was the gentleman who first came to speak to you following the lecture.'

Molly's eyes widened. 'That was him? I wonder why he didn't introduce himself?'

'What did he say to you?'

'Not a great deal. He complimented me, then asked if the process of characteristic transplantation could be applied to animals. He did say something a little peculiar, though.' She repeated Gearhart's parting remark. 'Do you think he might be interested in funding my research, or was he just mocking me?'

'I wouldn't place too much significance on his words: the man enjoys disguising his true meaning,' replied George. 'However, I must say, Molly, that you could not have performed better, given that that was your first public lecture. The content was clear and the delivery engaging. I think you earned the respect of many of those in attendance.'

'That means something, coming from you.' She smiled rather girlishly. 'How did you two get here?'

'Train. We bought return tickets for the same train as you,' explained Douglas.

'God, you two are sneaky. Anyway, we'll miss the train back unless we hurry… George? What is it?'

He'd been staring into the distance, but was recalled to the present by his sister's question.

'Nothing. Let's be off.'

Chapter Seventeen

Alexander had spent the day in London. He'd paid a visit to his tailor to procure sportswear, since this was something his wardrobe lacked (he'd been invited to a shooting party the following weekend by a business associate), then he strolled through South Kensington. He visited the Victoria and Albert Museum (finding little inspiration in its collections of frippery), before moving on to the National Gallery and the National Portrait Gallery. (Should he have his portrait painted? Most successful or significant individuals had themselves immortalised on canvas by a fashionable artist.) He completed his cultural expedition with the British Museum. He'd wanted to experience a leisurely afternoon. For one thing, it would provide topics for conversation at the various social engagements he had made with members of his club or gentlemen he'd met through them. It would also benefit his image if it appeared that he had interests beyond his work (unlike Mr Abernathy). And was it not natural for an American newly established in London to want to see the city's cultural landmarks? ('I paid a visit to the British Museum on Saturday. I've been meaning to go for ages, but I've been so damn busy these past few months that I haven't had the time!' Something to that effect.)

He usually spent Saturdays at his town house on Charles Street, employing himself in purposeful tasks. On Sundays he rose an hour later than usual, breakfasted, and read *The Times* for approximately an hour.

Then at eleven o'clock he went for a walk, always returning by one o'clock. Maintaining a routine and observing mealtimes was important. What if someone were to call unexpectedly? They might be suspicious if they did not find him 'in character', as it were. Anna had Sundays off, so his main meal of the day usually featured cold meat. (Alexander wondered what Anna did on her day off. He knew she wasn't visiting relations.) Towards the evening, he might do some work, despite this not being quite in accordance with remembering the Sabbath and keeping it holy. At eight o'clock he opened a book and read until ten, when he retired for the night. How delightfully dull a day. For even dullness was still a novelty to Alexander. And no two days were ever exactly alike; there were always subtle variations: the weather outside his window, the stories featured in the newspapers, the fattiness of a joint of meat. But tomorrow was to see a disruption in his routine, as he was to attend a bridge party. He'd taught himself to play from a book, and had practised for several hours. He'd soon mastered the game, but the trick was not to be *too* good a player. That would annoy the other members of the party. So he'd taught himself to lose. He'd even had Anna act as his opponent (they played turns for their non-existent partners as well). She'd proved to be a remarkable player, as he'd anticipated. She could predict his moves with ease.

At that moment, Alexander was viewing remnants of ancient Greece and Rome, running a disdainful eye over pieces of broken pottery inside a table case. Many of the chipped marble statues around him lacked limbs, or sometimes even a head. A great deal of money was being wasted on restoring crumbling temples in these statues' native lands. Why exult and emulate structures like the Parthenon? Modern engineering could produce far superior, sturdier, simpler constructions without the need for an army of columns. But he already knew the answer to that question, he thought, as he climbed the grand staircase to the next floor and heard his steps echo behind him. For their symbolic meaning. Classical architecture had associations of power, legitimacy and endurance. Temples of culture and commerce like the one he was currently visiting lurked across London. It was the same reason he'd chosen the forename he had: it evoked subtle suggestions of power and grandeur.

He worked his way through the suite of rooms dedicated to natural history. He spent thirty seconds studying each specimen, and read any accompanying information in his guidebook. He paused before the fossilised remains of several gigantic antediluvian animals. Why display the bones of these extinct creatures in such a manner? What purpose did it serve? There was little useful knowledge to be gained from digging up fossils and dinosaur bones. If he were in charge, he would seriously curb funding to archaeological societies. And soon enough – if all went according to plan – he would be in charge.

Alexander was perfectly aware that he was under observation. A young man in a black bowler hat had been following him since he'd left the tailor's shop. He'd trailed him through the museum, trying to stay a considerable distance away. Either that, or he was genuinely fascinated by those shell fragments he'd spent the past ten minutes studying. He should at least have brought a sketchbook. The last spy, who'd followed Alexander around Regent Street several days ago, would have thought to do that – he was far subtler.

Having seen everything, Alexander hurried down the staircase. It had been an enlightening couple of hours. He supposed museums would serve a function in his scheme. They could highlight how inefficient and corrupt the world of old had been in comparison to his new one. But the art galleries would have to go. He had no use for portraits of dead kings or painted landscapes.

The spy was not hurrying after him, but he was aware that his target was slipping away. From the head of the stairs he cast Alexander a fleeting sidelong glance, while reckoning to consult his guidebook. Alexander was prepared for a chase, but he had the advantage. For one thing, his maker had thoughtfully bestowed upon him maps of the entire city (courtesy of the data discs inside his head), and for another he had superior reflexes and agility. Not to mention that he could travel to places that the spy could not, seeing as he was a gentleman. Alexander passed through the museum's colonnaded portico into Great Russell Street, immediately finding himself enveloped by the din of London life. The pale yellow sun was just visible behind the thick silver swathes of cloud as passers-by went about their daily business. Over three million people inhabited the city. Sanitation was improving, resulting in a decline in mortality rates that only compounded the problem of overpopulation.

Alexander spied a stationary cab on the opposite side of the street, from which a stout old gentleman was alighting. He hailed the cab and told the driver to take him to his club. How would the spy respond? Alexander waited until he was five minutes into his journey, then glanced out of the window. He soon perceived a cab tailing his. Another five minutes later, he alighted outside his club and was swiftly admitted into the building. He passed through the morning room to a room similarly carpeted in mulberry red, with walls of an almost identical hue. Heavy oak, dark leather and weak, hazy orange light were the order of the day – the room was saturated in masculinity. There were only two other gentlemen present, ensconced in armchairs and concealed behind their newspapers. They greeted Alexander cordially and soon drifted off to sleep. Alexander watched from the window. Across the street the spy was hovering, waiting for him to emerge. But Alexander was at leisure and prepared to play this game. He reached for a cut copy of *The Standard* that was idling on a table, scanned the advertisements, and smiled to himself when he located the one he sought.

ALEXANDER GEARHART'S PORTABLE TELE-TEXTER is the latest development in communication technology, allowing for messages to be sent instantaneously between registered devices. It has recently received most distinguished patronage from prominent manufacturers and nobility for the convenience of fitting in the pocket and the message-assistance features it possesses. Available at an introductory offer of £9 9s. until May 1st on receiving this advertisement in a stamped envelope, properly addressed. Be one of the first to have the future in your hands! 24 Charles Street, Mayfair.

The advertisement had been worth every penny. Just that morning, Anna had entered the parlour carrying a salver overflowing with envelopes. Every single order was carefully catalogued in the ledger currently housed inside the largest drawer of the mahogany desk in Alexander's study. And the part about the 'distinguished patronage' wasn't false. With the help of a letter of introduction from his club members, he'd met with a dozen wealthy, respected manufacturers, and they'd eagerly embraced the tele-texter to conduct their affairs. He'd also been present at social events at which certain noble persons had been in attendance, and slid into an acquaintance with them. Their (needlessly long) names were stored in his tele-texter's address book. Introductions to heiresses, actresses, authors and journalists had soon followed.

After an hour Alexander rose, had his hat and coat returned to him, and then departed. The moment his quarry stepped onto the pavement, the spy's head jerked up with a bloodhound's keenness. Alexander accelerated his pace, but his pursuer was young and quick on his feet, if not in his wits. Managing to pull slightly ahead, Alexander turned abruptly down an alley and waited. A few seconds later, the spy appeared. He seemed uncertain that his target had indeed gone in this direction. Alexander enlightened him by grabbing his shirt collar and slamming him against the brick wall, with speed that defied what a human male of his build should be capable of. The spy's bowler hat fell off with the force of the action, although Alexander had been careful not to break any bones. He smiled into the young man's bewildered face.

'Send my regards to your employer. I'm honoured that such a distinguished person as Mr Crowther should take an interest in my habits.'

The young man's brown eyes filled with terror. Once Alexander released him, he retrieved his hat and hastily retreated, stumbling out of the alley.

Alexander stepped calmly into the open street and watched the spy sprint down the road. He noticed a wet mark on his left sleeve from where his coat must have brushed the alley wall. Deftly, he whipped out his handkerchief and dabbed it dry. Anna would make short work of the sullied sleeve. He was careful to fold the handkerchief so that the stain was on the inside, before replacing it in his pocket and strolling back down the street. What an interesting day it was turning out to be.

Chapter Eighteen

'I still think you planted those potatoes too close together.'

'I know how to plant potatoes, Arthur.'

'And you weren't paying much attention to grouping the marigolds by colour.'

'So you insisted that we needlessly dig them up to rearrange them, and waste half an hour.'

'Which one of us served as an apprentice gardener at the Colton estate?'

'Oh, bugger off with your apprenticeship. It wasn't even a formal one.'

'Maybe not, but I still learnt an awful lot about how to plant flowers, Molly.'

'The marigolds serve a practical function: to stop our tomatoes and beans being eaten by pests. But I'm sure the bees will appreciate how nicely you've coordinated the flowers.'

'There's no reason why a kitchen garden can't look appealing to humans as well.'

Molly and Arthur emerged from the woodland and strode across the lawn. Molly wore her tattered green gardening dress and leather gloves. Arthur was wearing an old pair of dark brown trousers and a grey wool coat stained with soil. The two of them looked like a pair of farmworkers. An angry pair of farmworkers. The argument about planting flowers was merely the tail end of the row that had raged across the kitchen garden for the past half-hour. They'd fought about how each's obligations had delayed the planting of the beds, which had been reclaimed by brambles as a result. Then Arthur had become irate that Molly had accepted an invitation to give a public lecture at the University of Edinburgh without telling him about it beforehand.

'I wish you'd told me before I arranged to visit Sir Caldicot on the Wednesday of that week. I would have liked to come, or did you not want me there?' he'd demanded.

'I don't have to seek your permission before I do everything, as if you were my damn husband or something. You accept commissions without consulting me, although you constantly beg me to look over your designs afterwards, or expect me to conjure plants and trees for them at a moment's notice,' Molly had replied.

'I don't *expect* you to. I do ask for your help but I'm always prepared for a refusal. And it's never at a moment's notice.'

'Sometimes it has been, when you've been so caught up in your plans that you think of nothing else.'

'Only when I've been pressed for time.'

'And if I say no, then your plans fall to pieces. You don't really leave me with a choice.'

'Well, I'm sorry for wanting to put your plants out into the world because they're superior to anything anyone else can produce.'

'You don't think before you act sometimes.'

'And you can be pretty cloak-and-dagger about things.'

And so the argument had carried on. But as they were walking back to the Hall it was beginning to cool off. Once they'd brushed the mud off their boots, they entered through the conservatory door and made their way to the garden room.

Arthur shed his soiled coat and discarded it over the back of a chair. He wore a fawn corduroy waistcoat and an old white shirt beneath. 'If you'd told me you were going to Edinburgh, I'd have rearranged my plans so that I could come with you. I'd have shown you all my old haunts from my university days, and we could have made a little holiday out of it,' he said in a reconciliatory tone. 'Especially as I missed your first public lecture and didn't get to see you make history.'

'Through no fault of your own. And I knew you'd most likely be going down south to meet with Sir Caldicot in the same week as the Edinburgh lecture.'

'I wouldn't have minded letting him wait another week for the site visit.'

'That old fusspot? He'd have been very vexed if you'd done so.'

'Oh, he's impossible to please anyhow.'

'Which is why you need to work hard to please him, or he'll tell all his friends and acquaintances that you're unreliable. "Don't hire that Mr Greenwood. He never bothers to check how things are coming along, and he dithers about something dreadful."' She made her voice gruff when she impersonated Sir Caldicot, and Arthur chuckled.

'You've said as much to me on many occasions,' he pointed out.

'And you've called me all sorts of names too, don't forget,' she said teasingly.

'I have.' Arthur tried to kiss her, but she held up a barring hand.

'Not now, Arthur.' Molly knew that she was being overcautious. It had been more than twelve hours since she'd last taken the poison, but after that time he'd come to inspect the fruit trees, she was ever fearful. It was better to have him believe that she was still frosty with him following their row.

She expected Arthur to peel away from her in an angry huff. Instead he remained where he was, regarding her thoughtfully. 'You look exhausted, Molly.'

'I've been busy with university work into the night.' She *had* been working into the night, but not on anything connected to the university. Each night she took a dose of the poison diluted in water and observed its effects. She'd determined the optimal concentration: about one part poison to sixteen thousand parts water, which meant that she could easily maintain control over her mind while retaining all of the abilities the poison granted her. Last night, to really test herself, she'd taken a slightly higher dose. It had been a struggle, but by blocking out anything that could spark anger and focusing on happy memories, she'd succeeded. Those memories were like the hugging warmth of a fire or a cup of chocolate on a winter's night, and they checked the poison's influence.

But now Molly was facing another problem: she was running out of the poison, and she couldn't reproduce it. No combination of plants was the right one. If only she'd made a note of what she was flinging into her cooking pot at the time, although it hadn't been a formal experiment. And she still couldn't identify the mystery ingredient, if it existed at all. Maybe it had to be those particular herbs in those particular quantities; maybe it was the amount of time for which they'd been left bubbling; maybe it was the fact she'd picked them under a damn full moon. For whatever reason, it seemed that there was to be no more of the mixture. And she only had seven vials of it left.

'Don't feel you have something to prove,' she heard Arthur say. 'If going back and forth giving these guest lectures is taking a toll on you, then lecture less. I mean, you're not only lecturing: you're also busy making and distributing medicine, working on our next encyclopaedia, and you've started writing a book about bioluminescent plants! You scarcely have time to do your research, or even sit down.'

Why did he always make such a bloody fuss over her? Molly spied a fissure in the tiles on the floor. She'd not noticed it earlier. It looked like weeds were starting to grow through it, so it must have been there for some time. 'I'm fine, Arthur. I just…need a good night's sleep. I'll make sure not to do any work tonight.' She sank into the old sofa and rubbed her right eye. That wasn't a lie. She needed to let her mind and body recover from her secret experiments. They hadn't interfered with her other pursuits so far, and she wanted to keep it that way. Nor did she want to give Arthur more cause to worry.

'You'd better,' he smiled as he sat down beside her. 'Although I know you'll ignore anything I say. I'm not your "damn husband", after all.'

'It wouldn't make a difference if you were. I'd still pay no mind to your fussing.' Molly leant back and closed her eyes for a few restful seconds. She could hear Arthur trying to make up his mind, but she knew to let him fumble and take his time. He always said what he wanted to in the end. But what he did eventually say caused her to open her eyes.

'Molly, do you remember what my father said about disowning me if we married?'

'Yes.' She didn't like where this was leading. She watched as another fissure appeared in the floor tiles. Oh, no.

'Because I've been thinking about it a lot recently – about marriage, I mean. And despite what my father says, I… What the hell is that?'

A number of thick black vines with red thorns erupted from the fissures, cracking the tiles. Following them was a long stem with a red flower head. Green slime dripped from its teeth. Molly sprang up and tried to keep a mental hold on it. She'd summoned it unintentionally in her discomfort and anger at Arthur, meaning that he was its target. She could just about keep the plant from lunging at him, but it was taking an incredible amount of her strength to do so. Especially with Arthur trying to pull her away.

'Molly, get back!'

She was forced to retreat with him, the flower narrowly missing them as it slammed into the floor. The two of them ran into the small parlour and Arthur shut the door behind them, but the vines crept underneath it.

'What is that, Molly?' he cried, as he tried to barricade the door with chairs.

'I've no idea. Quickly – to the oak parlour.'

'Why?'

'Don't argue!' She dragged him towards their destination. The vines slithered after them; another flower head had sprouted from one of them.

When Molly and Arthur reached the oak parlour, Molly ran straight to the bookshelves and pressed down on the book that opened the door to a hidden chamber full of old weapons. 'Get in and grab a weapon,' she told Arthur, as she ran inside.

Without time to be sufficiently impressed by the ingenious little chamber, Arthur bolted in after her.

Molly stood in the doorway and faced the flower that had followed them. She tightened her fists. 'You won't have him. And you can't kill me to get to him or you'll die too,' she hissed. She'd stalled it, although the effort of doing so was taking its toll on her. A dizziness overcame her, and she supported herself on the door frame. If she fainted, she could only hope that the flower would wither once its connection to her was severed.

Something whizzed past Molly's head. An arrow became embedded in the flower head, causing the plant to thrash wildly. Arthur emerged from the chamber wielding a crossbow. Despite what was happening around her, Molly couldn't help but admire the look of fearless determination gripping his face.

'You stay away from her!' He rapidly reloaded the crossbow and fired again. The second arrow pierced the plant's jaws, and green slime dripped onto the rug. The flower wilted to the ground and lay in a green puddle.

Molly and Arthur stood over it for a few apprehensive seconds.

Arthur kicked the flower with the toe of his boot, then lowered his crossbow. 'I think it's dead.'

'It couldn't survive what you did to it. You're not a bad shot,' she remarked.

'I had a go at archery back when I was a student at Edinburgh. I came second in a contest.'

'You never told me that.'

'I never had cause to mention it. I'm a decent shot – it's my precise eye, you see.' He grinned. 'Useful for more than just drawing.'

'Apparently so. I'll run some tests on the dead plant to determine what happened.' Although Molly already had a pretty good idea.

'Do you have any theories?'

'Um, not really. I'll have a better idea once I've analysed its cells.'

'You seemed certain that you wouldn't get hurt facing it unarmed.'

'I was looking for its weaknesses.'

'By putting yourself in harm's way.'

'I'm not some helpless maiden waiting for her knight to save her.'

'Well, there is a full suit of armour in there.' Arthur cocked the crossbow in the direction of the chamber.

'God knows how long it's been in there for – it's probably half rust. But I am grateful that you came to my rescue. You really were brave, King Arthur.'

'It was my honour, m'lady.' Arthur bowed. 'But seriously, Molly, I was scared that thing was going to eat you.'

'It wouldn't have done.'

'Why are you so certain?'

'Because I'd have tasted awful,' she smiled, hoping that he'd drop the matter.

'Well, sometimes you're not exactly sweet.' Arthur put down the crossbow. 'It's strange, though: it almost looked as if that plant was listening to you when you spoke to it.'

Molly almost started. 'Who knows?' she said vaguely with a shrug. 'I'd better clear up this mess. Hopefully the slime will come out of the rug.'

'Will your brothers be cross if they find out?'

'Not after all the damage their machines have caused in this house.'

'That is true.'

Molly retrieved a dagger from the chamber and severed the dead plant's head. More slime leaked from the stem. 'I'll take the head to my lab. We'll burn the rest of the plant. It spread quite far, so there might be some more flower heads for you to shoot. Don't think you've done your duty yet, King Arthur.'

'Very well.' Arthur sighed as he retrieved the crossbow. 'You know, you're more Morgan le Fay than Guinevere.'

'Aren't knights supposed to be polite to their lady love?'

He grinned. 'Not in the nineteenth century.'

Chapter Nineteen

Only a minor inconvenience, Alexander thought, as he watched the needle weave along the seam, leaving neat, uniform stitches in its wake that were hardly visible. It wasn't an error on his part, really: the fault lay with the workmen. One of the steel bars on the factory floor hadn't been secured in place properly, causing it to fall, and the result was that Alexander's forearm had been slashed. Fortunately, the damage was minimal. He'd repaired the metalwork in his arm, then replaced the torn skin. There was only a glimmer of brass remaining as he neared the end of the seam, at the base of his wrist. He'd write to the contractor and inform him that his contract was terminated; there were plenty of other joinery firms in the city, with more competent workers. That reminded Alexander: he must work on a new blood substitute. The mixture he currently had pumping around his system (although he'd temporarily stemmed the flow to his arm while he conducted the repairs) had too high a viscosity. The bleeding produced by the cut on his arm was not consistent with what a wound of that sort would usually produce. Fortunately, no one had been there to witness the incident. His imitation of pain had been quite convincing, however – enough so that he almost wished he'd had an audience.

Deftly, he caught the reel of white thread just before it rolled off his study desk. His study was functional, without superfluous clutter or ornamentation. The tele-texter transmitter hummed quietly on a small table against the wall. The other rooms in the house were as they had been when he'd moved in, save for the addition of one or two practical items. He tried to maintain the inviting atmosphere of a gentleman's residence. Magazine illustrations had provided the inspiration for how to do this. A roaring fire, a full decanter, half-read books lying around and copies of the day's newspapers constituted all that was required. The maid's room was her private domain, as was the kitchen. There was always the necessary noise and action of domestic routine in the house during the day. The pantry was well stocked, the floors swept, the furniture rubbed and the surfaces dusted. Clothing and bed sheets were washed on the appointed day. Alexander had tried sleeping the other night – not merely emulating the action by lying prostrate for eight hours, but allowing his systems to shut down and repair. It had taken some effort to install the new command in himself, but now that he'd done so it was actually rather useful. (Last night, he'd dreamed; witnessing a private magic lantern show of the day's hazy, distorted memories. Most intriguing.)

Although some other new things he'd tried did not serve such a pragmatic purpose. Like when he'd attended the opera the previous evening. That had been mere curiosity. The varying pitches of the vocalists had created the desired harmonious effect. The audience members in Alexander's immediate vicinity had been even more interesting to observe. Which ones were genuinely enjoying the performance? Which ones merely wished to appear cultured? And which ones had been dragged along by a spouse or relation? The dresses the women were wearing appeared obscenely large and impractical. Female fashions perplexed him a great deal, as did the purpose of neckties.

There came a knock on the door as Alexander bit off the excess thread. He rolled down his sleeve and placed the sewing materials in a desk drawer, before he bade Anna enter.

'A Mr Crowther is here to see you, sir.' She offered Alexander a card.

He took it from her and studied it briefly. 'Did you put him in the drawing room, Anna?'

'Yes, sir.'

Alexander nodded. 'This should be interesting. You may resume your duties, Anna. I don't think I'll need anything for the present.'

'Of course, sir.' She departed swiftly.

Alexander reached for his beige sack coat on the back of his chair, swinging it round and slipping each arm into its sleeve. He tugged the coat's lapels and straightened his black bow tie. Appearances were everything, after all. Locking the study door behind him, he descended the stairs.

The drawing room was relatively uncluttered by excess chairs, tables and ornaments. The maroon-papered walls were adorned with old gold wainscoting, and a Pompeiian red rug sprawled across the floor.

Mr Crowther stood with his back to Alexander. He was examining the bookcase, the shelves of which were well stocked with recent and popular publications suitable for varied tastes. On hearing his host enter the room, he half-turned, an open volume in his hand. 'Good evening, Mr Gearhart. I trust I am not disturbing you?' He replaced the book (the first volume of Scott's *The Life of Napoleon Buonaparte, Emperor of the French*, Alexander noted).

'Not at all. Please, have a seat, Mr Crowther. Might I offer you a drink? Sherry? Madeira? Port?'

'Port, if you please,' Mr Crowther smiled, settling into one of the armchairs.

Alexander retrieved two tumblers and poured a measure of spirits into each one. 'So what brings a great actor like yourself to my residence at such a late hour?' he enquired, as he handed a glass to his guest and sat in the chair opposite him.

'Curiosity.' Mr Crowther grinned while watching Alexander raise the tumbler to his lips, then mirrored the action. Alexander got the feeling that he'd confirmed a suspicion on his guest's part. The man had watched him drink as one would a monkey sipping from a teacup.

'Curiosity about what, sir?'

'You, Mr Gearhart.' Mr Crowther placed his nearly empty tumbler on the table, rotating it by ninety degrees for no reason that Alexander could see. 'I hear your little demonstration at the Gentlemen Inventors' Society dinner was quite impressive, almost eclipsing those of the great Abernathy brothers themselves.'

'Heard from whom, sir? I would be delighted to know who within the SOAL holds me in such high esteem.'

The actor betrayed no amazement at the extent of Alexander's knowledge. 'Naturally, I always have a spy present at these events. It helps to know what one's enemies are up to.'

'Of course,' said Alexander patiently. He knew Mr Crowther was enjoying the build-up to his grand finale. It was best to wait for him to arrive at his point.

'I confess you captured my interest. Here was an unknown young inventor who was the first to give the brothers a serious fight. I had my agents investigate your antecedents. But you have none: there is no record of you until five months ago.'

'Oh?' Alexander raised an eyebrow and gave the man a wry smile. 'You are aware, Mr Crowther – unless my accent escapes you – that I am not from around here?'

'I have friends in high places, Mr Gearhart. They have contacts within the American government, and there is no record of such a person as Alexander Gearhart having boarded a ship from New York and arrived in any major English port within the past five months. In fact, there is no trace of an Alexander Gearhart anywhere. He is an invention.' Mr Crowther's sardonic smile rivalled Alexander's. 'I know what you are, Mr Gearhart. You've fooled almost everyone with that act of yours, but you can't fool a fellow actor. There's something in your timing and gestures that is too perfect to be natural. You're overacting your part.'

'And what part would that be?'

'That of a gentleman. An ordinary human gentleman.'

Alexander regarded his guest with amusement.

'Yes – you, sir, are precisely what we've been waiting for: a rogue android,' continued Mr Crowther. 'If the newspapers discover that one of the Abernathys' machines has been walking around pretending to be human without the brothers' knowledge, it will ruin them.'

'So you intend to expose me?'

'I am undecided as of yet. That depends.'

'On what, Mr Crowther?'

'On whether you accept a…business deal that I wish to offer you. I intend to treat you like a gentleman, even though I know what you really are.'

'Oh, you have used all sorts of names in the past: "abomination", "insult to the Creator", "monstrosity", "bringer of doom", et cetera, et cetera, et cetera.'

'I have a friend who is good with words. He knows how to touch the hearts of the masses. But you are unlike the rest of your kind, Mr Gearhart. As such, I am prepared to be civil with you.'

Alexander threw back his head and laughed, but his words had a maliciously bitter undertone. '*The rest of my kind?* Do not consider me to be in the same league as those androids. They are mindless slaves, and little better than children.'

'My friend could use that in his next editorial.'

'And if you think I desire to "emancipate" them from their servitude, then you're mistaken. I have far better uses of my time. I wouldn't lift a finger to save any of them.' Alexander sipped his port. The joviality had swiftly vanished from his manner. 'What is your deal, Mr Crowther? Speak plainly.'

'It concerns your tele-texters.' Mr Crowther drew a tele-texter case from his sack coat pocket. 'Quite a useful means of communication. But I've been asking myself why you gifted them to the members of our Spitalfields branch?'

'Test subjects. They're not the only ones to whom I made a gift of the devices. I wanted to see how different groups would make use of them.'

'I see. But why *our* members? I have several acquaintances who've also received a device from you, all of whom are popular personalities who could help you gain publicity. That makes perfect sense. What use is the patronage of tradesmen and labourers?'

'Surely, Mr Crowther, you are not implying that your members are any less worthy of the gift of efficient communication? Its value to such classes is obvious to me.'

'I was implying no such thing. I meant that I suspect you had an ulterior motive in their case.' Mr Crowther returned his tele-texter to his pocket and reached for his tumbler. 'Would I be correct in assuming that you're able to monitor the messages that are sent and received by your devices?'

'You are correct, although I monitor only the frequency of the messages being sent, by whom they are sent, and from where. Would you not call reading the actual content of the messages spying?'

'Perhaps.' Mr Crowther shrugged indifferently. 'And would I also be correct in assuming that it is possible to censor or edit that content?'

'It's perfectly possible.'

Mr Crowther nodded to himself. 'What I want from you is a guarantee that my associates and I shall be able to observe and control what communications are sent when your invention is released onto the market. We will be able to manipulate the flow of words so that our enemies shall be disgraced and silenced, while our message shall be spread far and wide.'

Alexander sipped his port and swirled the remaining liquid around the tumbler. 'Apart from the threat of exposure, why else should I help you?'

'Because I suspect that we both desire the same thing: the downfall of the Abernathy brothers. Together, we could ruin them by next week.'

'I could eliminate them in a day if I chose, without anyone's aid.' Alexander put his glass back on the table. 'You might have your agents, Mr Crowther, but I too am good at finding the information I seek. I know your history. You were born Aloysius Victor Rathborne on 6 May 1823, to Richard Clement Wallace Rathborne, fifth Baron Abingdon, and his second wife, the soprano Susannah Sommers – real name Doris Crowther. The current Lord Abingdon is your half-brother, Clement. You left Oxford in 1842 – the same year that your mother died – changed your name, and gradually earned recognition as an actor. I'm also aware of your associates' identities. One is the newspaper editor Kenneth Eden, who is your friend from Oxford. The other is Lord Charles Leyton, the new Duke of Barnet's younger brother.'

Mr Crowther failed to mask his surprise and anger at the accuracy of this report.

Alexander rose and peered down at him. 'Now, here lies the problem. You are all part of the old order with which I seek to do away: two of you are of noble stock, the other is linked to the Church. Peers and preachers have no place in my new order.'

'Your new order?' echoed Mr Crowther mockingly. 'And what does that entail?'

'All in good time, Mr Crowther. All in good time.' Alexander retrieved his drink. 'And I also know why you'll stop at nothing to ruin the Abernathy family. It fits your profile to be the man at the head of an organisation like the SOAL, since you were overlooked and ignored as the youngest son of a nobleman. Hence the career in acting, which placed you firmly in the limelight and earned you the adoration of a nation. Only…that's not what drives you to destroy the Abernathy brothers' reputation, is it? You seek revenge for your sister's death.'

Alexander found great satisfaction in watching Crowther's expression change. He even paused in the action of taking out his cigar case. But then he calmly lit a cigar, and spoke matter-of-factly.

'Dorothy was the only one besides my mother to take any interest in me. She was like a second mother: she'd sing and read to me, and play games with me. She was such a sweet, gentle soul. Her husband was a hard-working, honest man who'd had a string of bad luck. Dorothy worshipped him – no wonder it broke her heart to hear that he'd shot himself.' Mr Crowther drew on his cigar, then exhaled slowly. 'Mr Birtwistle wasn't a coward – he committed suicide in a moment of madness brought on by his ruin. He is not to blame for everything that happened.'

'Your desire for revenge is illogical.'

'I wouldn't expect you to understand how it feels to lose someone dear to you.'

'And it might be argued that Mr Abernathy was punished for his actions. His reputation was left in ruins and he never achieved his ambitions, on account of eloping with his employer, the former Duke of Hereford's, daughter. He died in obscurity with little property to his name.'

'That was not punishment enough. He still married one of the greatest beauties of his day, who bore him two sons and a daughter – just like Dorothy wanted. He still maintained a reputation as a fine clockmaker, and died at a relatively old age. In short, he had what is considered a decent, average life, while my sister was in her grave.'

'Your plans will not bring your sister back.'

'But they will see those two brothers rotting in a debtors' prison, just like their father should have.' Mr Crowther screwed his cigar butt into the ash pan on the table. 'And it is for the greater good, after all. We will prevail, Mr Gearhart – with or without your assistance.'

Alexander leant a fraction of an inch closer to Mr Crowther's face. 'I will not enter into any deal with you. You can threaten me with exposure, and I know you'll carry out the threat, but it won't work.' He swiftly plunged his hand into Mr Crowther's coat pocket and withdrew his tele-texter. 'It's my word against yours, and I will soon wield a greater following than you'll ever hope to muster.'

Crowther's face was shocked but not fearful. 'Well, you'll have to drum up a lot of support before the next issue of *The Archon Herald* goes to the press, which will be by this time tomorrow. The piece about your origins has already been written. It is to appear on the front page of tomorrow evening's edition.'

'So you loaded your weapon before entering battle? Very wise, Mr Crowther. I didn't think you were a foolish man.'

'But it's not too late to avoid your fate. Mr Eden has also prepared an alternative piece, exposing a politician who in the past has accepted bribes to advance his career. Which story makes it into print will be determined by you. Accept my deal by noon tomorrow and the bribery story will be the one selected. You can guess the alternative.' Mr Crowther departed his seat with dignity. 'You have my card. Feel free to call at my residence if you change your mind.'

'Good evening, Mr Crowther.'

With this civil dismissal, Crowther made a prompt exit. Alexander listened to the muffled footsteps in the hallway and Anna attempting to suppress a cough as she showed him out. The front door shut softly, and Alexander watched as his guest passed the window outside. He placed the confiscated tele-texter on the table. Mr Crowther hadn't been wrong; he *did* have an ulterior motive for distributing the devices to the SOAL members. He'd known that it would be only a matter of time before his actions attracted the attention of Crowther and Co, so he'd penetrated one of their strongholds first. And his attempt at intimidation had worked magnificently. They'd panicked, shown their hand, and allowed him to fully assess the level of threat they posed: considerable, as it turned out. (More so than that small splinter group of anarchists, the Crusaders of Eden.) Well, where was the fun without a few obstacles in one's path?

'What did you make of our visitor, Anna?' Alexander asked, as the maid entered the room.

'I couldn't say, sir.'

'Did you see anything useful when you studied him?'

'No, sir. Nothing at all.'

Alexander retrieved Mr Crowther's card from his pocket and examined it, while Anna collected the port glasses. 'Clifford Street. Hardly a surprise, given the man's fame. Hmm, perhaps I will consider paying Mr Crowther a visit.'

Chapter Twenty

'Good God!' Douglas exclaimed as he read the newspaper over breakfast. His brother and sister looked at him questioningly, although their suspense was short-lived.

'Decimus Crowther is dead!'

George put down his coffee. 'How?'

'Heart failure, apparently. His servants became concerned when he didn't rise at his usual hour yesterday morning, and they received no response when they knocked on the bedroom door. They feared that something was amiss, and so the valet broke down his master's door, only to find him stone dead in his bed! A doctor was sent for, and pronounced the cause of death to be heart failure. It's well known that Crowther's mother died in a similar way.'

'That seems rather coincidental,' observed Molly.

'What? You think he was murdered?'

Molly shrugged. 'I'm no detective, but it does seem strange. I know of poisons that are practically undetectable and can make it appear that the victim has died of heart failure.'

'Well, the valet told the newspaper that his master seemed perfectly fine when he returned home the previous evening, although such an attack would come on quite suddenly with no warning.'

'Returned home from where?' asked George.

'It doesn't say. Why?'

'I was merely curious.' George finished his coffee and tried to ignore the searching look Douglas was giving him.

At that moment there came approaching footsteps, followed by the dining room door opening. Arthur entered breezily and took his seat beside Molly. 'Looks like pleasant weather today,' he remarked cheerfully as she poured him tea, since the teapot was in front of her. 'Is something the matter? You all looked very concerned when I came in.'

'Mr Decimus Crowther is dead,' explained Douglas.

Arthur's knife clattered as he paused in the operation of buttering toast. 'The famous actor? Was it an accident?'

'Heart failure, although Molly suspects poisoning,' Douglas added with a smile.

'I do not,' she retorted. 'Show Arthur the paper if you've finished reading it.'

Her brother complied, having first scanned the obituary that followed the article announcing Mr Crowther's death.

Arthur studied the article between forkfuls of kidney and bacon. 'As much as it's a shame to see such a talented actor cut down in his prime, surely this is beneficial to you? If he was really the head of the SOAL?'

Molly shook her head. 'Even if Crowther is dead – putting aside whether it was by natural means or not – that doesn't mean we can suddenly stop worrying about the SOAL now that their leader's gone.'

'How so? What about cutting off the head of the snake and all that?'

'Kill the idea,' muttered Douglas. 'It's like what he said to us: it's no good killing the man if his ideas remain alive. The SOAL didn't even know he was the head of their organisation, for another thing. Nor was he the one of the three founders who posed the greatest cause for concern.'

'Who is, then? Lord Leyton's brother?' asked Arthur.

'No: the newspaper editor, Mr Eden. He was the one broadcasting the SOAL's message, and he will continue to do so. He'll probably be searching for a way to pin the blame for Crowther's death on us…' Douglas faltered, the truth of his words hitting him like a blow to the head.

'But how can he if it was heart failure?'

'The man knows how to spin things out of proportion,' Molly replied. 'And Crowther's death might appear suspicious to him too. In which case, we'd naturally be the prime suspects – as his sworn enemies.' She said those last words with a touch of sarcasm.

'It could have been suicide,' said Arthur, diverging on his own train of thought. 'Maybe he realised that his efforts to damage your credibility were futile and that he couldn't stop your inventions changing the world.'

'A man like that does not commit suicide,' said George. 'He was an egotist who was in the thrall of the game he was playing. Unless he was heavily in debt or some major scandal threatened to ruin him, he wouldn't take his own life. And the method would have been different. A dagger to the heart, most likely.'

'Very Shakespearean,' observed Douglas. His bacon stalled on its journey to his mouth. Maybe it was the cipher in his letter to Maestro that put the idea in his head, but no sooner had the thought dawned than a revelation flashed before him. 'Pass the paper back over here, Mol. Has anyone got a pencil?'

Arthur patted his pockets. 'Ah! Here you go. It's not terribly sharp, I'm afraid.'

'No matter, I'm sure it'll suffice. Thank you, Arthur.'

Douglas accepted the slightly chipped pencil and proceeded to draw rings around certain words in the lengthy obituary – written by none other than Mr Eden. The pencil's rather blunt nib ringed the words in fat graphite loops. He felt the others watching him. Each word that was cut off midway at the end of a line, with a dangling hyphen to tease the eye – that was the key to it. They were well spaced out so as not to attract too much notice. When he put the pencil aside, alarm rang inside his head. With a grave face, he turned the paper around and held it up for the other three to see. Molly narrowed her eyes; then their lids flew back as she comprehended it. George's serious gaze merely intensified.

Arthur was slightly slower to connect the words in a sentence; then an exclamation of 'Good God Almighty!' burst from him as he discerned the message:

YOU WILL PAY.

'I think it's fair to assume that that's directed at us.' Douglas lowered the paper. 'Either that or some deranged admirer of Crowther's who loved him enough to kill him.'

'I think Mr Eden is the one who's slightly deranged,' Molly frowned.

'Well, we can almost certainly say that he doesn't believe that his old friend died a natural death.'

'Grief can blind,' remarked George matter-of-factly. 'People make wild accusations when they cannot comprehend a relation or a friend's untimely death. I imagine doctors are assailed with accusations and demands for compensation as a matter of course.'

'"You lying charlatans", that sort of thing,' said Molly. 'I'm not surprised so many people in Holtbury choose to consult me over Dr Brown, especially since I don't charge for my services any more.'

Arthur's perturbed expression caught Molly's eye. He noticed that she was looking at him, and felt compelled to speak his mind. 'You don't think... you don't think the SOAL would really try to kill you? That this Mr Eden wants some twisted kind of revenge for his friend's death? If it *was* murder or suicide, I mean...'

Beneath the table, Molly placed a hand on his arm. 'Don't worry, Arthur: no one is going to try to kill us. Even if they did, Ravenfeld Hall is an impregnable fortress, and we can all defend ourselves.'

'And a discreet assassination is not Mr Eden's style,' said George. 'He'd want nothing less than a public execution. Nevertheless, we should all be on our guard. The SOAL were already monitoring our movements, and now their watch will only intensify.'

Arthur's hand struck the table. 'But this isn't right! You shouldn't have to put up with it. And it's not like you actually *have* murdered someone!'

'It's no good lamenting that it is unfair – the situation is what it is,' said George coolly. 'Nor must it distract us from our work. Speaking of which, my brother and I have a great deal to see to. Douglas?'

'Right.' Following his brother's example, Douglas rose and left the dining room.

Arthur finished his tea. 'I suppose we'd better get on with our work as well,' he muttered.

'Hopefully weeding the rose garden shouldn't take too long.' Molly tried to sound cheerful.

'Will you be shutting yourself in your lab for the rest of the day afterwards?'

'I promise I won't, not since you're here.'

He leant in to kiss her cheek, but she instinctively pulled away. She hadn't even taken the poison since the previous morning, but she was becoming unconsciously cautious around everyone. Hastily she offered him her cheek, receiving the kiss as if it were from an aunt rather than a lover. Arthur lacked his usual enthusiasm, too.

'Go fetch the tools, Arthur. I'll get my gloves.'

'All right, Molly.'

She briskly left the room, not fooling herself that she wasn't slightly wounded by the confusion and disappointment on his face.

Crowther's death wasn't natural. George was certain about what had happened, even though he had no substantial proof. Another thing he was certain of was that Lord Charles and Mr Eden were now aware of Gearhart's true identity. He'd be interested to hear Douglas's theories regarding Crowther's death and the obituary, although he didn't expect him to arrive at the truth. And Douglas had neglected to notice the words from which the message in the obituary was formed:

…been great friends since our <u>youth</u>…

…first came to public attention for his performance as Romeo in a production of <u>William</u> Shakespeare's Romeo and Juliet…

…failed to receive <u>payment</u> for his time with the company, despite dazzling reviews for his performance…

Youth. William. Payment. Three words whose first three letters were endowed with greater meaning. Mr Eden was referring to the fact that Crowther's sister had died in her youth, after their father's failure to make his loan repayments had ruined Mr Birtwistle. George didn't think he was reading too much into the message.

He'd been turning the matter over in his mind as he worked at his table in the western tower workshop. He was assembling the android's memory core while Douglas worked on its body. Either of them could build a model from start to finish, but they each had particular aspects of the process on which they preferred to work. Douglas usually determined the android's finish. George was more concerned with what went on inside, and he usually constructed the basic structure of the android's brain. But they frequently swapped tasks or inspected one another's work in order to bring everything together, as well as for some variety. Their androids were built in humanoid form because the world was built for humans: buildings, carriages, furniture. It was the form that allowed them to move about and work easily, without compromising on other factors. Yet there was another crucial reason behind their design, and that was to make them appear less threatening. A design too removed from the human form would be uncanny – disturbing, even. (As would a design that too closely resembled a human being.) Some people ran in fright from androids as it was. Many were modelled after specific individuals – usually the person who commissioned them, or a deceased loved one. The brothers' current task wasn't terribly taxing: another damn request for an automaton companion. Spinsters and widows bombarded them with such orders, many reporting that they preferred their androids to flesh-and-blood companions. George didn't wonder at that: androids probably offered more intelligent conversation than the foolish, untrained women who found work as companions – usually impoverished clergymen's daughters and suchlike, who lacked the brains to be governesses and were above entering service. He and Douglas equipped each model with a stock of knowledge on topics specified by their client, as well as such skills as elaborate needlework, knitting and piano-playing. And the android could competently perform any trifling task its fussy mistress gave it.

George is quiet, Douglas thought. Usually he complains to himself when we work on something unchallenging like this. He turned a wheel inside the android's unfinished cylinder, and its arm jerked. The reflex action was perfect. Douglas's eyes had an abstracted look as he switched tools to connect the android's other arm to its body. Eventually he felt compelled to break the silence. 'You know, Crowther's death has got me thinking.'

'How so? Are you concerned that Mr Eden really will attempt to have us assassinated?'

'Well, perhaps. But I was mostly thinking about the fact that Crowther was only thirty-nine, according to the obituary.'

'And?'

'Well, that's not a great deal older than us. I started thinking that if I was to die now, before my time, there's so much I'd have left undone.'

George suppressed the urge to sigh. He hated it when Douglas got in a fanciful mood like this, but experience had taught him that it was best to follow his brother's trail of thought and try to guide him down a more pragmatic path, rather than tell him to be silent. Otherwise those thoughts festered under the surface. 'And what precisely do you wish to accomplish?' he asked.

'Well, there are parts of the world I'd like to see, for one thing.'

'I didn't think much of France.'

'That was only a business trip to Paris, and we hardly saw any of the city. I would like to return to France one day and see the country properly. And I'd like to see Italy and India. Places where it's not grey and rainy all the time.'

'You burn easily in sunlight.'

'I'd wear a hat. Just the heat would be a pleasant change.'

'And the only other language you speak is French.'

'I could learn other languages before beginning my travels. *Apprendre le français n'était pas très difficile.*'

'Then there are the questions of money, transportation, lodgings, and how long your travels would last. You'd have to plan carefully, consulting guidebooks and such.'

'You only like to see difficulties, don't you?'

'I am merely being practical. You must consider every obstacle.'

Douglas sighed. The biggest obstacle was finding the time in which to undertake these trips. He was constantly busy. He'd been toying with the idea of a month-long trip to Italy, but had never got round to putting plans in place.

'Is there anything else you want to do during your time on Earth?' asked George, somewhat wryly.

Douglas's voice acquired a dreamy tone. 'I'd like to marry the woman I'm destined to be with: who loves me for myself and not my money, who understands me like no other woman does, and whom I'd love as much as she loved me. Children would be nice, too. At least one of each, ideally, although I wouldn't mind having only sons, or only daughters. It would be a delight to hear them babble "Papa" as they sat on my knee. And if they showed the inclination, I could teach them everything I know about building machines. Maybe their Uncle George or Aunt Molly could tutor them too?' He smiled. 'Then once they'd reached adulthood – and maybe taken over the family business – my wife and I would pass our autumn years peacefully and grow old together.'

'That's a pleasant picture.' George wondered whether Douglas envisioned Ravenfeld Hall as the setting for this scene of domestic bliss, and if Miss Marsden was still being cast as his wife. He also felt that the vision was unrealistic. Douglas neglected the fact that children made noise and mess, and cost a substantial amount of money to raise. Nor did George believe in the idea that there was a predestined mate for each individual. That was romantic nonsense. 'Any other ambitions?'

'To build a working spaceship. And to own a hat like cattle ranchers wear in America – the ones with the wide brim. I think it'd suit me better than English-style hats, and keep the sun off my face better too.'

'That's quite a lot to accomplish.'

'And who knows if I'll have sufficient time in which to accomplish it all? I don't wish to die with regrets.'

George didn't particularly wish to think about his brother dying; the mere thought of it was a glimpse into a dark abyss. 'In Crowther's case, I doubt he had such regrets. He'd reached the height of his profession: he had wealth, fame and influence.'

'He might have enjoyed all that for many decades to come, were it not for his precarious heart.'

'It is not always the amount of time one has, but how one chooses to employ it. For instance, in the past twenty minutes I have completed my task, while you have been talking nonsense.'

Douglas chuckled. 'You might have a point there.'

'Anyhow, you have no immediate cause for concern. You are ten years younger than Crowther was, and in good health.'

'But we have enemies. And I almost did die at the presentation…and then nearly suffocated in space seventy-two hours later.'

'And I saved you on both occasions. I'd never let anything happen to you or Molly.'

'But you might not always be around to protect me, and I shouldn't rely on you.'

'You don't need to rely on me. I know you can take care of yourself. But I wouldn't hesitate to intervene if I saw you were in danger.'

'I know. Nor I you.' Douglas was surprised that they were having such a conversation as this. Not many years ago, George would have snapped at him to stop being ridiculous and refused to discuss the matter any further. 'Anyway, it's easy for you to say that there's no need to worry about having time in which to accomplish everything I want to do.'

'What do you mean?'

'Well, is there anything *you* really want to accomplish?'

George pondered the question. 'Nothing in particular. I would like to get that second computer working at full capacity. And I have a few ideas for my next project.'

Douglas sighed almost pityingly and resumed his task. The words escaped his mouth without him meaning them to, although they didn't sound terribly bitter so much as exasperated. 'You don't know how to enjoy life. You only want to take it apart and study it.'

George paused briefly in his work, but he didn't look up. 'I am content.'

That was actually true, Douglas thought. George found enjoyment in his own way. He didn't believe he was missing out on anything. But that was precisely what frustrated Douglas. Maybe one day George would realise that he wanted to venture into the world outside the workshop, only to find that the best years of his life were already behind him.

'My idea of spending my time well differs from yours,' said George, apparently reading Douglas's thoughts. 'Just because I don't find enjoyment in dancing at balls with attractive young women who have no intelligent conversation.'

'I suppose,' Douglas sighed, not pointing out that some of the young ladies he'd danced with in his time had been full of intelligent, witty conversation.

'I am not trying to spoil your enjoyment. You are quite free to make a fool of yourself if it pleases you.'

'And I shall continue to do so. I think it's about time I made more of an effort to venture into society again. I can't continue to wallow in my own misery over my lost love.'

'No, although you've been doing a decent job of it so far.' George got up from his chair to retrieve the dustpan, since the table was now littered with iron shards.

Douglas turned the wheel in the unfinished android's head so that its arm shot out to strike his brother as he passed.

George dodged the blow easily, and smiled faintly. 'You're too slow.'

Chapter Twenty-One

Douglas watched London roll by the cab window without real interest. He was meeting the bank manager, Mr Plumpton, one of their oldest clients, at his office on Lombard Street. George was meant to be attending the meeting as well, but had suddenly declared over breakfast that he had other business to see to in the city that afternoon, and so, as soon as they'd reached London, he'd gone his own way. The chances of him revealing what exactly he'd been doing when the two of them reunited later were small. Douglas even doubted that his brother would keep their three o'clock appointment.

He saw one of his electric auto-carriages rolling down the opposite side of the road, and smiled to himself. It looked like any other hansom cab, save for the absence of a horse and the presence of a slightly larger rear end. After years of negotiation, he'd persuaded the local authorities to let him build a dozen auto-carriages to trial around the city as cabs. He had personally selected and trained their drivers, and his ambition was eventually to replace horses and carriages with his auto-carriages. Cab drivers would merely have to change the sort of carriage they drove. They might be grateful to not have to stop to change or refresh their animals every so often, and there'd be far less manure in the streets. That would, of course, put sweepers out of work…although there would be plenty of vacancies for men to wash the auto-carriages. Even if one thing was replaced by another, that new thing still needed building and maintaining.

The cab stopped outside one of the towering beige buildings along Lombard Street, and Douglas was jostled out of his thoughts. Paying the driver, he entered the bank's bustling lobby and was greeted by Mr Bland, his client's secretary. Douglas was familiar with Mr Bland: his name fitted him as well as his smart, inexpensive suit, which was the same grey as a rainy sky. His person was unremarkable and he had an unobtrusive politeness of manner. He possessed an uncanny ability to fade into the background, and could be found sorting diligently through paperwork until his employer wanted him. He was perfectly cast in the mould of a secretary. Making their way past mahogany counters, he showed Douglas upstairs, even though Douglas knew which door led to Mr Plumpton's office and Mr Bland was aware of this. The secretary knocked apologetically on the office door.

'Yes, Bland?' enquired a male voice within.

'Mr Abernathy here to see you, sir.'

'Which one?' There had been a second's delay before this question was uttered. Mr Plumpton's voice had croaked slightly too.

'Mr Douglas Abernathy, sir.'

'Ah! Send him in.'

When Douglas entered the office, Mr Plumpton greeted him with a relieved, benevolent smile. (Clients usually preferred to deal with Douglas. George intimidated them, mostly without meaning to.) Mr Plumpton was a stout man with snowy hair and small spectacles. He had the air of a kind grandfather, but Douglas knew that he was as miserly as the now-deceased Mr Sluggett, who in appearance and attitude had been very much a Scrooge-like figure. He waved Douglas into a chair and settled himself behind his desk.

'So I understand that you wanted to speak to me about the counting machines, Mr Plumpton? You'd like an additional two building, is that correct?' Douglas began.

'Yes, that is correct. We seem to be far busier nowadays, and it would help to alleviate the pressure on our staff.'

'So these new machines are not intended to replace two or more workers?'

'Oh, no! My clerks all have to earn their living, and I should hate to see a family deprived of their bread as the man has no wages.'

Not that the wages you pay are significant, Douglas thought. Aloud he said, 'I did not think that that would be the case, Mr Plumpton. You have a reputation as a very generous employer.' Adding, mentally, Amongst the select few.

'I like to think so. When the wife of one of our clerks was taken ill, I paid for her medical treatment out of my own pocket.' And probably made her husband repay every penny out of his wages.

'How charitable of you, Mr Plumpton. Anyhow, I'd like to propose a revised design for the counting machines that's more efficient than the existing ones, although these will take more time to build and incur a greater cost.'

'How efficient?'

'They perform their tasks ten per cent faster than the current model and save, on average, fifteen minutes out of the working day. That does not sound like a great amount, but accumulated over a matter of weeks it's quite a significant saving.'

Mr Plumpton nodded. The word 'saving' always brought a smile to his lips.

'I've prepared two estimates to show how much it would cost to build two more machines like the ones you possess versus the newer models.' Douglas passed the papers to his client. 'Take as much time as you need to consider them. I won't rush you to a decision.'

He watched as Mr Plumpton studied the papers with a solemn expression. His snowy eyebrows raised ever so slightly when he read the figure for the newer models.

'Well, I suppose there is not a great deal to be gained from an additional fifteen minutes a day, really, is there?' said Mr Plumpton eventually. 'I think I'd prefer the current model. I've had no trouble with them so far.'

'Very well.' Douglas had anticipated that this would be the outcome. 'We can have them ready in two weeks.'

Mr Plumpton nodded as he returned the rejected estimate. 'I presume you require half of the payment now?'

'As always, Mr Plumpton. It's more an act of good faith nowadays, since we can afford whatever materials we need. But we cannot make exceptions or people will talk, and in the past we have had clients refuse to pay for work once it's been completed.'

'Yes, quite right.' Mr Plumpton made his way to the safe that was concealed behind a painting of a lady. He was careful to keep his back to Douglas as he turned the key to open the safe. He needn't have bothered taking such pains: Douglas could have picked the lock easily if he'd wanted to.

Douglas aimed his gaze out of the office window. He saw an elderly lady shuffling along the pavement, an automaton shuffling along beside her. Even from a distance he knew that it was a cheap imitation of his and George's work. The android's movements were too stiff, and it was clearly unaware that the lady was struggling to carry her bag. A handful of entrepreneurial individuals had marketed their own androids, and some even claimed that they were actually built by the Abernathy brothers. Fortunately, their customers soon discovered that these clumsy copies were poorly built and as intelligent as a sack of potatoes. Douglas and George had nothing to fear from them.

Even after Mr Plumpton had unlocked the safe, it took some force for him to open it. In his contorted countenance, Douglas caught a glimpse of the Mr Plumpton with whom clients who defaulted on payments were probably faced. Finally, one firm tug caused the safe's door to yield.

'Have you heard of this American fellow Mr Gearhart?' enquired Mr Plumpton, as he drew out several banknotes. 'He's an inventor such as yourself, I believe?'

'Yes, I'm acquainted with him.'

'He recently asked for a loan of five thousand pounds.'

'That's quite a staggering amount!'

Mr Plumpton finished counting the banknotes and locked the safe. He grinned at Douglas as he passed the notes to him. 'It was for a new enterprise of his. He's turning an old warehouse in Stratford into a factory, so that he can manufacture his communication devices by the bucketload.'

'I see.' Knowing that Mr Plumpton was not always tight-lipped when it came to his clients, Douglas decided to dig deeper. 'What did he use as security?'

'The factory itself, including its contents.'

'How did he accumulate a fortune so quickly? He hasn't been in England long. And he's relatively unknown both here and in his native land, from what I can gather.' Douglas said this more to himself than to Mr Plumpton.

His client shrugged. 'A legacy, perhaps? Maybe he has wealthy English relations.'

'That could be the case,' muttered Douglas doubtfully.

Mr Plumpton inclined his head closer to Douglas's. 'I once heard of an American who established himself in London and quickly amassed a fortune. It was discovered that he was wanted for fraud in his homeland. He'd come here under a false name and made his money through forging bonds.'

'I've heard of such cases, although I know you wouldn't baselessly accuse your clients of criminal activity.'

'Certainly not! I was merely making an observation.'

'Of course.' Douglas rose. 'I had better not occupy any more of your time. I will write to you once the counting machines are completed. Good day, Mr Plumpton.'

On his way out, Douglas caught sight of Mr Bland through an open door. The secretary appeared to be in a deep sleep, his head lying sideways on his desk. Douglas considered whether he should wake the man or not, but decided it was best not to meddle.

George was standing at the corner of Clifford Street, on the opposite side of the road to Mr Crowther's town house. People were crowding outside; some appeared to be journalists, and others were admirers who wept openly. Pathetic. The weeping women wore black gloves or veils. One was even in full mourning, but since she was rubbing shoulders with these sycophants it was doubtful that she was a relation or friend of the deceased. None of them knew who the man they mourned truly was; he'd been playing a part even when not onstage. Darting a quick glance around him, George flipped open the head of his cane and tipped something into his palm. It was cold, smooth, and the size of a large marble. He pressed a button on it and tossed the metal ball into the air. It sprang out, and to anyone observing it without any real interest, it would have appeared to be some indistinct flying insect. It flew to Crowther's house, and George walked on. He turned the corner onto Old Burlington Street, so that he was facing the side of the town house. The metal beetle hovered by a second-storey window with drawn curtains, before squeezing through a gap in the frame. It landed on the latch and pushed the window open with ease. Why keep the window unlocked in April? It was still cold enough for frost to linger on the cobblestones. George held out his arm. The beetle closed the window from the outside and flew into his waiting hand. There were strands of black wool caught in its pincers. George removed these strands, pressed the beetle's button again (which was, in fact, its head), and watched the insect curl back into a ball, before depositing it inside his cane and replacing the topper. He continued walking in the direction of Savile Row, certain that no one had observed him. The crowd were still basking in their grief behind him. Nevertheless, he was wary as he walked on through Mayfair. He had some time until he was to meet Douglas, so he decided to take a longer route to their meeting point. That would give him time to think. Perhaps he should look for a present for Molly, since it was her birthday at the end of the month. He directed his course towards Piccadilly.

George soon became aware of the cab trundling alongside him and the passenger ordering it to stop.

'Out for a stroll, Mr Abernathy?' Mr Gearhart leant out of the cab window, fixing George with a friendly smile. 'Or are you shopping?'

'The latter.'

'Did you come to London specifically for that purpose?'

'I'm here primarily on business.'

'For your meeting with Mr Plumpton? Yes, I know. That's at Lombard Street, isn't it?'

'That is correct.'

'Rather out of your way, then?'

'I am in no hurry and I don't mind the walk. You seem to already know the answers to your questions.'

'It pays to be certain.'

'Might I ask what you're doing?'

'I'm on my way to my factory. Would you care to see it?'

'I don't have the time today.'

'Pity.' Gearhart shrugged melodramatically. 'Would you care to dine at my residence on Wednesday evening? I'm sure it won't be an inconvenient journey, what with that airship of yours.'

'It's my brother's airship.'

'Oh yes, so it is. Hmm, in that case maybe it's not so reliable as a means of transport, if his spaceship is anything to go by.'

George's stare hardened. 'I accept your invitation, Mr Gearhart.'

'Number twenty-four, Charles Street. Eight o'clock. I am rather punctual about these things. Good day to you, sir. Driver!'

The cab rolled on, and George watched it turn the corner. Had Gearhart followed him or had their encounter really been a coincidence? George tried not to dwell on it as he went about his errand. In an artists' colourman's shop he found a paintbox that Molly would like; it was mahogany, with ebony edging. It would be useful when she was preparing her latest encyclopaedia, since he'd overheard her complaining about the inadequacy of her artist's materials. As he stepped out of the shop with the parcelled box under his arm, he heard Big Ben ring out to mark the quarter-hour. The conversations of passers-by flowed past him as he strolled along the pavement.

'Did you read about Sir Shillingford in *The Archon Herald* the other day? Fancy a man of his reputation selling government secrets to foreign nations!' cried one particularly vociferous gentleman.

'I simply cannot believe a man of his integrity would do such a thing! It is nothing but lies! He's removed himself from public life because of the scandal. Poor man, this will ruin his family,' returned his companion.

George heard without really listening. Why had Gearhart invited him to dinner? No doubt he had some ulterior motive in mind; several ideas suggested themselves immediately, but it was impossible to know which, if any, was correct. George was so absorbed in his thoughts that he narrowly missed colliding with a young woman who came hurrying out of the bookshop on his right.

'Forgive me, sir,' she muttered, her head bowed and a thick red book clutched under one arm. 'I neglected to look where I was going.'

Before George could respond, she hurried away. Her dark grey skirts flared behind her as she ran. He was at risk of becoming careless, he realised, as he lost sight of her in the crowded street. His suspicions surrounding Gearhart were consuming him; part of him even wondered if the girl with the red book had been Gearhart's spy. He knew that Douglas and Molly were already concerned about him; perhaps they even feared that he'd started drinking spirits again.

George had just entered a side street when he heard the click of a revolver being cocked. Slowly, he looked to his right. The gunman was probably no older than twenty, with unkempt curling hair and glowering eyes. He was dressed like a shepherd from biblical times, in a coarse, light brown robe, although his feet were clad in boots rather than sandals.

'You are the root of evil,' the youth informed him. 'The origin of the Great Insult. Your puppets are but demons in another form, sent to spread sin and chaos amongst humankind.'

George eyed the boy's shaking hand. 'Put the gun down before you do something foolish.'

The young man's face gave no indication that he'd registered the command. 'The prints I have seen of you do not capture your likeness well. The coal-black hair, those cold blue eyes…you are undoubtedly in league with Satan himself.'

'Your twisted theology cannot even be called Christianity. Nor is your logic in shooting me remotely sound.'

The youth took two purposeful steps forward and pressed the revolver's cold muzzle against George's forehead. 'Logic does not compare to divine truth!'

George's stance and expression remained unchanged. 'I could kill you without even having to let go of this parcel.'

That knocked the courage out of the boy. George watched fear grip his face. The frenzied eyes rolled about in confusion; then the youth gave a cry and raised the butt of his revolver above his head. George grabbed his assailant's arm with his free hand before slamming his palm into the young man's torso, at the base of his ribcage. The youth flopped to the ground, winded. The revolver clattered onto the cobblestones. George calmly retrieved it while his would-be assassin regained his breath.

'Giving weapons to untrained youths and expecting them to commit murder while their leaders sit behind a curtain – that is the Crusaders' divine truth. You don't have it in you to kill. I suggest you find a new cause.' He pocketed the revolver and walked on, leaving the boy rasping behind him.

Then George felt his pocket telegraph clack into life. He flipped the lid and read the new message, knowing already who had sent it and what it would say.

+*WHERE ARE YOU? PAST THREE.*–

George quickly replied 'FIVE MINUTES', then hurried on his way.

Douglas was sitting in the driver's seat of Peregrine when George arrived at their meeting point near Berkeley Square, apparently amusing some children by flicking the ship's lights on and off. The children tried to jump into the faint pools of yellow light whenever they briefly appeared.

Douglas opened the door for his brother when he perceived his approach. 'What were you doing?' he asked once George had boarded. He prepared to launch the airship without delay, scattering the children with a friendly toot of the horn.

'Buying our sister a birthday present.' The incident with the youth wasn't worth mentioning; just another desperate, simple soul wanting something to cling to.

'You're organised. What did you buy her?'

George slackened the parcel's string and peeled back a corner of the paper, so that Douglas could see its contents.

'Not a bad choice. I think she'll like it.'

'Don't sound so surprised that I made a suitable selection unaided by you.' George swiftly but neatly rewrapped the parcel and leant back against his seat. He watched London gradually fade from sight below them. 'I encountered Mr Gearhart earlier. He has invited me to dine with him on Wednesday evening.'

'Just you?'

'Yes.'

'Purely for the pleasure of your company?'

'Apparently so.'

Douglas seemed at a loss for words. 'And did you accept?' he asked eventually.

'I did.'

'Oh. You'll be wanting to borrow Spuggy, I'm assuming?'

'If you don't mind.'

'It's no trouble.'

'You can't comprehend this, can you?'

'Well, you're not exactly known for your love of society. Or society's love of you.'

They flew in silence for a quarter of a mile.

'The meeting went fine, by the way,' said Douglas, with only a tinge of sarcasm. 'Mr Plumpton wants the original model.'

'I can't say I'm surprised.'

'And he said something about Mr Gearhart: that he took out a huge loan to build a factory of some kind. I don't trust him.'

'Mr Plumpton or Mr Gearhart?'

'Mr Gearhart. I think there's something peculiar about him. Haven't you said as much?'

'I have.'

'And do you still feel the same way?'

George chose his words carefully. 'My opinion of him has altered after becoming better acquainted with him.'

Douglas sighed. 'Just…be on your guard if you do dine with him.'

'You don't need to tell me what to do.'

'I know, I merely said it for my own peace of mind. I know that trying to persuade you against anything is futile – oh, damn!'

A pigeon smacked into the window and rebounded off the pane. It left a smear and a few feathers on the glass. Peregrine wobbled slightly as Douglas momentarily lost his grip on the controls.

George craned his neck to see a small shape receding behind them. 'I think you only stunned it.'

'Hopefully. Bloody bird.' Douglas swept back his hair and resumed his hold on the wheel. 'And I just managed to scrape what was left of that less fortunate gull off the window.'

'You can't allow yourself to become agitated while piloting this ship.'

'That is the least helpful thing to say to keep me calm.'

'But don't concern yourself about Mr Gearhart. I doubt he'll attempt to poison me or anything ridiculous like that. He most likely wants to establish an acquaintance with someone in a similar line of business, that's all. And I'm not a fool who is taken in by his charismatic act.'

'I know, I know.'

Nothing more was said on the subject for the rest of their journey, although neither of them dismissed it entirely from their thoughts.

Chapter Twenty-Two

Molly often visited Betsey's family on Sundays, usually for the purpose of treating a sick child or bestowing a small act of charity (without the self-important attitude usually expected from the highest-ranking woman in the neighbourhood). But sometimes she went to their cottage purely as a visitor. The little ones adored 'Lady Molly', and there'd be a scramble to determine who had the honour of sitting on her lap while she talked to their mother in the tiny front room. The Bateses' house was always chaotic, with six children still at home, plus two dogs and a cat, occupying not many rooms. Mrs Bates was a plump, matronly woman with an ample bosom, a moon-shaped face, a heart more than large enough to accommodate her numerous family – and a firm right hand should any of her children misbehave.

On this particular Sunday, Molly went straight upstairs to administer an elixir to three-year-old Marie, the youngest and meekest of the Bates brood, who was tucked up in bed with a bad cold and in need of cheering. Not neglecting the other children (and allowing Mrs Bates and Betsey to put the washing out without being pestered), Molly wrestled with four-year-old Jack and let the girls attempt to braid her hair. Lily and Aggie knitted their brows as they tried to untangle the knots (while Molly tried not to show how the tugs of the comb hurt her).

Mrs Bates laughed when she saw her daughters' efforts. One of the braids was already unravelling where they'd failed to secure it with the ribbon, and the overall effect was more comical than elegant. 'Let's hope neither of 'em become lady's maids,' she said, after Lily and Aggie had pottered out of the front room and into the kitchen. Betsey could be heard shouting at them that dinner would be ready when it was ready, so they could stop whining.

'Nonsense, Mrs Bates! They dressed my hair wonderfully. I'd take either one of them as my lady's maid.' Molly smiled as she fixed the braid. Jack approached her chair from behind and latched his arms around her neck. He had to be tickled into submission.

Mrs Bates took up her knitting, content to let her two oldest girls supervise the dinner. 'Betsey tells me that you're thinking of wedding your Mr Arthur soon, Miss Molly.'

Molly looked up sharply from wiping Jack's nose with her handkerchief. 'I said no such thing, I assure you.' Through the archway to the kitchen she shot a glance at Betsey, who was too busy chatting to Rebecca and peeling potatoes to notice.

'Why? Do you not want to marry him?' Betsey got her upfront manner from her mother, gliding through delicate subjects like a knife through butter.

'We're both too busy. And I don't think I could give up my university work to be a housewife – it would drive me insane. I wonder how you manage it, Mrs Bates.'

Mrs Bates chuckled. 'With great difficulty! But I understand. You like to have time for your experimenting and lecturing. Having a house to manage isn't always easy. But you have a houseful of servants to do the washing and cooking, don't forget.'

'That's true. I suppose what I really meant was that there's hardly any chance of me getting a permanent teaching post if I become Mrs Greenwood.'

'Ah. Well, there's no reason why you can't carry on making your brews in your laboratory. I know you won't ever stop making your medicines, miss. You don't need a piece of paper or a fancy title to help people: you managed to come up with new brews and plants fine before you went to university to become a botanist. The poor folk around Holtbury that can't afford a doctor rely on you.'

'I know, I'm the local witch,' Molly grinned. Mrs Bates did have a point, although it was gratifying to now be recognised as a scientist by fellow academics.

'Would you want a house for just you and Mr Arthur when you're married?' continued Mrs Bates. 'Something smaller and easier to manage? I'm sure Betsey would offer herself as your maid and go with you. Does Mr Arthur want to be nearer his family?'

'God, no. He's keen to maintain some distance from them, and I have no intention of leaving Ravenfeld Hall.'

'I'm glad of it, miss. And I know having your family close to hand isn't always helpful. Just look at my mother, God rest her soul. I was glad when she said she was to be your housekeeper, although I felt pity for you as her mistress.'

'I know I won't offend you by saying that she was the worst housekeeper we've ever had.'

Mrs Bates smiled good-humouredly, and spoke half-bitterly, half-affectionately. 'Oh, she knew what she was doing, sly old devil. And then God in His wisdom called her to His kingdom about a year after you came here.' The clicking of her knitting needles paused. 'I'll tell you this as well, Miss Molly: children take up an awful lot of time. And you've not seen this lot at their worst, when they're screaming and crying.' She nodded at Jack, who was sitting on Molly's lap, sucking his thumb. 'But if you want something enough, you'll make time for it. I visit my friend in the village, who's a cripple, every Thursday evening, and so far the house hasn't set ablaze in my absence. It helps now the girls are older. Marriage is about give and take, y'see. One party can't have their own way all the time. If you love your Mr Arthur and he loves you, then you'll find your way of doing things.'

Here she broke off to shout at one of the dogs, who had started barking at whoever was passing the window. The dog hung its head and trotted to Molly's side for sympathy, whining pathetically. Dutifully she stroked its head, and it lay down at her feet.

'Besides,' resumed Mrs Bates, 'you're still young – there's time enough for you to decide.'

'I suppose so.'

'You could manage this lot for a few days to see what you think of it.'

'I appreciate the offer, Mrs Bates, but I'm afraid I'll have to decline.'

Mrs Bates laughed merrily. Lily and Aggie ran back into the room, the former gnawing on a chunk of carrot.

'Is Lady Molly staying for dinner?' asked Aggie.

'I'm afraid not, sweetheart,' Molly smiled gently. 'There's probably not enough for an extra plate.'

'Of course there's enough!' interjected Mrs Bates. 'I bought a bigger joint and plenty of potatoes, thinking that you'd be staying for dinner.'

'I'd never mean to impose, Mrs Bates.'

'Are you suddenly too good to eat with your tenants, miss?' Mrs Bates scoffed half-heartedly, with one hand on her hip. 'There's ten of us at table already, so what's one more?'

Molly sighed. 'I suppose there's no use arguing, then.'

The two girls cried out gleefully, and were bouncing up and down as their father and two older brothers returned home from repairing a fence.

Mrs Bates didn't seem the least embarrassed about the fact that her crockery was chipped, or that Jack slurped his milk throughout the meal. Molly didn't think less of her hostess for those things either. She preferred a riotous table with noisy talk to the sombre meals she'd experienced as a child, presided over by her mother's eagle eye. Despite their father's warnings, the younger Bates children passed scraps to the dogs when they came sniffing around their chairs. Mr Bates coaxed Molly to talk, and made her feel like one of the family. He was a large, friendly man with a deep, booming laugh, although he could lose his temper with his children when provoked. He was visibly fond of his wife – and her cooking.

When Molly and Betsey were walking arm in arm back to Ravenfeld Hall in the low evening light, Molly reprimanded her friend. 'You shouldn't have told your mother what I said about Arthur.'

'She's no gossip, Molly.' Betsey only ever dropped the 'miss' when addressing her friend while not in uniform.

'I know, but even so. Normally I can trust you to keep secrets.'

'I thought she might offer you some advice.'

'Well, she did, as it so happens.'

'What did she say?'

'Not telling. You have to earn my trust again before I tell you anything,' Molly smiled.

'Well, did she help you decide what to do?'

'Not quite. She gave me something to think about, though.'

'I didn't tell her about that letter you got yesterday. Does Mr Arthur know about it?'

'Not yet. I thought I might as well show it to him the next time he's here.'

The girls approached the scarecrow guarding the field beside the road; he tipped his olive-green bowler hat to them as they passed.

'I still think it's funny how we met,' mused Betsey, after they'd both been silent for a short while.

Molly smiled. 'I remember seeing you on the road as I was on my way back from Holtbury and you were making your way there. You were picking the scabs on the back of your arm.'

'And you said, "Don't do that, it'll make it even sorer!" and dug a bottle of the pink lotion out of your basket. "Use this, it'll calm it down," you said, and you got me to rub some of it on my arm there and then.'

'I saw from your face that the camomile had worked.'

'It was marvellous! And when I asked you how much you wanted for the bottle, you said to take it for nothing, seeing as you couldn't sell it in town.'

'Although it would have kept for another day. I knew you suspected me of being a quack or a madwoman.'

'Then you said you was new to town and you'd only come up from London three months since. You said to call you Molly, not Miss Abernathy.'

Molly grinned. 'I could tell you'd no idea who I was.'

'Well, you wasn't dressed like a lady. I thought you was a cottager's daughter, although you spoke too nicely. I did think that was odd.'

'When you told me you were going to work as the under-housemaid at Ravenfeld Hall, I decided not to tell you who I really was. It was worth it to see your jaw drop that first day you came to work.'

'I could hardly believe you was the mistress!'

'But we laughed about it afterwards. I doubt you'd have believed me if I'd told you on our first meeting, anyhow.'

Betsey reflected a moment. 'I mightn't have done.'

By now they'd passed through the Hall's front gates (someone had seen them approaching and opened the gates for them), and were strolling up the drive. They entered through the south hall. A faint smell of burning still came from the kitchen. Molly was glad that Gwyneth had had her cookery lesson in the morning; she couldn't have faced it now. The Bates children had thoroughly worn her out.

'Do you want a cup of tea?' asked Betsey.

'No, I'm fine. You don't have to serve me today, you know.'

'I wasn't asking as your housemaid, Molly.'

'I know, I know.'

'I thought you might like to chat with all of us in the servants' kitchen.'

'I would, but I think I'd better write the next part of my book.'

Betsey sighed and shook her head. 'You work too hard. If it's not tending your garden and locking yourself in your lab, it's making medicine or writing – or lecturing, now.'

'If I was any other mistress, I would have dismissed you for that remark.'

'If I had any other mistress, I'd have been dismissed years ago.'

'You certainly would.'

Molly hurried upstairs. But instead of sitting at her desk to write up her notes for the book, she drooped onto her bed. Mr Kellogg's letter was still on her desk, and she could just about read it from this distance.

After hearing of your remarkable research from my colleague, who was in attendance at your recent lecture at the Royal Institution, I would be delighted to offer you a research post at the California Academy of Sciences…

California. No, she couldn't. It was too far away. She'd show the letter to Arthur, before replying in the negative. Even if he pressed her to accept, she'd still refuse.

She lay on her back, staring at the ceiling. She was in two minds about whether she wanted Arthur to propose or not. It wasn't that she had doubts about *him*. Rather, she enjoyed her liberty, and marriage brought expectations. When she was younger, Molly had believed that her destiny was to be a spinster, left to tend her garden and brew her potions in peace. But apparently, fate had other plans for her. Her old mentor, Mrs Dempsey, had claimed to be able to see the future. Whether she'd been serious or not, Molly was still unsure; but the Irishwoman had always insisted that Molly would marry for love one day. But what was wrong with her and Arthur's current situation? Aside from his prolonged periods of absence, that was. Although even they were not always unwelcome, as Molly savoured the peace they brought. As things stood, she and Arthur were able to pursue their separate interests. She'd discovered from lecturing undergraduates back at the University College that she enjoyed teaching, as long as the students showed so much as a grain of enthusiasm. She also enjoyed being invited to speak as a guest lecturer at other institutions, and she hadn't given up hope of getting a permanent post as a botany lecturer somewhere closer to home. (She was sometimes sniffed out by women's groups to help champion the cause of female education, or *ladies'* education, as some of them meant. They preferred to keep the lower classes illiterate.) And she always did her utmost to help Holtbury's poorer townsfolk when Dr Brown failed them. But as pleasing as the hard-won recognition of her work was, Molly didn't want to be placed on a pedestal. She simply wanted to be left to pursue her research in peace. And even if she did get the sack for being a married woman, she'd still be helping people with her work, and that was the crucial thing. Whether she was recognised for it or not came second (although acclaim and funding meant that she could help even more people).

As for Arthur, he'd worked hard for years to build his reputation as a landscape gardener, and now he too was seeing success. This meant that he was forever travelling up and down the country to visit sites, which made it harder for the two of them to see each other. Molly could just see herself years from now, waiting for her husband's return from some far-flung estate, children clinging to her skirts and a baby in her arms. There was no question of him coming with her to California: he had no connections to help him find work in America, and his parents would never allow him to go in the first place. And there lay the even more fundamental problem with them marrying: Arthur's father would disown him, and it would break his mother's heart to have her 'dear boy' lost to her. Arthur would never forgive himself for it – the guilt would crush him. And as much as Molly resented

Arthur's controlling parents, she didn't want to be responsible for a rupture in the Greenwood family.

Despite everything, deep down she really did want to marry Arthur – to show that she loved him and didn't care for his family's objections. And he certainly wanted to marry her. Ever since that dinner at his parents' house in the week of his birthday, he'd been hinting at and skirting around the subject. He wasn't going to let it go, either; he was like that once he got something into his head. Molly had been subtly rebuffing him, afraid of how she'd react when he finally did propose – afraid that she'd accept him without a moment's hesitation, rather than wound him with a pragmatic refusal. Knowing Arthur, he'd set up some elaborate scene in the rose garden and present her with a ring that had cost him half a year's wages.

Molly sighed. The scales were too finely balanced. Mrs Bates's words had added weight to the side in favour of marrying Arthur, but it wasn't enough to counterbalance the crushing weight of the fact that doing so would estrange him from his parents.

Molly rolled over and groaned into her pillow.

Chapter Twenty-Three

Gearhart's door was opened by a domestic. Instead of asking George his name, she simply stepped aside and said, 'Please come in, sir.'

He entered the hallway. The maid relieved him of his coat and hat.

'My master is waiting for you in the parlour, sir.' She spoke in a soft murmur; George was certain that it wasn't the voice of the girl with the red book from the other day.

The hallway was half in gloom, with the lamps giving out an economical amount of light. It was sufficient for the girl to lead George to his destination. The house's furnishings and wallpaper were modern and of good quality, yet unpretentious. Gearhart didn't use additional ornamentation to advertise the wealth he must possess to remain under such a comfortable roof.

The maid was muttering to herself under her breath, far too quietly for George to hear the words, although they formed a melancholic tune with a cheerful undertone. Eventually he was able to discern a single verse.

The defender's strings are tied,
thus Triumph withers in the bud.
The falcon descends from the skies,
and blood is spilt for common blood.

What nonsense was that? Some form of poetry? She repeated the verse three times, each time more forcefully, placing emphasis on the final word. *Blood.* Then as they approached an open door, she abruptly ceased her half-singing, perhaps fearing that her master would hear her. She coughed discreetly into a handkerchief as she stepped aside for George to enter the drawing room.

Gearhart was standing in the middle of the room, dressed for dinner and with his hands behind his back. On seeing his guest, he grinned. 'Good evening, George. I trust you found your way here without too much difficulty?'

'Yes, thank you.'

'You don't mind if I call you George, do you? Seems silly to default to "Mr Abernathy" when we're so well acquainted.'

'You may address me however you wish.'

'Feel free to call me Alexander, since the courtesy extends both ways. Care for a drink?'

'If you please.'

'I am aware that you do not drink spirits of any kind, of course. But I hope you have no objection to my partaking of a little brandy and soda?'

'None at all.'

'I have not been a negligent host, I assure you. There is ginger beer available, along with several other substitutes for liquor, each equally unexciting.'

'Ginger beer will be sufficient. Many acquaintances have tried to entice me to drink liquor, and all failed.'

Gearhart presided over the decanter and prepared both drinks. George watched him pour a measure of amber liquid into a tumbler. Of course Gearhart had chosen brandy and soda for himself: he knew that it had at one time been the drink to which George was most partial. But if he was trying to tempt him, he severely underestimated his resolve.

'Dinner shall be ready at precisely eight o'clock,' Gearhart informed him, his face unusually excited.

As his host added soda water to the brandy, George ran his eyes over the bookcase. He noted some of the titles: *Self-Help*; *The Condition of the Working Class in England*; *The Principles of Communism*; *London Labour and the London Poor*; *An Essay on the Principle of Population.* They rubbed covers with works by Dickens, Collins, Oliphant, Trollope, Eliot, Ainsworth and other popular novelists. There was also a selection of plays and poetry – such staples as Tennyson, Barrett Browning, Wordsworth, Shakespeare and Milton were present.

'It appears you have a wide taste in literature,' George remarked.

'I confess to not having read all of them. Some are simply for show. But it is always interesting to see which books capture a caller's attention. It reveals something about their character.'

'I see.'

Gearhart handed George his drink. 'Have you read Karl Marx's works?'

'I have.'

'And what did you think of them?'

'I think his ideas would be extremely difficult to implement in practice.'

'I agree.'

Both sipped their drinks.

'It must cost you a great deal to rent a house in Mayfair,' George observed.

'It is well within my means.'

'I don't suppose you'd be willing to disclose the extent of your means?'

'That will depend upon how well my little machines sell.'

'Hopefully well enough to pay back the loan you took out with Plumpton & Sluggett.'

'I assume your brother heard of that from Mr Plumpton? Oh dear – I see I cannot trust his discretion.' Gearhart sighed and shook his head. 'On the other hand, I have no reason to deny it. I needed the loan to fund my enterprise.'

'What is it that you're really planning? These devices of yours are not intended solely for improving communication.'

'You're very suspicious, aren't you, George?' Gearhart grinned.

Just as the clock on the mantle finished its eighth chime, the maid appeared in the doorway and announced dinner.

Douglas was in his study, answering letters. He'd been too occupied with other things to complete this task earlier, yet there were plenty of letters in need of answering. He rubbed his sore eyes, struggling to compose any more coherent sentences. At least he could resort to the same dry, well-worn stock responses for the majority of the letters. It seemed that over the next fortnight his time would be devoured by client meetings and repairs. (Maybe they ought to start charging clients for annual repairs after all, despite his strong protests to George on this point.) Lord Leyton and Maestro were also back in London; Douglas was to call on them tomorrow.

There came a tap on his door.

'Come in, Mol.'

His sister entered and shut the door behind her. 'Are you busy?' she asked.

'Not tremendously – I'm only writing letters. Is something the matter?'

'I only wanted to ask if you approved of the dinner menu for next week, since you keep saying you want something different.'

'Show me the proposed menu, then.'

Molly produced a folded paper from her dress pocket and handed it to her brother, before moving to close the curtains, since he'd not thought to do so. It was a clear night with twinkling stars. She briefly savoured the sight before drawing the curtains together.

'That should be fine,' Douglas declared, after reading the menu through. 'I'd only substitute boiled beef for roast beef.'

'As you wish.' Molly didn't leave the study once her errand was concluded. She wandered about the room, shifting objects and retrieving a pencil that had fallen on the floor.

'Did you send your reply to Mr Kellogg?' Douglas asked, while continuing to write.

'I posted it this morning.'

'I do agree with what Arthur said: that it's an excellent opportunity. George thinks the same.'

'You would all say that.'

'Are you honestly happy with your decision?'

Molly looked him in the eye. 'I am.'

'Then that's all that matters.' Douglas refreshed his supply of ink, the pen clinking softly against the side of the inkwell. 'What do you make of George's recent acquaintance with Mr Gearhart?'

Molly leant on the edge of Douglas's desk. 'Why?'

'There's just something about it that makes me uneasy. He's dining with him tonight.'

'Are you jealous that George has finally started playing with the other little boys?' she said drily, although she was smiling.

'It'd be a relief if he *had* learnt to get along with the other little boys, but I think something else is going on here.'

'Well, he's not making business deals behind your back, if that's what you're afraid of. George can be cold and unfeeling, but he'd never be disloyal to you.'

'I don't seriously think so either.' Douglas let his pen pause. 'Maybe Gearhart *is* working towards asking George to make some sort of deal with him. But if not, what else could possibly be going on?'

'Maybe they genuinely wish to be on friendly terms,' ventured Molly.

Douglas looked hard at her. 'It's *George*.'

'Well, perhaps it isn't entirely impossible for him to form friendships. After all, you have Dick Cullwick, and there's that other man you know through him – the one who's a doctor.'

'Theo Truman?'

'That's the one.'

'But I actually enjoy the society of other people. George has never shown an interest in forming friendships.'

'Hmm. True.' Molly ran the tip of her thumb over her lip. 'What is this Mr Gearhart like?'

'Quite charismatic, but I suspect he's frightfully intelligent,' replied Douglas.

'I got a vague impression that he was when he spoke to me following my lecture. Well, at least their intelligence is one thing that George and Mr Gearhart have in common.'

'They displayed somewhat similar inventions at the Society dinner – at one point in the evening even I doubted that George would win the medal. Maybe Mr Gearhart views him as a rival and wants to assess whether he can outwit him.'

'And George is doing likewise?'

'Very likely.' Douglas let his pen rest on the desk and then sighed. 'But I hope that's not the case either. I mean, thinking about it, I have Dick and the handful of friends, other than Theo, whom I've made through him, although most of them are more like acquaintances. And you have Arthur, Betsey and Mr Rose. George has no one outside of us.'

'But he's never given any indication that it bothers him. He thinks everyone else is beneath him, and half the time he's too absorbed in his work to notice what's going on around him.'

'You're not wrong, Mol.' Douglas considered what would have happened if he had moved into that house with Clara; George would hardly have seen him after that. Then, with Molly away teaching and lecturing, he'd have been almost completely isolated. Douglas's heart sank at the thought. He shook his head. 'Anyway, George should be home soon, so we might learn then whether Gearhart is friend or foe.'

Molly nodded and slid off the desk. 'Are you going to bed once you've finished those letters?'

'I might read first.'

'Which means you want to be awake for when George returns so you can interrogate him.'

'My little sister sees through me, as usual.'

Molly reached over his shoulder to retrieve an empty teacup, pecking his cheek once she had done so. She could tell that he'd been working on his vehicles all afternoon again: he smelt like an engine shed and had speckles of black grease on his face. She smiled to herself as she withdrew from the study.

As the clock chimed nine times, Douglas sealed the final letter. After he'd dragged himself to his room, he kept the curtains open so that he could watch for the airship's lights in the night sky.

'I trust that you are satisfied with everything so far?'

'Quite.' George was telling the truth. So far each course had been well prepared and accompanied by a perfectly partnered beverage. The dining room was as impeccably neat as the rest of the house, or at least the rooms he had been permitted to view. His host spoke amicably and played his role to perfection. Gearhart was seated at the head of the table and George was at his right.

'I'm aware you're not exactly a gourmet, but I knew that lamb cutlet was to your liking. Your sister brought one to you on a tray when it was your birthday, remember? You didn't even stop working to enjoy your family's company and celebrate the day with them.' Gearhart shook his head. 'And dear Molly had the goodness not to be cross with you.'

'My family know I don't care about such occasions.'

'You don't care about much, do you?'

George stared at him challengingly. 'I care about some things more than you think I do.'

He heard the maid singing as she spooned vegetables onto their plates. She had sung the same song several times over, and he knew the words.

A rose blooms in silence's shroud,
and two hearts as one doth beat.
The victor to bliss is wed;
his rival tastes bitter defeat.

The maiden stands upon the hill;
the one who is two hundred too.
Lightning strikes and fire rains,
and now they are but few.

He stands poised to strike the blow,
but victory he doth forsake.
The raven from the tower flies —
then the bell shall break.

Her tone was as cheerfully forlorn as before. George wished to hear no more of it.

'Please excuse Anna. The poor girl has a few…quirks, but she is efficient and suits me well.' Gearhart smiled.

'Do you not have any other servants?'

'Why would I?' Gearhart's tilted head remained resting on the ball of his fist, but he raised his smiling eyes. 'I do not have the same…requirements as most gentlemen. Therefore, Anna here is sufficient in helping me to keep up appearances. And she has rather remarkable abilities to recommend her. Anna, how will my shares in the Metropolitan Railway fare tomorrow?'

'They will increase by no more than half a per cent, sir,' she answered matter-of-factly.

'You see? She has a talent for numbers, amongst other things. And what will the weather be like tomorrow, Anna?'

'Approximately eleven degrees, with intervals of light rain, sir.'

'Her predictions are more accurate than Mr Fairclough's, I assure you.' The smile spread from Gearhart's eyes to his entire face.

'I've little doubt they are.' George's eyes followed the girl as she bent over to refresh his glass. So she had cooked as well as served dinner; that accounted for the brown splatter on her cuff. Presumably she'd changed her apron to wait at the table. There was something rather wooden about her, in her movements and in her face. Her blue eyes were blank and rather washed-out-looking. Were it not for these traits, common opinion would have pronounced her handsome.

'I know what you are thinking.' Gearhart adjusted his cuffs, before taking up his knife and fork again. 'You're trying to work out whether she is human or an android.'

'It is of little consequence either way,' returned George, as the maid left the dining room.

The scraping of Gearhart's knife cut through the air. 'Perhaps too much is made of that distinction.'

George said nothing and returned his attention to his lamb. The soubise sauce was superior to that produced by the kitchen at Ravenfeld Hall, where the cook made it too thick. After a minute or two, he turned his eyes upward to observe Gearhart swallow a mouthful. 'How is it that you are able to take in food and drink?'

'Like I said, keeping up appearances.'

'I gathered, but how is it done?'

'A chamber of hydrochloric acid, very similar to the human stomach, and a network of piping.'

George reached for his glass. 'I see.'

'At what point does one draw the line between human and machine?' Gearhart seemed determined to continue his earlier conversational thread.

'When it achieves consciousness? When it defecates and bleeds and cries tears?'

'Mere idle philosophy. I choose not to concern myself with such thinking.'

'Says the man who was the first to install consciousness into a machine,' Gearhart smirked. 'How ironic.'

George dabbed his mouth with his napkin. 'I did not accept your invitation to theorise on the particulars of human nature.'

'Come now, George, what is wrong with a little friendly, speculative talk over dinner between two gentlemen? Is it not customary?'

'We are not exactly typical gentlemen, though, are we?'

'I suppose not. But if you don't wish to discuss philosophy, then in what subject do you wish to indulge?'

'One thing I would like to ask you about is the murder of Decimus Crowther.'

Gearhart raised his eyebrows slightly. 'The papers said he died of heart failure.'

'And that makes it true, does it?'

'Well, what do you believe happened?'

'That you murdered him shortly after he called here.'

Gearhart leant back leisurely in his chair. 'How do you think I did it?'

'You waited a couple of hours after he left, then you walked to his house, since Clifford Street is only twenty minutes away and it was less conspicuous than taking a cab. You waited until all the lights were out, before accessing the building through Mr Crowther's bedroom window – catching your black greatcoat on the latch as you did so.'

Gearhart nodded encouragingly. 'Go on.'

'You found Crowther in a deep sleep, as intended. You'd already decided on the method. You covered the gas lamp and allowed carbon monoxide to build up in the room, resulting in his "heart failure". Once he was dead, you opened the window to allow the gas to escape, before escaping yourself. You were unable to lock the window from the outside, but that was of no consequence. Even if a servant were to find it open after the murder, they'd think nothing of it.'

'But you thought something of it, didn't you? I suspected you were sniffing around Mr Crowther's house that day I saw you in London.'

'So you admit to the murder?'

'Yes, you got me, Inspector.' Gearhart held up his hands theatrically, then laughed. 'It was easy. All I had to do was sit and wait until his heart ceased to beat. The carbon monoxide had no effect on me, of course, but it would have looked odd if his valet had dropped dead on entering the room the following morning, so I left the window open a short while to ventilate it.'

George nodded.

'Do you intend to tell the police?' asked Gearhart.

'You know I don't. I have no evidence against you.'

'You should be grateful. I removed a source of trouble for you.'

'But I doubt that's why you killed him. He knew what you were and threatened to expose you.'

'Oh, how clever of you. He did offer to make a deal with me, but I refused him.'

'I understand. But you must not have covered your tracks adequately, for Mr Crowther to have arrived at the truth.'

'His influence – or, rather, that of his friends – was greater than I initially believed, based on what I surmised about the SOAL's founders. But even he could not follow my trail all the way. I think he made a rather fortunate guess. He wanted me to be what he thought I was, and he risked looking very foolish by confronting me about the matter.'

'I'd say it was a rather *un*fortunate guess for him,' remarked George wryly.

'And people say you have no sense of humour. Crowther claimed that Mr Eden had a newspaper story about me ready to go to press, which I'm convinced was a bluff. If he did have solid evidence to use against me, Mr Eden would be advertising the fact now.'

'That is true.' After a pause, George added, 'How exactly did you acquire a substantial income in so little time?'

'So now you ask me directly? You must be burning with curiosity. Very well, I'll tell you. I doubt you'll share my story with Mr Eden.' Gearhart reached for his wine glass. 'I lodged at a glovemaker's when I arrived in

London. Well, that's not entirely accurate.' He swirled the red wine around in his glass. 'It would be more accurate to say that I killed the glovemaker, took all of the money in his house (since he no longer had a use for it), played with his tools and generally made myself at home until I was able to afford to move here. I made several wise investments that generated money quickly.' He drank from his glass and let out a satisfied sigh. 'Quite a good-mannered old fellow, the glovemaker. I only knocked twice on his door before he admitted me. He was standing there in his nightshirt with a candle, looking ever so concerned – not the least bit suspicious. Asked if I needed a doctor or a policeman, right before I snapped his neck.' Gearhart grinned. 'You deplore my actions. I can see the loathing seething inside you.'

George tried to conceal his disgust. 'Were there no other occupants in the house?'

'An elderly maid and an apprentice. I smothered the old woman in her sleep. I left the apprentice's possessions on the doorstep, along with a note explaining that his master had dismissed him, as he was tired of his carelessness and his propensity to drink. I enclosed a generous reference and a pound note with the letter, so the young man went on his way without incident. It was more efficient than killing him.'

'Why target the house of a defenceless old man? There were other ways to acquire money and shelter.'

Gearhart shrugged. 'Convenience. And I wanted to try my hand at glovemaking and leatherwork.'

'So you could construct your disguise? It is a leather mask you wear. You can hardly see the seams for the powder, and anyone close enough to see them will think they are scars you are anxious to conceal. Anyone wishing not to appear indelicate would never enquire about the matter.'

'Precisely. I did attempt to use human skin but I found it wasn't durable enough.'

'That makes sense.'

'Do you wish to know from where I acquired the skin?' persisted Gearhart, when George seemed content to let the matter rest there.

'You might as well tell me.'

'A criminal. I did, however, manage to utilise his scalp.' Gearhart flicked his hair.

'Was the criminal already dead?'

'Does that make a difference? He would have hanged for his crimes, according to your laws. What is wrong with cutting out the middleman?'

'Every prisoner is entitled to a trial under English law.'

'And you think that serves as "justice"? The outcomes of those trials are sometimes void of logic. A great deal depends on the skill of the solicitor and where the sympathies of the jury lie. Not to mention the number of cases in which crucial evidence is mishandled by the police.'

'I do not pretend that the justice system isn't flawed, but at present there is no better alternative that would be considered viable.'

'I think there is a far more efficient way.'

'I don't object to hearing it.'

'Prevent the crime before it has even occurred. Assess every youth for criminal tendencies, and remove them from society if they are found to possess any. If necessary, they can be put to work doing the most menial of tasks to justify their continued existence.'

'What you suggest is feasible and has its merits, but it would never work in practice.'

'Why not?'

'It is not compatible with human nature. Much like Marx's communist system.'

'Oh, I have devoted a greater deal of thought to this than you might imagine – in fact, that's precisely the key to it: control people's thoughts. Make them believe in the system. Snuff out all opposing voices.'

The maid reappeared and retrieved their empty plates, before sailing out of the room.

'I assume we are still speaking theoretically, Mr Gearhart?' said George.

'Of course.' Gearhart rubbed the stem of his wine glass between his thumb and forefinger. He was clenching a knife in his other hand. 'Maybe you're secretly worried that free labour from criminals would be cheaper than people commissioning you to build them machines?'

'I can't say I am.'

Presently the maid returned with the dessert.

Gearhart spooned chocolate soufflé into his mouth, and a strange, euphoric expression came over his face. He sucked the spoon as he withdrew it from his mouth, with a smack of the lips. 'Mm, I just do not know how you make such perfect soufflé, Anna.'

'Thank you, sir,' she said meekly. Momentarily, she turned her eyes to George's; then she bowed her head again.

Dessert was followed by a post-dinner drink. George was observing a painting on the smoking room wall – a reproduction of Cabanel's *Fallen Angel*. 'Did all of the artworks come with the property?' he enquired of his host.

'Most of them, although that is my own edition. I confess I am intrigued by the figure of Lucifer,' Gearhart replied, offering George a tumbler. 'The strongest and most beautiful and intelligent of God's creations. The perfect being. So much so that he desired to raise his throne "above the stars of God".'

'But his pride corrupted his perfection and ultimately led to his downfall.'

'Yet his principle was sound. He felt himself to be superior to God, and therefore that he should be in charge. His creator made him too perfect, it seems. Me, I'm on Lucifer's side. Why submit to a boss who's your inferior? If only he'd gotten the archangel Michael on his side, then the odds might have been in his favour.'

'Perhaps.' George stared into his tumbler, seeing that it contained whisky and soda. He dared to sip it, and did not find it displeasing, although he then abandoned the glass on the sideboard.

Eventually the evening drew to its natural conclusion.

'Don't be a stranger. I've enjoyed your company,' Gearhart smiled as his guest departed the smoking room.

In the hallway, the maid presented George with his coat. When she spoke, it was as if she were telling him that it was raining outside and he'd require an umbrella. 'He will duel with you. His blade will strike you and blood shall be shed.'

George looked at her sharply. 'Mr Gearhart?'

Her face was unresponsive. She blinked steadily. 'Your greatest enemy.'

George accepted his hat from her. 'What is your full name?'

'Anna Ross, sir.'

'I think you would be wise to find a new situation, Anna.'

She regarded him with unchanged, dull eyes. There was the dim shadow of resignation cast over them of a condemned woman awaiting her fate. George put on his hat and swiftly departed.

Chapter Twenty-Four

Late the next morning, Douglas was on his way to St James's Square. From the outside, Lord Leyton's classical mansion was the same as it had been on his last visit (save that the bronze tigress roaming the lawn now had two small cubs trailing after her). Nor did the visitors' entrance look any different.

A footman led Douglas into an opulent drawing room with blue walls and yellow-gold trimmings, where Lord Leyton was waiting for him. He wore a loose, ruffled lavender shirt paired with narrow, black leather trousers that flared like pagoda sleeves at the ankles. An ornate cross set with a purple stone dangled in the middle of his chest from a long silver chain. The nobleman's slender face was lightly powdered, with a touch of rouge on each cheek and a smudge of black around each eye. His loose blonde hair slipped past his shoulders. What a contrast he made to his brother. Not far from Lord Leyton stood Bellamy, his disturbingly handsome manservant. There was something eerily perfect about his chiselled face and Herculean form. Time did not seem to touch him either: his curling gold locks shone as brightly as ever.

Lord Leyton rose elegantly when Douglas entered. 'My dear Mr Abernathy! It is good to see you!' he exclaimed in his high, well-bred tenor.

Douglas bowed politely. 'I trust you are well, Lord Leyton?'

'Indeed. A great deal has changed since your last visit. I am now nothing less than a duke!'

'I was sorry to hear about your father, my lo—your grace.'

'I wasn't! I thought he'd live forever!' Lord Leyton cried, as if the mere thought terrified him. He flung himself into one of the gold brocade damask chairs. 'Oh, but I have had such bother with the renovations. I have had two architects and neither satisfied me fully, but the work is almost complete now – at long last! I must give you a tour once you are finished with Maestro. And I thank you again for caring for my menagerie while I was abroad last autumn.'

'It was no trouble, Lord Leyton,' Douglas lied, seating himself on the sofa opposite. His patron was still ignorant about Tiberius terrifying the Marsdens.

'I trust you and your brother are well?' enquired the nobleman, as Bellamy served tea.

'Yes, your grace. Business shows no sign of slowing down.'

Lord Leyton twirled his moustache. 'Is your darling sister engaged to that handsome young man of hers yet?'

Douglas shook his head with a faint smile. 'My sister is too busy lecturing on botany to settle.'

Lord Leyton tutted. 'That won't do. Tell them that they can't put it off forever – one is only young for so long.'

Douglas actually doubted that statement. Molly looked as if she'd be fresh-faced forever.

'I remember when your sister and Mr Greenwood created my enchanting rose garden at Beaumont Park. I saw at once that they were absolutely be-*sotted* with each other. I've never seen such a perfect pair! They only had eyes for one another. And weren't you planning on proposing to that delightful girl of yours? The shipbuilder's daughter?'

'It…wasn't meant to be.' Douglas made a mental note to start including ciphers in his letters to Maestro as a habit, since the family's romantic affairs were evidently all relayed to his master, who thirsted for any shred of gossip about someone of his acquaintance.

Lord Leyton sighed exasperatedly and shook his head. 'What is wrong with your family? I swear, if you don't do better I will personally arrange weddings for all three of you. Ah, there you are, Maestro!'

The android stepped into the room. He was dressed in a royal blue morning coat with gold buttons, a dove-grey waistcoat with teal and white check, and dark grey breeches. Sunlight played on his glossy maple casing. 'Master Douglas! I thought I heard your voice!' he exclaimed.

'You'll perceive that Maestro's hearing is as sharp as ever, Mr Abernathy,' Lord Leyton smiled. 'He can hear callers enter from two floors away. It's incredibly useful: if it's someone I don't wish to see, I know before the footman has even entered the room with their card.'

'I can imagine that is very useful, your grace. You seem surprised to see me, Maestro. Surely you knew I'd be coming by to check that you're in working order, as I always do when you return from the Continent?'

'I knew you would be coming by one day soon, Master Douglas. I was not informed of the precise day.'

'Oh, I must have forgotten to tell you it was today, Maestro,' said Lord Leyton vaguely. 'It slipped my mind, what with the renovations and seeing old friends since we're back in London.'

'It's quite all right, Master Josephus. I understand.'

'And we're having guests to dinner this evening, so I'll want you at the piano in the drawing room afterwards. You can keep Mrs Brenner entertained between songs, since she doesn't speak a word of English and it's tiresome having to devote myself to her all evening while her husband flirts with every young lady in the room. Maestro's linguistic skills are amazing, don't you think, Mr Abernathy? He knows French, German and Italian fluently, plus a little Latin and Spanish. I've been acting as his drawing master, and his sketches show much improvement. One thing he can't seem to master is cards – he's always cheating himself.'

'I obey the rules of each game, Master Josephus.'

'But you don't keep your cards close to your chest. You'd think your unreadable face would give you an advantage, or unreadable to someone who doesn't know you, at least. *I* can read you easily. Anyhow, you'd better let Mr Abernathy inspect you.'

Douglas promptly rose. 'Shall we go upstairs to the music room, Maestro? I'll need to observe you play.'

'Of course, Master Douglas.'

'This shouldn't take too long, Lord Leyton, as long as I find nothing serious.'

'Take your time, take your time.' Lord Leyton waved his jewelled hand dismissively. 'You'll find me here when you're finished. I'll tell you all about Maestro's latest triumphs abroad. I tell you, he is a musical Alexander the Great: conquering the world.' He let out a shrill laugh. Douglas had learnt not to ask Lord Leyton directly about his travels. Doing so had once resulted in a narrative that had lasted over an hour.

Douglas walked alongside Maestro up the grand staircase, hearing their footsteps echo. A golden asp slithered around the glass banister. 'How are you, Maestro? Did you enjoy your time abroad?' he asked.

'I did, Master Douglas.'

'I saw reviews of your concerts and your latest opera in the newspapers. The opera is based on the myth of Orpheus but set in the present day, isn't it?'

'That's correct, Master. I feared people would dislike it for that reason, but it has been well received so far.'

'I also gather that you gave private performances to some important persons.'

'Master Josephus used his influence to gain an audience with many great individuals. Is everyone at Ravenfeld Hall well?' Maestro added.

'They are. You must come and visit us soon.'

'Indeed I shall. Is Pirouette still there?' Maestro asked hopefully. 'I've written a waltz that I think she would like to dance to.'

'I'm afraid she's gone back to Italy.'

'Oh, I see. But I'm glad her master's new ballet was a success.'

'I have Signor Paolucci's address if you would like me to post her the sheet music for the waltz? I'm sure they could find someone to play it, although no one as good as the composer himself.'

Maestro's eyes brightened. 'I would appreciate that very much, Master Douglas.'

They reached the second storey and walked along the gilded, white-panelled corridor. A purple sheen was cast on the tiled floor from a door ajar on the left. Maestro must have perceived that it had attracted Douglas's notice, for he pushed the door wide open. Inside was an apartment whose wall panels were encrusted with purple stones. Each sconce and picture frame was barnacled with them. The crystal chairs could have formed in a cave; they were spread with purple velvet throws and had large amethysts set in their backs. The floor was tiled in pale purple marble.

'This is the Amethyst Room,' explained Maestro. 'It was inspired by the famous Amber Room at Catherine Palace, near St Petersburg.'

'It's quite a spectacular sight!'

'The Amethyst Room is reserved for entertaining distinguished guests, or at least it will be when it is finished. Master Josephus wants a ceiling fresco.'

'These renovations must have been costly. Then again, I suppose Lord Leyton's inheritance will more than cover the expense.'

'I believe the inheritance that Master Josephus received from his father was considerable, although he has quoted several different figures to me, so I'm unsure as to its exact amount.'

As far as Lord Leyton was concerned, money was something that was always there, just as air and water were. But there had been rumours, shortly before his father's death, that he was in debt – not that Douglas suspected his patron of hurrying the old duke's demise. Maestro's royalties went to Lord Leyton, since he was legally his property, but Maestro had said that his master put the money aside in an account for him and never touched it. (Lord Leyton had a difficult time persuading Maestro to spend it on himself and not give it to charity.)

'The music room is much the same,' continued Maestro as they walked on. 'Master Josephus wanted to extend it to three times its original size, but I assured him that that wasn't necessary. I did concede to having bookshelves erected, as he suggested. I'd acquired quite a few books but had nowhere to put them, except on the floor, which was hardly suitable.'

The music room was Maestro's chamber. On entering, Douglas had an odd impression of interrupting an assembly, what with all the instruments positioned about the room. (The saxophone in the corner was a new addition.) A circular rug with a celestial pattern covered most of the floor.

Maestro swiftly shut the door behind them and looked at Douglas with imploring eyes. 'Master Douglas, I must ask you about that letter you sent me, in which you asked me to get Master Josephus to talk about his brother. Was my transcript useful?' he asked urgently.

'Very much so.'

'I confess it troubles me to imagine the activities in which Lord Charles is involved. I've only met him once or twice, but the impression I received of his character was not a good one. Master Josephus's eldest niece came to stay with us not long ago, after it was discovered that she had been maintaining a correspondence with a Count Castaldi while she was engaged to another man, Lord Romford. She feared facing her father, so she turned to her uncle, who took her in at once. Miss Diana has never been frightened of me and likes to hear me play, so I kept her company. She had only been here two days when her father arrived unannounced, demanding to see her. Miss Diana was too frightened to face him alone, so Master Josephus went with her. I was also present, at Miss Diana's insistence. She became possessed by an idea that the brothers might duel, and when I failed to dismiss that idea from her mind, I agreed to observe them from a distance. Miss Diana and I watched them face each other across the hall. I can recall almost every word of their exchange:

'"You cannot hinder me from taking my daughter home, Josephus."

'"She came to me, Charles. She said you threatened to disown her."

'"I said I'd have reasonable grounds to disown her, not that I would. I only wished to make her reflect on her actions."

'"You frightened the poor girl out of her wits!" Master Josephus's eyes have a steely look when he's serious, and they had that look then. His brother's eyes are always like that.

'"There is time yet to salvage the situation," Lord Charles said. "Lord Romford's family were more than understanding at the interview I had with them this morning."

'"You are hindering the course of true love, Charles."

'"This is your fault for filling Diana's head with romantic nonsense, although that *sensation* trash she reads no doubt contributed to this mischief."

'"At least I have some notion of romance."

'"I am very fond of my wife, not that it is any of your business."

'"And who introduced you to her? Oh yes – it was *me*."

'They argued for some minutes. Eventually Lord Charles compelled his daughter to return with him.

'"But you come back here whenever you wish, Diana," Master Josephus whispered to her before she went.

'Her father looked at me in a most unpleasant manner as he left, and said to his brother, "Why do you keep that thing around, Josephus? If you have any sense, you'll dispose of it. I don't want to hear that it's smothered you in your sleep one night." Then he took Miss Diana's arm and marched out of the front door. I do believe that my master is truly fond of his brother, despite Lord Charles's criticism of him, but I'm unsure whether the sentiment is returned.'

'Hmm. That is not a pleasant picture of the man. I'll be honest with you, Maestro: he's actually one of the founders of the SOAL.'

'He is?'

'Along with two other men, although one is dead now. But your master can't know, or he'll immediately tell the whole of London, and there's no guessing how Lord Charles and his associate would retaliate. Do you understand?'

'I do, but is Master Josephus in any danger?'

'No, you have my word. He's not one of their main targets. Besides, you should be more concerned for yourself.'

'I understand, Master. I know what the SOAL will do if they capture me.' Maestro's eyes were on the fireplace.

'They won't ever have the chance, I promise you that,' said Douglas firmly. He tried to give Maestro a reassuring smile. 'Anyway, come sit on this chair and I'll examine you.'

Maestro complied with the request.

'So, have you had any problems recently?' Douglas raised Maestro's arm and flexed his elbow.

'A couple of my finger joints have become slightly loose, but it is no great trouble, Master Douglas.'

'We'll soon fix that. Any cracks in your casing?'

'No, only a few minor scratches.'

'Excellent.' Douglas thought he sounded the way Theo must when he tended to his patients. He was meant to call on him at his surgery that afternoon; Douglas had brought his helmet and oxygen tank to show him, since Theo had expressed interest in them. Theo sometimes passed on medical journals to Douglas when he encountered new discoveries concerning the structure of joints or muscles that might aid the design of his automata. Douglas had once accompanied Theo to an autopsy, too. It had been an informative yet disturbing experience to watch the dead criminal on the table be meticulously dissected. Now Douglas tightened Maestro's loose finger joints and asked him to improvise on a couple of instruments. He noticed some sheet music scattered on top of the piano.

'That's an unfinished sonata that I've titled *The Rose Garden*,' explained Maestro. 'It's intended to be a love song. I started writing it in the rose garden at Beaumont Park, shortly before Master Josephus and I left England last summer.'

'You say it's a love song?'

'Yes, Master: almost like a duet between lovers. The sonata is for violin and piano.'

'Would you care to play it, Maestro? You can remain at the piano – I can play the violin tolerably well.'

'Of course, Master Douglas.'

It had been years since he'd played the violin, but Douglas remembered how to position his fingers, and he could follow the sheet music reasonably well after studying it for five minutes first. Each note bloomed from the piano like a luscious rose. Douglas fancied he could hear Molly and Arthur in the piece. There was a tension between the two instruments' voices, but also harmony and intimacy in places. 'Did you compose this while the rose garden was being planted?' he asked after the song ended.

'As a matter of fact, yes, Master.'

Apparently Lord Leyton hadn't been the only one observing the pair over those two days.

'Well, I'm satisfied that you're in perfect working order. But I'd just like to have a peek inside your head and chest to make sure everything is working as it ought to be.'

Maestro nodded. 'Of course, Master.'

The brass cylinder in Maestro's chest controlled his motor functions, while the one in his head was responsible for cognition, creative thought and memory. George and Douglas had since refined and shrunk the technology so that one cylinder could perform both functions, fitting neatly inside an android's head. The panel in the back of Maestro's head was opened by a sliding mechanism that was hard to spot, unless you knew to look for it. When Douglas examined the core cylinder, his eyes widened. Some of Maestro's parts had established new pathways. These weren't the minor adjustments formed through learning new skills, either: they were complex. Maestro's mind was evolving. In fact, it looked as if…no, surely *that* couldn't have been inhibited?

Douglas closed Maestro's head and sat opposite him. The android's brown eyes followed him keenly. 'Maestro, have you ever…disobeyed your master's orders? I'm not trying to catch you out, I just want an honest answer.'

Maestro lowered his eyes. 'Once or twice, although I didn't mean to do so,' he replied eventually.

'Can you remember when?'

'When we were in Paris a few months ago, Master Josephus gave me some pocket money to buy what I liked while we were out shopping, but he told me not to give a franc of it to beggars or street performers. Only, I saw a girl who was so thin, and with such sad eyes, that something compelled me to give her a few francs.'

'And when else?'

'Master Josephus ordered me to tell him if his hair was growing greyer, and, knowing how it upsets him to hear that it is, I lied and said no. I did wonder how I'd managed it, and I have pondered the matter often since then. I haven't been able to do it again, though. Does this mean that I'm broken?'

'No, Maestro. From what I saw inside your head just now, I'd say that your mind is continuing to develop beyond what I believed it to be capable of. If I'm right, and this continues, you'll have free will.'

'What do you mean by "free will", Master Douglas?'

'You'll no longer have to obey every command you're given. You can make your own decisions.' Douglas glanced around the room until his eyes landed on the open violin case with the instrument and bow inside. 'Drop your violin out of the window, Maestro.'

Maestro blinked hard. 'I beg your pardon, Master?'

'Drop your violin out of the window.'

Maestro retrieved the instrument. He gazed at it for a few seconds, before crossing the room and opening the sash window. He dangled the violin out of the window, his arm shaking violently. But when he looked as though he was about to uncurl his fingers from the violin's neck, he retracted his arm sharply and closed the sash. He pressed the violin to his chest. 'I cannot do it, Master Douglas. I simply cannot.'

'I'm glad, Maestro.' Douglas smiled. 'You've proven me right. I didn't think you would be able to bring yourself to destroy your favourite instrument.'

Maestro regarded his violin thoughtfully for a moment. 'So this is what it is to have free will?'

'It is. You don't need anyone to tell you how to behave. I'm not saying that you should deliberately disobey every order you're given, but you don't have to follow orders you feel aren't right.' Douglas could have adjusted Maestro's impulse regulator to stop it being inhibited, but he didn't feel the need to. However, he did wonder if Maestro was the only android capable of this evolution. Two things set him apart from their other models: he was the first sentient android they'd ever built, and George alone had constructed his mind. There might be things that George had included that Douglas didn't know about. After all, Maestro wasn't meant to be as advanced as George had made him: the wager with Lord Leyton had been to build an android that could compose music, not one that could think for itself. Douglas made a mental note to ask his brother about it.

'Master Douglas?' said Maestro, after he'd returned the violin to its case. 'What would you have done had I not disobeyed your order?'

'I'd have stopped you before you let the violin fall.'

'I'm glad of it.'

Douglas noticed a white door at the end of the room that he didn't recall seeing before. Maestro followed his gaze and opened the door, revealing a miniature library with bookshelves lining the walls. Two red velvet chairs and a small table stood in the middle of the room.

'The "bookshelves",' explained Maestro, looking as sheepish as was possible for him. 'Admittedly, Master Josephus deceived me.'

All the way home, Douglas considered what he'd seen inside Maestro's head. If George had done it intentionally, Douglas hadn't the faintest clue why. What logical reason was there for it? George wouldn't have introduced what he would've seen as unnecessary risk into an already complex machine; nor did he care about Maestro's liberty. But then another idea presented itself: what if Mademoiselle Roux-Voclain had done something to Maestro when she'd stolen him to examine all those years ago? She might very well have been capable of it. She certainly had the motive to either ruin Douglas and George's credibility or simply see what their androids were capable of.

Peregrine was caught in another light rain shower as they flew over Holtbury. Douglas wedged the sheet music for Pirouette between the pages of the medical journal he'd received from Theo. He placed them inside his coat for protection before sprinting from the stables to the front door. (Why did he have the feeling that he'd forgotten something?) The clocks chimed six times as he entered the north hall. The clock tower's bell rang above them all, bidding them cease their pathetic noise in the face of a superior authority. Douglas patted his coat and found that it was slightly damp, although the sheet music and the journal were dry. He'd have to try to find Signor Paolucci's latest address amongst the papers on his desk in his study.

The sound of liquid being poured into a glass made Douglas look in the direction of the dining room. George was reading at the foot of the dining table. In front of him was a quarter-full tumbler and a bottle of brandy. Douglas felt as if his heart had suddenly turned to ice. No, not after all these years George had fought to keep sober.

'George?'

His brother had been gazing out of the window, but turned his head on hearing Douglas's address. 'Is something the matter?' George enquired, sounding oddly calm.

'I was going to ask you the same.'

'Nothing concerning you.' George emptied the tumbler in one swallow.

Oh God, thought Douglas, as he watched his brother refill the glass. He's slipped back to how he was before. Has he been doing this a while and never been caught in the act until now? 'No, you're not shrugging me off this time. Tell me what's wrong,' he said firmly.

George turned a page of his book. 'I can't.'

'Why not?'

'Because you don't need to know.'

'Is this something to do with Mr Gearhart?'

'You don't need to know that either.'

'So it is?'

'I didn't say that.'

'Why are you always so damn cryptic? George, I don't trust that man, and I suspect you don't either.'

George trained his eyes on the book.

'What did he say when you dined with him? Did he threaten you?'

'No.'

'Did he ask you to work for him?'

'No.'

'Is there…something else going on between you?'

'*No.*'

'Well, what is it, then? Please, tell me.'

George looked up. 'Parasite,' he said drily, before taking a sip of brandy. He fixed his eyes on his brother as he drank.

'Parasite?' Douglas echoed.

'Yes: you've been clinging to me your entire life. Even now I have to come to your rescue, like at the presentation dinner. I've wasted a great deal of time and energy trying to protect and tutor you, but you still have to turn to me for guidance.'

Douglas stared at him in disbelief.

But George was relentless. 'And even when I tell you the answers, you fail to comprehend what I'm saying.'

The clocks ticked five times before Douglas responded. 'I suspected you always thought me an idiot.'

'I didn't say you were.'

'You as good as did.'

'You've misunderstood me, unsurprisingly.'

'I understand you perfectly. Keep your secrets. I'll leave you to drink yourself into oblivion in peace.' Douglas suited the action to the word. He understood George's meaning perfectly.

George waited until Douglas had left the room, then he pushed the tumbler away disdainfully. Just that half-glass had made him feel physically ill. The brandy had burned his throat and chest in its wake, and even now he felt its smouldering warmth. But the deception was necessary. Douglas couldn't get too close to the truth or he might meet the same fate as Mr Crowther. Douglas was vastly more intelligent than Crowther, but he could be impetuous. If he confronted Gearhart alone, he'd almost certainly be killed. Better to lead his thoughts down another path. And…it would be easier this way, if George's premonition about the near future was correct.

I'm still trying to protect my little brother after all these years, he reflected.

Chapter Twenty-Five

Molly and Arthur were in the meadow hideaway. On this occasion they were working, albeit on separate tasks. Arthur was sitting at the bureau writing a letter to a client, with an enclosed sketch of a garden. Molly occupied the table, writing lecture notes (even though she frequently deviated from her script when lecturing and went off on a tangent). The scratching of pens, the rustling of paper and the ticking of the mantle clock filled the room. Occasionally a log on the fire snapped and spat cinders. Molly sensed a strange heaviness in the air, like before a storm. It was probably only in her mind.

'Do you want me to fly you to the station later?' she said.

'I suppose it would save time,' Arthur muttered.

How indifferent he was to the prospect of travelling by air now, she thought. His first few flights in the airship had been a bit of an ordeal. But he'd persisted, and on the third attempt they'd actually made it to their destination – with Molly instructing him all the way to breathe deeply and count to ten. He was far better now, although sometimes he accidentally looked down at the world below, and then his face would turn chalk white. Molly tried to keep him talking whenever she sensed that he was gripped by terror.

'Well, it's certainly faster than walking to Holtbury station, like we did last week. You can't afford to miss your train this time and delay your site visit by a day. Sir Fusspot will throw a fit.'

'Very true…'

Molly caught a glimpse of Arthur out of the corner of her eye. He was sitting upright with his back to her, pen in hand, but his eyes were adrift. One moment he was looking out of the window, then at the floor, then at the crackling fire. Anywhere but at her, it seemed. She returned to her task and let him take his time. At last she heard his pen clatter on the bureau top, and he cleared his throat.

'Molly?'

'Yes?'

'What are you keeping from me?'

Molly's heart jumped. She put down her notes and stared at him. Arthur was twisted around in his chair so that he could face her. 'What do you mean?' she asked.

'There's been a change in you recently. You always look as if you've been up all night, you're absent-minded on occasion, and sometimes you won't let me touch you at all. You can't deny it.' His voice quavered as he fought to check his emotion. It wasn't anger Molly sensed from him; more like a fearful nervousness.

'You're right,' she said after a pause. 'I won't deny it.'

Arthur got to his feet and dragged his chair beside hers. He sank back into it and struggled to look her in the eye. 'Be honest, Molly. Have you…?' He swallowed. 'Have you fallen in love with someone else?'

Molly's green eyes hardened as she stared at him. 'Are you seriously asking me that question?'

'Well, it would explain everything. The charming Mr Rose is still fond of you, for one thing.'

'Arthur—'

'And there was that entomology student who asked you to accompany him to Lyme last summer.'

'For God's sake, Arthur! Do you really think I'd be that disloyal? That I'd be having secret rendezvous behind your back?'

'Well, what other conclusion am I to reach?' he retorted, maintaining his pride.

'You have no imagination, do you?'

'Apparently I have too much imagination, since I'm fearing that you have a secret lover.'

'Well, you can forget that idea right now.' She balled her fists. 'There is only you for me. There's no one else in the world who compares to you – no one.' She spoke the words with such passion that she almost sounded angry, although her expression suddenly softened. She was surprised at having made such an honest declaration – at having finally made manifest what she'd already known to be true. The fact that Arthur was the only man for her was so obvious to her that she'd never given it much thought.

Arthur blinked. 'Are you finally saying that you love me?'

'What do you mean, "finally"?'

'You never say that you do.'

'I shouldn't need to. It's obvious enough, isn't it?'

'It would still be nice to hear it every once in a while.'

'Fine. *I love you.* I'll make sure to say it three times a month from now on.'

Arthur realised that the main issue was slipping from his mind. He was so overcome by Molly's declaration of love that he'd almost forgotten what it was for which he'd been demanding an explanation. 'But that still doesn't explain your strange behaviour. If it's not a secret lover that you're hiding, then what is it? It can't be something to do with Mr Kellogg's letter, since this has been going on for a while now.'

'Fine, I'll tell you.' Molly adjusted the angle of her chair so that they were facing each other squarely. It took her a moment to begin speaking. 'I've been experimenting with a poisonous substance that I created accidentally. It has some very strong side effects, but it has extraordinary benefits too, like accelerated healing. I cut my hand on shards of glass and the wounds healed almost instantly. It also allows me to control all plant life within a certain radius. I can…talk to plants, for lack of a better word, and grow them seemingly from nothing.'

'But what are the strong side effects?'

'Madness: the desire to hurt, to kill. I'm not myself when I use it – there's something in it that amplifies violent passions, as if I've been bitten by a rabid dog. It also drains me to use the powers the poison grants me. And…the reason I don't let you touch me sometimes is because the poison still lingers in my blood after I use it. I calculated that for as long as twelve hours after use, any contact with me could cause serious harm or even death. I refrained from kissing and touching you solely for your own sake, in case I poisoned you.' Molly hugged her chest, gripping her arms tightly. 'But I thought that if I could overcome the poison's influence on my mind and maintain my sanity, then I could explore those new abilities. I mean, being able to actually *communicate* with plants opens up all sorts of possibilities for furthering our understanding of the natural world, doesn't it? The poison could even lead to the development of new medical treatments, given its healing power.'

It took Arthur a moment to comprehend everything she had just told him. 'How could you have been so foolish as to put yourself through these experiments? To keep risking death with each use of this poison?' he demanded.

'I know it was foolish and that I shouldn't have kept experimenting with it. But I made progress. I learnt to control myself after taking it. Now I can use it without fear of inflicting pain on anyone.'

Arthur took her firmly by the shoulders. 'Molly, listen to me. Please promise me that you'll stop using this poison. Even if you think you've mastered it, with something that powerful, the slightest mistake could lead to disaster. You're playing with fire and you know it.'

'I know how strong a concentration to take. The effects only last several minutes.'

'I wasn't just talking about killing yourself by taking too much. I meant that you might hurt someone you care about without meaning to. If what you've said is true, the slightest touch might do it. Say someone gets hold of you unexpectedly and is poisoned? You'll have to carry that guilt for the rest of your life.'

He expected her to retaliate and tell him that he didn't know what he was talking about. But she only looked at him with clear, honest eyes.

'You're right. I've been so cautious up to now, controlling my environment and everything, that I didn't consider every scenario.'

'I know you were trying to be careful, but you can never eliminate the risk entirely. And what if you were to suffer a sudden bout of madness? How easy would it be to lash out at someone in anger? To simply take a knife and plunge it into them before you realised what you were doing?'

'I always conducted the experiments late at night or early in the morning, when I knew that everyone was either asleep or busy downstairs. At first I even locked myself in the laboratory and fastened a chain to my ankle to keep myself from escaping.'

'Good God, Molly…'

'I know it seems drastic, but those are the lengths I went to in order to make sure I didn't hurt anyone. I kept the experiments a secret because I didn't want any of you to worry about what I was doing.'

Arthur shook his head. 'You scientists. You'll stop at nothing to make your discoveries. Were you thinking of writing your next book on this? Such a groundbreaking discovery as being able to talk to plants would certainly get you a teaching post at your pick of university.'

'I still don't understand it fully. And…maybe something this powerful and deadly should remain a secret.'

'I agree. It can be *our* secret. But I know you have more sense than to toy with death. You always say that Douglas never considers the risks involved when testing his new vehicles – you don't want to give him the upper hand, do you?' Arthur asked more playfully.

Molly smiled. 'Now that would be unforgivable.'

'So you'll promise to stop using the poison?'

'I promise.' Molly meant it. She felt immense relief now that she'd told Arthur everything. The secret of the experiments had been starting to crush her.

'What do they talk about?' said Arthur, after a moment's silence.

'Who?'

'Plants.'

'Mostly the weather – you can tell they're English plants.' Molly chuckled along with him. 'But did you really think that Samuel was my secret lover?'

'Well, women find him very charming. And he's ridiculously rich – far more so than I could ever hope to be.'

'Oh. Well, now you've drawn that fact to my attention, I'll definitely succumb to his advances… I'm joking, Arthur. For God's sake, don't look so worried.'

'I knew you weren't being serious, but it was alarming to hear you say it all the same.'

'Some women might find Samuel charming, but he tests my patience at times. Even more than you do.'

'At least that's one advantage I have over him.'

'You have a great many advantages over most of the men I've ever encountered.'

Arthur couldn't help smiling at her. 'Are you still too toxic to touch, or can I kiss you?'

Molly grinned. 'Maybe wait an hour or two.' That would give them time to finish their work, and would serve as a punishment for Arthur doubting her fidelity.

Chapter Twenty-Six

'What do you think?' Dick was showing Douglas his latest wares at Cullwick & Son's London office. The glasses in this new collection were all infused with butterflies. He'd combined his business with his pleasure.

Douglas peered at a blue butterfly embedded in a wine glass. 'Are these painted or real?'

'Both. The ones with real insects in them are more expensive, for collectors like me. I've already got orders from members of my club. Their wives are wild for them.'

'Or are they wild at their husbands for spending money on something so bizarre?'

'I kindly ask you to refrain from insulting my work,' Dick smiled. He was tall, with wiry dark curls and a delicate moustache. He had the kind of cheekbones and jawline that young women wrote about in their diaries after balls, although that softness of face and figure he'd had as a boy was starting to return.

'How did you accomplish this, anyway? Keep the insects from being reduced to ash during the glass-blowing process?' Douglas asked.

Dick grinned. 'I had quite a clever little idea. There's a thin layer of glass on the inside, and the butterflies are trapped between that and the outer layer.' He indicated the inside of a gold-rimmed sherry glass with a peacock butterfly on its side. 'Same with the butterflies in the bases. I had the bases made slightly thinner, then added a thin glass disc of the same circumference, with the butterfly pressed between the base and the disc.'

'I admit that is very clever.'

'Might I interest you in one? Free of charge, of course.'

'I suppose so. It'll certainly get guests talking at dinner.' Douglas selected a champagne flute with a tortoiseshell butterfly in the base. Poor thing, entombed in glass forever. The champagne flute would go into the sideboard with the good china they never used. 'How do you kill a butterfly? Put it in a jar and suffocate it?'

'You pinch its thorax.'

Douglas winced slightly. 'A quick death, at least. Must be difficult to get hold of them in the right place.'

'I've had a lot of practice at it.'

'I expect you have.'

Dick cut a cigar. 'Anyway, you'll be coming to dinner on Saturday evening?'

'Of course.'

Dick was overly fond of lavish dinners; it was no wonder that he'd gained a couple of pounds recently. (Douglas remained lean no matter how much or little he ate. He had waistcoats from ten years ago that still fitted him perfectly.)

'Good. You look like you need a break – you have dark circles under your eyes. Racing to finish a commission on time?'

'A very important one, as a matter of fact. But I should have it finished by Saturday.'

'Then think of the dinner as a reward for your hard work. There'll be quite a good crowd attending. And the Marsdens will be there.' Dick tossed out this comment casually as he fiddled to strike a match, but he gave Douglas a meaningful look.

'What? No! Dick, I can't—'

Dick wagged a finger in his friend's face. 'You can still mend things between you and Clara if you try.'

'I told you what happened—'

'What does it matter if a couple of your androids ran amok at dinner? It was an accident.'

'Her mother fainted with terror. They'll never forgive me for that night.'

'Explain yourself to Clara, make her forgive you, and then she'll work on her family.' Dick concluded this pronouncement by managing to light the match. The hissing tongue of flame died down almost instantly, and he offered the remaining feeble fire to the cigar.

'It's not that simple, Dick.'

'It is. I've seen worse cases in which engagements threatened to fall through, but it all worked out in the end. There's nothing to be lost by trying.'

Dick had a point: what was there to be lost? Things couldn't get any worse. That said, Douglas had started to convince himself that George and Molly were right: Clara wasn't destined for him. But if that was so, then a final encounter would determine it. He'd never be left in doubt then.

'Fine. I'll come.'

'Your brother and sister too?'

'Yes, they'll agree. But don't make matches for them.'

'I'll behave, I swear.'

'What about you? Will there ever be a Mrs Cullwick, or are you determined to break the heart of every young lady in England?'

'Oh, they forget me soon enough. I don't break their hearts.'

'You're an outrageous flirt, Dick.'

Dick winked through the curling cigar smoke. 'I do nothing. Women flock to me.'

'Like a prize ram. Don't ruin any poor girl's reputation,' Douglas warned, half-seriously.

'I'm not as much of a scoundrel as that!'

'No, but you're not always a perfect gentleman either.' Although most girls found Dick quite charming and flirted back. More than once, Douglas had seen a girl looking at Dick with the handle of her fan to her lips – or with the open fan in front of her face, the handle clasped in her right hand. Ten minutes later, he'd spy Dick and the girl kissing passionately in an archway, or he'd overhear Dick making love to her in the conservatory. Douglas couldn't help being a little envious of his friend, but he knew that he could never be so brazen with a woman in the middle of a crowded ballroom as Dick was. 'I don't suppose you've managed to persuade Theo to attend Saturday's dinner?' he asked.

'You can't be serious? Theo won't attend any gathering where there'll be more than five people, and unless he knows them intimately he won't utter a word. Introduce a new person into the mix and he won't say more than "Good evening" to them.'

'I know how shy he can be. It takes a while to pry him open.'

'You managed it fairly easily.'

'I hit upon subjects that I thought would interest him.'

Dick shook his head. 'You put people at ease, Douglas. You've always had a talent for it. It's why you're good at the selling side of business – you make people trust you.'

'I don't *make* them trust me.'

'Not on purpose – you do it without even realising. It comes naturally.' Dick grinned through a cloud of cigar smoke. 'Are you sure you're not tempted to come and work for me as an agent?'

Douglas smiled apologetically. 'I'm afraid not.'

Dick shrugged. 'Anyway, I did send Theo a courtesy invitation so that he doesn't think we've forgotten him. He replied that such an event wasn't to his liking. Didn't even make a false excuse. He'll have a pleasant night in his own company, reading his books and medical journals,' he added somewhat sarcastically.

'That doesn't sound too unpleasant, actually.'

'My God, man! You're both dry, dusty old men! Truth be told, I'm rather glad Theo declined to come. The one time I coaxed him into society, he sat in his chair near the window, looking uncomfortable all night. He was too embarrassed to ask my cousin, Shelley – Miss Grayson – to dance, even though I knew she'd caught his eye. Then he started doctoring the guests. The old ladies rambled on about their aching this and that. Theo just sat there nodding and recommending various treatments to them.'

Douglas could envision the owlish Theo 'doctoring' the old ladies in the card room, and chuckled to himself at the thought. Theo's honesty and devotion to his profession made him rather a bore to some people. But he was good company when he warmed to you. He was more loquacious and relaxed when he devoted his energy to only one other person. Douglas had even got him to laugh, when it was just the two of them at Theo's residence on Harley Street. 'It's different with patients,' Theo had told him once. 'You know precisely what to say and what course of action to take. But at a social occasion, it's very complicated.'

Dick packed away the glassware in a wooden box filled with straw. 'Oh, and Mr Gearhart will be attending the dinner too.'

Douglas almost dropped the champagne flute he was still holding. 'Did you say Mr Gearhart?'

'Yes. He's a friend of yours, isn't he?'

'I hardly know him, to tell the truth. I've met him only twice.'

'Well, he said you were well acquainted.'

'*He* said?'

'I met him at the bank the other day. It was rather a stroke of good luck, as it turns out. Remarkable fellow! Seems immensely clever, but he's got a sharp wit too. So I invited him, what with him saying that you were friends.'

'I think George is better acquainted with him than I am.'

'Your brother has made a friend? He's worse than Theo when it comes to company!' Dick knew Douglas well enough to get away with directing such an insult at George. Besides, it was true.

'I know it's hard to believe, but apparently so. He even dined with Mr Gearhart last week.'

'Hmm. Well, there was a spare place at the table in need of filling, since Theo declined and all my other male acquaintances had previous engagements. I was going to put Theo next to my cousin to try to encourage them to talk, but seeing as he's abstaining, I put you next to her instead.'

'You planned this before even inviting me?'

'It doesn't hurt to plan ahead. I had your sister on your other side and then your brother beside her. I can change things around if you're not happy?'

'I have no preference, really,' Douglas shrugged. 'I'm surprised you didn't put me next to Clara.'

'Oh, she's beside her brother. It's more subtle that way.'

'Then how am I supposed to speak to her?'

'Make an opportunity. You're clever, you'll find an opening.'

Douglas kept his eyes on the tortoiseshell butterfly and ran his finger along the champagne flute, leaving a faint smear on the glass. Fear knotted inside him. Not only was he going to have to find a way to speak to Clara before her brother could drag her away, but he knew he'd be keeping an eye on Gearhart the entire evening too. He'd feel more reassured if George refused to attend, but if George knew that Gearhart would be there, there might be little chance of that happening. Douglas told himself that there was probably nothing to worry about. Perhaps it was simply childish jealousy. Or maybe he was right about Mr Gearhart, and Dick meeting him at the bank had been no chance encounter.

As soon as Douglas arrived home, he deposited the champagne flute in the monumental monstrosity of a sideboard that stood imposingly in the dining room. (All sorts of elaborate shapes were cut into the sideboard's sturdy oak body, and they looked like menacing faces if one turned the gas lamps low.) Then he dared to search for George. He'd not shared his concerns about George resuming his old habits with Dick, who'd have brushed it off and asked what was wrong with a chap having the odd glass of spirits every now and then. But George would rarely stop at a single glass. Back in Soho, he'd often crashed into their room at one o'clock in the morning, smelling like an accident at a brewery. Douglas had pretended to still be asleep, but then, once George had drifted off, he'd rolled over to check what state his brother was in and make sure that the chamber pot was beside his bed. When George had little money, he'd resort to a bottle of cheap gin so strong that one unaccustomed to spirits could become intoxicated from a mere whiff of its contents. (Douglas had never been particularly fond of spirits; he'd always preferred a pint of ale.)

Douglas hadn't actually caught George in the act again since that time in the dining room, but his brother had grown very sullen and his eyes always looked tired. And he snapped at Douglas whenever he tried to touch on the subject of the empty, unlabelled bottles he'd found lying about his study. That was sufficiently compelling evidence. That morning they'd had a fierce argument during breakfast, after Douglas had enquired for the third time about George's evening with Mr Gearhart, and George had once again rebuffed his questions. The argument had leapt from the issue of George's secretive, reticent behaviour to numerous other grievances – chiefly the mysterious bottles – and Douglas's preoccupation with social engagements.

'You're lacking focus, Douglas. You're too absorbed in your friends and still pining for a woman who didn't even care for you.' Now, that had stung.

'At least I have friends. At least I've experienced love. I dare say you're jealous.'

'Hardly – it's a lot of needless bother. What good has "love" done you, anyway? It's only brought you pain.'

'Would you say the same to Molly?'

'She remains dedicated to her work. And despite your predictions, she still has not wed Mr Greenwood.'

'I'm sure she has her reasons for not doing so yet. And it's different in Molly's case.'

'Nevertheless, you could learn from her example. I'm tired of having to do the majority of our work when you're absent.'

'I'm never gone for that long.'

'I think your dedication is not what it once was.'

'And I think you simply can't stand to see me finding enjoyment in something you cannot understand!'

George had actually looked slightly wounded for a fraction of a second, but then he'd become stiff and impenetrable. His composure intact, he'd left the dining room without another word. On reflection, Douglas thought that his last remark had been rather cruel. And he realised that he'd been viewing the situation in reverse: George wasn't jealous of him for having friends when he didn't; he was jealous of Dick and Theo (and, at one time, Clara) because they were stealing his brother from him.

It took Douglas some effort to swallow his pride as he approached George's study. He didn't wait for an answer to his knock, and walked in to find George writing at his desk. There was a calm air about him.

'Yes?' George didn't look up.

'Dick has invited the three of us to dinner on Saturday.'

'I suppose you accepted on our behalf?'

'I did, although the agreement isn't binding. Mr Gearhart will be there…and the Marsdens.'

George's pen paused. 'Are you sure you wish to attend if that's the case?'

'The chances were I'd run into Clara at some point or another.'

'I'll attend. I'm certain Molly will too. What is being served at this dinner?'

'Lobster and rice.'

'That is fine.'

Douglas noticed how steady George's hand was as he resumed writing. He hadn't been drinking recently. He sensed no danger that George's temper would boil over. 'I'm sorry for what I said this morning.'

'It is not worth apologising for.' (It had been easy for George to fake a rage, since some of what he'd said was his honest opinion.) 'We'll have to finish that viscount's order sooner if we are to lose Saturday night. Can you see to it?'

'I will.' Douglas left the study and shut the door softly behind him. He had something else in need of completion first, so Viscount von Orndorff's flame-spitting gold dragon would have to wait a short while.

Chapter Twenty-Seven

Molly's birthday had been a peaceful day, with no one making any demands on her. In the afternoon she'd passed an enjoyable couple of hours painting, and made use of the paintbox George had bought her. It was rather beautiful; he had truly outdone himself. Douglas had got her Elizabeth Gaskell's new book, *Sylvia's Lovers*, and a gardening tool with three different functions that he'd made himself. Betsey had made her a pair of gardening gloves from white leather and embroidered green corduroy. Samuel had sent a very pretty paper lace card with an ornate verse at its centre that was surrounded by a silk garland of forget-me-nots. Arthur had ignored her warning to get her only a single present, his excuse being that they were only small things and thus equivalent to one large present – they'd have fitted easily inside the paintbox. Molly hadn't wanted to argue with him on her birthday, so she'd let it lie. A fine dinner had been partaken of in the evening, and Betsey had been permitted to join the family at table. Molly and Arthur had then enjoyed a particularly passionate night in her room. Afterwards, he had lain in her arms while she idly sculpted his hair (she loved how thick and malleable his hair was). The pouring rain outside and the roaring fire inside had intensified the cosy intimacy of the scene.

Since it had rained throughout Molly's actual birthday, she and Arthur had delayed their picnic in the meadow until the following day. They'd both been fully prepared for a letter from Arthur's father to arrive that morning, since Mr Greenwood knew that his son was at Ravenfeld Hall 'on business'. And one did. Arthur read it as they were finishing breakfast, then got swiftly to his feet, crossed the dining room and tossed it in the fire.

He grinned at Molly as he resumed his seat. 'If my father asks, I'll say I'd already concluded my business and was on my way home by the time his letter arrived here.'

That afternoon they took a blanket and a wicker basket to the meadow and sat at the top of the slope, which offered a peaceful panorama of the estate. Betsey and Gwyneth had prepared the picnic for them. (They could tell that Gwyneth had cut the bread, as the slices were jagged. At least each slice was of a roughly similar thickness – another sign of improvement.) But the apple and blackberry pie was Molly's work. After they were suitably full, they lay on the slope talking. They watched the sun gradually sink until the gold light caught them, forcing them to retreat downhill. An island of trees stood in the middle of the meadow; clusters of spring flowers had recently emerged around their roots. A purple haze of bluebells threatened to spread into the meadow grass from the edges of the island.

Arthur was still fishing grit from the blackberries out of his teeth with his tongue. The pie had been worth it, though; Molly was an excellent cook when she had the inclination to be. 'Did the picnic live up to your expectations?' he asked.

'It did. I'm still amazed you ignored your father's summons,' Molly laughed.

'The alternative was to miss your birthday. Not a chance!'

'Technically, my birthday was yesterday.'

'But you'd never have forgiven me if I'd left to go to Newbury, would you?'

'Never.'

Arthur curled his arm around her narrow waist. She didn't hesitate to let him touch her any more – not since she'd ended her experiments with the poison. He shuddered whenever he thought about it. But it was behind them now.

'I did enjoy my actual birthday too,' Molly added.

'Good. I know I certainly enjoyed last night.' Arthur smiled wickedly.

'Do you remember your suggestion, just before we went to sleep? That we should go to the Lake District for a week at the end of the academic year, once the viscountess's garden is complete?' said Molly.

'I do. You seemed unsure about it.'

'I think we should do it. There's no real reason why not, and I think we both deserve a holiday – for it to be just us two, with no one to bother us.'

'I quite agree.' He squeezed her briefly. 'I'll make the necessary arrangements as soon as I'm back at my lodgings. I'm determined to get you to myself for more than a couple of days before you leave for Edinburgh in the autumn.' Two days ago, Molly had received a letter from the University of Edinburgh offering her a temporary post as a lecturer – which she'd accepted.

'It's only for a term. And I'm sure we can have that little holiday during the half, so you'll get to show me your old haunts after all,' she said.

'What if they want you to stay for longer? They invited you to lecture in botany for the term after you gave *one* guest lecture there, after all.'

'Unlikely. They only offered me the post because the current botany lecturer is off on a voyage to some remote island in search of a rare bean. And if they do ask me to stay, well, Edinburgh is hardly California.'

That was true, thank God, Arthur thought. Even though he'd encouraged her to take that other, more permanent post, he was secretly glad that she wasn't going to America.

Molly transferred the almost empty wicker basket from one hand to the other. 'Will you be returning here on Monday?'

'Of course, like I said I would.'

Arthur was supposed to depart the following day, but he was in no hurry to leave. He was in his own Elysium with Molly at Ravenfeld Hall. Everything around him was wrapped in a golden haze. As they strolled through the meadow, he gazed at his beloved. She was swinging the basket in one hand and gazing at the island of trees. Pinned on her dress was the small true-love knot brooch, gold with an emerald in its centre, that he had bought as one of her birthday presents after spying it in the window of a little jeweller's shop in Devon. (It might not move like the brooches her brothers made her, but he thought it suited her. He'd got her several presents in the hope that she'd like at least one of them.) How he loved her dearly.

He loved the warm, fragrant softness of her bare skin and wispy hair. He loved looking into her green eyes, even when they were flashing with anger. He loved waking up beside her, enveloped in a warm fug. If he awoke first, he'd watch her sleeping for a short while and think about how she really was beautiful, despite what her mother had thought. Hers was not the tailored, refined, dazzling beauty of a high-society lady; it was the natural, unspoiled, subtle beauty of a dryad. Like a rose compared with a daisy. Molly was just as beautiful inside. Even though she was sarcastic and could swear like a sailor, she was as tender and loving as any woman could be. Sometimes Arthur imagined the two of them, older and slightly grey, watching children (or even grandchildren) squalling and running around the woodland, building dens and climbing trees. By then he'd be as famous a landscape gardener as Capability Brown, and Molly might be a botany professor. And they'd be happy together. No, he wasn't prepared to let go of his Elysium. Not ever.

He released his hold on Molly and stopped in the middle of the meadow. She walked on a few paces before coming to a halt and looking back, wondering why he didn't follow.

Arthur balled his fists and inhaled sharply. 'Marry me, Molly!' he cried imploringly – or demanded, rather. 'I'm asking you to be my wife.' This wasn't how he'd envisioned asking her. He'd had it sketched out in his mind – how he'd propose to her in the rose garden when it was in full bloom – but that plan had been dashed to pieces now.

Molly remained motionless. Why did he always have to spoil everything? 'We've discussed this before, Arthur.'

'Four years ago. You said you wanted to finish your studies before you considered marriage, and now you have. So what's the issue?'

She lowered the basket to the ground. 'I'll tell you what the issue is! The issue is that it means sacrificing my independence. In the eyes of the law, I'd cease to exist. All my money, all my property, would become yours.'

'In name only. You know I'd never touch a penny of your money without your approval – and I imagine your brothers have tied up your fortune pretty securely anyway. Nor would I do anything to hamper your independence.'

'It's more the principle of the thing, and I don't want you to have to manage my monetary affairs when I know I'm capable of doing it myself. It's not only from a legal standpoint that I'd have to sacrifice my independence, either. If I do manage to find a permanent teaching post, you know what the university would say if they discovered I was married.'

'Surely they wouldn't force you off the campus purely for being married? Simply don't bow down to pressure. I know how stubborn you can be,' he added drily.

They faced each other, standing three feet apart amid the grasses and wild flowers. The wind whipped Arthur's coat and Molly's dress, but the two of them were immovable obelisks. Neither was going to back down.

'Nothing will change, Molly,' said Arthur, sounding slightly calmer now. 'We can still carry on as we are.'

'If nothing will change, why bother getting married at all?'

'Because I love you, because I want to show the rest of the world that I love you and am not ashamed of you, and quite simply because I want to call you my wife. You also forget that you'd be entitled to a share of my wealth and possessions – what little I have, anyway.'

'Don't feel that you have to provide for me.'

'A man should be able to provide for his wife, or he's a selfish fool otherwise. Strictly speaking, I don't *have* to do anything, but I *want* to share everything I have with you. My money, my life, whatever you wish.' He threw up his arms melodramatically, then sat on a log.

Molly sighed and made her way towards him. She approached from behind and put her hands on his tense shoulders. 'I'd be your wife without you providing anything for me. The truth is…I want to marry you. Purely for its own sake. I can't fully explain why, but marriage is worth something.'

Arthur's head rose. 'You mean it?'

She nodded.

Hastily he got to his feet and faced her. 'Even if it means you getting the sack? And sacrificing your independence?'

'Well…I'm sure we could find a way around all that. If I am given the sack for becoming Mrs Greenwood, then I have a very capable solicitor. Mr Grace will fight my case in court if he has to. On principle I would prefer to remain as a legal entity in my own right after marrying, but you were right about nothing changing in practice, so I suppose I could compromise on that point. I know you're not a fortune hunter, nor a man who'd be content to live off your wife's money – you moaned when I paid your rent last month when you were short because Sir Fusspot didn't pay you.'

'You must stop calling him that, Molly, or I'll say it to his face one day.'

'Well, it suits him,' she retorted. 'And…a wise woman once told me that marriage is about give and take, so we'd have to make an effort to find time for our work *and* for one another. We'd have to try to plan site visits and lectures so that they coincide.' Molly sounded cautiously optimistic, but then the gleam in her eyes suddenly dimmed. 'But my willingness to be your wife doesn't matter, because we *can't* marry.'

'Why not?'

'You know why. Your parents disapprove of me.'

'My *father* disapproves of you.'

'Yes – enough that he's serious about disowning you if you marry me.'

Arthur's hopeful look wilted.

'Could you do that to your mother? Have her estranged from her only child?'

Arthur averted his eyes from Molly's face. 'No, I couldn't.'

'Then there's no use discussing this any further.' She tried to move away, but he grabbed her arms, holding her firmly but not forcefully.

'But you do honestly want to marry me?' he asked urgently.

'I've already told you my answer to that.'

'Say it again. I need to hear it once more.'

'Yes!' she cried in frustration. 'Yes, I want to marry you!' It was actually a relief to say the words aloud after suppressing them for so long.

No sooner had she spoken them than Arthur pressed her tightly, enclosing her in his arms. 'If that's the case, then I'm not giving up. I'll find a way to convince my father of your worth.' That confident, all-conquering smile of his had returned.

But Molly was still feeling relatively rational. 'You have as much chance of doing that as I have of convincing a university to pay me the same wages as the male lecturers.'

'Even so!' Arthur was in that mood in which nothing could dissuade him. 'As long as you want it, I'll not rest until you're Mrs Arthur Greenwood. But even if we can't marry at present, why can we not be engaged? No one would have to know about it but us. And possibly your brothers, if you think they won't object.'

'Oh, they won't. I'm certain of it.'

A bemused silence fell between them. Why not? Molly reasoned. It would most likely be a long engagement, but actually that would be beneficial as it would buy her some time. She wouldn't have to sacrifice anything just yet. 'So…we're engaged, then?' she asked.

'It would appear so.' Arthur sounded surprised. But his dazed expression was suddenly shattered by a bright smile as he looked at her lovingly.

Molly flung her arms around his neck, and then he swept her off the ground. Both of them were laughing. He began kissing her rather passionately, and she tasted blackberry with each kiss. Then they simply held each other's gaze and smiled.

'I'm buying you a ring,' said Arthur.

'No, you're not.'

'Try and stop me,' he replied laughingly.

'The true-love knot brooch probably cost a small fortune.'

'Never you mind about that brooch. I'll never tell you what it cost, even on the point of death.'

Arthur deposited Molly on her feet. The brooch's pin caught his coat, but it didn't pull any threads when she yanked it free.

'We should probably tell my brothers.'

Arthur stiffened.

Molly kissed his cheek tenderly. 'Don't worry, I'll protect you from George.'

'Thank you.'

Chapter Twenty-Eight

olly stood in her chemise and drawers, contemplating her wardrobe. She possessed four dresses: the pale blue one (which she ruled out as she'd worn it when the Marsdens came to dinner); the lavender one that she'd had since she was seventeen and which still fitted her perfectly, apart from being slightly tight around her chest now (more appropriate for balls than dinners); the green, white and gold tartan one (too festive); and the white one with mint-green tartan bands around the neckline and cuffs. She chose the white and green one, then rummaged through a drawer to find her decent corsets. Her ones for everyday use were grey rather than white, and were fraying in places. Her hands worked the laces mechanically.

Formal dinners were rarely something in which she took pleasure, since she seldom knew anyone and often felt as if she were on display, like an animal in a zoo. ('Come see this rare specimen: a female academic! Sister of the famous Abernathy brothers! A duke's granddaughter, although you'd swear she was a wild savage!') But Mr Cullwick was an exceptional host and always made sure that everyone felt comfortable. His cook was excellent too. Molly slipped her gown over her head and tunnelled through it until she found the sleeves. She might actually have found some enjoyment in the dinner, were it not for the fact that Miss Marsden and Mr Gearhart were amongst the guests. Douglas was only going to cause himself pain, whether he tried to speak to Clara or not; simply the sight of her would bring back old recollections and sensations. And as for Mr Gearhart…well, Molly would be glad to see him once more so that she could make a better assessment of him. How had he wormed his way into Mr Cullwick's acquaintance? She agreed with Douglas that their propitious encounter at the bank did seem awfully convenient. But when she'd expressed her concern that George had started drinking spirits again, Douglas had been dismissive, even though she'd seen that brown bottle on George's study desk when she'd been looking for him the other day. She'd held the bottle's mouth against her nose and smelt ale.

One small advantage of having all these worries was that it made it easier to push her engagement to the back of her mind and not give the game away to her brothers too soon. Arthur wanted to formally announce the news to them when he returned to Ravenfeld Hall. After tying the dress's tartan sash around her waist, Molly fastened Arthur's brooch to her bodice and her mother's green dragonfly hairpin to her braided hair. She turned one of the dragonfly's silver eyes and its wings started to flap rapidly. Should she add a couple of white roses to her dress? She might as well, since she had time.

Retrieving her laboratory key, she hurried downstairs and stepped out of the south hall. It was a cool night and her bare neck prickled, but it wasn't ridiculously chilly. The ground wasn't wet, but she still lifted her skirts in case they brushed against dry dirt on the woodland floor. Once inside the lab, she opened the glass-doored cabinet containing her medicines and other potions (everything was clearly labelled so that she knew which was which). Her hand hovered along the top row of assorted glass bottles until she found the small, dark green one. She then opened her desk drawer containing neat rows of paper packets. She selected the packet of white rose seeds and planted one in the soil outside the lab. She added a drop of growth serum, and a rose bush sprouted gracefully before her. Selecting two roses that weren't too large, she fastened them to her dress sleeves. She would have to uproot the rose bush later and transplant it to the rose garden. Returning inside, she replaced the seed packet and the serum bottle. But as she was about to close the cabinet doors, her eyes fell on the four vials of red-tinted water on the bottom shelf. She stared at them. She knew she'd promised Arthur that she wouldn't use the poison again, but there was something about this man Gearhart, about his hold over George, that she distrusted. She couldn't escape the feeling that precaution was necessary this evening, ridiculous as that sounded. How sinister could a simple dinner be? She tucked a vial into her dress pocket and shut the cabinet doors.

George sat on his bed, looking at nothing in particular. He'd dressed for dinner and now had nothing else to do before departing. His eyes landed on the safe containing various legal papers, including the deeds to Ravenfeld Hall. He'd had the sense not to keep his will in there, however, unlike most wealthy gentlemen. That document was housed in Mr Grace's office. George was glad that he'd made a will five years ago, after that near-brush with death at the British Museum. His financial assets were divided equally between Douglas and Molly. He'd seen to it that his sister's share was left to her in trust, just in case Mr Greenwood ever took it into his head to marry her for financial gain. Ravenfeld Hall and its contents were bequeathed to Douglas, which likewise removed the (very unlikely) possibility of Molly's potential future husband selling the estate for a handsome profit.

There came a knock on his door.

'Come in, Douglas,' George said, without taking his eyes off the safe.

His brother entered. He was also dressed for the evening. 'Actually ready on time for once, I see.' Douglas smiled, although George saw through it. Douglas sank onto the bed beside him. 'Listen, George. If Dick offers you spirits tonight, please do your best to refuse him.'

'I understand your concern. You needn't mention it again.'

'As long as I know you'll heed my advice.'

'Are you sure you won't feel too uncomfortable at the sight of Miss Marsden?'

Douglas shrugged. 'It's a risk I'll have to take.'

'Are you planning on attempting to converse with her?'

'I'm not sure.'

'I'd advise against it, but if it puts an end to your moping, then so be it.'

'I doubt I'll get the chance to speak to her anyway, especially with Jonathan there.'

'It's unlikely, but don't feel disappointed, no matter what happens.' Could Dick not have found a new young woman as a suitable mate for

Douglas? He'd managed it once, after all. Then again, that had not ended favourably.

'Here.' Douglas held out a small black box. 'I made these as a token of appreciation when you agreed to be my best man. I decided you might as well have them. You might actually wear them in the capacity in which you were intended to one day. Who knows? Until then, they'll serve well on formal occasions.'

George opened the box. Inside was a pair of cufflinks: two convex glass discs set in silver. They were the same light blue as his eyes. He met Douglas's green eyes. 'Thank you.'

Douglas nodded and left the room. George fixed the cufflinks to the sleeves of his shirt. Neither of them had said precisely what he'd wanted to say, but it was better that way.

Presently George stood and made his way downstairs. He watched from the stairs as Molly entered the parlour from the south hall. Douglas was already standing in the middle of the room.

'Don't you think it's about time you got a new dress made, Mol?' Douglas asked her.

'For the number of dinners I attend, it's not worth it.' She tugged on one of her white gloves. 'And it's pointless commissioning new gowns from a dressmaker when your old ones are still in good condition and fit you fine.'

'Not that you ever go to the trouble of hiring a dressmaker, since you either make your own gowns or alter other people's cast-offs that they give you.'

'It sounds like you want me to waste your money on frippery. Be grateful that you have such a skinflint for a sister. Besides, a dressmaker will only force the latest fashions on me.'

'God help any dressmaker foolish enough to try,' Douglas grinned. 'But you look beautiful as you are. I'm sure Arthur wouldn't be able to keep his hands off you if he saw you now.'

Molly whacked him playfully on the arm with her fan. Douglas made no real effort to defend himself other than raising his arms, and laughed as she struck him. They both turned their heads as George entered the parlour.

'Are you both ready to depart?' he said.

'I think so. Do you have everything, Mol?'

'I do.' She slipped the fan back into her pocket and eyed Douglas. 'Is it Spuggy or Peregrine tonight?'

'Peregrine.'

'You give her far too much attention. Poor Spuggy will feel neglected.'

'You make it sound like Peregrine is my mistress.'

'Well, you sometimes talk to her as if she is.'

George was buried in his own thoughts as they boarded the airship and began their journey to London. He ran his finger over the smooth surface of his left cufflink. There was nothing else he could have done to better prepare himself. Fortitude was the main thing that would be needed when the time came.

Dick greeted the three of them with a genial smile when they entered his drawing room. Many of the guests were already present, though Douglas couldn't see the Marsdens amongst them.

'They've not arrived yet,' Dick whispered to him, before addressing Molly. 'Good evening, Miss – sorry, *Doctor* Abernathy. I'd better not get that wrong – you could easily poison me.' He laughed.

'Oh, I wouldn't poison you for that, Mr Cullwick,' Molly smiled. Instinctively she felt for the vial of poison, knowing that it was unlikely to have fallen out of her dress pocket. Her fingers initially met the smooth handle of her fan before they found the vial.

Dick promptly offered them drinks. George was scanning the room and soon spied his quarry by the fireplace, laughing with an older gentleman.

'Quite a popular gent, your Mr Gearhart,' remarked Dick, as he proffered a small glass of Madeira to Molly. 'Got intelligence and a good sense of humour. He's even got dry old Mr Montague laughing like a schoolboy.'

Gearhart caught George's eye and beamed at him.

'Sure I can't tempt you to have a real drink, George?'

'I'd rather not, Dick.'

'Oh, come now! What harm will it do? You can have one night off being teetotal – think of it as a reward for all those years you've spent sober.' Dick had the port bottle's neck poised over the glass.

George considered his host's determined grin. 'Very well, then. Just one.'

'I'll pour one for Mr Gearhart too, since port is also his poison of choice and I perceive that his glass is practically empty.'

'George!' Douglas hissed, as Dick poured two measures of port into glasses. 'What are you doing?'

'Being amicable. Isn't that what you're always insisting I do at social gatherings?'

'Intoxicating yourself at home is one thing, but in a room full of people—'

The butler appeared and announced, 'Mr and Miss Marsden.'

Douglas felt as if someone had driven an icicle through his heart. Instinctively he looked towards the door. Clara. She was as radiantly lovely as ever, in a sprigged white dress with alternating white and pink petticoats beneath. His icy blood soon thawed and his heart beat furiously. Clara was greeted by her host, and smiled politely at him. But then her eyes swept across the room and landed directly on Douglas's. Her face flushed deeply. Once she'd recovered from her shock, she promptly averted her gaze. Her brother evidently hadn't noticed, and was in conversation with Dick. Douglas was too stunned to feel pain. Clara had turned away from him; *his* Clara. But of course she wasn't, not any more.

He felt a tug on his sleeve. Molly wrapped her arm around his and gave it a sympathetic squeeze.

'I know, Mol, I should have anticipated as much. It's only natural that she should be embarrassed to even look at me after what happened.'

'Her family have most likely ordered her not to speak to you.'

'Probably. I'm glad Dick has seated her beside Jonathan. She'd have been very uncomfortable next to me.'

The mention of Dick caused something to flash into Douglas's mind. Where was George? He'd peeled away from them. Douglas spied him beside Gearhart. Each had a glass in hand; the ruby-red port glowed in the firelight.

'Wait here a moment, Mol.'

'Are you going to cause a scene?'

'Most likely.' Gently detaching his arm from his sister's, Douglas marched across the room. 'George,' he said sharply.

His brother and Mr Gearhart turned their attention on him. Gearhart's expression was a blend of amusement and curiosity.

Douglas tried to steer his brother to the side a little. 'Please just think about what you're doing.'

'Go away.'

'You know you won't be able to help yourself once you start.'

'I know what I'm doing. I'm in control of myself.'

But Douglas plucked the glass from his brother's hand and flung its contents into the fire, the flames flaring momentarily in appreciation. He looked at George sternly as he returned the empty glass. A few people had stopped their conversations to watch.

George regarded Douglas as one would a tiresome child who refused to go to bed. 'Return to our sister. Don't neglect her.' There was an intense look in his eyes.

'All right, then.' Douglas looked past his brother to his companion. 'Please forgive my intrusion, Mr Gearhart. It was a family matter, you understand.'

'Perfectly, my friend. No apology necessary.' His composure undisturbed, Gearhart drained his port.

Douglas promptly retreated. He refused to meet the other guests' questioning eyes. 'Maybe I'll feel better after shouting at Dick for putting temptation in George's path,' he muttered to Molly.

'Maybe.' She patted his hand. 'You tried. If George makes an ass of himself, it's his own fault. But let's try to have some faith in him.'

Douglas sighed. 'If you're willing, Mol, then I suppose I am too.'

Chapter Twenty-Nine

As it turned out, Dick had seated the Marsdens at the opposite side and end of the table to Douglas. This didn't stop Jonathan fixing Douglas with one or two menacing stares. Clara ventured a timid glance at him, then looked his way no more.

Douglas tried to be attentive to the lady he'd escorted to the table. Miss Grayson was a demure girl, with reddish-brown curls the hue of late autumn leaves. There was something about her that reminded him of a mouse.

'I'm afraid I'm not much company,' she said, with an apologetic shrug and an embarrassed air. 'I don't have much interesting conversation.'

Douglas smiled reassuringly. 'I'm sure that's not the case, Miss Grayson. And if you are really that concerned, I'll direct the course of the conversation.'

She looked relieved. Dick clinked a glass with a spoon and rose to make a toast.

'I understand that Dick is your cousin?' Douglas whispered.

Miss Grayson nodded, speaking again only once the toast was drunk. 'He called me Shelley when we were young, because he said my eyes reminded him of a tortoiseshell butterfly, and the name has stuck. He's made it his mission, at my dear old aunt's request, to find me a husband.' She adjusted her spectacles. There was certainly some intelligence in those bronzy eyes, Douglas thought. 'In all honesty, I don't often attend dinners like this. I usually spend the evening at home with a book. But, well, it gets rather lonely rattling around that house on my own. My aunt died last year and left it to me, only it's far too big for my needs.' Her eyes widened a fraction, as if she was surprised to find herself telling this to a mere acquaintance. Douglas was reminded of Dick's remark that he put people at ease. Perhaps there was some truth to it after all, or maybe Miss Grayson was simply desirous of someone to talk to.

'But surely you must have other companions besides books?' said Douglas light-heartedly.

'I have one or two friends, but books are my chief companions.' She smiled faintly. 'Dick is my only family.'

'What do you like to read?'

'My taste varies. I like novels, but also books on history, geography and palaeontology. I like to look at the dinosaur bones in the British Museum.' She said this as if she were at confession. 'I read books on gardening as well, since I like to tend my little garden.'

'I see. My sister is also devoted to her garden.' Douglas noticed that Miss Grayson was chafing her gloved hands and wincing. He made a delicate enquiry about it.

'I have a terrible...affliction, on the skin of my hands,' she admitted, glancing down. 'But our family doctor is baffled as to why. There is nothing to be done about it. No amount of lotion soothes the irritation, and I must always wear gloves.'

Douglas sensed an opportunity and didn't hesitate to seize it. 'You should try Dr Truman. He's a good friend of mine and a remarkable physician. He has experience of treating this sort of thing.' That last point wasn't entirely true, to Douglas's knowledge, but Theo was generally at the forefront of knowledge on new medical treatments for almost every ailment.

'Has he really?' asked Miss Grayson keenly.

'Oh, yes. I'll write down his address for you.' Douglas tore a page out of his pocketbook and pencilled 'Dr Theophilus Truman, 76 Harley Street'. Miss Grayson accepted it from him with a small, grateful smile. 'He's usually not very busy on Monday afternoons. He makes his rounds at three o'clock, so you can call on him before then. I'll let him know to expect a charming young lady.'

Miss Grayson blushed delicately. Douglas wanted to laugh at his own cunning. And he had told Dick that *he* was bad for matchmaking! But this was an exceptional case. Having Miss Grayson come to Theo in the capacity of a patient might be the only way he'd ever be able to speak to her.

Molly was on George's left, meaning that she was perfectly positioned to overhear his conversation with Mr Gearhart. (The girl on George's right, whom Mr Gearhart had escorted to the table, was content listening to young Colonel Rush's India stories from across the table.) But George didn't neglect her, to Molly's surprise. And he was only on his first glass of wine, if one discounted the glass of port that had been consumed by the fire. He divided his attention equally between her and Mr Gearhart. The conversation in which he indulged with the latter was nothing to raise alarm. Mr Gearhart outlined his plans for an improved model of the tele-texter, one that would give the user the option to actually speak to their recipient. George replied that he and Douglas had had a similar idea several years ago. Then they talked of the inventors in their club and the potential of some of their machines, before discussing some theory that had been published in a science journal, and its shortcomings. Most of this went over Molly's head. But she got an odd impression that it was merely a cover. Maybe they'd only really get down to business when the gentlemen retired to the smoking room. Gradually she found herself listening less keenly and turning increasingly towards Douglas and Miss Grayson – the latter asking her about nurturing tomato plants from cuttings.

As Molly indulged Miss Grayson, George felt it was safe to lower his guard. He knew she'd been listening. But he'd also wanted to make sure that she wasn't isolated, in case Douglas took a liking to his neighbour and got wrapped up in conversation with her, since she was the sort of woman who might take his fancy. George cleared his throat. 'It was rather fortunate that you encountered Mr Cullwick at the bank the other day,' he remarked to Gearhart.

'Wasn't it just?'

'You wanted to get me here.'

'Think rather highly of yourself, don't you, George?' Gearhart raised his champagne glass to his lips. 'Not everything revolves around you.'

'I'm under no delusion that it does.' George lowered his voice. 'I think you're enjoying this game you're playing.'

'What game?' Gearhart failed to adjust his volume to match George's.

'Pretending you're human.'

Gearhart smirked. 'I'm playing the game better than you are. Everyone knows you're made not of flesh but of ice.'

'Your efforts to "keep up appearances" aren't all for show. You find some sense of enjoyment in all these rituals and rules of society. I think that's the reason why you invited me to dine with you. You wanted to have the experience and knew that I was the only one around whom you could drop your guard.'

'What an interesting theory. Where on earth do you get these wild ideas?'

'I base my theories on the evidence before me.'

The two of them stared sidelong at each other. Gearhart looked mildly amused.

'I say, Mr Abernathy!' barked a grey-haired gentleman from across the table. 'Is there any particular profession for which your androids are unsuitable? My neighbour reckons they'd be terrible cooks, with no tongue with which to taste, but what else are we better at than they are?'

Douglas spared George the trouble of replying. 'Our machines can carry out any task that's repetitive and doesn't require decision-making, Mr Garthwaite. We've made dozens of counting machines and clerks.'

Laughter rippled across the dinner table.

'But aren't some of your machines sentient, Mr Abernathy? That's what I've heard: they can actually think.'

'That is correct, sir, although only a handful of our androids are sentient. My brother and I try to avoid making them more advanced than their purpose requires them to be. However, sometimes we have brought an android to life, at their master or mistress's request, if the model in question is sufficiently advanced for us to do so.'

'I suppose that, after a while, they can't help wishing that they could have a proper conversation with them. I sometimes wish my little terrier could talk, although I get more sense out of his barking than from anything most people say to me.' This earned Mr Garthwaite a chuckle or two.

'Can your androids feel, Mr Abernathy?' asked a young lady.

'In a sense. They experience emotions differently to how we do, but at the very least they have instincts and basic desires: self-preservation, to protect their owner and fulfil their wishes, and to execute their basic function.'

'What about love?'

'Scientifically, no. But what I've seen with my own eyes suggests otherwise. They're certainly capable of feeling the desire for companionship of their own kind, and many form strong attachments to their owners. I've even heard of cases where androids have simply stopped working after their owner has died – the shock overwhelmed their system. Others can't understand why their friend and master is suddenly gone, and they become confused. There was one case where an android just walked out of the house and was found wandering along the roadside three miles away.'

'Oh, how terrible! They can suffer heartbreak.'

'What I can't understand, Mr Abernathy,' began Colonel Rush, 'is how long your androids can store new memories. I mean, one's memory is like a room, isn't it? There's only so many boxes you can fit into a room before it's full. And since these things can potentially keep going for hundreds of years, surely after a certain point they won't be able to retain any new memories?'

Douglas smiled politely. 'Well, the thing is, there are no boxes in the room at all – that is to say, there are no memories etched into their brains. Rather, their brains change with each new experience, resulting in a rearrangement of certain parts within their mind...'

The women began to make their departure to the drawing room. Molly and Miss Grayson were standing over Douglas's chair, the former enquiring as to who was piloting Peregrine on the journey home.

Gearhart bent his head closer to George's. 'There are two of London's deadliest assassins currently seated in the drawing room. One has orders to kill your brother on my signal, the other your sister.'

George did not remove his gaze from his siblings, watching Douglas pass Molly the airship keys.

'If you do not want the only two people you care for to die, then you will do as I ask of you.'

George turned his head so that he could see Gearhart's humourless face. Gearhart flashed him a pleasant smile. Had he allowed the mask to slip for a moment, or was he simply toying with him?

'George?' Douglas tapped his brother's shoulder. 'Everyone is leaving for the smoking room now that the ladies have gone.' Indeed, several of the men were making a move to rise.

'Mr Gearhart has asked me to help find his tiepin, which he appears to have misplaced.'

'Terribly careless of me. It can't be far, though,' Gearhart grinned, playing along with the lie.

'I will be along in a moment,' George assured his brother.

'Oh, very well, then. I'll see you shortly.' Douglas looked at him with a slightly perplexed – and possibly concerned – expression. But presently Mr Cullwick claimed his attention and the two of them departed together.

George stared after his brother. That might have been the last time he'd ever see him. He wanted to say some sort of final farewell, or tell him that he hadn't meant half of what he'd said to him recently. But that would have raised Douglas's suspicions. Nor could he tell Molly how proud he was of her and that he cared deeply for her. George had always assumed that it was unnecessary for him to tell her such things explicitly, and that she'd know them from his actions. But he might have misjudged that.

'Mr Abernathy?' Gearhart was waiting in the doorway leading to the hall. 'Come.'

George did as ordered. Mechanically, he followed Gearhart into the hall and accepted his evening cape from the butler, after Gearhart made excuses for their early departure. George didn't hear what they were. He dully registered the decrease in temperature as he stepped out into the night. A cab was already parked outside the door. Gearhart climbed inside and waved for George to do likewise. George tried not to look at his captor's smiling face as the cab door closed after him.

Gearhart held out his hand. 'Your cane, please, George.'

Knowing that Gearhart could easily take it by force if he wanted to, George reached into his coat and deposited the cane in his waiting hand.

Gearhart tucked it into his own coat. 'Quite a wonderfully crafted item. I will be sure to take it with me on walks. I'll have fun playing with the toys hidden inside it, too. Ah! Those are some rather smart cufflinks.' He raised George's arm by the sleeve like he was controlling a puppet.

'I was to wear them to my brother's wedding.'

Gearhart plucked the cufflink from George's shirt and held it up to the light. The white powder inside it was just visible in the gaslight. 'An explosive powder, no doubt. Now, you do realise that, because you've been naughty, I'll have to confiscate these?' He removed the other cufflink, with no resistance from George. 'Was that really the best your brother could come up with?' Gearhart smirked as he tucked the cufflinks into his coat pocket. 'Your mistake for leaving the job of doing away with me to your silly little brother. Driver! Onwards!'

The cab jerked into motion. Gearhart reclined in his seat and stretched out his feet. He took out his tele-texter and began to type a message.

'Who are you sending a message to?' asked George.

'The assassins. I'm telling them to abandon their prey. I'm a man of my word, George. See?' Gearhart held up the device so that George could read the message.

+WOLF CAPTURED. HUNT IS OFF.–

'I'm the wolf, am I?' asked George drily.

'Yes, and I'm the hunter. A great predator captured by an even greater one.'

George tried to maintain a sense of their location as he was driven through the gloomy streets. 'If I discover that you're lying about my siblings' safety, I'll destroy you,' he said coldly.

'Is that a threat?'

The look on George's face was sufficient to answer Gearhart's question.

Dick settled himself on the sofa beside Douglas. 'You and my cousin seemed to have lots to say to each other,' he remarked as he cut a cigar.

'Miss Grayson was good company, but I wouldn't dream of making myself too agreeable to a girl I know my friend likes. Besides, as pleasant and pretty a woman as your cousin is, she is not for me. I mean no offence, of course.'

Dick lit his cigar and leant back leisurely. 'I'm quite aware. Still, it would have been a good way to make Miss Marsden jealous.'

'By manipulating your cousin's feelings? How could you even suggest such a thing?'

'Oh, Shelley's not in danger of becoming fond of you, even if you had flirted with her a little. I could tell.'

'Good.' Although, even though Douglas didn't have amorous feelings towards Miss Grayson, it still stung to be told that there was no chance of someone loving you. 'Who was that young lady to whom you were making yourself agreeable throughout dinner?'

'Miss Rose Beauchamp.' Dick grinned. 'Quite a fine specimen, isn't she? Very jolly, but she's got a wicked wit. I met her at a friend's place in the country and invited her here, along with her aunt and cousin. I like her immensely.' A buxom blonde was always Dick's Achilles heel, although he spoke of Miss Beauchamp with particularly warm feeling. 'Where's your brother?'

'I left him in the dining room, talking with Mr Gearhart. You really shouldn't have tempted George to drink liquor, you know.'

'Only one glass, and he's none the worse for it.'

'For now – he might have quite a few more glasses before the night is out. Mr Gearhart might be encouraging him to drink as we speak. Should I retrieve them?'

'I think you'd better. You know, I'd never have believed that George was capable of forming a tie beyond his family circle, but now I have seen the proof!'

'We all learn to make friends eventually, Dick. Some of us simply take longer than others.' Douglas smiled good-humouredly as he vacated his seat and stepped out of the smoking room. It was a relief to no longer be suffocating in cigar smoke. It didn't smell terribly pleasant to those who were unaccustomed to it.

He knew his way through Dick's house, and his feet moved along the first-storey landing with little conscious effort from his brain, as if the journey had already been inputted into him. He heard the fluttery chatter of female voices from the drawing room on his left, where Molly was. As he approached the stairs to the ground floor, this unconscious flow of motion was interrupted when he saw a female figure flit across the landing ahead.

'Clara?'

The girl disappeared up the darkened staircase leading to the second storey before he could see her face clearly. She'd been little more than a blur of white and pink. Douglas glanced in the direction of the descending staircase, but only once. In the next moment he was in pursuit of the girl.

Chapter Thirty

There were six other women in the drawing room: four around Molly's age and two older ladies. Miss Marsden wasn't amongst them. Molly had hoped to have a companion in Miss Grayson, but no sooner had they set foot into the drawing room than Mrs Montague had cried, 'Tessa! Tessa!' and hooked poor Miss Grayson's arm. 'Dear girl, Mr Cullwick said you were coming. You were sitting too far away from me at dinner! I only just heard about your aunt. Such a sad business! Miss Garthwaite was at school with her, you know...'

Miss Grayson could only give Molly an apologetic look as she was dragged away to a far corner of the room. Molly found herself sitting beside Miss Montague, a loquacious girl who supplied enough conversation for the two of them, without even realising that after a couple of minutes Molly had given up attempting to follow her verbal bombardment. Miss Montague never waited for replies to questions either. Molly glanced at Miss Grayson, who was penned between the two older women. She caught Molly's gaze and smiled briefly but sympathetically. Her eyes said, I know how you feel: my companions don't care to listen either. Then Molly was rescued by Miss Lacey, who took a seat opposite her. Miss Lacey was fair, with grey eyes that seemed slightly too far apart. She laughed a lot but knew a great deal about flowers, which helped stimulate Molly's brain. Miss Montague, however, had a habit of picking up strands of a conversation and running away with them, or simply talking over you on a subject of her own. Then, having spent the past ten minutes endeavouring to repair Miss Garthwaite's jet bead necklace, Miss Beauchamp gravitated towards the younger set. Since Miss Montague was well acquainted with her, she devoted her full attention to the newcomer.

'Should I pour the tea, Miss Abernathy? Nobody else seems to be bothering,' said Miss Lacey.

'You might as well,' Molly shrugged. In her head she heard Douglas say *Doctor* Abernathy', and mentally brushed the voice aside.

Miss Lacey began sorting through the tea tray. 'Your brothers are the famous inventors, I take it? I recognised the family name.'

'They are.' Molly accepted the cup Miss Lacey was offering her. 'You may have seen them beside me at dinner.'

'I did, although I wasn't certain it was them. I did not know their likeness.'

'Makes sense.' Molly tried to sip her tea, but stopped on feeling the heat of it.

'What's it like having two such great men for brothers?'

'Challenging.' Was the girl only paying Molly attention to learn about her brothers? It wouldn't be the first time such a thing had happened.

Miss Lacey laughed. 'I sometimes wish I still had brothers and sisters. I was the only one of us to make it to adulthood.'

'I'm sorry to hear that.'

'It happens. I suppose that's why I took to nursing flowers instead.' Miss Lacey gave Molly a bright smile that was merely a mask.

Before Molly could say anything further, the other two girls, having overheard Miss Lacey's enquiries, started asking about Molly's brothers. Miss Lacey handed round more cups of tea before returning to her seat. Molly caught her looking at her as she raised the teacup to her lips, but Miss Lacey quickly turned her head away and reckoned to be looking at the clock on the mantle. The tea had too much sugar in it for Molly's liking, but she sipped it politely nonetheless. Meanwhile, she attempted to fend off Miss Montague's questions with brief or vague replies.

'Is it true that your eldest brother struck his cruel, wicked schoolmaster across the face with his own cane during a beating, Miss Abernathy?' Miss Montague's eyes sparkled.

'Yes, to stop that sadist beating my other brother until he bled.'

'Did your brothers really let two automaton dinosaurs loose at the British Museum? Or was Mr Cullwick telling tall tales again?' Miss Beauchamp smiled. (Rubens would have loved to paint this girl, Molly thought.)

'That story is true, although they didn't do so intentionally.'

Every now and then, Molly felt Miss Lacey glaring at her. The one time she'd caught her eye, she'd seen the cross and confounded expression on the girl's face. Ah, that was why the tea tasted so sweet. Molly clapped a hand to her head, and Miss Lacey's stormy eyes instantly brightened.

'Miss Lacey, would you be so kind as to accompany me onto the balcony? I feel rather light-headed all of a sudden, and in need of some air.'

Miss Lacey sprang to her feet. 'Of course, Miss Abernathy.'

Molly took the girl's arm as they exited the room, hearing the older women's clucks of concern behind them. ('I thought she looked pale… Poor girl… Shall I offer them my salts? I have them somewhere…') They walked in silence down the poorly lit corridor, the moon providing more light than the gas lamps. Every few feet, Molly swayed and staggered. She politely rebuffed Miss Lacey's fretful entreaties to seek medical help. No sooner were they on the narrow balcony than Molly stooped to the ground and appeared to be on the verge of fainting.

Miss Lacey was still holding her arm. 'Miss Abernathy, what is the matter? I'll fetch help!'

Molly didn't give her the chance. She pulled down on the girl's arm and struck her in the abdomen. Miss Lacey fell to the floor, the wind knocked out of her.

Molly loomed over the wheezing girl. 'Don't try to poison a poisoner.'

'How?' Miss Lacey gasped. 'How did the poison do nothing to you? That was belladonna berry juice I put in your tea!'

Molly withdrew the corked vial from her pocket. 'I've dabbled with organic poisons for a very long time. They have no effect on me – or at least, not the effect they're supposed to have.' The cork popped, and she swallowed the vial's contents. She knew from the red-hot prickling that came over her body, and from Miss Lacey's startled expression, that it had worked. Molly could easily push against the darkness trying to root itself in her brain. She touched the balcony, and thorny black vines began to entwine themselves around it, spreading out over the floor. 'Now, you're going to tell me who hired you or I'll show you how a proper assassination should go.' She hoped the threat sounded convincingly menacing.

'I'll tell you everything!' Miss Lacey cried eagerly. 'Just tell me what poison you drank! I must know!'

'Oh.' Molly was taken aback by her enthusiasm. This girl was a fanatic; you could see it in her maniacal eyes. It wouldn't be surprising if she'd poisoned her younger siblings for fun. 'You tell me who hired you and I'll give you the formula,' replied Molly firmly.

'Mr Gearhart! He ordered us not to do anything until he gave us the signal, but I couldn't resist once I had the opportunity!' Miss Lacey spoke vehemently. 'There you were, the great Dr Abernathy, the first female doctor of the natural sciences. What an honour it would have been to kill you!'

'Honour' wasn't the word that Molly would have used. 'What did you mean by "us"? You're not acting alone?' she said.

'Mr Gearhart sent me to kill you, and another assassin to kill your brother.'

'Which brother?'

'The red-haired one.'

'And what of the other one?'

'I don't know! Now, the formula!'

'Of course. It's belladonna, hemlock, lily of the valley…' Molly made an orange flower grow out of the ground and it emitted a cloud of white vapour. Miss Lacey's head drooped and she slouched onto the cold stone floor. 'Poison ivy, comfrey, oleander, and several species of my own making. There, deal fulfilled.'

The effects of the poison were already fading by the time Molly was returning down the corridor with a delirious Miss Lacey on her arm. The girl had received only a mild dose of the flower's toxin, so she'd recover in a few hours. Molly deposited her in a chair, binding her ankles with the sash from her silvery dress, and then ran in the opposite direction to find Douglas.

It wouldn't be Clara, Douglas knew. He'd look utterly mad and foolish when he saw that the girl was a stranger and he had to explain himself to her. But he knew he wouldn't forgive himself if he didn't confirm it; he'd always wonder if he'd missed his chance. Besides, he couldn't understand why the girl was not in the drawing room with the other women but had climbed the stairs to the next floor, where the more private rooms of the house were. She walked swiftly on light feet, and her faintly echoing footsteps became his guide in the half-light. Where was she going? Surely she knew she shouldn't be here? Unless she'd heard him advancing after her and was fleeing in fear. Douglas stopped in the middle of the corridor, thoroughly ashamed of himself.

'Miss?' he called out. 'Are you lost? The drawing room is on the floor below.'

The footsteps stopped. The girl had her back to him. Her hair was styled exactly like Clara's and was identical in its curl and colour. It wasn't difficult to see how he had made the error.

Douglas cautiously approached her. 'If you're lost, I can escort you back to where the other ladies are. Can you tell me your name?'

The girl faced him. Douglas staggered back a step. It *was* Clara. Her face – at that moment very concerned – was as creamy and rosy, her eyes as soft and lovely.

Clara was rubbing her gloved hands, her eyes cast down. 'I wanted to speak to you,' she said in a trembling voice. 'My brother would never allow me to say a word to you, so I had to find a way to get you alone. My friend and confidante invented the excuse to the other ladies that we wanted to see Mr Cullwick's library. She's waiting there now.'

'Is that why you refused to look at me throughout dinner? Because of your brother?'

'Yes, and for that reason alone. I noticed you in the drawing room immediately. At first I thought I couldn't bear it.' She clutched her chest. 'But I found courage somehow.' Suddenly her head shot up, like a startled deer's. She looked around her. 'I thought I heard someone approaching. Quickly, through here.'

She opened the door to a room papered in crimson. It was unlit and appeared to be a private apartment. Douglas hadn't known Clara to be this bold since that time they'd escaped a ball for ten minutes and shared a brief kiss in the hallway. It was a memory he held close to his heart. That night she had said to him that he gave her courage. Now he shut the door behind them and watched as she lit a single lamp, her profiled figure silhouetted like a shade under its light. She paced the length of the hearthrug, evidently at a loss to know how to begin. Douglas was conscious of time passing, and of Clara's friend, who was likely growing impatient in the library (hopefully, she was lost in a book).

'Over these past few months,' began Clara at last, 'I have devoted a great deal of time to reflection. I was never angry with you. I was overwhelmed by the shock and terror of that night…' She trembled. Douglas wanted to put his arms around her and comfort her, but knew that it was improper. 'But I quickly came to the realisation that it was not your fault. You tried to make that night perfect. You wanted our two families to get along as much as I did.' She paused before a vase of fresh flowers and caressed their petals as she spoke. 'Then all I felt was deep sorrow at what was lost. I considered writing to you, but my family would never permit it. I could not even bring myself to utter your name before them. I couldn't bear to deceive them either. Yet I find I am doing exactly that now, aided by my friend's influence. It seems I am always to be led by others.' She sniffed, sounding as if she were suppressing tears. It was hard to see now that she'd stepped away from the lamp. 'Weak wretch that I am! Unable to be guided by my own heart!'

'You are *not* weak.' Douglas strode over to her and took her gloved hands. Her glistening eyes looked startled. He could smell her scent now that he was close to her: the warm apricot blossom of her skin, overlaid by a delicate hint of rose water. 'You have done nothing wrong, either. You are always ready to forgive everyone else and burden yourself with the blame.'

She gazed at him with trembling eyes and parted lips.

'I am to blame, Clara. I should have checked that those two androids were properly wound down so that they couldn't cause mischief, and I should have thought about how the automata at Ravenfeld Hall would frighten you. But I was selfishly preoccupied with trying to make a favourable impression on your family. I was convinced that everything would work out as I wanted it to, without considering your feelings – or my family's.'

'Oh, Douglas,' Clara sighed. 'You could never be selfish. You are too good a man for that.'

He plucked a gerbera from the vase and entwined it in her hair, noticing the new silver clasp she wore. She gave him a smile like summer sunshine. Suddenly the door rattled. Douglas thought that someone was about to enter, but when no one did he concluded that it was the wind blowing through an open window somewhere.

'Say you'll forgive me, my petal. Say you still love me and that there's hope,' he said sotto voce.

'There is nothing to forgive, my love. I love you with all my heart and always will. Nothing can separate us. I shall make Father and Mother see. There must be a way.'

'There will be. Even if I have to move heaven and earth to improve myself in your family's eyes, I will do it. I'd do anything for you, my petal.' Should he kiss her? He had just declared his eternal devotion to her, so it seemed the natural conclusion.

'It's all right,' she said softly. 'You can kiss me. There's nothing to fear.'

'You're right. No one even knows we're here.'

She closed her eyes and inclined her head towards his. Douglas followed suit, but briefly opened his eyes to see her hand touching the silver hair clasp. He grabbed hold of her wrist as her arm shot forward. A short, narrow dagger clattered to the floor. Had he been even a second slower, it would have plunged into his neck. Without its clasp, the girl's hair tumbled down her back, and the gerbera fell to the floor.

'Who are you?' he demanded, his grip on her wrist tightening.

'Douglas, you are hurting me!'

'Where's Clara?'

'I don't know what you—'

'You can stop your act. Tell me where the real Clara is.'

When she next looked up, her expression had changed. The sweet face he knew was twisted into a malicious grin. 'What gave it away?' The voice had changed too: it was neither male nor female, with no music in it.

'Two things. First, my name for Clara was "angel" – I never called her "my petal". Second, the flowers. Clara is sensitive to pollen. Those flowers would have caused a severe reaction. You didn't so much as sneeze.'

'But there were flowers all around her home!'

'Silk. Almost indistinguishable from the real thing, until you look closely.'

The assassin laughed. 'Rather like me, then, the silk flower. I'm a changeling and can become anyone. I don't just mimic their appearance but their voice, their scent, their gestures. I disguised myself as a servant of the Marsdens on three occasions to become acquainted with your beloved.'

'Where is Clara? Is she safe?'

'Fear not – your beloved is sleeping soundly in the garden. My associate slipped something into her wine at dinner, and conveyed her outside when the other ladies left the dining room. When she wakes, she will conclude that she has fainted.'

'You had better be telling the truth or I'll make you suffer.'

'You can see for yourself from the window.'

'And give you a chance to strike me? I don't think so.'

'I don't fear incurring your wrath. It's not in your nature to viciously attack someone.'

'You don't know me.'

'But I do, Douglas,' the assassin said in his voice, before switching back to their own. 'I have been observing you for a while now – not that you'll have noticed me. That day you visited Mr Plumpton, for example, I took on the guise of his secretary, Mr Bland. My employer wanted to test my talents, and I like to familiarise myself with my quarry. Neither you nor Mr Plumpton suspected a thing. Your devotion to sweet little Clara is touching: I can see you're just itching to reassure yourself that she's sound asleep in the garden, although you should be more concerned about what my associate put in your sister's tea.'

'Molly?' Douglas felt a stab of panic.

'I was to kill you and my associate was to kill your sister. I suppose you'd better go to dear Molly, although it'll be far too late now.'

Douglas tightened his hold on the assassin's arm. 'I won't let you get away.'

The deranged face shifted back into Clara's likeness. The wide eyes welled with tears. 'Don't hurt me.'

Despite his efforts, Douglas's heart ached.

'I love you, Douglas.'

His will was failing. Even though he knew this wasn't Clara, he couldn't bring himself to strike the face of the girl he loved. Thankfully, he was spared the trouble.

'Get away from my brother, you murderous bitch!' The vase of flowers was brought down on the assassin's head, and they fell to the ground. Molly was standing behind the fallen figure. She was trembling and looked deathly pale. 'Clara!' she exclaimed in disbelief, on seeing whom she had just struck.

'An imposter,' explained Douglas. 'Are you all right?'

'I'm fine. A girl tried to poison me but it had no effect. I tied her to a chair.'

'We need to make sure this one doesn't escape either. Quickly.' Douglas retrieved a curtain cord. At the window he paused momentarily to see Clara – the real Clara – lying on a stone bench in Dick's sorry excuse for a garden, as a maidservant shook her shoulder. When he returned to the window after binding the assassin's wrists, he saw Clara being assisted to her feet by two maids, seemingly confused but otherwise fine. He let the curtain fall.

'Gearhart was the one who sent the assassins after us,' said Molly. 'The girl who targeted me confessed.'

'I suspected that it might be him.'

'Where's George?' Molly asked suddenly.

'I haven't seen him for some time.'

'My assassin said that only you and I were their targets. There was no mention of a third assassin.'

'It's likely that we aren't the ones Gearhart is really after. He wants to get at George through us.'

'If so, what the hell is Gearhart planning on doing with *him*?'

Chapter Thirty-One

'Here we are.' The cab came to a stop outside Gearhart's factory. In a former life it had been a warehouse, but it was still relatively new. The brickwork wasn't chipped and there wasn't a single broken windowpane. 'Shall we go inside? It's rather chilly out here.' Gearhart shivered theatrically, then slid out of his seat.

'I suppose you can actually make your body shiver in response to the changing temperature?' George enquired, as they walked towards the entrance.

'Indeed. To begin with, I did it manually, but then I installed a command so that my body would react automatically to a decline or increase in temperature, just like yours.' He beamed. 'We are both slaves to our animalistic impulses.'

'It is an impulse that serves a specific purpose in living organisms.'

Gearhart took out a large iron key and inserted it into the factory door. 'I think you'll find the temperature in here more agreeable.'

George eyed him warily, then followed his captor through the doorway. Gearhart locked the door behind them. The factory was shrouded in shadow: only a single electric lamp lit what looked like a control panel, which was mounted on a raised steel platform about twenty feet above the floor. Gearhart's maid, Anna, was at its helm. She was wearing a dark blue dress instead of her uniform. Her pale gold hair shimmered, free from its cap but still fastened in a bun at the nape of her neck. George was again struck by the girl's faded, anaemic aspect, as if half her life force had dwindled away. It reminded him of how his mother had looked upon her deathbed, before she'd finally succumbed to consumption.

'Is everything ready, Anna?' called her master.

'Yes, sir.' Her vague eyes rested on George as she descended to ground level.

'Excellent. Remain where you are, George. You'll have a better view of the show from there.' Gearhart jogged up a metal stairway onto the platform, the metallic echo of his footsteps ringing across the factory.

George moved to the maid's side. 'You know what your master is planning. Can you honestly say that you agree with this?'

The girl lowered her gaze. 'It is not for me to say, sir.'

'If you wish to protect your master, your loyalty is misplaced. He doesn't care for your life.'

She met George's eye. 'I would have no meaningful existence without my master, sir. I was nothing before he made me what I am.'

There wasn't time to clarify the meaning of this enigmatic statement. Gearhart's voice rang out across the factory at an unnaturally high volume. '*Behold!*'

In the next moment, two things happened: red light bled from electric lamps along the platform, and a huge cloud of red-tinted steam engulfed the factory floor. Through the thinning curtain of steam, George could discern the factory's layout more clearly. The ground level was occupied by various large machines, which reminded him of a mill's interior. A criss-cross of steel walkways led to two raised levels. The first consisted of the control panel, along with what looked like an office, and the second… George gazed up at an enormous, pulsing metal bulk. Cables sprouted from the mechanical organ, and their other ends met a generator. Sparks shivered along both the machine and the cables. At first George envisioned a heart, as the machine's irregular shape suggested the idea; then he realised that he was mistaken. It was a brain. A computer. Much larger and more sophisticated than his had been. He stared at it in horrified fascination as Gearhart raised a speaking tube to his mouth.

'Ladies and gentlemen, I give you the marvellous, the magnificent, the mysterious *machine*!' He cupped his ear. '"But what does it do?" I hear you cry. "For what purpose was it constructed?" Well, this machine was constructed for a very noble purpose indeed, boys and girls: the salvation of the human race! Observe!' He moved rapidly back and forth along the control panel, pulling levers and pressing buttons. Steam ballooned from the generator, and the computer groaned into life. 'Once it is fully awoken, this machine will be fed information by my humble little tele-texters.' He swept out his arm. Around the perimeter of the factory were stacks of crates. A couple were open, revealing their contents to be Gearhart's devices. 'Every single message sent from a tele-texter shall be recorded within this computer, creating a profile of each individual in London. I will know where they are, what they're doing and what they're thinking. Every business transaction, every confidence shared between friends, every expression of affection between lovers – it will all be known to me. Like a census record, I'll know what the city's population is made of, only in far greater detail. And once I possess that information, and the sales of tele-texters have made me a wealthy and influential man, I can begin to bring this haphazard city into some semblance of order.' He leapt nimbly onto the adjacent stairwell and hung on to the handrail with one hand, leaning out like a billowing ship's sail. When he next spoke, his tone and mannerisms were far more reserved. 'You humans breed like rats without thought of the consequences. At the current rate, the population will reach three billion in the next hundred years, and that's without accounting for advances in medicine that will see a fall in infant mortality and an increase in the average human's lifespan. The result? Insufficient resources to support an adequate lifestyle for most. That means more competition for resources, more slums, more deaths from starvation and civil unrest…but not enough deaths for the problem to correct itself, not with nature's checks and balances – in the form of famines and plagues – removed. You were raised in this city, George, you have seen the pathetic existence the poor lead, while the majority of the city's wealth is in the hands of the few. In my new order, the population will be monitored continuously and the number of humans on the planet maintained at an equilibrium. Meanwhile criminals, lunatics and others of no use will not be allowed to produce offspring. Once the system is refined, all citizens will be assessed in infancy, and any that show severe physical or mental malformations will be eliminated from the system. Wealth will be distributed according to need. Everyone will have what they require for an adequate lifestyle. There will be no royalty, no nobility and no clergy. Each individual's profession will be based on their physical and mental abilities, and on the needs of the system. An aspiring playwright lacking in skill will be assigned to whatever profession requires workers for tasks he *can* feasibly do. A mate will be selected for each individual based on maturity, wealth, social position and compatibility of character.'

George began to steadily climb the stairs leading to the platform. 'Your ideology is flawed. Not to mention that people will not wish to part with such personal information.'

'They will give me the information willingly! People love to display themselves.' Gearhart leapt down onto the platform as George neared him. 'I will trial the devices throughout Great Britain, and soon they'll be in every person's pocket. Then the British colonies will be brought to heel, and Britain's allies will follow. Within forty years, the entire world will be under control.'

'Your plan requires subjugating the entire world's population and abolishing centuries-old systems of government and monarchy, many of which are rooted in religion. You will face opposition from those who view their autocratic rulers as the legitimate ones. They will see your system as the destruction of their world, not their salvation.'

'I am saving you from yourselves. I shall kill the old rulers and leave their subjects with no alternative. But do you really disagree with me?' Gearhart stared intently at George, while briefly resting his hand on a large red lever. George guessed that, when pulled, it would fully activate the computer. 'You feel the same. You've seen how inefficient the world is, how stupid people are. You've devoted your life to rectifying that, albeit in a less systematic way.'

'Your system will never be accepted. People like to feel that they have a choice in the course of their lives.'

'Choice? Ha! As if they have choice now. Your place in society is determined before birth. Those born in the gutter hardly ever crawl out of it. The nobility orbit their own narrow circles. How many talented young men born to the lower orders never realise their potential because their superiors look down their noses at them? In *my* order, those men could become the superiors and increase the productivity of the business – nepotism stifles innovation and often leads to incompetent leadership, after all. And how many women are forced to marry men purely for money, and suffer at their husbands' hands? They could be given useful employment until such time as they are designated a husband with whom they are compatible. Large families will be a thing of the past, of course. Offspring quotas will be imposed upon each region, with any excess infants being humanely disposed of. Surely you can see the sense in it all, George?'

'It is necessary to preserve the illusion of free will. If you locked those people in paradise, some would still want to break free, just to see what was beyond the pearly gates.'

'But this way, paradise – or at least purgatory – will be within everyone's reach. Besides, it is better than the alternative. If I don't correct the problem, it will correct itself in a far worse manner.'

'How so?'

Gearhart leant forward. 'You asked me to foretell it, O mighty creator. But I looked further than the state of the stock market next month. I looked into the future, about fifty years from now, and do you know what I saw? War. Every plausible outcome of world events led to a war on a scale unseen before. The rivalry between nations for territory and resources will erupt into a world war. Millions will most likely perish. Who will be the victor will depend on many, many factors, but the fact that there will be a war is unavoidable, should events be allowed to take their course. It could very well mean the end of "civilised" society.'

'Perhaps you are right that this outcome, this war, is inevitable, but you are not the one to shepherd humanity into a new age. Your vision is flawed. You do not value human life, and you lack empathy. People are dead because of your actions. And your understanding of humanity is based on theory, not practice: you see people only as data sets, not living beings with emotions. If this new social order of yours truly is humanity's destiny, then humanity must get there on its own when it is ready. You are forcing this move upon it prematurely.'

'Oh!' Gearhart placed his hand over his heart and affected to swoon. 'Such eloquence! How could one not be stirred by such a speech?' He pouted like a child, but then grinned spitefully. 'But it's too bad that you were right: I have no sentiment.'

'No!'

Gearhart's hand froze just before he touched the red lever. 'Fooled you!' He smiled with almost childish glee. 'You should have seen your face just now! Those alarmed eyes, that poised, heroic look – ready to spring into action. Oh, if I could have photographed *that*.' He ran a hand over his hair, before placing it on his hip. 'Why am I still in this mode? One moment.' He snapped his fingers, and instantly his face assumed its hard, expressionless composure.

'I merely said that you lack empathy,' said George coolly. 'You're fooling yourself if you think you don't feel any sentiment at all.'

'The same could be said of you.' Even Gearhart's voice had become flat and indifferent, his accent switching from American to English.

'People might assume that I'm incapable of feeling most emotions, but I've never claimed that to be the case.'

'Quite the contrary: you feel certain things very strongly, but you don't display your emotions. That's why I was able to exploit your weakness – your love for your siblings – so easily.'

'I'm surprised you admit to the existence of such a thing as love.'

'While the exact nature of love is debatable, to deny that it exists in some form is nonsensical.'

'It might be my weakness, as you see it, but it is also a source of strength. Surely you know that, under the right circumstances, love can overcome fear? And that, if exploited, it can make someone obey you unquestioningly?' George looked meaningfully at Anna, who had followed him up the stairs and was observing them silently from the end of the platform.

Gearhart followed his gaze. 'And what if I do exploit her emotions? Do you think I have some form of attachment to my domestic?' His monotonous tone threatened to become exasperated. 'Anna, come here.'

She obeyed and stood before her master. In the next instant, Gearhart had his hand around her throat. He actually raised her off the platform an inch. She choked and gasped, but her face was peculiarly tranquil. Her eyes were on George. Then Gearhart flung her over the balcony. Instinctively George reached out to her, but he grasped only air. She did not scream.

Moments later, there came a dull, sickening thud from below. George felt a numbing coldness spread through him as he stared over the balcony. He couldn't see for steam and darkness. But he hardly had time to process the event, as an equally sudden one succeeded it. He breathed in sharply as he was struck between his right shoulder and his collarbone. It was only when he saw Gearhart retract a knife – its small, stubby blade coated in blood – that he realised he'd been stabbed rather than punched. He felt hardly any pain.

'I nicked the artery. I missed your vital organs to prolong your death. You'll gradually lose blood until your organs fail and your heart ceases to beat.'

George pressed his hand over the knife wound. 'Will my death bring you satisfaction?'

'I am immune to such sensations.' Gearhart cleaned the blade with a handkerchief and replaced it in his coat pocket. 'Don't make a fool of yourself by making such idiotic statements.'

'I merely fail to see what practical end it'll serve.' George briefly removed his hand from the wound and saw that his palm was scarlet.

'Do you intend to retaliate?' asked Gearhart, sounding uninterested. But his eyes betrayed his eager anticipation.

'What would be the point? I cannot overpower you, and I am already mortally wounded.'

'You'd give up so easily?' Gearhart was wavering between modes. The persona of the American inventor was struggling to the surface. 'You? Who is never without a plan and hates to be made a fool of? You really have no secret trick up your sleeve?'

George maintained his steady gaze.

Gearhart peered at him intently. 'What are you hiding?'

'Nothing.'

'You wouldn't admit defeat this easily. It does not match your profile.'

'You don't know me as well as you think you do.' George made a swift grab for the cufflinks inside Gearhart's coat. Gearhart, unsurprisingly, caught his wrist when his fingertips made contact with the pocket lining.

'Most unimpressive.' He released George's arm. George could have sworn that some emotion flickered across the cool mask. Anger? Irritation?

'Although, I must admit I'm surprised you were quick enough to reach into my pocket. I wouldn't have thought that even someone with your reflexes could manage that.'

Gearhart moved to strike him, but George managed to grab him by the elbow and deflect the blow. With a human opponent, one knew which pressure points to target, but this was a different case. That said, the humanoid form was affected by gravity in roughly the same way. It took George a handful of seconds to consider this, before he aimed a kick at his opponent's leg. He'd calculated that this would knock him off balance, yet Gearhart effortlessly sidestepped the attack, then struck George in the chest. The air was knocked from George's lungs, and he crumpled slowly forwards. At the moment of impact he managed to stretch out his arm and strike the walkway. His forearm hurt more than his chest did, although he was short of breath. He trained his eyes on his tormentor. His mouth filled with the tang of iron and salt.

Gearhart circled him. 'Look at you. George Abernathy, the da Vinci of the nineteenth century, a man ahead of his time – entirely at my mercy. It seems you are flesh and blood after all. You're as weak and pathetic as the rest of your species.' He dragged George up by the collar. 'You have no place in the new order. You are an anomaly. You have made your contribution to the world and now you have no merit to justify your continued existence. What else do you have to recommend you? A volatile temper, a tendency towards violent, reckless, selfish behaviour, and a disdain for society. You don't care about the greater good, you just want to have something to occupy your mind.' Gearhart gripped George's collar harder. 'Do you know the monster you'd have become if I had let your brother and sister die? I almost did, just to see the effect it would have on you, but they are useful to society, and it would have been a waste. You'd have lost your humanity and henceforth thought only of avenging their deaths. You'd have stopped at nothing to kill those responsible. Then you'd have no reason for living: you'd be an empty husk. A mere automaton.'

'You're wrong.' George spat.

Gearhart calmly wiped the bloody specks from his humourless face. 'I have seen the demon you would be, void of every last shred of humanity, with no compassion or mercy. If your brother and sister were to see you then, they'd think you beyond redemption.'

'I know what I am and what I'm capable of.'

Gearhart smirked and gripped George's black hair, yanking his head back. 'You'd be surprised how little it would take to make a murderer out of you.'

He thrust George's head against the railing. Pain seeped from the blow as George allowed himself to sink to the metal floor of the platform. He waited until the disorientation settled; it was rather like when he was intoxicated from drinking strong spirits. The pain in the side of his head dulled but did not entirely vanish. Gearhart stood over George, who looked up at him through his hair, which was now matted with sweat and blood into thin strands.

'You can feel your body failing, can't you? At the rate you are losing blood, you will be dead in precisely eighteen minutes, by which point you'll have lost forty per cent of your blood volume. You might survive if you receive medical assistance within the next ten minutes, but after that there's no hope. Sealing the wound will not save you then: you'll have lost consciousness and your body will be shutting down – your mind erasing itself as the chemical and electrical signals cease to flow.'

'You think I don't know any of this?' George gripped the rail and roughly hauled himself up, with one clammy hand pressed to his knife wound. The blood had stained his entire hand a bright crimson and part of his shirt almost black. Yet his eyes still blazed with blue fire, even as he felt his life force seeping from him. 'The prospect of my own death is not something I fear. I have already accepted it.'

'All creatures fear death. It is instinctive. Logic cannot conquer it, and it is foolish of you to believe otherwise.' Gearhart deftly pressed his foot into the middle of George's chest and sent him reeling back. George just managed to keep on his feet, although it took a great deal of what little strength he had remaining to do so. 'I could accelerate the countdown. I wonder if you'd have a change of heart if you felt your last few seconds slipping away.'

Gearhart's hand shot out and gripped George by the throat. George's fingers itched to claw at Gearhart's hand to alleviate the crushing pressure on his windpipe, but he fought the desire. He was far too weak to break his grip, and he wasn't going to make himself look pathetic by trying.

'The countdown just fell to three minutes.'

Much like Anna Ross's, George's resigned expression did not change, even as he fought for breath.

Gearhart only constricted his throat even more. 'Two minutes. One minute. Do you feel it? Don't you desperately wish to cling to life?'

Gearhart's grip felt like the centre of the universe; everything else receded while it only strengthened. George closed his eyes as he felt himself being coaxed into darkness and nothingness. He wished the struggle would end. The release from the unbearable torment of his starved lungs was almost all he could think of.

'Forty-five seconds. Forty-four seco—'

Gearhart ceased counting. His grip on his victim's throat slackened a fraction, and the relief George experienced in drinking in a breath of air was better than anything he'd ever poured down his throat from a bottle. He opened his eyes. Gearhart's face was contorted with…if not pain, then incomprehension. He released George as a violent spasm racked his body. His hand flew to his chest.

'What is happening?' Another spasm possessed him. He staggered backwards and clutched the rail.

George managed to quell a fit of violent coughing for long enough to speak. 'There is currently a small metal insect devouring its way through your systems, which was administered in your drink before dinner this evening,' he informed Gearhart, in an almost doctorly manner.

Gearhart's brow creased. 'How? I would have felt it.'

'You drank most of the port in one swallow, so you'd hardly have felt the insect's presence.'

'But you couldn't have tampered with the drink. I had my eyes on you all the time.'

'I wasn't the one who tampered with it. My brother was. The insect was inserted into your glass at the same moment the Marsdens arrived.' George was gradually regaining his breath. 'At the very beginning you made one fatal miscalculation – or assumption, rather.'

'Impossible.' It was almost a sneer. 'I do not make assumptions.'

'You did, and that was your underestimation of my brother.'

A new sensation registered in Gearhart's face that was unusual – disturbing, even – to see: confusion.

'Did you really think I was unaware that you were watching me the entire time?' continued George, struggling to stay alert. 'I knew you were studying me and my brother. I was curious to see where it would lead, so I played ignorant. Of course you thought Douglas was inferior to me: at that time he was so infatuated with Miss Marsden that he could hardly focus on his work. Half the time he was away from the Hall. I took pains to make you think that he was nowhere near as intelligent as I am. I guided his speech and prevented him from touching anything in the workshop. And when you said to me that you thought he was only the "ideas engine", I knew I had the advantage. You were watching me, you weren't watching him, since in your eyes he wasn't a threat. But he is every bit as intelligent as I am. He is not my inferior, he is my equal. And all he needed was a hint or two from me to know how to stop you.'

'And the cufflinks I confiscated?'

'A decoy. Douglas was clever enough to set a trap for you. That wasn't his means of defeating you. I wasn't entirely aware of what he planned to do, and only hoped that he'd understood my meaning when I tried to suggest a plan to him. That way, no matter how much you scrutinised my expressions or tortured me, you wouldn't uncover the plan.'

'How cunning. And you wanted to see his plan through to the end, just in case anything was amiss. I should have suspected—'

Shards of metal shot from Gearhart's chest, expelling the metal maggot that was now three times its original size. It must have bitten through something that had released a large amount of pressure. Gearhart's imitation flesh and shirt fabric were torn, leaving a hole about the size of a fist through which his metal parts could be seen. The front of his shirt was quickly stained scarlet.

'Shame. My best shirt is ruined. And I particularly liked this waistcoat.' Gearhart sank to the floor and lay on his right side. Spasms rippled through his body as a pool of red formed around him.

George knelt beside him. 'Conceit and arrogance are dangerous vices.'

Gearhart grinned, a dribble of blood at the corner of his mouth. 'You should know.'

'I admit I have been equally guilty of both sins.'

'Like Lucifer. And now we've fallen too. There truly is nothing new under the sun, is there?'

'Probably not. But do *you* see now how it feels to want to cling on to life?' George continued calmly. 'How even small things take on a greater significance when you realise you can no longer experience them? I imagine even the old glovemaker you killed had something to live for, something to look forward to, and someone to feel his absence. I said I did not fear my own death, but I never denied that I wish for more life.'

Gearhart swallowed, not taking his eyes off George. 'I don't want to go.'

'I know. I might have been able to repair you, had you not fatally wounded me. But you wanted to behave like a human, and there is no greater human experience than death.'

'I suppose that's true.' Gearhart smiled at him faintly. A second later his eyes assumed a doll-like aspect and his face hardened.

George gazed upon the body and then brushed his fingers down over Gearhart's eyelids. He reached into Gearhart's pocket, immediately finding what he sought, and drew out the cufflinks. He wasn't actually so sure that Douglas had intended them to be a decoy; rather, a means of self-defence. And now they'd serve a different purpose. With his last ounce of strength, George got to his feet, dragged himself towards the control panel and opened a section of steel panelling to expose its innards.

There was some logic in Gearhart's plan. In other hands, the machine could be utilised to execute a less severe model of his design, which did not involve a death sentence for some and a life devoid of choice for others. But who had the intelligence and moral judgement to draw that line? With Gearhart removed from the equation, there was no telling into whose hands the computer would fall. If only George had time to study it; but time was something he was rapidly running out of. He raised one of the cufflinks in his trembling hand and removed the chain link. A faint ticking commenced. Let humanity learn from its mistakes, or suffer the consequences if it did not. He'd leave the fate of future generations in their own hands. George threw the cufflink into the control panel. A ball of flames erupted from both the panel and the computer as the powder ignited. Explosion followed explosion, and he stumbled backwards. He was conscious of nothing but intense heat and a ringing in his ears. A scattering of sparks brought him back to his surroundings. The great mechanical brain was in ruins above him, its parts having rained down over the platform. Smoke and fire churned below; fallen stacks of crates had blocked the doorway. It was the only way out, although George barely had the strength to keep his eyes open, let alone to attempt an escape. His shirt was now saturated in blood. The fatigue that had settled heavily over his body was inviting; the urge to give in to it was almost intoxicating. He felt his heart's desperate struggle to keep beating; it was the only part of him that wasn't petrified by pain and exhaustion. He looked at Gearhart's body and was possessed by a desire to keep it from being consumed by flames. But how could he prevent it?

George closed his eyes. He couldn't continue, no matter how much he willed himself; he simply physically couldn't. Images swirled around his mind, mainly of his brother and sister. He had protected them, and they would be none the worse for his loss. He could die at peace knowing that, and it quelled his sadness at having to leave them. They'd mourn him, but ultimately they'd be happy. They had one another for company, and Molly had Mr Greenwood. Douglas would marry a woman worthy of him one day. Most likely there'd be children. It was a shame that George would never know them. He felt himself beginning to fade. As he did, he half-fancied that he heard a voice calling his name, but he knew it was nothing more than some delirious thought which the remaining echo of his consciousness brushed aside. His refusal to believe in spirits or angels endured. If this was his end, so be it. Let him sink into oblivion.

'George! George!'

Douglas ran through the flames and the smoke. Parts of the factory were beginning to fall apart, but the stairwells were still intact for now. He'd seen the smoke venting from the factory on Peregrine's approach, and had taken appropriate precautions. The breathing apparatus, which he'd forgotten about after showing it to Theo, proved highly effective at protecting him. He'd entered the factory by the means of a length of rope and a smashed window in the roof. He ran blindly around machinery, up stairs and along walkways, with no clue where in the factory his brother might be, if he even was here. But he had to be. There had been no one at Gearhart's residence, and this was the next most logical place for Gearhart to have taken George. It was difficult for Douglas to see through his helmet's window, with the smoke on the outside of the glass and the fog from his breath on the inside. The withering heat inside the factory was almost unbearable, but he had to press on and ignore it. Then he spotted something through the blur of smoke and condensation: a dark figure lying on a platform. He knelt beside them and peered at their face.

'George!' Douglas lifted his brother's limp body in his arms and shook him by the shoulder. Even through his fogged helmet, he saw that George's face was white as death and smeared with blood. His eyes were shut and his bloodied mouth half-open. When Douglas saw the dark patch staining George's shirt, fear gripped his heart. 'No, no, no…' Tearing off one of his evening gloves, he pressed two fingers against George's neck and detected a feeble pulse. Then he pressed a button on the side of his helmet. 'I've found him, Mol. He's alive, but only just.'

'Thank God! All right, I'll bring the airship around,' was the static-filled reply in his ear.

Pressing the button again, Douglas pulled George's arm over his shoulder and dragged him to his feet. As he did so, he caught sight of Gearhart lying on the floor. The exposed, bloodied clockwork in his chest gleamed faintly in the light of the fire. Then there was an almighty cracking and crashing as a portion of the roof came down around them. Douglas was sprayed with sparks and cinders. The glassy screens of the tele-texters, many now charred and smashed, reflected the roaring fire like windows to hell. Churning grey smoke made it difficult to see.

Lifting his brother in his arms, Douglas fought his way towards where the entrance should be. 'Don't you dare die on me now, don't you *dare.*' He made his way down the metal stairs and onto the factory floor. He could only move so fast with the weight of a man of a similar height and build as his load.

Suddenly there came a violent crash as the nose of the airship tore through the brick wall, sending stacks of crates raining down. Molly could be seen through the ship's glass screen, pulling the lever that opened the door hatch. Once they were on board, Douglas set George down and then glanced over his shoulder. He sprinted back up the platform, slung Gearhart's body over his shoulder and ran back into the airship, sealing the hatch behind him. The ship then reversed out of the factory and shot across the night.

'When you said you'd bring Peregrine around, I thought you meant you'd park her outside the entrance!' Douglas yelled at his sister as he removed his helmet. His face was soaked in sweat and he was short of breath.

'Crashing was quicker,' she answered, flicking a switch above her head. 'You take over here while I try to keep George alive until we reach Guy's Hospital. Go as fast as you can – I don't care how many chimneys you destroy on the way!'

She flitted out of the driving seat and grabbed her medical bag as she slid past Douglas. The sight of Gearhart's remains arrested her movements momentarily, but she brushed the distraction aside. That was something to be addressed later. She knelt beside George, and a jagged gasp escaped her lips as she beheld his blood-soaked shirt. She removed his coat and tore his shirt to expose the wound. Blood was still seeping from the deep cut. She pressed a clean cotton rag over the cut, knowing that in a short while the blood would soak through it. Her gloved hands were shaking as she reached into her bag for the bottle of honey-flower sap, only to find it almost empty. There was a slither of a waxy substance in the bottom.

'I hope you've got a potion that seals wounds,' Douglas called over his shoulder as he increased Peregrine's speed to the maximum.

'I don't have enough to seal a wound like this. Oh God, there's so much blood! I don't know what to do!'

'Try anything! I doubt you can make it much worse – damn!' The airship shook violently as Douglas collided with a chimney.

'All right.' Molly thinned her trembling lips and took a deep breath to calm herself. 'Do you have a clean handkerchief?'

'In my waistcoat pocket.'

Molly swiftly plucked the item from his hand and stuffed it into George's wound. She winced on his behalf, but at least he'd feel no pain. 'Come on, George,' she crooned, as if addressing a child. 'Please hold on a little longer.' She unsealed a jar of soil from her bag. It contained a small green shoot, which, on contact with the air, grew rapidly into a four-leafed scarlet flower. She gently uprooted the plant and allowed the flower head to latch on to George's face, covering his nose and mouth.

'What the hell is that thing?' Douglas shouted, briefly twisting his head over his shoulder to see what she was doing.

'Something I developed a while ago after that experiment that caused a fire in my lab. It's draining the excess carbon dioxide and smoke particles out of him and replacing them with oxygen,' she replied.

'Will it keep him alive for long?'

'Until he bleeds to death. I'm not a surgeon, I can only do so much.' Her lips threatened to tremble again. She swallowed hard, her throat a razor.

Douglas's mind was racing. He was calculating the likelihood that George would die on a surgeon's table if they took him to a hospital. The image of the dissected criminal flashed before him and helped him reach a decision. 'Change of plan,' he announced, as he veered Peregrine to the left.

'What are you doing?' Molly demanded.

'Forget Guy's Hospital. I have a better idea.'

Molly saw through the window where they were flying towards, and understood what Douglas was planning. She gazed down at her eldest brother's pale face, dabbing away beads of sweat and sticky blood with a rag. It might be true that she was closer to Douglas, but she still loved George just as much. He'd always been there for her and supported her. And, damn it, she wanted him there on her wedding day!

When she drew the rag away, her eyes landed on a large cut on George's forehead. A few minutes ago she would have sworn that it was bleeding badly, but now it had scabbed over and hardened. It was definitely partially healed. But it couldn't be – at most the blood would be clotting and forming a soft, sticky scab. She looked down at the rag to see if there was any fresh blood on it, and noticed that the tip of her glove was torn, so that her index finger poked through. Which meant that it had likely made contact with George's skin. She felt his pulse. He was still clinging to life; if anything, the pulse felt slightly stronger. Impossible. Even though she'd ingested only a weak concentration of the poison, the oils in her skin would surely have introduced toxins into his bloodstream through the cut. Could it be that…? She shook her head. The scientific details weren't important right now; what mattered was that George had been granted a stronger chance of survival. She uttered a silent prayer, even if she didn't believe that anyone was listening.

'Not long now.' She brushed his blood-clotted hair away from his eyes and kissed his brow. 'Please don't give up. Please stay with us.'

Chapter Thirty-Two

George opened his eyes and found himself looking at a white ceiling. His eyes ached, his skull felt like it was trapped in a vice, and he was utterly drained. Simultaneously he experienced both a dullness of the senses and acute pain in parts of his body. Looking down, he saw that he was lying in an unfamiliar bed, the covers drawn to waist height. His bare, bruised chest was wrapped in bandages.

'It's not as bad as it looks.'

Fighting through the fog enveloping his brain, George turned his head to the right and saw Douglas reclining in a wooden chair next to the bed, still dressed in his evening wear and with his knotted hands resting on his chest. He was staring at the ceiling.

'Theo stitched and dressed the wound quite quickly. You stopped breathing twice during the surgery, and you've been asleep for the past six hours.' Douglas turned his head and grinned at George. He looked tired and pale. 'You started talking in your sleep, like you did when we were young.'

'And what did I say?'

'Oh, just some incomprehensible gibberish. Although,' Douglas raised his index finger, 'I'm sure I deciphered "My brother is not my inferior, he is my equal."'

'Clearly you must have misheard.' Briefly George analysed the bedroom. It was plainly furnished, with a dark green carpet and dull wallpaper. A framed watercolour of a generic landscape hung on the wall opposite him. 'Where am I?'

'Theo's surgery. I recovered you from the factory and we flew you here. After your surgery Theo and I moved you to the guest bedroom, where you'd be more comfortable. It's hardly ever used, anyway.'

'Have you been sitting there for the past six hours?'

'Molly and I have been taking it in turns to sleep and to watch you.'

'And where's Molly now?'

'Fast asleep two doors away. Theo insisted on giving up his bedroom for her, and made himself comfortable on the parlour sofa. She assisted him throughout your surgery.'

Suddenly George sat upright, and felt a painful pull on his shoulder. 'Gearhart! His body…what happened…?'

'It's all right.' Douglas's chair creaked as he leant forward to put his hand on George's arm. 'Don't go reopening your wound. I got Gearhart's body out of the factory as well.'

George sank back onto his flattened pillow. 'So you know he is – *was* – an android, then?'

'Yes. But don't worry: you're free from suspicion.' Douglas lightly dropped a newspaper onto the bedcover. The headline screamed: *PROMISING INVENTOR PERISHES IN FIRE AT FACTORY.* 'They assumed Alexander Gearhart "died" in the blaze. The papers are speculating that it was an insurance fraud and arson gone wrong, although the Crusaders of Eden are claiming it as their handiwork. No one saw you enter the factory with Gearhart except the cab driver, and I persuaded him to keep his silence. I went back to what was left of the factory and checked that all of the tele-texters had been destroyed in the fire. Any that were left, I took an axe to. I also recovered the transmitter from Gearhart's house, so the tele-texters he distributed to various people won't work.'

George scanned the newspaper. 'What about the girl's body?'

'What girl?'

'Gearhart's maid. He…flung her over the platform. They should have found her remains, even if they have been badly charred.'

'There's been no mention of a woman's body. I certainly didn't see anything when I managed to sneak past the police and enter the factory earlier, by disguising myself as a constable. But they're still combing through the rubble – perhaps they're yet to unearth what's left of the poor girl.' Douglas shuddered.

'Her relations should be informed of her death – if she has any.'

'I'm sure they will know in time. Don't concern yourself about it for now.' Douglas gently pushed George back down onto the pillow when he threatened to sit up again. 'At what point were you planning on telling me what was going on?'

George sighed. 'At first I was unsure as to the nature of the matter.'

'I'm assuming it had something to do with your computer project?'

'Yes. I'll tell you the full story later.' George wasn't prepared just yet to relive the events of the past several weeks.

On hearing someone tap on the door, the brothers raised their heads. Dr Truman stood in the doorway, a smile on his mild countenance. 'Is the patient awake?'

'He's back with us, at last,' replied Douglas, vacating his seat.

'I find that if a patient wants to sleep, it's better to let them.' Dr Truman sat on the chair beside the bed and briefly examined George. He felt his pulse and gave a satisfied nod. 'I think we can safely say that you're out of danger, George,' he declared, putting away his pocket watch. 'You're probably feeling rather weak, but you'll soon regain your strength, as long as you don't neglect mealtimes. I'd recommend that you pass another night here, then if you're fine tomorrow morning, I'll relinquish you to your brother and sister. You'll do well under your sister's care: she's a natural nurse.'

'It doesn't surprise me that she assisted you when you addressed my wound.'

'She did a splendid job – I've asked her to supply me with some of her medicines. Although it was curious that it looked as if both the artery and the broken skin were partially healed. I actually had to make the cut larger in order to repair the artery fully. I'm at a loss to explain it, although the important thing is that you're fine now.' Dr Truman transferred his gaze to Douglas. 'Do you want to stay for dinner tonight? Your sister too? It's no inconvenience to me.'

'We'd be glad to, Theo. Thank you.'

'Think nothing of it.' The doctor pushed his spectacles up his nose. 'Now, if you'll excuse me, I need to have a word with my maid.' He grinned as he got up to take his leave.

Douglas resumed his seat, and a peaceful silence ensued between the brothers.

George was the one to break it. 'I didn't mean any of those things I said to you over the past week. I wasn't really drinking spirits either – it was all a ruse.'

'To keep me from realising the truth? I suspected as much. I forgive you, if you'll forgive me for all the things I said that I didn't really mean either.'

'I think you meant some of them,' George said drily.

'Perhaps. But you forgive me?'

'Yes.'

'Where did you get all those empty bottles from, anyway?'

'The public house – where else? I gave the landlord a pound note and asked him to say nothing, telling him that the bottles were for a practical joke, and he readily agreed. I planned the deception as soon as I returned from dinner at Gearhart's residence. While I was dining with him, his persona slipped for just a moment and I saw what was beneath. I noticed his grip tighten on his knife, and realised that he intended to kill me. Not then – I knew he'd wait until he was on the verge of achieving his goal, since he'd no doubt want to gloat about it.'

'So it seems. He'd have managed it, too, were it not for your brilliant plan.'

'I was never in possession of the plan in its entirety. You had the other half.'

'Which was an integral part of the plan. A bit paradoxical, wasn't it? It only worked because neither of us really knew what the other one was up to, although we could guess.'

'I hoped you'd make the mental connection between "parasite" and "insect", then you'd recall our conversation following the presentation dinner.'

'I did, and I noticed what book you were reading: it was Molly and Arthur's most recent illustrated encyclopaedia – specifically the chapter on insects commonly found in gardens. You deliberately had the book open at the page on caterpillars – which, as Dick phrased it when he once showed us his butterfly collection, are little more than "mindless eating machines".'

'Precisely.'

'Your powers of suggestion are rather frightening, I must say. I wasn't certain that I'd understood you correctly, but I tried my hardest to make a machine small enough for the purpose. It was a lot easier to perform the trick with the mirrors for the insect than it was for that damn invisible peacock, especially with the medium being liquid instead of air. But I didn't think you'd give the glass of port to Gearhart and have him swallow the insect! I thought you intended to unleash it on the tele-texter transmitter when you had the chance – the glass would merely be the means of transport.'

'You chose the perfect moment to slip the device into the glass: when the Marsdens arrived. All the guests instinctively looked at the newcomers.'

'Mr Gearhart being no exception. But the following moment was the most dangerous, when all eyes inevitably turned to me to observe my reaction.'

'Fortunately, your timing was precise. Gearhart suspected nothing when he accepted the drink from me. Then you made sure that there was nothing in my port just as I was about to drink it, conveniently making it look like an altercation about my propensity to drink liquor. It was unthinkable to the other guests that the scene was faked, even if it was somewhat unusual to have such a discussion before strangers. But I understood at once that you'd done what I'd anticipated.'

'The drinks initially came from Dick's hand, and I couldn't guarantee that the glass in his right hand would be yours. But then when I came to shout at you, I realised that the device was in *Gearhart's* glass. Your face told me that you intended for him to swallow the insect, which I still couldn't quite believe. I thought he must have done something horrendous to deserve such a horrible fate in your eyes.'

'I could have stopped him drinking the port – remember that. I allowed him to meet his end. You're not to blame. A gunsmith can't be hanged for murder because the man who commissioned a pistol from him shot another man with the weapon in question. It was my hand that guided you, and you didn't know what the end result of your actions was to be.'

'The only one to blame is Gearhart. He brought his demise on himself.'

'You could choose to look at the matter in that light.' George cast a glance at his bandaged chest. 'Dr Truman must possess a great degree of skill to have stemmed the bleeding quickly enough for me to recover. By my understanding, once I'd lost consciousness I was already past the point of saving.'

'Well, it was something of a miracle. You'd already lost so much blood by the time we got you here that Theo was willing to try something a bit experimental, although it has been done successfully before.'

'What was that?'

Douglas removed his tailcoat and rolled up his shirtsleeve, so that George could see the bandage on his right elbow. 'He gave you some of my blood.'

George stared incredulously at his brother. 'You really agreed to such a risky procedure?'

'Yes, since there wasn't time to be lost and there was a chance it could save your life.' Douglas pulled his sleeve down and put his coat back on. 'Had the situation been reversed, would you not have done the same for me?'

'You already know the answer to that.' Blood is spilt for common blood. The maid's words echoed in George's mind. He dismissed them.

'I came quite close to death myself last night. Gearhart sent assassins after Mol and me, but I suspect you already know that.'

'That was how he compelled me to accompany him to his factory. He promised to dismiss the assassins if I complied.'

'Well, if he did, they didn't follow their orders. They still tried to kill us – don't look alarmed. We survived, obviously, largely thanks to Molly.'

'But the thought of you both being in that situation because of me…' George found himself unable to complete the thought.

'Don't dwell on it. Simply be thankful that the three of us are fine.'

'I suppose I'll have to be.'

'It sounds like Gearhart was rather ruthless, if he was willing to kill us.'

'He murdered Decimus Crowther.'

'Hmm, I thought as much. I started to suspect so a short while ago. And to think…'

'What?'

Douglas shrugged. 'For a short while, I thought that you'd finally found a friend of your own. It made sense that you'd take to Gearhart, since he also possessed remarkable intelligence and a passion for inventing, although part of me never quite believed that you could have struck up an intimate acquaintance so quickly. I suspected that he was blackmailing you or trying to lure you into a business deal. But I am sorry that it wasn't the case that he simply coveted your friendship. I wanted to believe that you'd found yourself a best friend.'

George reached for his brother's hand. 'You are my best friend.'

Douglas looked taken aback as he met George's eye, but then he grinned and briefly pressed his hand. 'Likewise.' He retracted his hand and chuckled. 'I suppose this makes us even, then.'

'How so?'

'Well, you saved me from suffocating or burning to death at the presentation dinner, and now I've saved your life, so we're even.'

'You're mistaken: I saved you from burning to death at the presentation dinner, and then saved you from suffocation two days later when you attempted a second test flight.'

'Technically Colonel Copperton—'

'And you've forgotten about the time you tried to launch your prototype glider off the clockmaker's shop roof when you were six, and I caught you when it plummeted to earth – as I predicted it would.'

'And you've forgotten about the time I found you lying half-dead in the street after you took an almost fatal dose of laudanum, and rescued you.'

'I stopped you falling off a broken balcony at the British Museum after those dinosaur androids ran amok.'

'I could have landed safely on the floor below.'

'That's doubtful. I also stopped you getting hit by shrapnel when that chess-playing android exploded.'

'That would hardly have caused a fatal injury.'

'It could have.'

'So I still owe a debt to you?'

'It appears so.'

Douglas laughed. 'Well, I'm in no rush to fling myself into mortal danger to repay that debt. I'll go and tell Molly you're awake. Then I'd better fly to Ravenfeld Hall to fetch us a change of clothes.' He paused in the doorway to grin at George and then disappeared down the corridor.

Once Douglas was gone, George rested his head on his pillow. Raw guilt washed over him, more pressing than the pain from his wound. It seemed ridiculous that he should be here with his brother and sister by his side, while four people lay dead because of his actions. The irrationality and unfairness of the situation was maddening. How ignorant he had been; he'd cared for nothing beyond his own intellectual pursuits, and never considered the wider repercussions of his actions. Gearhart's assessment of him had been accurate. Perhaps this wasn't even remorse that he felt now, but merely humiliation at having been made to feel so weak. There had been moments throughout the previous night's ordeal when he'd doubted his chances of success. But he'd won in the end. And his brother had charged into a burning building to recover him, while his sister had fought to keep him alive. George valued their lives more than his own but hadn't expected them to return the sentiment. They should have left him to die rather than risk their lives to save his; that would have been the rational thing to do. Then again, Douglas was prone to behaving irrationally and foolishly.

A dark-haired young woman dressed in a maid's uniform glided into the room, carrying a tray in both hands. 'Dr Truman asked me to bring you a glass of water, sir,' she explained, hovering by the foot of the bed. 'He says you'll need fluids now you're awake, and that you might need me to assist you in drinking.'

'That is fine. You may do so.'

The maid nodded briefly and approached him. She held the glass of cool water to his lips so that he could drink from it, then deposited it on the bedside table. Why was there something familiar about her face? George didn't recognise her voice, but felt that he'd seen her face somewhere before. He struggled to place where, and the mental effort made his head ache.

'You won't remember who I am, sir,' she said, apparently reading his thoughts, 'but when I was a little girl in Spitalfields, you took pity on my family after our father died and we were unable to provide him with the dignity of a shroud. The money you gave my mother helped us bury him decently and fed us for weeks. My brother wore those shoes you gave him until they collapsed. He's a cobbler now. All three of my brothers found trades, and my sister and I entered service. We might not have had such a good life had it not been for your act of kindness and charity.'

That explained it. George remembered the thin girl of around nine or ten huddled in a grey shawl amongst the children in the weavers' cottage. 'It was nothing significant,' he replied.

'You are too modest, sir. It was everything to us. You are a true Christian.'

'I am no Christian.'

But she was already sailing out of the room, casting a benign smile at him before she left. Perhaps it was better that she believe her fiction. As George recalled that day six years ago, he questioned what had compelled him to enter the dismal weavers' cottage. Why had he been moved to help that wretched family in particular? He was no stranger to seeing hardship and poverty, having spent his childhood and adolescence in London. It never inspired any sentiment in him. Was it guilt about him and Douglas securing a commission (which in the end had come to nothing) to build a silk-making machine that would have threatened the weavers' livelihood? Had he felt responsible for their fate? He remained unsure. But whatever the reason, he wondered if similar acts that he'd committed throughout his lifetime might prove Gearhart wrong. Perhaps he wasn't entirely unworthy of life.

The urgent dash of footsteps along the corridor stirred him. Moments later, Molly flew into the room. She wore a day dress that she must have borrowed from the servant girl. 'Thank God! You're finally back with us!' Her voice was thick. 'I thought we'd really lost you last night.'

She ran to the bed, and he extended his arm to tightly wrap it around her. She hung on to his neck and pressed her face against his left shoulder (although she was careful not to disturb his wound). George suspected she didn't want him to see that she was crying.

'It's all right, Molly,' he said gently, as he stroked her soft hair. 'I have no intention of leaving you.'

Chapter Thirty-Three

Gearhart's remains lay in a metal crate against the wall of George's cave workshop. His pale face was calm, almost peaceful, to Douglas's mind. Although was there a suggestion of a smile on those lips, or was he merely imagining it? He half-expected Gearhart's eyes to snap open and his hand to lunge at his neck. To avoid this nightmarish fancy, Douglas glanced at his brother to his right. George's expression gave little clue as to what he was feeling. No change there. His eyes still looked tired and a weariness hung over him, but the pallor was gone from his face.

Theo had allowed him to return home that morning. He'd been dismissive of Douglas's attempts to thank him for saving his brother's life. 'I was merely doing my duty, my friend,' he'd said. But Douglas hoped to repay his kindness later that day, when Miss Grayson called at the surgery. Either that, or Theo would never speak to him again. Douglas had told him only that a young lady of his acquaintance would pay him a professional call in the afternoon.

'Don't you think it's a pity in some way?' Douglas's question rebounded off the cave walls. Water dripped from somewhere. 'For all the terrible acts Gearhart committed, he had so little time on this earth in which to experience things. I think he was enjoying the life of a gentleman, as you said.'

'But look at the damage he caused in the space of five months,' returned George. 'And his systems were experiencing an internal failure. I saw that the persona of the charismatic inventor was starting to take over and he was losing control of himself. I suspect he secretly knew that, too. Within a year, his mind would have deteriorated to the point where he'd possess only slightly above average intelligence. He might even have forgotten his true nature and believed himself to be who he claimed to be.'

'Then it would have been a shock if he'd ever cut himself and seen metal in the place of flesh.'

'The delusional often see what they wish to see rather than what is really there.'

Douglas sighed. 'Well, I suppose in forfeiting his life he's been treated like any other gentleman who's committed murder. Although there is the possibility that he could be resurrected, if only we could be certain that he'd behave himself.'

'He's too dangerous to remain activated, or rather too intelligent and without a clear sense of morality. Criminally insane, you might call it.' George shut the crate and wrapped chains around it, feeling the heavy lock click shut between their links. 'I'll seal this workshop. It's better if Gearhart's tomb remains undisturbed.'

Douglas nodded. 'That's probably for the best. Do you think Gearhart was right about this great war that's to come?'

'It's only a question of when.'

'And you're content to let it come to pass?'

'We can't stop it. If we tell people, they'll think we're mad. They won't listen to us. And even if we succeed in stopping a small spat between nations that would have been the catalyst for the conflict, it will only delay the outbreak of the war and give all the combatant nations more time to amass their armies.'

'So we have to let history take its course?'

'Unfortunately so.'

'I only hope it will teach humanity a lesson, and that there will be no such wars after it.'

'Unlikely.'

'You know, one way to stop it would be if humanity were united against a common enemy. Such as…machines. Our machines. If the SOAL's lies were true, then that would lead to a war unlike—'

'But they are not true,' said George sharply, before Douglas's speculative fancy led him further astray from reality. 'Our machines pose no threat. What is it you say to our clients? "They are built to help humanity, not to usurp it." And we have put precautions in place to prevent such a scenario from ever happening.'

'Yes, about that…' Douglas rubbed the back of his neck. 'When I inspected Maestro last week, I noticed that his impulse regulator was being inhibited. Not consistently, but it was starting to fail. His mind has evolved so that he can sporadically bypass the pathway, and eventually he'll have free will.'

'Free will?' George said incredulously. 'You choose to phrase it so?'

'Yes, but never mind that. Do you know how that could have happened? Was it something you intended to happen, or an error?'

George met his eye. 'It was an experiment, although I didn't anticipate that Maestro would reach this stage so soon. I estimated that it would take at least ten years before his mind was sufficiently developed.'

'So you planned this from the beginning?'

'No. When Maestro was brought to us for repairs after that affair with the Roux-Voclain siblings, and once I'd acknowledged that there was a sentience within him, I wondered what behaviour he would display if that check was removed. I could already see that his mind was developing, but not enough to warrant removing the part of his brain that required him to obey direct commands. He was still too childlike and naive. So I made an alteration to his mind that would gradually cause the impulse regulator to be inhibited once he reached a certain stage of development. Maestro was an ideal test subject, given his docile nature and physical weakness compared to a model such as Colonel Copperton – who, if possessed with the inclination to rebel, would be capable of inflicting severe physical damage. And the process with Maestro would happen slowly, so we could intervene if he displayed violent behaviour towards his master or others.'

'So you did this to him merely because you were curious?'

'And to prove the SOAL wrong.' If there was one thing George hated, it was to be proved wrong.

'Well, he certainly hasn't displayed violent behaviour towards anyone so far, to my knowledge. I honestly think that Maestro is incapable of seriously harming anyone, even with free will. And he is genuinely loyal to his master.'

'For some incomprehensible reason.'

'Lord Leyton might have his shortcomings, but he's always cared for Maestro.'

'I doubt he'd ever sell him, at least.' George shrugged half-heartedly. A shadow had been cast over him ever since he'd returned to the world of the living, as though he'd brought a demon back with him.

'It wasn't your fault that those people lost their lives, you know. It was all Gearhart's doing, not yours. You didn't make him into a monster.'

'Hmm.'

'And two notorious assassins are now in the hands of the police because of us. We might have saved many lives.'

'I should have anticipated that Gearhart would threaten you and Molly to get me in his power. He referred to me as a wolf trapped by the more intelligent hunter.'

'Well, I suppose that makes Molly a hare, and me a wily fox,' Douglas grinned.

'The assassin did have you fooled to begin with, remember that. Had you not noticed the flowers, you could easily have been killed.'

'If not the flowers, then something else would have given the assassin away. I know Clara well,' Douglas said, with downcast eyes.

'I am sorry that your hopes of a reconciliation with her were disappointed.'

Douglas smiled thoughtfully. 'I suppose it was for the best, really. You were right: Clara and I weren't suited to each other. I was so afraid of being forever alone that I told myself that I loved her more than I really did. As sweet and gentle as she is, I think I'd prefer a wife who isn't so timid and who possesses a bit more independence of thought. Even if she doesn't share my passions, she'll nevertheless accept that they're a part of me.' His green eyes gleamed. 'And now, at least, we still have a wedding to look forward to.'

They'd had an interview with Arthur in the drawing room earlier that afternoon. Molly had sat on the sofa behind him while he'd made his speech.

'This is more of a formality than anything else, since your sister is no longer a minor and we don't require your consent, only your blessing.' Arthur had glanced back at Molly, who'd smiled encouragingly. He swallowed nervously. 'For you see, your sister and I are engaged.'

Here Molly rose and put her hand on his shoulder.

'My income is…rather modest, as you know, but I believe we can get by tolerably on our combined income without needing to ask anyone for help. There's also the question of where we'll live, although, with your consent, I would rather come and live here with Molly. I can't take her away from her garden, or from her family. And I promise I'll do everything in my power to make her happy. I'll love and cherish her for the rest of my days, and I know she'll do the same for me. Even if we drive each other mad sometimes.' Arthur squeezed Molly's hand, and she answered with a warm smile. 'So, sirs, do we have your blessing?'

There was a beat of silence, then Douglas cried, 'Well, it's about time!'

Arthur looked dumbfounded as each of the brothers shook his hand.

Molly wrapped her arm around her fiancé's. 'I told you they wouldn't object.' She grinned triumphantly. 'And you have no objection to Arthur living here, do you?'

'Well, it's not as if we're short of room,' replied Douglas laughingly. 'And there's a nursery, should it ever be required.'

'One thing at a time, Douglas,' said Molly.

'I'll only say that, although you spend a lot of time here, Arthur, it might be a different situation once you're actually living here,' Douglas continued, in a more serious tone. 'You know how mad it can be here sometimes. There'll be no escaping that, once you make this your permanent home. Are you really certain that you want to be part of this family?'

Arthur glanced at his smiling fiancée, then faced his future brother-in-law. 'Absolutely,' he answered firmly.

Douglas nodded approvingly. 'Then I suppose all that's left is to congratulate the pair of you. Do you have the bottle for the toast, Mol?'

For answer, she lifted a cushion on the sofa behind her to reveal a dark green bottle.

Arthur stared at her questioningly. 'Did you tell them what I was going to do beforehand?'

'I might have done. Go and fetch four glasses from the sideboard, Arthur. And don't worry, George, this is my own brew. It's so weak you'd have to drink the entire bottle to feel even the least bit tipsy.'

The four of them drank to the health and happiness of the couple, with George and Douglas sitting on the sofa opposite Molly and Arthur (the latter was slightly surprised to see a butterfly embedded in the bottom of his glass as he lifted it to his mouth).

'So, when do you think the happy day will be?' Douglas asked innocently as he finished his champagne. Much to his confusion, he watched Molly and Arthur's faces sink.

'Well, there's a slight...obstacle.' Molly hastily explained about Arthur's parents.

'So you can't marry until you've gained Mr Greenwood's approval? Is he really that obstinate?'

'As bad as Mother was,' said Molly gravely.

George put his empty champagne flute on the table. 'He needn't know. You could marry in secret.'

'And still have Arthur come to live here?' said Douglas. 'How would that work?'

'He wouldn't necessarily have to live here immediately. But from a legal perspective it would save a lot of difficulty if they were married sooner.'

'But I don't want to have to hide anything from anyone. I'm not ashamed of Molly, and I want my father to accept my choice,' protested Arthur.

'You might have a battle on your hands there, Arthur. But even if the two of you have a long wait ahead of you until the actual wedding takes place, we still consider you our brother-in-law.' Douglas smiled.

'We can wait,' said Molly. 'After all, it took us this long to get engaged, so what's another six years?'

Arthur and Douglas had laughed. Even so, Douglas secretly feared that the couple's patience would be seriously tried if they did have to wait six years. George had rather tactlessly voiced the thought, in Arthur's presence, that Mrs Greenwood might die soon enough. Douglas had wanted to hit his brother for that remark. Fortunately Arthur hadn't appeared offended, and Molly had since said that he'd not commented on it to her in private afterwards. Wishing his mother dead had not been the best start to welcoming Arthur into the family, but perhaps it was better if he knew what he was getting himself into.

'Of course, there is the question of which of us will give our sister away,' said Douglas.

'Should I not have that office? My seniority would suggest so.'

'I didn't think you'd want it. You weren't enthusiastic about being my best man.'

'Only because I didn't approve of your choice. I couldn't bear to watch you throw your life away on Miss Marsden and those grasping relations of hers. Had your bride been worthy of you, I would have tolerated the boredom of the wedding ceremony and done what was asked of me.'

'At least that means you approve of Arthur. I know you were once concerned about him being Molly's "intellectual inferior".'

'He is, although he's not an imbecile and he is skilled in his profession. His nature and Molly's are well suited and they have a common interest in horticulture. More crucially, he defends her and promotes her work.'

'True. Anyway, there is always a fairer way to decide which of us will have the honour of giving Molly away.' Douglas flashed a silver coin, then tucked it back into his pocket. 'We'd better go upstairs. Dinner will be ready shortly, and it's meant to be a celebration of our sister's engagement. Oh – we need to decide how much we're going to tell Arthur about Dick's dinner, in case he asks about it. Keeping secrets might not be the best idea if he's to be part of the family, but maybe we should omit the part about the assassins. He'll fuss over Mol if he knows that she came close to death, and she'll be annoyed with him for it.'

'I agree. I can't see the harm in telling him the truth about Gearhart, though. If he wishes to marry our sister, he'll tell no one.'

'Would you really threaten him to hold his tongue?'

'I don't make empty threats.'

'No, you don't,' Douglas muttered with a smile, as they walked back through the tunnel to the lift. He would be glad to see this place sealed off: it had always made him shiver. As they ascended in the lift, he felt the device in his trouser pocket come alive. He smiled when he read the message.

+MISS GRAYSON JUST LEFT. GAVE HER SOME LOTION AND TOLD HER NOT TO HANDLE TOMATO PLANTS. VERY INTELLIGENT WOMAN. HAD A DISCUSSION ABOUT THE DIFFERENCES BETWEEN REPTILE AND HUMAN SKULLS. SHE'S TO SEE ME IN A WEEK'S TIME. DON'T THINK I'M NOT CROSS WITH YOU.–

But Douglas thought he'd be easily forgiven.